"Spare me your sweet words," Sophie hissed.

"Well enough do I know that you ply them at will to win your way with me."

"Me?" Hughes demanded sharply. "'Tis not I who have had my way, milady, I assure you, for when you cannot control the scene, you want naught of it."

"What nonsense is this you speak?"

"Think you that I have not seen how you turn away in revulsion from my touch?" Hughes whispered.

"But I——" Sophie attempted to argue, but Hughes summarily interrupted her.

"Spare me *your* sweet words," he spat. "And spare me also your mad tales of destiny, your sultry looks and the tempting sway of your buttocks. Well you know that I would have had you a hundred times these past days had you not turned me aside with your maidenly distaste. Different I thought you, Sophie, woman enough to admit what you wanted, but in truth you are like any other *lady* I have known, promising what you cannot or *will not* deliver!"

Dear Reader,

This month brings you *The Sorceress*, by popular author Claire Delacroix, an intriguing medieval tale of dreams and magic. It's the prequel to the author's *Romance of the Rose*, the first of the Rose series.

And from Merline Lovelace comes the next book in her Destiny's Women trilogy, *Siren's Call*, the story of an Athenian sea captain and the Spartan widow he claims as his captive. And when Rafe Sugarman returns home to Mississippi, he finds peace in the arms of Serena Quinn, in *The Sugarman*, by author Mary McBride.

And last but not least, our fourth title this month is *Brides for Sale* by Ana Seymour, a rollicking Western where a woman arrives in Seattle with high hopes for a respectable marriage and ends up falling for the town's most notorious bachelor.

As always, Harlequin strives to bring our readers the finest stories and the most memorable characters. We hope you enjoy them.

Sincerely,

Tracy Farrell
Senior Editor
Harlequin Historical

Please address questions and book requests to:
Harlequin Reader Service
U.S.: 3010 Walden Ave., P.O. Box 1325, Buffalo, NY 14269
Canadian: P.O. Box 609, Fort Erie, Ont. L2A 5X3

CLAIRE DELACROIX

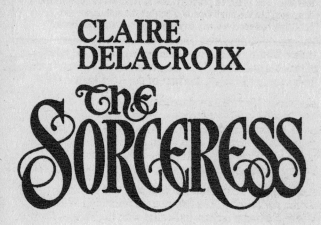

The SORCERESS

Harlequin Books

TORONTO • NEW YORK • LONDON
AMSTERDAM • PARIS • SYDNEY • HAMBURG
STOCKHOLM • ATHENS • TOKYO • MILAN
MADRID • WARSAW • BUDAPEST • AUCKLAND

ISBN 0-373-28835-2

THE SORCERESS

Books by Claire Delacroix

Harlequin Historicals

Romance of the Rose #166
Honeyed Lies #209
Unicorn Bride #223
The Sorceress #235

CLAIRE DELACROIX

An avid traveler and student of history, Claire Delacroix can be found at home when she has a deadline, amid the usual jumble of books, knitting needles and potted herbs.

For Donna,
who loves to venture off the beaten path
as much as I do

Chapter One

Bordeaux, October 1226

Mist rolled lazily over the hills and Sophie shivered in familiar trepidation, powerless to resist the allure of the low summit before her. The shadowy outlines of large shapes became discernible as she moved closer, although she had known all the while that they were there, waiting silently in the falling darkness. As usual, the fog obscured them and she had little more than a sense of their presence, their coldness raising goose pimples on her skin, their chill towering above her as she stepped cautiously between them.

Sophie shivered anew, as much from the cold as from her growing fear of what would come, her curiosity compelling her to continue. As far as the eye could see the countryside was shaded in subtle tones of blue, green and gray, all draped in a secretive cloak of ethereal mist. She was not alone in her anticipation. It seemed the very earth held its breath and awaited something of import.

Something that would come to pass in this clearing, on this night.

Sophie listened and heard the rhythmic pounding of the sea, the waves breaking on the shore close at hand, and she fancied she could smell the salt. She paused when she gained the summit, aware that she stood within a circle of massive shadows. She swallowed with difficulty at the thought of what she must do, desperately trying to quell her rising terror as she turned slowly, even though she knew the sight that would greet her eyes.

Expecting the presence of another did not lessen the shock of finding the mysterious cloaked figure there, awaiting her acknowledgment with its usual watchful patience. No greeting hailed her, simply the weight of the other's silently assessing regard upon her. Sophie's gaze tripped to the coals of a fire between them that had burned down to glowing embers and back to unsuccessfully seek some hint of the other's eyes amidst the shadows of the cowl.

She swallowed nervously, her heart racing, as the motionless form stirred to life and stepped forward. It strode purposefully toward her in the mist, the dying blaze casting it in a warm golden glow from one side, a light so at variance with the damp blues and grays of the surrounding scene.

Sophie caught her breath at the realization that there had been a subtle change. The one approaching her was much larger than usual and could not possibly be the woman she had always assumed it to be. She forced herself to hold her ground as the space between them diminished, to wait despite her fear as she struggled to make some sense of this unexpected change.

The heavy wool cloak rippled as the other approached with methodical steps, and Sophie's heart quickened to first match and then exceed the rhythm of the footfalls. Her pulse pounding in her ears drowned out the sound of the sea, but she could not have moved to save her life, struck motionless like the great shapes around her. The silent figure drew nearer, his features still hidden, and Sophie's fingers clenched her surcoat with trepidation.

An arm's length away he stopped abruptly, broad shoulders silhouetted by the fire now hidden from view, casting a cold shadow over Sophie. She shivered beneath his gaze, enduring that long, expectant moment with increasing difficulty. He towered over her like the encircling shadows, those mysterious shapes wrapped in their own shroud of mist, but gradually Sophie became aware of the heat that emanated from him.

A very human warmth 'twas, unlike the menacing cold of those mysterious stones, and for the first time Sophie was not afraid of what might come to pass. But not a moment had she to savor that unfamiliar sense, for one gloved hand lifted slowly a heartbeat later toward the rim of his hood.

Sophie panicked anew, certain she was not ready to face this unveiling. Curiosity fought against fear and she half turned away, her heart in her throat. She forced herself to endure one last agonizing moment, catching the barest glimpse of thick tawny hair and blue eyes keen with intelligence before she bolted and ran.

She gasped in alarm and abruptly sat up, her heart hammering as though she had run all the way from the city gates. Her breath caught painfully in her chest as the looming shadows in the mist dissolved into the familiar shadows of her own room.

She was home.

And safe.

It had been naught but the dream again.

Sophie released the air trapped in her lungs and took a deep, shaky breath as she untangled her fingers from the bed linens, reassuring herself with a quick inventory of the familiar room. The chest, the armoire, the steeply pitched roof with its broad, dark beams, all were there.

Home, serene in the darkness.

Sophie closed her eyes with relief and clasped her knees to her chest, filling her senses with the safe aura of the sleeping town and letting it dissipate her terror. She dropped her forehead to rest on her knees as her heart slowed its pace and felt the dampness of her own tears against her skin. Her stomach rolled ominously as it always did after such an encounter and she sighed while her frustration rose to the fore.

One day 'twould all make sense, this she knew within her heart. Then and only then would the dream cease its torment, but she wondered now, as she had countless times before, how she would endure the waiting. 'Twas too much to keep living this nightmare, for she was certain 'twould make her old before her time.

But what of the change this night?

Sophie frowned to herself, lifted her head from her knees and peered into the shadows It *had* been different. She was sure beyond a doubt that the figure had been that of a woman every other time she had had the dream. Why had the tale changed this time, after being identical so many nights?

Would she ever know the truth of it?

Sophie shivered against the chill in the autumn air and rolled out of bed to close the shutters, certain that she could feel the moonlight touch her skin when she stepped into the glow it cast into the room. In mingled horror and wonder, she watched the goose pimples rise on her skin under the silver light before she hastily closed the shutters to lock out the moon's knowing eye with a sudden and irrational fear.

'Twas true the dreams made her fey, just as her mother had claimed from the beginning. Fey and flighty. 'Twas no manner for a woman grown, especially one born to a hard-working and practical household such as this. Sophie closed her eyes and forced herself to breathe at a normal rate once more. Would that she could just dismiss the dream and bid it torment her no more, she thought with gritted teeth, knowing she would not sleep again that night.

Perhaps there was someone else awake, she reasoned. She listened for an instant and fancied she heard voices rising from the kitchen below.

She immediately drew her surcoat over her shoulders and stepped out into the stillness of the hall, the familiar rumble of men disagreeing good-naturedly sending her hastening down the stairs for the reassurance of human contact.

''It cannot be good for business'' came the assertion as Sophie gained the bottom of the stairs. Naught was good for business as far as her eldest brother was concerned, but for once she refrained from pointing that out, and simply savored the welcome contrast of such practical and earthly matters to the questions left by her dream.

Something must be afoot for all four of her brothers to be gathered around the table at this late hour with their parents, and Sophie slipped into her seat as she listened.

"As long as the Franks do not interfere with the shipping," her father growled from the head of the table.

"'Tis the first thing they will do, have they a whit of sense among them," his firstborn claimed flatly, and Papa slanted an unappreciative glance in his direction.

"They will likely ravage the vineyards first," another of the boys pronounced before Papa could comment.

"They would not dare," her eldest brother declared, but his voice lacked conviction as he lifted his mug.

"What has happened?" Sophie demanded, and six bright pairs of eyes turned upon her. All of them spoke at the same time and only years of survival in this busy household left Sophie equipped to follow the conversation, although she had yet to find a way to interrupt her brothers once they began.

"Have you not heard the news?"

"Lost in daydreams, 'tis our Sophie all over."

"Sophie," Papa chided, "you must take more notice of the world about you. Louis is dead and his child will be king."

"More likely his wife will be queen."

"Think you not that she will take us all well in hand?" A ripple of laughter rolled around the table at that comment.

"I confess I still do not understand," Sophie interjected.

"The *entire* town is talking about it, Sophie."

"Where have you *been* this day?"

"Mooning about with Gérard the stonemason, likely as not."

"A stonemason?" Papa seized on those words angrily.

"One would think with her looks, Sophie could do better than a *mason*."

"But *this* mason has all the women watching him."

"Gérard is a hard-working young man," *Maman* observed evenly, her no-nonsense tones restoring order in a single stroke. She set a stoneware carafe of wine in the middle of the table with a deliberately heavy hand and cast a quelling eye over her brood. "The lot of you ought to know the value of that." Silence reigned a moment longer, until Papa shifted uneasily and frowned at the wooden table.

"A good living they make," he conceded with obvious reluctance.

"But little stability for hearth and home with their travels."

"And work only when times are good."

"Not like vintners, who prosper in good times and bad."

"Aye, folks will either celebrate or drown their sorrows."

"You need not trouble yourselves on that matter, for there is naught between Gérard and me," Sophie protested, knowing the objection was futile even as she spoke the words.

"Naught?"

"Woho! Mayhap that is where the trouble lies!"

"But a *mason*."

"Aye, she is pretty enough to do better, for all her faults."

"Surely you trust Papa to find a better match for you than a mason?" her eldest brother demanded, his words followed closely by Papa's horrified demand.

"Surely you have not compromised yourself?" he demanded sternly.

All fell silent at that thought and Sophie felt their eyes upon her. Fighting the urge to squirm beneath their perusal as it would only be misinterpreted, she held her father's gaze determinedly and ignored her brothers.

"Of course not," she declared flatly, and watched the tension ease out of Papa's shoulders at the surety of her declaration. "Should you trouble yourselves to listen to me, you would know in truth that I have no regard for the man."

"Indeed?" Papa gave her a lingering stare, but Sophie did not flinch.

"Should you truly have some regard for this mason, now is the time to speak your mind," *Maman* advised in a whisper, but Sophie could only shake her head.

"In truth, I have naught," she whispered back and her mother nodded slowly. Sophie had an uneasy sense that something was in the wind, but *Maman* turned away before she could ask for an explanation and Papa was returning to the business at hand once more.

"Perhaps 'twould be best for all of you to help the Norman cause," he advised his sons matter-of-factly and they groaned collectively.

"Already do we toil all the day," the youngest protested, spreading his hands palm up to show his calluses.

"And the vines are to be pruned again this week."

"Aye," Papa agreed easily. "But be assured that your assistance will be required."

"How?"

"What could *we* do?"

"More will I know after the town council meets tomorrow eve," Papa maintained calmly.

"I will accompany you," the eldest concluded with a terse nod, but Papa, to the surprise of all, shook his head adamantly.

"No. 'Twill be Sophie who accompanies me."

Sophie looked up in surprise and met the conviction in her father's eyes even as dissent broke out around the table. Why was she being so singled out? Her mother reached over and patted her hands, and Sophie had again the sense that something was afoot.

"Enough." Papa dismissed his sons' questions with a wave. "The matter is decided and 'tis time enough you found your beds. After all, a full day do I expect from you all on the morrow. As Bernard reminds us, the vines have to be pruned and the lot must be done by the end of the week."

Her brothers groaned dramatically as they pushed to their feet, the youngest slanting a glance across the table to his sister.

"Lucky you were to be born a girl," he muttered and Sophie smirked at that. Both of them missed their mother's sharp intake of breath.

"Some compensation there had to be for having brothers such as you," she teased, prompting him to grin unrepentantly.

When she turned to make a comment to her mother, Sophie was surprised to find that she had disappeared.

Hugues dismounted in front of the church the townspeople used for their meetings, handing his des-

trier's reins to his squire with all the nonchalance he
could muster. Certain that all who watched him were
aware of the nervousness coursing through his veins, he
removed his gloves deliberately and spared a casual
glance to the darkening sky above the tiled roofs as
though he had not a care in the world.

Far from the truth that was, he conceded to himself.
Indeed, Lady Blanche could hardly have granted him a
more difficult mission than to gain a pledge of support
from these skeptical townsfolk. Hugues was not looking forward to this meeting with the town leaders. Why
could the woman not have chosen one of the skilled
diplomats from her ranks of aides instead of himself,
the one knight least able to handle a delicate matter such
as this?

Politics were a tangled business here in Gascogne, the
nobility halfheartedly maintaining their old ties to the
Capetian king with his closer demesne, the townsfolk
naturally influenced by the strong links between their
vineyards and the Norman court.

Trust the Normans to attempt to take advantage of
the Louis' death to gain full sovereignty over this terri-
tory. Evidently they knew naught of Blanche of Castile
if they thought her a less worthy opponent than her de-
ceased spouse. Hugues grimaced at the realization that
the nobles of Gascogne evidently had missed that les-
son, as well, for they too played games with their allegiance in recent days.

Like as not, Hugues would set his foot square in the
middle of this mess, and well he knew it. Give him room
to swing a blade and he was fine, but set him amidst
politicians and he was quickly lost in the labyrinth.

Hugues openly acknowledged his shortcomings, but the lady had apparently thought him overly modest.

He supposed she would learn the error of her judgment soon enough.

All the way from Paris he had racked his brain in the vain hope he could avoid a disastrous betrayal of the lady's trust, and still he could find no compelling argument to persuade the people of Bordeaux to rally behind the French crown instead of the Norman one. He frowned at the sky and made some inconsequential comment about the weather to his squire, praying that none could see the rivulet of sweat making its way down his back.

More than tradition was on the Norman side, for they had levied a painfully severe tax just one year past and Hugues knew the townspeople would quite naturally expect from them more than one year tax free as a result. 'Twas unlikely indeed that the Capetians could match that, for part of the appeal of gaining the towns was admittedly the increase of revenue.

If only the virtually bankrupt Normans could manage to send an emissary to these wealthy townsmen demanding yet another tax, then Lady Blanche's side would certainly gain a better reception.

Hugues stepped forward, then hesitated on the threshold of the church as the fullness of that thought struck him. He considered the possibility for a long moment and acknowledged that it might possibly be accomplished. The Normans were certain to come begging for money sooner or later due to their financial straits, and perhaps he could arrange that their envoy *not* be detained. Hugues permitted himself a fleeting smile and slapped the leather of his gloves against his palm with satisfaction.

'Twould work, he knew. And hopefully 'twould happen soon enough that he could get to Paris and home to Pontesse again before his cursed sister Justine managed to entangle herself in another mess.

By the time she walked behind her father to the church, Sophie had contrived a dozen reasons for Gaillard's insistence that she accompany him, but not a one that pleased her or satisfied all of her questions. Neither of her parents seemed inclined to enlighten her, and she could not manage to dispel a sense of dread that lingered from the night before. Was it just the lingering remnants of her dream or had her family's insistence on discussing Gérard made her overly sensitive to any sign of matchmaking?

"Stand tall, child," her father scolded under his breath as they approached the church doors. Sophie had an uncanny feeling that her sense was right and her heart sank.

"And uncover your hair." That last demand clarified the matter beyond a doubt, for Sophie's blond tresses were her most marketable asset in this southern town.

Her father had brought her along to meet someone. At eighteen, she was slipping past eligibility, she knew, but to her mind 'twas not fair that she should be so singled out. Only the eldest of all her brothers had a betrothed and every one of the boys was older than her. And what sort of man would arrange to meet her through her father instead of addressing her directly?

None that she would care for, of that Sophie was certain.

At her father's quelling look she lifted her chin proudly, not missing the flash of disapproval in his eyes when she did not smile.

A young boy ducked forward to open the door for them and Sophie granted him a thin smile. Her gaze naturally followed the length of reins grasped in his other hand to the largest gray horse she had ever seen. She stared for a moment, amazed that a horse could be so large, that its coat could be so sleek or its caparisons so rich, before her father impatiently nudged her across the threshold.

The church was dusty and dim as usual, the last rays of light slanting through the stained glass, the scent of incense burned daily since its consecration lingering in the air. Sophie genuflected with her father before turning to join the group of men clustered in the shadows at the back of the church.

There was an alcove there used frequently for such gatherings, its walls lined with simple chairs. As Sophie turned, one of the men lit a tallow candle and the nook leaped with golden light. She helped to distribute flickering candles around the alcove, acknowledging with a nod several of the vintners who regularly commiserated with her father in the kitchen over sun, rain, soil and pestilence. The men seemed quieter than she would have anticipated and Sophie wondered whether they were as uncomfortable as she was.

"Begin we must if we are to see this matter through," the mayor proclaimed, and all hastened for seats. Sophie slipped silently into a chair beside her father and determinedly kept her eyes downcast.

"This eve we have the privilege of greeting Hugues de Pontesse, an envoy from the Queen Regent herself," the mayor continued when the shuffle had settled. "I would ask you consider his words carefully before you respond."

A ripple tripped through the assembly of thirteen men and Sophie wondered which of them her father had intended she should meet.

Surely not the aging Mayor Odet, for he had been a widower for as long as she could recall. And a healthy business the women at the east gates had built with his patronage alone, she thought, smothering her smile at the recollection of the gossip she had heard.

And surely not Pascal with his great hairy arms. 'Twas rumored his dark hair continued right down his back, and she shivered at the very thought. Surely it could not be him.

"I would thank you for your courtesy in assembling this night that I might extend my lady's offer to you," came a deep voice from the other side of the room. Sophie glanced up almost absently, her thoughts summarily dismissed when she met the incisive gaze of the cloaked figure from her dream.

'Twas fate, there could be no other explanation for his appearance both here and in her dream.

Sophie caught her breath in excitement, her gaze running quickly over him to confirm what she already knew was the truth. He was as tall and broad as she had seen him just a night past, his hair cropped at the nape in an unruly tangle of tawny gold. His skin was tanned, his brows lightened to gold, and it seemed from his size, coloring and the way he fairly growled when he spoke that he was some heraldic lion from a distant lord's standard come to life before her eyes.

She waited impatiently for his acknowledgment and finally his eyes flicked almost casually to hers.

Sophie felt every fiber of her being leap to life in the instant that their eyes met. Meant for each other they were and she knew she saw the realization of that truth in his expression, too. She boldly held his gaze for what seemed an eternity, her heart in her throat, but his eyes flicked away as though she were no more significant than a fly on the wall.

'Twas the company, she resolved quickly, and her heart was buoyed up with that thought as she scanned the assembly of men quickly. No forum was this to discuss the way the fates had ordained that they should meet and be together.

Sophie nodded to herself in the fullness of her understanding, filling with appreciation that he had kept his wits about him enough to follow social convention. Her heart glowed with pride that such a man was destined for her alone and she fought against the victorious smile that struggled to claim her lips.

She folded her hands together tightly in her lap and let her knight's voice roll over her as she studied him, a thousand tiny details coinciding with those in her dream. The almost lethargic way he gestured with one hand while he spoke was reminiscent of the way that same hand had lifted to pull back his cowl. The smooth way his words flowed reminded her of the keen intellect she had glimpsed in his eyes in her dream. So often she had despaired at thoughts of growing older without a mate, but now all those worries seemed for naught. Indeed, she had just been waiting for the destiny and the man that was her due.

And now he was here. And her future would begin.

He did not look to her again, but Sophie did not hold this fact against him, for she could see the evidence of his nervousness and assumed her presence was at the root of it. Somehow, after the council, they would have to meet and she busied herself with planning for the inevitable moment that she would speak directly with him.

What was the man thinking to bring his wife to such a meeting?

Hugues refused to fidget, forcing himself to concentrate on reciting his carefully rehearsed proposal and continuing to look each man in the eye in turn. The hairs on the back of his neck prickled with the awareness that the woman opposite was still watching him avidly, and the unexpected jolt he had received when those unusual violet eyes had met his still made his innards writhe.

But why would the man bring her here? Although if she looked at all men as though she would devour them whole, perhaps her husband was wise to keep her within sight. Hugues glanced over her without seeming to, and noticed once more the vast difference in the pair's ages, disliking that it bothered him. None of his business that was, he thought dismissively, forcing himself to continue with his presentation of the Queen Regent's proposal.

How was this being accepted by the council? In truth, Hugues could not tell, for his mind was consumed with his awareness of the woman opposite and her avid gaze.

And what of the older man seated so casually beside her? Was it really any of Hugues' business that their ages were so disparate?

Certainly not. 'Twas the way such things were done, particularly in these smaller towns, though he had never had much use for the practice. Hopefully *he* would have the opportunity to wed while he was yet young enough to choose a woman near his own age.

Not that any of that was relevant now, with his father still hearty if not hale, and indeed, Hugues knew he had no reason to even think of such matters, especially in this place and at this time. He glanced over the assembly, avoiding the opportunity to meet the woman's eyes again, and his heart sank when he saw that his offer was not being considered as seriously as he might have hoped.

Curse her for ruining his concentration when there was so much at stake! Leave it to a woman to foul up important matters with her nonsense. Hugues frowned to himself and addressed a man who seemed particularly skeptical, pouring renewed conviction into his argument with the hope that it was not too late to change the men's minds.

Just when Sophie thought she could endure the waiting no longer, the council meeting finally came to an end. The townsmen seemed particularly disgruntled, though she had not an inkling why; she had been so absorbed in watching her knight that she had neglected to listen to what was said.

Merely politics, she thought dismissively. She watched the knight answer a question of the mayor's while the other men gradually made their way out of the church, arguing heatedly amongst themselves. The mayor nodded thoughtfully at the knight's response and turned away. The knight summoned his squire with a quick gesture.

He meant to leave! Sophie panicked at the very thought that he intended to depart without speaking to her. Was he afraid to approach her before the others? Before her father? But where should she find him if he rode away without telling her his destination? Fear made Sophie even bolder than usual, and when her father turned to address one of the other men she slipped silently away from his side.

"Excuse me, milord, but I would speak with you."

Hugues knew without turning that 'twas the woman who addressed him and he steeled himself to meet that pale regard once more before he turned. What did she want from him?

"At your service," he responded with a polite inclination of his head as he turned, his heart taking a nervous leap when he saw that she stood alone before him. He flicked a quick glance over the emptied church and found her husband nowhere within view, much to his growing dismay. Was this some sort of trick to discredit him as a representative of the crown?

Hugues met the woman's eyes again, but her expression was devoid of guile. In fact, she smiled softly at him in a most disconcerting way, making him wonder if perhaps they had met before and he had been so gauche as to forget.

He studied her anew for some clue to trigger his faulty memory, noting now the honey gold hue of her skin, the slenderness of her figure beneath the draping of her kirtle, the delicate bones of her hands, so mismatched with the tan that could only have come from labor under the sun. He glanced back to her face and saw the resolve in the jut of her chin, the determination in those unusual violet eyes, but none of it struck a chord of familiarity.

"Have we perhaps met before?" he finally asked when she remained silent. It seemed to Hugues that she smothered a smile, but then she shook her head, leaving him more confused than ever.

"Nay, we have not," she replied simply. "But perhaps 'tis high time indeed that we did."

Hugues tried unsuccessfully to make some sense of that. If it had been some tavern whore before him, he would have known exactly what to make of her words.

An uneasy sense that he had missed some critical element in this exchange assailed him and he risked another glance to the woman, only to find her obviously fighting disappointment. He fidgeted restlessly, feeling unaccountably guilty even though he had no idea what she had expected him to do.

"Surely you have not decided to deny this?" she demanded unsteadily, and Hugues would not have been the man he was if that shimmer of tears in her eyes had not made him want to flee.

"Deny what?" he asked helplessly. He wished he had some idea of what was going on.

"Deny what?" she repeated angrily, one tear splashing over her cheek as she bit her lip in frustration and turned away for an instant. Hugues dared to hope that he had finally dissuaded her, but she seemed only to muster her strength in that moment and turned back on him with fury flashing in her eyes.

" 'Deny what?' you demand, as though there was naught between us," she snapped, her words strengthening Hugues's uncomfortable sense that he had forgotten something of import.

"I know not what you mean," he argued weakly, but his words were evidently not the ones she expected. She snorted with disgust and jabbed him in the chest with one slim finger, making the hard rings of his mail dig unexpectedly deep. Hugues did not dare to wince, but stood mute before her tirade.

"Who do you think you are, that you can so freely toss aside what mercies the fates would grant?" she demanded. Hugues knew he looked completely dumbfounded, for that he was.

"Play no games with me," she warned in a quieter tone, and when she leaned closer he saw once again the sparkle of tears in her eyes. "Can you not see that 'tis destined for us to be together?" she added and Hugues once again had that urge to run from Bordeaux as fast as he was able.

"Milady, indeed I meant no offense, but in truth it seems to me that you have erred," he argued hastily, taking a step backward to put some space between them. Just his luck 'twould be for her husband to return and find her hand pressed against his chest thus. To Hugues' dismay, she took a step to close the space and keep them toe-to-toe.

"I have not erred and this you know in truth," she asserted in a low voice, but Hugues folded his arms across his chest stubbornly.

"Then speak plainly of your meaning," he demanded. The shock that slid over her face before she hastily masked it made him feel the knave for speaking so boldly.

But no other way was there to hear the fullness of the tale, for clearly she thought he already knew something he did not. Unreasonable 'twas that he could have forgotten something of such significance as this woman and her intense manner, despite the weight of the matters on his mind, and he began to wonder if she was perhaps unbalanced.

"Destined we are for each other, for I saw it in a dream," she whispered with wide eyes, and Hugues' heart sank with the conviction that he had named it aright. Touched in the head she was, perhaps more than touched, and he felt a wave of sympathy for her husband that he must so closely tend his wife.

"You do not believe me," she said with disbelief, her low voice bringing Hugues abruptly back to the moment.

"Nay, milady, I do not," he agreed amiably. Something twisted inside him when again she seemed to fight her tears.

"But you *cannot* deny this," she argued. "I know it to be the truth in my heart and you must also know it within yours."

"Naught can one know with their heart," Hugues asserted firmly, welcoming the appearance of more familiar terms of discussion, "for 'tis an unreliable guide at best."

"'Tis the only voice that is reliable, for it alone speaks the truth," she countered in surprise, but Hugues only shook his head.

Trust the heart and its nonsense? 'Twas foolishness to follow such a path and certain to lead one into trouble. No matter how strenuously she argued, this slender blonde would not convince him otherwise.

"'Tis the intellect one must rely upon and naught else, milady, for 'tis logic alone that tells us of the greater truth," he argued, seeing incredulity light her eyes at his words.

"My heart tells me of a greater truth between us," she whispered almost reverently, but Hugues shook his head, determined to dissuade her from her foolishness, once and for all.

"A frivolous liar is the heart and you would do well to dismiss its tales," he retorted, but he had no time to savor a victory, for she immediately closed the remaining space between them and leaned into his chest with shocking familiarity.

He saw the glimmer of determination in her eyes just as he caught the scent of her skin, the smell of sun with a softly sweet undertone. Too late he saw that his resulting hesitation lasted just long enough for her purposes.

"'Tis your logic that tells false tales, milord, for this is a truth that will not be denied," she whispered as she leaned yet closer. Snared by the promise in her words, Hugues was powerless to pull away.

He saw her intent and managed somehow to turn his face slightly so that her lips landed on the corner of his mouth. Their softness and the way her scent assailed him almost proved his undoing. Hugues gripped her upper arms, fully intending to push her away, but instead his fingers curved around the strength he found there.

He was reminded of the willows he loved at Pontesse, so slim and supple yet strong beyond belief, and before Hugues knew what he was about, he had turned that last increment toward her and was tasting the fullness of her kiss.

She made some small sound of satisfaction at his gesture, but Hugues was lost in the ferocity of her demand, his own passion rising immediately to the fore. It seemed almost that she would devour him whole and Hugues crushed her against him as he answered her siren's call. No delicate maiden of the court was she, playing elaborate games of pursuit and barely tolerating the concession that she ultimately might feel compelled to grant. This one would rise to the occasion herself and the very promise of that kindled a fire in Hugues' loins.

No fear would he have of hurting this one, for she was not soft from years of embroidery like the women in Paris, and his mind immediately conjured an image of her splendidly nude. Despite his better judgment his hands seemed determined to aid the image, one slipping to the indent of her waist, the other to cup the firm curve of her buttock and lift her ever so slightly closer.

"Sophie!" barked a masculine voice from the portal and Hugues dropped the woman in shock. A glance across the room confirmed that 'twas indeed her husband come to fetch her and Hugues barely restrained a groan.

What had he been thinking? Indeed, 'twas nearly impossible to think at all in his current state and he spared a glance to the woman responsible, to find her looking similarly unsettled. At least he had not been alone in that, Hugues consoled himself, stunned when she laid a hand on his arm in a most intimate gesture.

"Your logic cannot explain that," she whispered unsteadily, but before Hugues could argue the point the man in the doorway cleared his throat angrily.

"Tomorrow, at Prime, at the east gate," she whispered, sailing across the room to her spouse before Hugues could agree or disagree to the liaison.

Astonishingly the man did not appear intent on calling Hugues out, at least not yet, and the two departed quickly. No wish had Hugues to be there when the woman got the tongue-lashing she undoubtedly deserved, but still he felt a modicum of guilt as he dropped bonelessly back into his chair once more.

Indeed, he had been partly responsible for the turn of events, for if he had managed to restrain his response, the kiss would not have endured as long as it had.

The kiss. Was that the only word for what had just occurred? Indeed, it seemed too light a term for that embrace, for the way he felt both exhilarated and drained in its aftermath, for the longing he felt already to taste her again.

Sophie, he thought, wondering how her name would roll off his tongue should he choose to voice it, before he abruptly dismissed that frivolous thought.

Hugues pushed to his feet and ran one hand through his hair in frustration, reluctantly conceding that 'twould probably make things worse for her if he showed up to defend her to her husband tonight. 'Twould be best if he simply retired to his room at the inn and left matters alone.

He snuffed the candles and ambled toward the door, somehow reluctant to leave this place, recalling suddenly her parting words. Everything within him leaped to life at the promise of that encounter before he stubbornly squelched his rising ardor. Such a meeting could only make matters worse for her and this he would not do, his own base instincts to the contrary.

"Sleep well this night, for we leave Bordeaux at Lauds," he sternly informed his squire, who waited at the portal, refusing to acknowledge the way the boy's face fell at the prospect of less sleep than usual.

"But the sun will not even be up, milord," Luc argued, earning himself a sharp glance from his master. He continued in spite of it. "Should we leave at Prime, mind you, the sun will just be rising and a full day for travel will there yet be."

"We leave at Lauds," Hugues reiterated firmly, his brows drawing together in annoyance. "And in the future, test not my patience with your arguments."

Chapter Two

Gaillard slammed the door to the kitchen so hard behind them both that Sophie jumped and glanced over her shoulder to find her father's brow furrowed into a thunderous scowl. *Maman* looked up in surprise from her endless mending, her brown eyes darting between daughter and spouse with concern as Sophie scampered to her side.

"No good can come of a child of the Maying," Papa growled in his wife's general direction. 'Twas the same charge he had made all the way home, though his enigmatic words had done little to enlighten Sophie. "This I told you eighteen years past, but naught did you listen to my counsel."

"What have you done, child?" *Maman* demanded curtly, but Sophie could only shrug.

"In truth, I know not."

"She knows not," her father muttered in annoyance, dropping into his customary place at the table and pouring an ample mug of wine from the carafe left at hand. "Whyever did you think I took you to the council this night?" he asked sharply. He fixed his daughter with a bright eye as he downed a draught of wine.

"I know not," she replied meekly, not daring to voice her suspicions in case she was wrong. Papa shook his head as though he were forced to deal with a particularly dim-witted individual and Sophie knew she was in serious trouble with her father.

"Was Gérard there?" *Maman* asked softly. Her words lent credence to Sophie's suspicions, but her spouse shook his head again.

"Nay, but he might as well have been for all the attention this one wasted on Rustengo."

"Rustengo!" Sophie repeated in amazement.

"Aye, *Rustengo,*" her father answered with a baleful glare. "A fine man he is with a prosperous enterprise, a man any other woman would be proud to stand beside."

"You would wed me to Rustengo de Cambris?"

At the confirmation in her father's expression, she dropped into a place opposite him in defeat. She had been right about her father's intentions, but that was small consolation now that he was so angry with her.

"Too old is he for me," she charged under her breath, and her father snorted in disgust.

"Little worry have you of him offering for your hand after this night," he retorted, then downed another mug of wine.

"Whatever do you mean?" *Maman* asked, putting her needlework aside and leaning toward her husband with increased concern.

"This child could not tear her eyes away from the queen's knight," Papa snapped with a wide gesture of his mug that set the remnant of wine within to splashing. At his wife's warning glance, he dropped his voice, muttering into his mug, "Eighteen summers and still she would turn aside all who come to the door."

"Sophie!" her mother chided. "Surely you did not ignore Rustengo?"

"No idea had I that I was to speak with him," Sophie argued. "Truly you should have told me of your intent."

"Ha!" her father snorted disbelievingly. "And willingly would you have followed me then?" he demanded. Sophie was forced to drop her gaze at the truth in his observation. "A veritable *knight* she eyes as boldly as a May Queen herself," he reminded his wife, quaffing yet another draught. "And no mere *local* knight for our Sophie. Nay. The man must be of the queen's own retinue."

"Sophie, what is this about?" her mother demanded when Gaillard seemed more intent on examining the bottom of his mug than imparting anything further.

"A knight there was from the Queen Regent," Sophie explained reluctantly, unwilling to reveal that she had recognized him from her dream. "Never have I seen one so finely arrayed," she concluded, feeling the inanity of the explanation as soon as she made it. "And such a beautiful destrier. In truth, I have never seen the like."

Her mother pursed her lips and examined her daughter thoughtfully across the table for a long moment before turning back to her spouse. "A simple enough explanation it seems to me," she commented mildly, earning another disbelieving snort from that man.

"Simple enough as far as it goes," Papa conceded and Sophie positively squirmed beneath the knowing expression in his eye when he turned back to confront her. "But 'twas more than that, was it not, Sophie?

Neither to the left nor the right did you look once you spied him and 'tis strange indeed that the man did not further acknowledge your regard."

"I know not what you mean."

"Indeed?" he asked archly, pushing resolutely to his feet. "Well enough do I know what I mean to compensate for us all. A child of the Maying you were eighteen winters past and still you are such. 'Tis but the blood of your kind asserting itself, for none of my seed could act in such a brazen manner."

With that he rose from the table to take his parting, but Sophie could not let him go. He was telling her something of import, this much she knew, but she would have the truth stated plainly before he left.

"What do you mean?" Sophie demanded as she rose to her feet.

"What do I mean?" her father repeated incredulously as he spun on his heel again to face her. "What do I mean? Let me state it plain so there are no questions left between us," he continued in a dangerously low voice. Sophie wondered in that moment whether it had been wise to demand the truth of him.

"No spawn of my seed are you," he declared with narrowed eyes, "but a child of the Maying, one born of trouble and certain to bring trouble, as I told Hélène all those years ago."

He placed his hand on his wife's shoulder and Sophie looked to her mother for a denial, but her gaze had dropped to the floor in silent confirmation. "A soft heart Hélène ever had and a yearning for a daughter we could not seem to bring into this world ourselves. 'Twas compassion alone that bade her listen to your natural mother's tale and compassion that saw you as a new babe enfolded in our home despite my protests."

Gaillard moved behind Hélène, his temper dissipating as he gripped both of her shoulders within his hands. Sophie watched his thumbs stroke the back of her mother's neck almost absently and something caught in her throat at the realization that the love dwelling within these four walls was no longer a part of her heritage, that in fact it never had been.

"Compassion. For so long even I thought it might be enough," Gaillard mused, suddenly piercing Sophie with a glance that seemed to go right through to her soul. "But 'tis within your very nature to disrupt the ways of men, child, just as the woman who spawned you bewitched some man and stole his seed."

"You are not my parents," Sophie managed to whisper through the tears that were rising to choke her. Gaillard's curt nod of agreement sent them spilling over her cheeks.

"No blood of ours do you share," he asserted flatly.

"And the others?" she had to ask.

"My sons are blood of my blood," he said, and the confirmation of what she already knew sent Sophie running out of the kitchen.

"Sophie!" Hélène cried, but Sophie could not stop her flight. Her mind was filled with unanswered questions even as she felt the surety of the pieces slipping into place, the certainty that Gaillard had told her the truth. All she could think of now was getting away, of finding time and space to think. She gained her attic room with relief, slamming the door and throwing herself across the bed in despair just as her tears broke.

The room had fallen into complete darkness by the time her sobbing ceased and Sophie sat up slowly, wiping the last vestiges of tears from her cheeks. She glanced around her familiar room thoughtfully, considering once again what it meant not to be born of this household.

Was she truly so different from the rest of the family even though they had raised her? Time and again over the years she had had the sense that she did not quite fit in, and now she wondered whether 'twas just fancy or fact.

Did Ramonet not tease her endlessly about being lost in daydreams, a pastime seemingly foreign to the other, more practical members of the household? Now her mother's look of concern when Sophie had first confessed to having the dream made perfect sense. Was it just the blood of "her kind" asserting itself as Gaillard claimed?

She flicked her hair over her shoulder, noting its wheaten color with a grimace, and wondered how she could have been so foolish not to guess her origins were different. What else could explain the fact that she alone was blond, that she alone did not have those flashing dark eyes the rest of her family shared?

Sophie stared at the coverlet with unseeing eyes and wondered what else her blood had granted her besides her coloring. Was this curious certainty of the veracity of thoughts that came unexpectedly a taint of her blood as well, or simply a part of herself at odds with her past?

Suddenly Sophie felt lost in a world not of her making, adrift like a boat without a rudder, for surely she belonged neither here in the comfort and security she had grown accustomed to, nor with the parents who had cast her aside eighteen winters past. She curled into a ball on the bed as she came to terms with this terrifying thought and struggled to make some sense of her life. Would she be alone, then, from this point onward?

And if she was no longer welcome here, where would she go?

Before she could speculate further on that question, a soft tap came at the door. Sophie rolled over to find Hélène framed in the doorway, her long hair unbraided and cast over one shoulder like a dark veil, her hand protectively cupping a flickering candle.

"I knew you had not a light," she said by way of explanation after an awkward pause.

The softly uttered words hung between the two of them for a long moment as each silently tried to gain a sense of the other's feelings. Sophie heard Gaillard's words as clearly as if he uttered them anew, though he was not even present, and she hugged her knees to her chest, unable to cross the room to the woman she had so long called *Maman*.

'Twere as though Hélène guessed her thoughts, for the candlelight caught the glimmer of tears in her eyes and she shrugged her shoulders apologetically as if she could not find the words. At that helpless gesture Sophie's own tears rose anew, but still she could not move.

"Never did I mean for you to learn the truth this way," Hélène murmured unsteadily.

Sophie closed her eyes against the flood of emotion launched in her chest by that confession. 'Twas absolutely true, then, and the knowledge that there would be no reprieve made Sophie abandon any lingering hope that Gaillard had merely spoken in anger.

"The truth will out," she contented herself with saying, her voice no more steady than the older woman's, and Hélène drew a shaky breath in turn.

The two women's gazes caught once more and held for a charged moment, then Sophie found herself on her feet and reaching for her mother. An instant later the candle was set on the floor and she was gathered close, the smell of Hélène's skin prompting a tide of childhood memories. Too much 'twas that this love was no longer hers to claim, and Sophie cried like a child once more, the recollections crowding into her mind making this revelation too painful to bear.

"So many times I wanted to tell you," Hélène whispered as she stroked Sophie's hair with practiced ease, and her head shook once in resignation. "But truly I knew not where to find the words." The older woman pulled back and cupped Sophie's chin as she stared into her eyes, compelling her to not look away despite her tears.

"I know at this moment the truth must seem of great import to you," she said softly, a ferocious undercurrent to her words, "but know this, Sophie. You suckled my breast as surely as though you were my very own and always have I thought of you thus."

Sophie had naught to say to that and swallowed with difficulty as she watched the tears rising anew in Hélène's dark eyes, even as the older woman smiled wryly and shook her head.

It seemed indeed that Hélène considered Sophie her own blood and Sophie marveled at the traitorous thoughts that flooded her mind. Regardless of who had suckled and raised her, Sophie knew with a flash of insight that some part of her, however small, had to carry an echo of the woman who had borne her. Hélène blinked several times in quick succession and glanced away for an instant, making Sophie wonder if her eyes had given her thoughts away, before Hélène snared her gaze once more.

"'Tis not in the making of men to understand this," she confided, "but know that Gaillard spoke in anger this night, as men are wont to do, and like I, he would not deny you even now."

"I do not understand," Sophie managed to say through the churn of her emotions, feeling more confused than ever. How could Gaillard speak so forcefully and not intend the words that crossed his lips? Hélène shook her head sadly and affectionately stroked the younger woman's cheek.

"Long indeed it has been since you came into our lives, Sophie," she mused, "and surely you know that we could not cast you out of our lives now."

"I know naught anymore," Sophie conceded uncertainly, having thought precisely that and earning another of those wan smiles from Hélène.

"I love you, child," she whispered urgently as she framed Sophie's cheeks within her palms. She frowned at the doubt in the younger woman's eyes and shook her head, with a resolution in her eyes impossible for Sophie to deny. "Regardless of how we began, 'tis here that we are now and a part of this family you are. A vow I made to raise you as my own, Sophie, and that vow I will keep until my last breath is drawn."

"But I am not your own," Sophie felt compelled to point out.

"Are you not?" Hélène demanded softly, but there was a new edge of determination in her voice despite its low timbre. "The creation of a child is a fleeting moment, but eighteen summers have I spent helping you become the woman you are."

When Sophie remained stubbornly silent Hélène continued. "Well do I understand that you feel a new loyalty to the woman who bore you, but think for a moment, child. Which woman in truth has given more? The one who abandoned you or the one who took you in?"

Unable to hold the older woman's gaze with such doubts running through her mind, Sophie pressed a kiss into each of Hélène's palms and turned away for a moment.

Was it true that she was a product of this household just like the boys, that her bloodline had contributed naught to whom she had become? Why then did Gaillard feel compelled to point out her roots if 'twas true there was no difference?

"What did Papa mean when he called me a child of the Maying?" she demanded through the tightness in her throat, seeing Hélène shake her head out of the corner of her eye.

"'Tis not the time for such things," she said simply, but Sophie turned back to face the older woman.

"I would know the truth of the matter now," she insisted. Hélène held her gaze for a long moment before she sighed and sat down heavily on the side of the bed as though the confession would cost her dearly.

"Naught is there for you with her, Sophie," she claimed in a voice that seemed now tired beyond her years. "Indeed, her days may be already passed for all we know. Truly I seek only to keep you from hurt."

"I would know the truth," Sophie insisted once more, and this time Hélène nodded in resignation.

"Then you shall have it, but blame me not should you not find it to your taste," she warned, and Sophie folded her arms across her chest to brace herself for the telling. The older woman fidgeted with the bed linens for a long moment, seemingly trying to find some way to begin. She frowned and Sophie bit her bottom lip to still its trembling, knowing without a doubt that she would *not* find this tale to her taste.

"'Tis said that in the north they still practice the old ways," Hélène began with obvious reluctance and Sophie stifled a frisson of dread at her mother's manner. "An old rite 'tis, to celebrate the return of the sun on May Eve."

"Still we dance on May Day," Sophie injected in confusion, finding nothing disreputable in the familiar tradition, but Hélène shook her head adamantly.

"'Tis but a shadow of the past," she asserted, "for the Church has removed much found objectionable to the Fathers." She smoothed a wrinkle from the coverlet and frowned to herself, as if she sought words to make the tale easier.

"'Tis thought fertility in the May Queen herself was promise of fertility of the earth," she blurted out more abruptly than was usually her manner. "Naturally, little was left to chance." Hélène fixed her daughter with a sharp look and Sophie braced herself for the worst of it.

"'Tis her task to welcome all between her thighs on that night of nights," she added flatly, turning to brush the coverlet almost absently while Sophie struggled against the implication behind her words.

"To what purpose?" Sophie croaked. Already had she guessed what the answer would be but wanted to hear the bald truth put into words.

"'Tis considered a divine sign that the land will be blessed should the May Queen round with child." Hélène tilted her head to one side to watch her daughter's reaction. Sophie paced to the window as her cheeks heated in humiliation and she tangled her fingers tightly together before her.

She was a bastard born of some ancient pagan rite. 'Twas shame alone that had compelled her mother to surrender her, and Sophie felt as though her lungs would burst with the strain of the knowing. She breathed deeply in the expectant darkness of her little room with its steeply pitched roof and forced herself to demand the rest of the tale, knowing she might never have the chance again.

"You said 'twas in the north," she said, barely recognizing her own strained voice. "How then did I come to be here?"

"The priest before Father Reisac—he died when you had seen but two summers—he knew that my heart yearned for a daughter," Hélène answered with some hesitancy. "His cousin was a parish priest in Bretagne and 'twas he who sought a home for the child. A home for you."

"Know you my mother's name?" Sophie asked quietly. The terse silence that filled the room behind her made her pulse accelerate in anticipation.

"Nay," Hélène declared flatly and Sophie turned, certain that the older woman was lying. She met the conviction in Hélène's gaze and her own surety died a quick death at the sight.

'Twas all she would ever know about her mother, apparently. A May Queen who had fulfilled her task and surrendered her babe in shame. Sophie watched the older woman rise to her feet and was disappointed that she knew so little about her mother. Hélène shot her a sharp look as though she had sensed the turn of her thoughts.

"Chase not the past, Sophie, for 'twill only bring you grief," Hélène advised in a low tone. Sophie nodded mutely in response, numb from all the revelations of this evening. Hélène smiled and stepped toward Sophie, cupping her chin once more and kissing her gently on each cheek.

"Sleep now, child, 'twill all look better in the morning."

"Yes, *Maman*," she responded unthinkingly, watching a tentative smile curve Hélène's lips.

"'Tis good to hear you speak thus," she whispered, sparing a final pat for Sophie's cheek. Sophie knew not what to say.

"Think this night whether you would have Gérard or Rustengo for dinner tomorrow eve," Hélène advised quietly, turning to pick up the candle and slipping from the room on silent feet.

Neither, Sophie concluded stubbornly as she dropped back onto her straw mattress, struggling to make sense of all she had learned. Disappointment threatened to overwhelm her but she forced herself to concentrate on the one bright spot in her evening.

A good thing 'twas that she and her knight were destined for each other, she reasoned with relief. Had there been no more than tender feelings between them, he might be distressed by her roots. Bad enough 'twould have been for her to be the spawn of a mere townsman in that case, for there would certainly be objections from his family to overcome, but to be a bastard of unknown parentage was incomparably worse.

Lucky indeed she was that destiny had taken the sting from this revelation so it could not foil their plans for a life together. Sophie hugged herself as she watched the stars through the open shutters, reminding herself to awaken in time to reach the east gates by Prime.

Her dream came again that night, but Sophie immediately saw that some cloud had been lifted from her vision, for everything was etched in new clarity. She approached the looming shapes and saw now that they were massive stones stood on end, arranged in the circle she knew she would enter, as well as in lines that stretched off as far as the eye could see.

Sophie nervously stepped within the circle of gigantic stones, disconcerted beyond compare by this clearer perception, fancying she could see the individual embers of the fire glowing to one side. She swallowed with difficulty and lifted her gaze to the opposite side of the clearing.

Her heart fairly stopped at the sight of the cloaked figure.

'Twas the woman again, and as she stepped closer Sophie was certain her new sight granted her the ability to see even the weave in the wool of the cloak. She knew she had not noted the deep plum shade of the cloak before, but all thought left her mind when the figure hesitated, then reached for edge of the cowl. Sophie forced herself to watch, hoping for a revelation, but the shock of what she saw when the hood fell back fairly stopped her heart.

No face had she, naught but a dark shadow revealed by the glowing embers of the fire. It could not be thus, and Sophie panicked as she stared at the figure before her, struggling to make some sense of it all. But when that hand stretched toward her, the figure clearly intending to draw her into its nothingness, Sophie parted her lips to scream.

She awoke with her heart pounding in her ears to find herself sitting up in her bed, the coverlet clutched to her chest and a cold sweat trickling down her back.

All Hugues' intentions were cast aside like leaves before the wind when he awoke to find the rosy tendrils of dawn creeping through his shutters to warm his face. Lauds had come and gone while they slept and now 'twas inevitable that he would meet that woman at the gates.

The realization brought him to his feet in alarm. He tripped over his unsuspecting and gently snoring squire, who did not stir at the disturbance, and barely restrained himself from shouting until the boy awoke.

'Twould serve Luc right for so blithely forgetting his instruction, but Hugues had not the heart to abruptly awaken him from his slumber despite the trouble he looked to be embroiled in. Instead Hugues satisfied himself with an eloquent stream of vulgarities muttered beneath his breath, then ensured that he made enough noise getting dressed that the boy could not help but awaken.

After all, why was he so distressed? 'Twas merely a woman he would cross paths with, a woman who had not even the weakest grip on the realities of this world.

A married woman whose touch made him forget all else.

Hugues fumbled with his hauberk in his haste to be safely on the road. A variety of options flitted through his sleepy mind and were discarded just as quickly. Remaining in Bordeaux was hardly an effective way to avoid the woman, and leaving by any other gate would send him leagues out of his way, an irrational choice that he refused to make to simply avoid crossing paths with a woman.

Even if her husband was certain to tear him from limb to limb should she land another of those incendiary kisses on him.

Hugues' normally nimble hands were all thumbs once more as he fastened on his scabbard, stifling a groan when he realized that his frenzied pace would land him at the east gate almost precisely at Prime. His squire stirred and rubbed his eyes sleepily and Hugues could not refrain from commenting.

"'Tis good of you to awaken in so timely a manner," he said, watching with satisfaction as Luc's eyes flew open and his jaw dropped in shock when he noticed the pinkening sky.

"Oh, milord, I am sorry," he apologized, all afluster as he immediately rose, hauling his tunic over his tousled head at the same time as he tried to rearrange his chausses. "'Tis all my fault that we are late to the road, for you charged me well with the task of awakening you before Lauds." The boy glanced out the window and back to Hugues with a look of such despair that Hugues almost laughed aloud.

"'Tis nearly *Prime,* I wager," he whispered with something akin to awe and Hugues nodded but once.

"Aye, that 'tis, indeed," he agreed. "Now cease your chattering and hasten yourself. We must make Saint Macaire in short order."

"Yes, milord." The boy bobbed a bow, scurrying out of the room with only one foot shod, pausing partway down the stairs to hop in place while he tried to haul on the other shoe.

Hugues watched Luc's departure with an indulgent smile, picking up the bread left by their host and tucking it into his pack lest the boy be hungry later. Already the lad learned quickly and they had been together but half a year. A good knight he would make one day, Hugues was sure of it. He took a deep breath as he recalled his own plight of this morning and squared his shoulders determinedly, reminding himself that he had naught to fear from a mere woman.

Even one seemingly as unbreakable as his beloved willows.

The church bells awakened Sophie and she rolled over with a groan, achingly tired after her restless night. She opened one eye warily when she realized that the house was silent, and came fully awake in a flash at the bright sunlight weaving through the slats of the shutters.

Nay! She could not have slept this late! Sophie threw open the shutters with dismay, the activity in the streets below telling her without a doubt that the bells were ringing for Terce and that Prime was long gone. Indeed, that merry old sun was climbing over the rooftops, well on its way to zenith. The silence in the kitchen made perfect sense now. Why had her family not awakened her on this day of all days?

Mayhap he had waited for her.

That thought alone had Sophie dressed and almost flying down the stairs in the blink of an eye. She paused in the deserted kitchen just long enough to hastily push her feet into her leather shoes and toss her cloak over her shoulders before bolting out the door and running for the east gates of town.

"Whoa, Sophie!"

Rustengo de Cambris gripped Sophie's shoulders to steady her as they collided just outside the door. Sophie regained her footing, dancing away from beneath the weight of his hands once she realized who stood before her. Rustengo smiled encouragingly, the expression in his eyes making Sophie recall Gaillard's plans and she knew not what to say.

"Good morning," she managed to say, and he nodded in greeting.

"And a good morning 'tis indeed to encounter you," he answered politely. "Although I regret that last evening we had not the chance to speak."

Sophie saw in his alert gaze something of what must have prompted Gaillard to accept the idea of the match. That glimmer of humor lighting his dark eyes reminded Sophie of her teasing brothers. Rustengo was well reputed as a hard worker and his polite manner toward her made Sophie realize that she might not have protested so much had she not already found her knight.

How lucky for destiny that she had met Hugues de Pontesse in time.

"'Twas indeed regrettable," she agreed hastily, impatient to get to the gates. "But I must not detain you from your business this morning."

"As my intention was to speak with you, 'tis unlikely you could manage that," Rustengo replied with a wry smile and Sophie thought quickly.

"'Tis unfortunate indeed that I have another task this morning," she countered.

"Indeed? Your father convinced me that you had naught with which to occupy yourself this morn."

Understanding dawned in Sophie's mind and she fairly stamped her foot in annoyance. So this was why she had not been awakened with the rest of the family. Did Gaillard not understand that he was meddling with the fates?

"Perhaps my father knew naught of my obligations." Before Rustengo could say something else, Sophie brushed hastily past him, determined not to give any further explanation.

"My pardon, sir, but I am terribly late," she excused herself, leaving her would-be suitor abandoned before the house, a puzzled frown puckering his brow.

And terribly late was truly what she was, Sophie acknowledged with a sigh when she had pushed her way through the jostle of the market only to find neither destrier nor knight waiting at the east gate. She felt her shoulders droop in defeat but forced herself to continue forward.

Certainly a knight in the Queen Regent's service could not afford to idly wait for her all day, Sophie told herself sadly. The very thought that he might think she had changed her mind made her want to drop to the ground and sob. She climbed the stairs to the scaffolded catwalk running along the inside of the thick stone wall and confronted the dark water of the Garonne right outside the city walls.

The bridge spanning the river was devoid of knights and Sophie scanned the horizon dispiritedly, knowing before she looked that she would be unable to see him, but helpless to stop herself from peering into the distance. Something flashed far away on the serpentine twist of the road and she fancied 'twas a knight's mail or his scabbard catching the sunlight.

Where had he gone? Sophie cursed herself now for not paying more attention to his words the previous night, for evidently he was on the business of the Queen Regent and might have made some mention of his path. How like her to lose interest in the words another spoke and miss some critical tidbit of information. She sighed and shoved her hands deep into her pockets, acknowledging how much she had been counting on being with him.

How would she ever find him again?

Had she perhaps put too much emphasis on her own sense that their togetherness was inevitable? Sophie reviewed their conversation in her mind, seeing now his hesitation, and cringed a little inside that she had not noticed earlier. Was it possible that he had not had the same feeling that their destinies were entwined? His condemnation of the heart's advice echoed in her mind once more and she closed her eyes against her own stupidity. Had she but paid attention to his protests, she would have realized last night that she had surprised him.

Had he deliberately ensured that they would not meet this morn?

The thought sickened Sophie, and she was suddenly glad that she had been late and could pretend to herself that he had been here at Prime. For she would not likely see him again. That sad thought, coupled with the realization that she had only herself to blame for sending him running, made her heart drop like a stone in her stomach. Destiny had been thwarted and 'twas all her own fault.

All of the concerns of Sophie's mundane life came back to roost in that moment and she leaned back against the wooden rail, unable to stand on her own any longer. She rubbed her temples in recollection of the way she had left Rustengo, knowing Gaillard would have plenty to say about that, especially since he had deliberately let her sleep late this morn that she might have a liaison with the suitor.

She would be in trouble on two fronts for that, for she was certain she had heard something of a ship leaving with the tide tonight and knew full well that precious little wine was casked for shipment. 'Twas her task to measure the wine, fill and seal the casks, and even though Gaillard himself was to blame for her not working this day, that fact would leave his mind were he angry with her, and angry he would surely be.

And what of this business of her parentage? Cursed to disrupt the ways of men, Gaillard had charged. Was it true that she carried some taint that had made it impossible for her not to give in to the impulse to kiss Hugues de Pontesse?

In truth, she had thought it the only way to convince him, and the intensity of the embrace had stunned her. From the look in his eyes when they had pulled apart, the knight had felt much the same, but Sophie could not imagine herself as the powerful temptress Gaillard spoke of. Indeed, she had kissed no other man than her knight and had never even wanted to do so. Was this truly some kind of witchery, as Gaillard maintained?

And with her knight well and truly gone, Sophie would have to decide for herself what to do with her life. Clearly if she remained here Gaillard would have her wed to Rustengo or some other should she refuse him and, at that realization, her lips pulled into a taut line.

She would have her knight or no one, Sophie resolved firmly. If the fates had decided to take him from her in retaliation for her foolishness, she would bear the punishment willingly, for he alone was the one intended for her.

This made it difficult to stay in Bordeaux, for Gaillard would not be denied much longer, now that the truth was on the table. Suddenly Sophie recalled her dream and that the knight had met her once in the mysterious clearing. Was it a sign that he would meet her there again? Did that clearing exist other than in her dream?

Chapter Three

"Too troubled you look for such a beautiful morning," came a familiar masculine voice, and Sophie glanced up with a start to find Gérard the stonemason beside her. He grinned when she met his eyes and Sophie smiled tentatively in return, not knowing what else to do.

"What could possibly trouble a pretty woman on a day such as this?" he demanded good-naturedly, folding his arms across his chest as he leaned against the rail alongside her.

Sophie looked to the bustle of activity below just in time to see one of Bordeaux's worst gossips turn away with a secretive smile and knew news of this encounter would soon reach Gaillard's ears. Would naught go right for her this day?

"I confess I was merely lost in my thoughts," she demurred when Gérard looked as though he intended to wait all day for her answer.

She would have departed with that comment, but Gérard showed no signs of moving and he effectively blocked her way to the stairs. Sophie met his eyes again, the twinkle she found there making her realize that he was well aware of her plight, and she settled back against the rail with a poorly concealed sigh.

"Your work here looks to be almost done," she observed for lack of anything better to say. He nodded in quick agreement, his gaze flicking over the stonework as if assessing just how much longer the repairs would take.

"Aye, 'twill be done afore the winter wind is up," he concurred, his manner almost expectant as he turned back to Sophie. She avoided his gaze, staring out to the point where the road disappeared into the smudge of the horizon, and tried to think of a way to make conversation. Anything to take her mind off the fact that he was watching her so intently.

"And whither then for you?" she asked without any particular interest, knowing that masons traveled constantly.

"Depends on a number of things, that does," he conceded, and Sophie felt his gaze upon her once more.

"I suppose one must take work where one can find it," she observed. Gérard made some small sound that could have been a sign of acquiescence.

"Aye, there is that, though there is always work for one who can use his hands," he maintained calmly. Something in his tone prompted Sophie to glance up, but he was staring down at his hands with a frown. The quick glance he abruptly flicked in her direction surprised her with its intensity, and she caught her breath.

"Easily could I be convinced to work the winter as a wright here," he said softly. "Wright's work there is aplenty in this town." His meaning was obvious and Sophie took a hesitant step backward, watching something in his eyes fade at her gesture.

"I would not falsely encourage you," she said quietly. He looked away abruptly, his mouth drawing into a thin line.

"At least you are honest," he muttered, and Sophie was dismayed that she had so easily hurt him. She laid one hand on his arm and he shot another of those quick glances in her direction before he cleared his throat.

"Gérard, 'tis not that I do not like you, for I do," she added, watching him square his shoulders, though he continued to stare into the distance. "'Tis simply that I have already given my heart."

That assertion captured his attention and his gaze swung to hers once more. Sophie wondered how much he could see as they stood silently regarding each other. Something mystical there was reputed to be about masons and their understanding of magical numbers, and she felt in that instant that he saw clear through to her soul.

"I would have you remember me should he fail you," Gérard said quietly, and now Sophie turned away that he might not see more.

"Tell me where you have been and where you will go," she urged, anxious to change the subject lest she be forced to face the fact that her knight might have already failed her. At the very least, he was gone and she knew not where.

Gérard chuckled dryly and out of the corner of her eye she saw him shake his head. "A lifetime 'twould take to tell you everywhere I have been," he said, not without a measure of irony, "and already have you denied me that. Of what would you like to hear, Sophie?"

At his words, an idea occurred to Sophie and she turned to regard him at the very simplicity of the thought. "Have you ever seen great stones stood on end?" she demanded, but Gérard simply smiled.

"Stones I stand on end every day when I build," he jested, but she shook her head.

"No, uncarved stones," she clarified. "In a circle or a line." Something brightened in Gérard's eyes and Sophie dared to hope in that instant that the place in her dream truly existed.

"Aye," he said thoughtfully. "Aye, tales I have heard of the stones of Bretagne, though I know not whether they be in lines or circles." He looked at Sophie hopefully and she could barely contain her excitement at what he revealed.

"Where are they?"

"West of Vannes, I hear, on the sea," he confided and Sophie's heart leaped at his unconscious confirmation of another detail from her dream.

She had heard of Vannes. 'Twas beyond Nantes where their ships often stopped to sell wine. Gérard cleared his throat expectantly but Sophie barely noticed, his next words taking her completely by surprise.

"I would take you there, should you wish to go," he offered in a low voice, rushing on when Sophie turned to him in openmouthed surprise. "Soon 'twill be too cold for the mortar to dry and the work here will be done at any rate. Together we could travel north, for I, too, would like to see these great stones."

"'Twould be most inappropriate," Sophie murmured, though she was half tempted by the offer.

"Not if we were wed," Gérard maintained stiffly. Sophie knew it could not have been easy for him to broach the subject again so close in the wake of her refusal.

"Already did I tell you I had granted my heart," she reminded him softly, surprised at the defiance that lit his eyes at her assertion.

"Think you that I cannot see your hurt?" he demanded. "'Tis there for all to see that already has this knave treated you poorly." His voice rose slightly with his insistence and he laid a hand on her arm. "Good 'twould be between us, Sophie, and well you know it. A fine living do I make and never would you know abuse at my hand."

Sophie shook her head stubbornly. She could have no other than her knight.

"Nay, I cannot."

"Nay, you *will* not," Gérard answered, his vehemence drawing Sophie's startled gaze to his.

"I must listen to my heart," she argued, angered when Gérard shook his head dismissively.

"Already does it lead you astray," he retorted, gripping her shoulders in his hands. "Answer me not now if you cannot, but think upon my words." He squeezed her shoulders briefly before he turned and leaped agilely down the ladder stairs.

"Hugues de Pontesse!"

Hugues almost jumped at the familiarity of that boisterous voice, and glanced up from the remnants of his meal just in time to see his brother-in-law land an enthusiastic hand on his shoulder.

"Jean de Fontaine!" he exclaimed with delight, rising to shake hands with the other knight.

Long indeed it had been since he had crossed paths with the man but a few years his senior and he cast an appraising eye over his sister's spouse, noting that he had changed little since taking over the management of

Fontaine. A few of the inn's other patrons looked on their meeting with interest, but the two knights were oblivious to their curiosity.

"Good indeed 'tis to see you," Jean asserted with a firm shake of Hugues' hand. One of his dark brows lifted speculatively when he caught a whiff of Hugues' meal and his eyes widened appreciatively. "God's blood, that smells good," he muttered and Hugues grinned outright as he gestured to the keeper.

"All is well at Fontaine?" he demanded, prompting a proud grin from his companion.

"Michel is *talking* since last you visited," he confided proudly, arching a brow to emphasize the import of his words. "High time 'tis we find you a bride so the boy will have somewhere to squire."

"Aye, aye," Hugues agreed easily, his mind flitting of its own accord back to the woman in Bordeaux. Only too well did he recall the disappointment that had surged through him when she had not been at the gates, and he pushed the recollection from his mind with an effort.

"Sit with me and tell me your news," he invited.

Jean dropped to the trestle bench opposite and braced his elbows on the table without further encouragement. He shoved back his mail coif with a tired gesture to run his fingers through his ebony hair and Hugues noted a few threads of silver now gracing his temples. Jean caught his eye and noted the direction of his gaze, grinning ruefully as he fingered the curly hair there, and shook his head.

"Louise ages me afore my time," he said with a mock sigh. Hugues laughed aloud at the reference to his tolerant sister, knowing full well that 'twas Jean's antics that would turn any other woman gray before her time.

"Aye, too often have I heard that complaint to put much stock in it," he teased. "And well indeed do I remember the enthusiasm of your courting." Jean grinned unrepentantly at that charge and Hugues shook his head indulgently.

"What brings you so far afield?" he asked, amused when his brother-in-law cast a covert glance to those surrounding them and dropped his voice.

"'Tis the wine," Jean confided, rolling his eyes and grinning when Hugues chuckled under his breath. The keeper chose that moment to deposit on the table a pewter tankard of said red substance along with a bowl of savory stew, and Hugues nodded silently that he would see to the charge.

"Naught will I hear of that," Jean protested, intercepting the gesture just as he lifted the tankard to his lips, but Hugues shook his head adamantly.

"Take your thanks to the Queen Regent," he explained as he tossed the keeper a silver denier, and Jean laughed aloud.

"Still in the envoy trade, then, are you?" he demanded jovially.

"Aye, and a hearty business 'tis indeed these days," Hugues agreed dryly, taking a draught of his own wine.

"Well, my thanks to the lady for her generosity," Jean said with a wink, "and you may confirm to her my loyalty to the crown."

"A pledge worth far more than a tankard of wine," Hugues pointed out with a smile, and Jean laughed again.

"Aye, 'tis my logic exactly," he agreed, lifting his tankard to touch Hugues' in toast. After they drank, Hugues braced his elbows on the table and fixed Jean with a quizzical eye.

"But your loyalty does not interfere with your acquisition of Gascon wine," he charged softly. This prompted a mischievous grin from his companion.

"As I see it," Jean confided, leaning across the table, his voice a mere whisper, "'tis my best and likely my only chance to fill Fontaine's cellars with fine wine while kings and queens squabble between themselves over this piece of turf."

"And what shall you do with it all before it sours to vinegar?"

"Oho." Jean chuckled and wagged one finger across the table at Hugues. "Well you know that Louise is but two months away from her time. Soon enough I shall be forced to entertain the lot of you hard-drinking folk from Pontesse. 'Twill be gone afore the Yule, should I not miss my guess."

"Without paying the tariff, to boot," Hugues charged without a measure of humor, but Jean swept that comment aside.

"'Tis not the tariff, for gladly would I pay it were the wine simply made available." He grimaced, and summoned the keeper once more with a gesture to the emptied tankards. "Those cursed Normans insist the better part of the vintage be shipped to their courts in Londres."

"Selfish lot. Right it is then that we should be at war with them," Hugues observed matter-of-factly.

Jean shot him a sharp glance at the unexpected irony in his remark. "'Tis not my imagination that you are less than yourself this night," he stated flatly as the wine splashed into the tankards. He slipped the keeper some silver before Hugues could retrieve his own, waving away his objections with ease.

"Readily will I accept our lady's graciousness when we discuss politics," Jean said by way of explanation, "but 'tis of personal matters I would talk now and only proper the fee should be our own. Unless 'tis this missive you deliver that has you so distressed?"

Hugues shook his head. "Nay, 'tis not that, though that goes not terribly well, either, now that I reflect upon it." Hugues sighed and considered the bubbles rimming the surface of his wine. He had not had much better luck here than in Bordeaux, though in truth 'twas a certain woman who distressed his thoughts more than any business of the crown.

What he needed now was a Norman envoy sent to collect a new tithe, he reminded himself sternly, deciding to head directly down the Garonne from here and see if he could not find one to deliberately let pass into the region.

"Well you know that you have my fullest attention, should you wish it," Jean interjected, and Hugues looked up with a start.

The intensity in Jean's gray eyes before he returned his attention to his ignored meal told Hugues more eloquently than words that the offer was sincerely meant. Hugues turned his tankard thoughtfully within the ring of dampness it had made on the table, knowing full well that the tale would go no farther should he choose to confide in Jean.

"'Twas a most unusual woman I met that has me troubled," he began quietly, not intending to say anything of the kind.

"A promising start, that," Jean commented with a flash of the devil in his eye, but Hugues frowned to himself in concentration.

"Aye, well enough it could have been so simple, but *something* there was about her...." His words faded as he knew not what to say, well aware that Jean was watching him with avid interest. Hugues frowned anew, trying to put his finger on exactly what 'twas that had so disturbed him about the blond woman.

"Indeed, it seemed I knew exactly the moment she looked at me," Hugues added almost to himself. Certain he was that the other knight would laugh at such fancy, but he glanced up in time to see both of Jean's brows rise in surprised acknowledgment.

"What is it?" he demanded. Jean leaned one elbow on the table, wagging a finger right beneath Hugues' nose as he spoke.

"Well you should know that Louise has done thus to me right from the start," he murmured. Hugues swallowed nervously at the implication of that. "'Tis a bad sign for a man not yet ready to wed," Jean commented idly. He took a long moment to study Hugues' features before he sat back and took another draught of wine, that speculative light still in his eyes.

"Have you spoken with her?" Jean asked.

Hugues nodded before he thought to do otherwise. "Aye," he confirmed. "And such a tale she spun of us being destined for each other that indeed she must be quite mad."

"Destiny?" Jean repeated skeptically.

"Aye, destiny." Hugues fairly spat the word he was growing to dislike intensely, his annoyance surprising him as it rose with the telling of the tale. "And when she kissed me, she fair turned me inside out."

"Perhaps I should buy enough wine for a wedding, as well," Jean muttered under his breath as he returned to his meat.

"Surely you jest," Hugues demanded abruptly, earning another of those doubtful looks from his brother-in-law.

"You have met her but once?" he asked in turn and, at Hugues' reluctant nod, Jean shoved aside his bowl impatiently. "'Tis not so premature as that for you to think to wed," he reasoned with apparent sincerity. His words sent a cold trickle of fear through Hugues's veins. "Louise has said the old man looks to be fading."

"Wait but a moment," Hugues protested angrily. "Naught did I say of marriage. 'Twas Sophie who seemed thus inclined, not I."

"Sophie?" A sly grin slid over Jean's features. "And why would you not consider marriage to this *Sophie* who ties you into knots with but one kiss? There are worse ways to find a wife."

"She is wed already, I fear," Hugues muttered irritably, feeling the color rising on his neck at Jean's teasing.

"And yet she thinks enough of her spouse to bestow upon you a kiss fit to turn you inside out? Unlikely indeed that seems, for surely if the woman held you in regard she would not see your health so endangered." Jean looked quizzical, but Hugues refused to indulge his curiosity.

"'Tis evident the woman is mad," he growled, wishing too late that he had not broached the subject.

"You could not have misjudged the situation?" Jean inquired with a cavalier air, but Hugues remained stubbornly silent. Jean spared an irreverent wink for the two women near the fireplace who had watched his antics. The women turned abruptly back to their gossip and Jean grinned wickedly across the table to Hugues.

"Just think." He dropped his voice to whisper conspiratorially. "She might be related to *vintners.*" Hugues eyed his brother-in-law warily, not in the least reassured by the merry twinkle in his eyes. "*Gascon* vintners," he clarified with evident relish and Hugues stirred himself to halt this conjecture.

"Naught do I know of her family," he protested but Jean waved a finger knowingly.

"And where did you meet the woman?"

"At the meeting called by the town council," Hugues confessed slowly, watching Jean smile.

"Surely all members of the council in Bordeaux are vintners?" he asked idly and Hugues felt his color heighten at the accuracy of Jean's guess.

"'Tis of no matter to you that the woman is clearly mad?" Hugues replied, but Jean only shrugged easily and drank leisurely of his wine.

"Aye, she must be mad to think herself in love with you," he countered practically. "Though 'tis undoubtedly an affliction many a man could see his way clear to living with."

"What about her class?" Hugues retorted angrily, uncertain why Jean's arguments were annoying him so much. Had he not been the one to broach the subject? "Does it mean so little to you that she is of a mere bourgeois background? And what if she is wed? Surely even you could not expect me to consider a woman who abandoned her match."

"To the wrong man are you speaking if you seek the voice of social convention," Jean commented with a grin.

"Aye, true enough that is," Hugues agreed dryly.

Jean laughed outright, leaning across the table in his confidential pose once more. "Mark my words," he advised, "for thoughts will surely change on these conventions. Better equipped are these vintners and merchants to retrieve silver deniers from the pockets of all and sundry than we with the expense of all our land and keeps to maintain." Jean cleared his throat and leaned closer. Hugues mimicked his gesture, that he might catch the other man's murmured words.

"Well advised would you be to take a glimpse at your father's accounts that you not be as surprised as I when the accounts of Fontaine passed to my hands," he advised quietly. When Hugues returned his regard uncomprehendingly, Jean shook his head and winced.

"Know you what it costs in hard silver to keep a single knight?" he demanded incredulously. "Shocked you would be, Hugues, and shocked I was to learn I owed no fewer than *ten* of such cursed expense to the crown. Ten," he reiterated grimly, flinging his hand wide in a gesture of dismissal, then drinking of his wine once more. "Well advised you would be indeed to consider the well-lined pockets of a bourgeois family when choosing a spouse."

"But, Jean, 'twould be scandalous to mingle the blood of a bourgeois with a noble line," Hugues protested, convinced that the other man had finally gone too far in his challenge of the way things were done.

"Scandalous?" Jean repeated skeptically and smothered a smile with difficulty. "Aye, 'twould be that," he agreed, too easy an agreement for the way he pinned Hugues with a bright eye. "For a month, or mayhap two. One could only hope the marriage would outlast the recriminations." That dark brow arched skyward once more and Hugues felt compelled to weigh his words for a moment.

Two months. Jean probably spoke aright, for there was always a new scandal to occupy the gossips. And the woman Hugues took to wife he would hope to have by his side for a lifetime. That thought prompted a recollection of Sophie's kiss, the very idea of a lifetime of those making it difficult to continue thinking rationally at all. He forced himself to wonder about Pontesse's finances and glanced up to find Jean watching him.

"The *work* I could give an honest vintner," Jean mused appreciatively as he sipped his wine, that bright gaze never slipping from Hugues' own. "Not to mention my friends' needs or those of the churches within my demesne."

"But, Jean, you cannot so readily dismiss the difference in class," Hugues protested.

"Wake up, Hugues," Jean commanded with a snap of his fingers, leaning across the table anew. "Not the first would you be to take this path and certainly you would not be the last. The land does not provide as it did in our grandfathers' days, consanguinity haunts the royal houses and time can only diminish our insistence on lineage."

"Consanguinity?" Hugues echoed, a little perplexed at the change in subject.

"I would not breed hounds the way we breed kings," Jean muttered in disgust.

"Jean!" Hugues was shocked, but Jean only chuckled anew at his outrage.

"Think upon it but a moment," he advised. "When was it last that they were paired in the seventh degree as the Church decrees?" he demanded, referring to the determination of the closeness of a couple's lineage. "I cannot even recall. Cousins they take to wife without reservation. And they wonder at the cause when their spawn are crippled or mentally inept." Jean shook his head and took a long, slow draught of wine. "Is it truly then a marvel that our politics are such a tangle?"

"Jean," Hugues warned under his breath. He recognized treacherous thoughts when he heard them and was more than aware of the mixture of the company surrounding them. "Hold your tongue, for you know not our company this night."

Jean cast an insouciant glance over his shoulder and flashed Hugues an irreverent grin. "Aye, you speak wisely, for Louise would surely have my hide were I not home in time for this arrival."

Hugues grinned himself at the reminder of how thoroughly his seemingly delicate sister had this great knight in hand. "How goes her confinement?" he asked, feeling a pang of jealousy at the way Jean's face relaxed into an affectionate smile.

"Well enough," he conceded, a flash of humor lighting his eyes. "'Tis *olives* she wants this time in the night," he supplied with no small measure of amusement, and rolled his eyes. "Olives. The woman will beggar me yet with her wild fancies."

"Aye, and fighting it you are, every step of the way," Hugues teased, drawing a laugh from the other man.

"Do not dismiss your thoughts of this Sophie so easily," Jean advised soberly, and Hugues distrusted the way his own heart leaped at the very mention of the woman's name.

"Convention is naught if she brings you happiness," Jean added a moment later, and Hugues avoided his gaze. He found himself wishing she had been at the east gates this morn before he took a draught of wine and stifled that errant thought.

Not that he was thinking of marriage, regardless of Jean's assertions. 'Twas simply another of Sophie's hot kisses Hugues desired, and naught more.

"Sophie!"

Sophie cringed in recognition of Gaillard's cry, knowing it was well past the time of reckoning for her treatment of Rustengo.

In truth, she could not believe the matter had been let alone so many days. Determined to face his annoyance now and be done with it, she straightened from the cask she was filling so Gaillard could see her more easily. With dismay, Sophie saw that his expression was positively thunderous but she held her ground, barely noticing the two men filled with self-importance who trailed in his wake.

"Did you fill the casks we shipped to Londres last July?" Gaillard demanded impatiently. His question was so unexpected that Sophie was momentarily taken off guard.

"Aye," she conceded with some confusion. "I filled all the casks this year so Ramonet could tend the vines." She referred to her brother who had tended this task before her.

"And you used the seal as he showed you?"

"Aye."

Gaillard harrumphed with what could only have been disgust and glanced over his shoulder to his two companions. Sophie followed his gaze, her heart sinking when she saw that the men wore the insignia of the Norman royal house.

"Is there a problem?" she demanded tentatively and Gaillard fairly exploded at her words.

"*A problem?* Aye, a problem there is and one of much consequence, should you care to know the truth of it. Our mark has been accused of shipping short!" This last he shouted and Sophie blanched.

"Always do I fill the casks to the measure," she argued weakly, but one of the gray-haired men behind Gaillard shook his head with precision.

"Nay, 'tis not the way of it," he argued as he scanned the roll he carried. "In truth, your mark has shipped four casks that were short of their measure in the last year."

Sophie sank onto one of the empty casks in dismay, unable to even imagine what this meant for their trade with the Normans. Gaillard glowered at her and she could not blame him, for this was a shame that a vintner could not easily shake from his reputation.

Was it possible she had made a mistake? Perhaps once or even twice she could have been daydreaming, Sophie conceded, but not four times.

"Perhaps there is some mistake," she dared to suggest.

The two clerks pulled themselves up with disdain.

"There is *no* mistake," the first maintained frostily.

"Absolutely impossible," claimed the second.

Sophie flicked a glance to her father, only to find that his anger had faded, leaving him looking defeated and uncharacteristically old. His earlier words rang in her ears and she wondered if she had indeed cursed his house.

It certainly seemed that no good *could* come of a child of the Maying, and her heart sank at her failure of those who had taken it upon themselves to raise her.

"What does this mean to the trade?" she managed, watching Gaillard flick an anxious sidelong glance to the two men.

"Naught to the likes of you," snorted the first clerk, and Sophie's heart leaped to her throat.

Would they blacklist Gaillard's mark?

"What do you mean?" Gaillard demanded, and the two clerks turned to him once more.

"Should you find another to manage your shipping, we would give you another chance to prove the reputation of your house," the second clerk offered, and Gaillard's shoulders sagged momentarily.

"One of my boys could assist," he suggested, but the first clerk shook his head with that neat precision once more.

"Nay, nay, 'twill never do," he insisted, indicating Sophie with the point of his dry quill. "Should she truly be the one who has packed your casks this year, then she must go or we take our trade elsewhere."

Gaillard turned to meet Sophie's gaze and she saw that despite his charges against her he was not willing to make this change. She shook her head mutely, not wanting him to sacrifice his trade simply to keep her at work, and that sadness grew in his eyes once more.

"Perhaps 'twould persuade you to know that our lord particularly favors your vintage," the second clerk whispered while the first nodded agreement. Gaillard swiveled to study them anew and the first managed a thin smile.

"'Tis that alone that prompted our offer of a second chance," he clarified briskly. "Three other houses have shipped short and their vintages are no longer welcome at court." It took but a heartbeat longer for Gaillard to make his decision once the realities were more clear, and

Sophie could not blame him for making the inevitable choice.

"The change will be made," he asserted grimly, making his mark without hesitation on the unfurled parchment where the first clerk indicated.

Sophie turned away, staring unseeingly at the casks around her while the men concluded their business. Was it true that she could not help but bring trouble upon Gaillard's house? And what would her role be now that she had naught to contribute?

Hugues had to wait but a day to find passage for himself, Luc and the two horses, and counted himself lucky at that, despite the small space on board that a goodly amount of silver ensured him. 'Twas late autumn and the ships were jammed with as much of the new vintage as they could carry for the last shipments before the winter squalls.

Luc regarded the vessel with deep suspicion as they coaxed the horses across the gangplank, and Hugues ruffled the boy's dark hair reassuringly, knowing he had seen naught like this before.

"'Tis only for a few days," Hugues murmured, watching the boy swallow nervously as he nodded.

"Aye, milord."

"And 'twill be close to the coast the whole of the way," Hugues lied to reassure the boy, whose gaze clung stubbornly to the shoreline.

Luc shot him an incredulous look and Hugues felt his color rise at being caught in his lie by a mere boy. He quickly followed a shipman's gesture to lead his destrier into the dark hold. When there came no response from Luc, he glanced back over his shoulder only to find the boy frozen in the portal, his countenance a curious green shade.

Just then Hugues became aware of the gentle rocking of the boat, a circumstance that had never troubled him. Was Luc to be cursed with the sickness? The boy made an ominous gurgling sound and Hugues knew the answer in that instant. Muttering impatiently at the unwieldy size of Argent, he tried to get around the warhorse in time to reach his squire, but mercifully the shipman was there ahead of him.

When Hugues gained the deck a moment later, the shipman was holding Luc's head over the side of the ship. He tossed Hugues a wry grin that was completely at odds with Luc's evident discomfort.

"'Tis the lad's first voyage?" he asked with good humor, his Breton accent thick enough that Hugues barely understood his words.

"Aye," Hugues agreed, folding his arms across his chest with a grin when Luc came up for air, looking sheepish. "The malady will pass, boy," he murmured reassuringly and Luc nodded without conviction.

"Aye, milord," he agreed halfheartedly. He took a deep breath and reached for his palfrey's reins again. The ship pitched gently as a bevy of casks was rolled onto the deck and Luc looked momentarily alarmed, glancing around nervously until the vessel settled. Hugues clapped one hand on the boy's shoulder and gave it a reassuring squeeze, hoping that his sickness would in fact ease.

"The horses should be settled, milord," Luc said unsteadily. His knuckles were white where he clutched the reins and Hugues felt a surge of admiration for the boy's pluck in the face of adversity.

"A fine knight will you make, Luc de Pamiers," he praised in a low voice. The look of delight that lit the boy's face convinced Hugues that they both were equally surprised by his assertion.

It took Sophie but a few scant hours to realize what she had to do and two long days to summon the nerve to do it.

She crouched behind the coiled ropes and stacks of empty casks on the wharf those two days later as darkness fell, willing herself to breathe so quietly that she made not a sound. To be discovered here would be the worst disgrace she could possibly imagine and she longed for this waiting to be behind her that she might be on her way.

It had not taken much imagination to see that she had to leave Gaillard's home, for not only was she not blood, not only did Gaillard himself think her a curse, but she had no useful role in the family since she could no longer fill the casks. Hélène managed the domestic tasks on her own, leaving Sophie naught to contribute, and she knew 'twould be only a matter of moments before Gaillard insisted that she wed.

And Sophie was determined that she would marry her knight or none at all. Who knew what would befall her if she openly defied the fates? Her knight's disappearance forced her to confront the rather strong possibility of spinsterhood, but Sophie was determined not to abandon her principles nonetheless. Should they truly be destined for each other, their paths would cross yet again. She was certain of it.

In the interim she had a purpose, for she was determined to find the great stones in her dreams. *North* Gérard had said, and north she would go. 'Twas foolhardy to travel on her own and Sophie knew it, though she would not encourage Gérard by traveling with him and she knew no one else who would go. So alone 'twould be, for lack of any better options.

'Twas not all bad to have had four brothers, for all her complaints, for Sophie had learned a practicality in matters of the world that might have been denied her in a more resolutely feminine household. Well she knew that traveling in her kirtle would only redouble the dangers of traveling unescorted. As a result, she had borrowed an old pair of chausses from the youngest of her four brothers and had tightly bound up her hair under her hood. No close scrutiny would her disguise endure, but Sophie had every intention of remaining out of sight.

And her brothers had taught her to fight with a knife long ago. She had pilfered the youngest's dagger tonight while he slept, knowing both that she might need it and that its disappearance would convince him that she had taken something with which to defend herself.

Perhaps then they would worry less about her.

Tears pricked the back of her eyes for the second time that evening and Sophie blinked them back stubbornly, refusing to speculate on what her family would think of her departure. No message had she left, for she knew not what to say, but hopefully they would realize her leave-taking was voluntary by her taking some clothes, the food and the knife. How hard it had been to gaze upon them one last time while they slept, one snoring openmouthed in typical fashion, and Sophie had almost wished they might awaken and discover her.

But that was not to be and she had slipped unobserved from the only house she had ever known, hugging the shadows as she made haste down the twisting streets to the wharf where the ships were being loaded.

Sophie peeked out from her hiding place, ducking back down when two men nearby shouted to each other. They were going home, she realized, risking another glance to the ship she had already selected as her conveyance north.

'Twas the largest one in the port and that admittedly was a fair measure of its appeal, for Sophie reasoned that there would be more places to hide on such a large vessel. And although she knew little of watercraft, she imagined that the larger one was more likely to be going out on the sea and up the coast to Londres, not simply to Royan at the mouth of the Garonne.

Hopefully it would stop somewhere between Royan and Londres, for Vannes, where Sophie wished to go, though not on the coast itself, lay between the two.

Silence fell and she gathered her small bundle of provisions nervously, taking one last cautious survey of the wharf before she stepped out of her hiding place and into the uncertainty of her future.

Chapter Four

Luc's sickness did not pass, much to Hugues' chagrin.

'Twas not that he minded tending the horses himself or that he needed the boy's assistance for anything. 'Twas simply that he knew not how to play the nursemaid. He was helpless to assist Luc and well he knew it, and though the boy seemed to appreciate having Hugues near, 'twas not the knight's way to tenderly wipe the brow of another. Illogical 'twas to think that such a gesture could help one overcome illness. Indeed, horses needed no such coddling, and Hugues felt uncharacteristically awkward in Luc's company.

At the boy's expectant look when he brought a bowl of soup into the cramped cabin, Hugues stifled a sigh and forced himself to sit on the edge of the bed. Luc smiled weakly and Hugues gritted his teeth as he helped the boy to sit up and held the bowl for him to dip bread into the broth.

This feeling of helplessness was something he could well live without.

"'Tis good," Luc whispered hoarsely. Hugues nodded uneasily, hoping against hope that today the meal would stay put, uncomfortably aware that there was naught he could do to affect the result. He fumbled with a cloth and clumsily wiped a bit of spilled broth from the boy's chin, wishing he was anywhere else on the face of the earth than here.

'Twas much as he felt in his father's presence these days, although truly Hugues' sire was a considerably less amiable invalid, snarling and shouting at all who dared to come within range. Perhaps he knew not how to deal with illness, either, and Hugues had a flash of understanding of the changes in his father's moods these past few years. Would Hugues not greet weakness in himself in much the same fashion, should he be cursed to be bedridden?

Hugues made a face and conceded that should such a fate befall him he would likely summon the herbalist for something to end his weakness once and for all. That thought brought to mind Jean's assertion that Louise thought the old man was failing and he grimaced anew, for his sister was observant about such matters.

He supposed 'twas a result of five years of illness that the very thought of his father passing away no longer shocked him. 'Twould almost be better to not see him at all than see what he had become. When last Hugues had been at Pontesse his father had insisted on drawing Hugues' sword to see its workmanship and Hugues had immediately agreed, knowing that his father would savor the weight of a blade in his grip once more.

The reality had been a far cry from what Hugues had expected. It had fair broken the younger man's heart to see the difficulty his sire had had in removing the sword from its scabbard. His idol, the man who had taught him to bellow loud enough to shake the rafters when he was but six summers green, could no longer even lift a broadsword.

Hugues had not been able to meet his father's gaze as he had replaced the blade, unwilling to let his surprise and disappointment show, but unable to think of anything to say. The older man had sighed with poorly concealed defeat and muttered something unintelligible under his breath before Hugues had hurriedly excused himself.

He had left Pontesse with the next dawn.

Luc sighed and closed his eyes, and Hugues studied the paleness of the boy's complexion for a moment before he hesitantly reached out to touch his brow. 'Twas hot as afore and Hugues frowned. He drained the remaining soup from the bowl as he studied his sleeping squire thoughtfully, wishing he was better with such trials.

He pulled the blanket over the boy's shoulders with less than his usual ease. 'Twas one of his own blankets and it smelled predictably of horses and stables and good hay. The scent reminded Hugues of the horses below.

High time 'twas he tended them, he reasoned, disliking how relieved he felt that he could leave the cabin in good conscience. The ship pitched unexpectedly as he reached the door and Hugues glanced over his shoulder in trepidation, but Luc slept on peacefully, and Hugues stepped out into the narrow passageway. The sea must be drawing near and he could only hope that that would not renew Luc's malady.

"Stowaway!"

The accusing cry, too close for comfort, brought Sophie awake with a start. Her heart sank when she met the startled gaze of a young boy etched in the poor light of the hold. Then he turned and shouted over his shoulder once more.

"Stowaway!" he cried again and Sophie panicked.

She stumbled to her feet, but her legs were woefully uncooperative after three days of being folded beneath her in her cramped hiding spot. Ignoring their protest, Sophie pushed past him and made to run, though she knew not where she would go. A burly man leaped down the ladder into the hold and lunged toward her. Her heart in her mouth, Sophie dodged to the left, but the pile of casks there left her little room for escape.

The seaman swore, and his strong fingers latched around her elbow, bringing her flight to an unceremonious halt. Sophie twisted to free her arm and when that was unsuccessful, bent to bite the offending hand. The gesture sent her hood tumbling back and at the sight of her hair, the man released her in shock.

"'Tis a woman," he gasped in horror as his hand fell away. Sophie glanced up, surprised at her unexpected release, to find both man and boy regarding her with something akin to horror.

"Woefully bad luck 'tis," the boy whispered. The older man nodded in ready agreement.

"And lucky we are that she was found afore we reached the sea," the older man concluded grimly, grasping Sophie's arm anew and shoving her toward the ladder.

"A woman!" cried another seaman at the top of the ladder, and Sophie looked up in time to see him cross himself. "The tides will turn against us, mark my words," he added, and Sophie wondered at this unexpected development.

Naught had she ever heard about seamen disliking women on their ships and she felt suddenly afraid. What would they do with her?

"I would speak with the captain about my passage," she said firmly when she had gained the lower deck, but the heavyset man behind her snorted with disdain.

"No silver will he take from a woman for passage," he asserted flatly. Well enough that was, for Sophie had not a single denier to her name.

"Then the next port will see me ashore," she countered, as though she truly had something with which to negotiate, but the man shook his head with finality.

"No docking do we make until La Rochelle," he retorted. Sophie could not argue the point, for she knew not where that town was. Seeing her lack of comprehension, the man shook his head again.

"You cannot go that far, for 'tis on the sea," he explained as though that clarified everything, his words creating a lump of dread in Sophie's stomach.

If she could not be put ashore and she could not stay aboard, what then would they do with her? The seaman regarded her for a long moment, then shrugged his shoulders and shoved her forward once more.

"One can only hope that a pretty lass like yourself has learned to swim."

When his meaning dawned on Sophie, she spun on her heel to confront him in shock.

"You cannot do this!" she charged, but his eyes only narrowed in determination.

"'Tis the way of the sea," he insisted in a dangerously low voice. "You would have done well to learn the consequences before you stole passage aboard." He gave her a little push once more and a new glint of determination lit his eye.

"Time 'tis that the captain met the likes of you," he muttered. Seeing no other options, Sophie turned and strode down the passageway ahead of him, her vision blinded with tears of defeat.

She had no idea whether she could swim, but it seemed she would shortly find out.

So distraught was she that she did not see the man advancing upon them from the other end of the dark passage until she barreled right into him. Annoyed that even a seaman would be so unchivalrous, Sophie glared up to see an expression of complete confusion cross Hugues de Pontesse's tanned face.

"Sophie!" Hugues whispered in shock, managing to put the pieces together in his mind to conclude that she must have been the stowaway they had discovered.

But why would she leave her husband? What was she doing here? He thought fleetingly of her insistence on destiny before he shoved the thought away, wondering if she had somehow contrived to follow him.

But the surprise on her face was as complete as his, before she smiled sunnily through her tears and unexpectedly hugged him close. Not knowing what to do against her assault, Hugues braced his hands on the walls of the passageway and stared down at her display of affection with amazement.

"Oh, Hugues, so glad am I to see you," she murmured against his chest to his complete astonishment. Hugues glanced up to find a similar sentiment etched on the faces of the three seamen before him.

"You *know* this woman?" the short, burly one demanded, and Hugues felt the color rise on his neck.

"Aye, we have met afore," he acknowledged awkwardly, not wanting to be rude and deny the woman. He did not even dare to imagine what she would say to that, and his heart sank in dread when she tut-tutted him under her breath.

"Hugues," she admonished, turning that confident smile on the three men behind her. "We are destined for each other," she informed them happily, and Hugues barely stifled a groan as three pairs of brows arched skyward in unison.

"Destined?" asked the same seaman with a skeptical glance to Hugues, who could only shake his head. Surely 'twould be rude to argue with the woman before others, he thought guiltily, wondering how to stop her from explaining her mad theory to them all.

"Aye, *destined*," she repeated firmly, and Hugues braced himself for the worst. "Hugues refuses to acknowledge the hand of fate," she breezily informed the seaman closest behind her. He exchanged a look with Hugues that spoke volumes before the captain's arrival interrupted the proceedings.

"What goes on here?" he demanded sharply from behind Hugues. Hugues stepped aside with some difficulty, as Sophie seemed disinclined to release her grasp on him.

"'Tis a stowaway we found in the hold, sir," a seaman who seemed to have appointed himself spokesman explained.

"A woman she is," interjected the boy unnecessarily, and Hugues watched the captain smother a smile.

"Aye, so I see," he said, his perusal of Sophie a little too thorough for Hugues' taste.

Hugues straightened, savoring the fact that he was taller than the captain, and deliberately placed his hand on the back of Sophie's waist. She pressed herself a little closer at his gesture and Hugues caught the faint whisper of that scent of sunshine in her hair, distrust-

ing the quickening in his loins that immediately followed.

"Acquainted you are, then?" the captain inquired
archly when he noted the gesture. Hugues nodded once,
for that was a more than adequate description in his eye.
Sophie stiffened and, knowing she was going to correct
the other man to her own detriment, he pressed the back
of her waist in warning.

To his annoyance, she blithely ignored him.

"'Tis more than mere acquaintance, for we are destined to be together," she informed the incredulous
captain. With a sinking heart Hugues watched the expression he was growing accustomed to seeing in response to these words flit across the captain's features.

"Indeed?" he inquired skeptically and Sophie nodded happily. "Bad luck 'tis to have a woman aboard
when venturing on the open sea," he said softly, the
threat in his voice no less for the quiet way he spoke.

"She will be put ashore?" Hugues demanded, already suspecting this was not to be, but unable to check
his dismay when the captain shook his head in curt dismissal.

"No time have I for such luxury," he said matter-of-
factly. "She will be cast overboard, as befits a stowaway."

"You cannot do this," Hugues argued, seeing all the
confirmation that the captain could do precisely that
reflected in the other man's eyes.

"Should you indeed be *destined* for each other..."
he began sarcastically, but Hugues interrupted him
flatly, shoving Sophie behind him as he confronted the
other man.

'Twas good silver that had gotten him on this boat
and no business had this would-be pirate to even

threaten to toss him overboard with Sophie. Indeed, Hugues had no doubt that more of that same silver would resolve this dilemma. At the very least, he had to try, for he could not stand aside and watch an innocent woman cast to her death.

'Twas in his vows, after all, to protect defenseless women and children.

"I would speak with you alone," he growled, and the shorter man considered him for a long moment before he nodded.

"Take charge of the woman," the captain ordered his men, but Hugues shook his head in disagreement.

"She will stay in my cabin," he stated flatly, and the captain arched one brow.

"I would be sure she not escape," he argued smoothly.

Hugues folded his arms across his chest in an uncompromising gesture. "I would be sure she not be raped," he countered.

Mercifully Sophie kept her mouth shut while the two men stared each other down. The silence stretched long between them before the captain nodded once again.

"Very well," he conceded with reluctance. "The woman will lock the cabin from the inside and Jacques will guard the door from the outside."

Hugues nodded in agreement and summarily hustled Sophie along the passageway to his cabin before anyone could change their mind. He groaned when the easing tension seemed to loosen her temporarily held tongue.

"Surely even you cannot deny that 'tis destiny's hand bringing us together at this time," she whispered excitedly. Hugues leveled one quelling look in her direction but it had absolutely no effect upon her.

"Surely naught else could have prompted your gallantry?" she demanded perkily, and Hugues counted to five under his breath before he spoke. The woman would drive him mad with her insistence on this preposterous tale.

"'Tis early to be jubilant, for the matter is far from settled," he said between his gritted teeth, perversely pleased when she looked momentarily dismayed. Did the woman not understand the fullness of the trouble she was in?

"You will convince him," she murmured confidently. The gleam in her eyes filled Hugues with a curious mixture of both pride and nervousness.

"The price of his conviction may well exceed the weight of my purse," he said gruffly, not wanting to build up her hopes. Instead he felt the knave when she paled at his words.

"Bar the door, open it only for me and do not even *think* to leave," he ordered under his breath, waiting for her to nod acquiescence before he turned back to the captain, awaiting him in the hall behind. Plenty of time would there be for apologies should he be successful in this endeavor, he reasoned.

The saints only knew what this was going to cost him, Hugues thought as he caught a gleam of avarice in the captain's eye. But what else could he do?

Hugues' muttered words almost took the wind from Sophie's sails before she decided that he was simply unwilling to admit anything before these other, *skeptical* men.

For her there was no longer any doubt, if in fact there ever had been, that her unwitting selection of the ship that Hugues was on clearly showed the hand of fate.

And that he should appear in the nick of time to rescue her from a certain death was more perfect a sign than she could have envisioned herself. She spun happily, sure beyond doubt that he would be successful. She stopped dead when she spotted the pale figure in the bed.

A boy slept there. For an instant Sophie thought that she had been shoved into the wrong cabin, until she recalled that Hugues had had a squire in Bordeaux. Of course, she thought crossly, though she had paid the boy little heed at the time. She took in his pallor, his dark hair as rumpled as his garments and bed linens. He looked young and particularly vulnerable as he slept. Sophie watched him for a long moment as she stood uncertainly with her back to the barred door.

So as not to startle him, she crossed the small room slowly, and bent to place her hand on his brow. The skin was but a shade warmer than usual and he stirred restlessly at her touch, his eyes flying open with a suddenness that surprised her.

"Oh," gasped the boy when he saw her, and Sophie's breath caught in her throat at that same instant. Then he frowned and fixed her with a quizzical eye. "You are the lady from Bordeaux," he affirmed with some confusion.

Sophie nodded. "Aye."

"How came you to be here?" he demanded, propping himself up on his elbows with interest.

"'Tis a long tale," Sophie said with a smile, and he smiled tentatively back.

"Will you be staying, then?" he asked pertly.

Sophie just barely stopped herself from answering in the affirmative. "I know not," she said instead, and he nodded with an understanding beyond his years.

"Luc I am," he introduced himself proudly. "Hugues says Chevalier Luc de Pamiers will I be when I earn my spurs."

"Sophie am I," she responded, smiling at the evident pride in his tone.

"How long have you squired for Hugues?" she asked, watching the boy's face brighten with pride.

"Not yet a year has it been," he enthused, "but already have I learned so much. Hugues says I clean his blade as well as he does himself and I can saddle Argent—"

"That great beast?" Sophie asked, smiling anew as she tried to imagine little Luc harnessing the destrier.

"Aye." He nodded solemnly. "He is most well trained and stands his ground. Never does he even kick at the smith," Luc assured Sophie, and she agreed that this was indeed an admirable trait.

"Hugues says 'tis best thus for battle, that a nervous steed will fail you when you least expect it." He repeated this as though 'twere the sagest thing he had ever heard in all his years.

"And why are you abed this day?" she asked softly, though she knew the answer all the while.

Luc looked shamefaced. "In truth, I have been ill," he admitted, his ears glowing red in his embarrassment, "but Hugues says 'tis not my fault to be troubled that the ship moves so."

Sophie leaned over and patted his hand reassuringly. "'Tis not that uncommon an affliction, I'm told," she informed him, and the words seemed to make him feel a bit better about it.

"Hugues is not ill," he observed as though he had failed somehow to live up to his ideal.

Sophie could only shrug. "Perhaps he is used to traveling thus," she reasoned, not expecting Luc's enthusiastic nod.

"Aye, likely that is, for Hugues has traveled the whole world over," he told Sophie enthusiastically.

"Indeed?" she responded. She wondered if 'twere indeed thus or whether the boy's evident worship of Hugues had distorted the facts in his mind.

"Aye, to Paris and Saint Denis and now to Gascogne," Luc affirmed. His lids drooped as the toll of his malady gained the upper hand. "And now we go to Bretagne, too," he mused, his voice dropping in timbre.

"Sleep," Sophie urged him in a whisper. "'Twill make you well again." It seemed to her that the boy sighed and nodded before he rolled to face the wall.

A muted rap at the door brought Sophie to her feet countless moments later and her heart accelerated in trepidation.

"Aye?" she demanded against the wood, sagging with relief at the familiarity of the gruff voice that answered.

"'Tis Hugues," he said shortly, and Sophie immediately lifted the latch.

He looked concerned and Sophie longed to brush the worry from his brow, though she knew somehow that he would not welcome the gesture. Hugues frowned anew and glanced over Sophie's shoulder to the bunk, and she instinctively reached to place one fingertip over his lips.

"He has fallen asleep again," she whispered when his gaze flew back to hers. The intensity in his eyes made her suddenly aware of the intimacy of her gesture. She pulled her hand away quickly and Hugues folded his arms across his chest as he remained in the doorway. The cabin seemed much smaller now than it had before and Sophie found herself painfully aware of how Hugues filled the compact space.

"What happened?" she asked nervously, his stillness bringing her earlier doubts back to roost. Had she assumed incorrectly that Hugues could make it all come right? He studied her for a long moment and Sophie almost panicked until he smiled down at her with a shake of his head.

"The captain has entrusted you to my care," he explained softly. "But you must stay here so as not to frighten the crew."

"But 'tis so small," she protested with a glance over her shoulder, then looked back to find a mischievous twinkle in Hugues' hazel eyes.

"Can you swim, then?" he demanded with a chuckle, and Sophie smiled herself.

"Nay," she admitted and he shrugged as he shouldered his way farther into the tiny cabin.

"Perhaps then 'tis a better option nonetheless," he observed amiably, making his way to the bed to feel the boy's forehead. "'Tis cooler," he muttered under his breath, and his relief was so tangible that Sophie felt a surge of affection for him. 'Twas almost overwhelming that this strong and gentle man was meant to be hers alone and she took the single step required to take her to his side. Hugues looked up and Sophie smiled encouragingly at him.

"Time will we have together then?" she asked hopefully, her heart sinking at the flash of outright fear in the knight's eyes.

"Nay," he said with a wild glance over his shoulder to the door. "Nay, you and Luc will have the cabin."

"And where will you sleep?" Sophie asked.

"On deck," Hugues answered hastily, but she shook her head stubbornly.

"This I will not let you do," she argued. "Already have you paid my passage as well as your own, and I will not take your bed."

"Already I explained that you must remain in the cabin," Hugues replied, and Sophie was certain she had had enough of his protests. 'Twas an unavoidable sign that they were both on this ship and if he refused to see the truth for himself, she would force him to.

"And so shall you," she murmured, cupping his face in her hands and locking her lips on his.

Hugues tried to bolt, but there was no room to maneuver and he found his back pressed against the wall. He struggled against the embrace for an instant before Sophie's scent deluged him, his mind conjuring up memories of what his hands would find should he touch her anew.

He cast around desperately in his mind for something to strengthen his resolve, but even the knowledge that Luc slept but an arm's length away was naught against the wild persuasiveness of Sophie's kiss. She forced her tongue between his teeth as though she sensed her advantage in that moment, and Hugues knew he was well and truly lost.

Conceding defeat, he closed his hands around her waist, the little sigh of satisfaction she made in the back of her throat enflaming him beyond reason. Hugues cupped her buttocks and lifted her against his arousal, his tongue plundering the sweet warmth of her mouth. The realization that she wore boy's chausses did little to

check his rising passion. Sophie grasped two fistfuls of
the hair at his nape and stretched up to her toes, her
nipples visibly taut under the fullness of her shirt, and
he ran his thumb across one, savoring the way she shivered beneath his touch.

Her eyes opened drowsily and Hugues stared down at
her, unable to recall any woman regarding him with
such adoration in her eyes. His gaze dropped to her
reddened lips and she stretched toward him as her lashes
fluttered shut. Hugues lifted her against him once more
that she might have no doubts of her effect upon him,
his pulse racing at the way she purred in response.

"Aye, Hugues," she whispered as though she had
heard his unspoken question, and Hugues needed no
further encouragement to partake of what she offered.

Had he not already paid a princely sum for her passage?

Had she not made the decision to leave her husband
of her own accord? Should she be so willing to exchange her favors for his temporary protection, who
was he to insult the lady with his refusal?

Hugues speared his fingers through the thickness of
her braid and backed her into the corner of the cabin,
his other hand quickly unlacing her chausses. His fingertips explored the warmth trapped within the wool as
he kissed her, his lips moving from hers to taste her
chin, her neck, her earlobe, savoring the intoxicating
flavor of her skin. Something leaped within him when
he discovered the slickness between her thighs, and the
flutter of her gasp against his throat when he first
touched her convinced Hugues that he could wait no
longer.

Sophie seemed to sense his intention, for she hastened to shed her chausses. The ripe curve of her but-

tocks when she bent to shove the garment over her feet made Hugues wonder how he would last. He ripped open his own chausses and clasped her around the waist, lifting her to her toes without another moment's hesitation.

Sophie twisted her tongue in his ear as she wrapped her legs around his waist and Hugues wondered briefly whether 'twas the ship that pitched and rolled or just his own equilibrium. He fingered her again and she writhed against his chest.

"Hurry," she demanded impatiently, her insistence redoubling his ardor.

Without hesitation Hugues did as she bade and drove himself deep within her. Sophie's little cry of pain made Hugues freeze in shock at the realization of what he had done.

A virgin.

His mind could get no further than that thought in his current state and he knew not what to do to right his error. He stared numbly down at Sophie for but an instant before she opened those pale eyes and smiled directly into his own confused ones.

"'Twill be fine now," she whispered and ground her hips against his.

Hugues could think no more when she did that, the kiss she landed on him making mere reason absolutely impossible. The reluctance that dogged his mind was swept away by sensation and he began to slowly move within her despite his reservations.

The tightness of her grip upon him brought the rush much sooner than he might have hoped. 'Twas more engulfing than Hugues could have imagined, its wake more devastating than he was accustomed to.

Mere heartbeats after her assurance, Hugues was leaning weakly against the wall, his brow beaded with sweat, his eyes drifting closed. Vaguely he was aware of Sophie disentangling herself and he tried to hold her fast to his side. Something he had to say to her, but he found himself unable to form the words, or even to recollect them as the drowsiness assailed him. He felt her warmth slide away and made one last reach for her, his fingers closing on empty air before he slumped against the wall.

'Twas a beginning, Sophie reasoned, drawing a deep breath while she refastened her brother's chausses and cast a glance to the sleeping squire.

Mercifully Luc had not awakened, and the loss of her maidenhead had been less painful than she had expected. Sophie glanced over her shoulder to the dozing Hugues and smiled affectionately, for he looked much a boy himself in this moment.

And when he had touched her *there,* it had been all she could do not to cry aloud. Sophie dared to touch that spot herself and the resultant surge through her veins made her skin tingle anew. She smothered a satisfied smile and leaned over to press a kiss to Hugues' chin. He stirred and murmured something unintelligible, but she sidestepped his outstretched hand once more, impulsively kissing the roughened fingertip that had caressed her before releasing it.

Aye, she would leave that spot and its curious sensations to her Hugues.

The reality of what he had done hit Hugues like a brick even before consciousness fully returned to him.

He awoke to find himself still slumped in the corner, and at his first glimpse of Sophie bending over Luc his guilt engulfed him like a wave breaking on the beach. The curve of her tight buttocks beneath those chausses aroused more than his guilt, and the telling path of his thoughts made Hugues furiously angry.

No reason had he to feel the knave, for Sophie had tempted him, deliberately he was sure, not only in offering herself, but in her insistence that he continue when his mistake was revealed and he would have pulled back. Not unreasonable had it been for him to assume that a married woman knew the way of things, and Hugues momentarily puzzled over her virginal state. His guilt redoubled and he cast the question from his mind, glaring once more at Sophie.

'Twas her fault he had erred, of that Hugues had little doubt, as little as he had that this had surely been part of her mad plan for them to be together. She intended to snare him, one way or the other, and the knowledge that he had been so easily made to do her bidding infuriated him beyond reason. Hugues vowed in his mind that she would not find him so willing to err so again.

No babe would there be to compel him to make an honest woman of her. An old trap was that, and Hugues would not play along, he vowed, ignoring the fact that he could not cease to watch her.

Although, there still remained the matter of her missing maidenhead and his own responsibility for its loss. The guilty twisting of his gut fed Hugues' anger and he straightened away from the wall, snapping the lacing on his chausses closed with an abrupt gesture. He could not stay here and watch her.

"How fares the boy?" he demanded sharply, and Sophie cast a surprised glance over her shoulder. Hugues refused to soften at the hurt in her eyes at his manner and stubbornly folded his arms across his chest.

"He needs but to sleep," she said softly, her eyes narrowing as she obviously tried to assess his mood. Hugues nodded with false confidence as though he had suspected as much all along. Despite his determination he found he could not hold her questioning gaze, and dropped his own with the pretense of tying the lace on his chausses.

"Where do you go?" she asked quietly, her tone making Hugues fight against his instinctive response to her hurt.

She had manipulated him, he reminded himself crossly, distressed to find his resolve against her made of less stern stuff than he had hoped. She intended to trick him by getting herself with child, he told himself, but the vision following close on that thought's heels did little to steel his resolve.

Would it be so bad to see her rounded with his seed?

But what of her husband? Hugues groaned at that complication, the very idea of another man raising his child repulsive beyond belief. And what other option was there? Would she have him challenge her spouse? But why was she here without him? And virginal?

The tangle of ramifications and possibilities was all too much for Hugues and he found himself craving the company of creatures he understood. Creatures with simple, straightforward needs.

"I must tend the horses." Hugues found himself wildly blurting the first excuse that came to mind. He spun on his heel and fairly lunged out of the intimacy of the cabin before Sophie could respond, taking a deep

breath of freedom in the passageway outside with relief.

As it became progressively darker in the little cabin,
Sophie forced herself to face the realization that Hugues
was not coming back. Luc tossed in his sleep and she
wiped the boy's brow absently, wondering what she had
done to earn the knight's displeasure. From her brothers' stories, she had always thought men liked the mat-
ing, but perhaps Hugues did not.

Although his manner had not exactly been that of a
man forced against his will, she recalled, and her pulse
took a little leap at the memory of his lips nuzzling her
earlobe. 'Twould be disappointing indeed to not further explore that sensation, she thought impatiently,
studying with displeasure the four walls that surrounded her.

Stay in the cabin. Sophie frowned and shoved her
hand through the remnants of her once-neat braid, acknowledging the grumble in her stomach for the hundredth time. She was famished and if Hugues was not
going to bring her anything to eat, then she *would* leave
this confining cabin.

After all, Luc needed to eat to regain his strength.
And a breath of fresh air would help to clear her
thoughts.

Sophie lifted the latch on the door and peered out
into the darkened passageway, a little surprised to find
no one standing guard there. The ship pitched a little
more enthusiastically than it had to date and she
gripped the wall to regain her balance.

Horses stamped in the hold below, a male voice
rumbled in reassurance and Sophie fancied she could
smell the beasts' fear. Running footsteps echoed across

the deck above and she reconsidered the wisdom of venturing out of the cabin. Mayhap she should stay put as Hugues had decreed.

Luc moaned, that plaintive sound renewing Sophie's resolve to find him a morsel to eat, and she darted into the darkness of the passageway. The ship rolled anew and she was thrown into one of the walls with bruising force, but still she continued doggedly toward the ladder hanging midway down the passageway.

'Twas the men's shouting above as she climbed the ladder that alerted Sophie to the fact that something was amiss. That and the lightning that starkly illuminated the deck with an unexpected flash. The light disappeared as suddenly as it had come, leaving Sophie hanging on the ladder as she blinked to restore her sight in the relative darkness, the resounding rumble of thunder shaking the ship she had thought so large and strong.

It took her but an instant to begin climbing again.

On deck 'twas yet more dramatic. Rain slanted across the boards, making the wood slick and slippery, and Sophie clung to the top of the ladder even as she marveled that she had not heard the storm below. It seemed all the men were on deck, and she carefully climbed out onto the wet planking herself, enjoying the feel of the wind whipping through her hair despite the inclement weather. She lifted her nose to the tang of salt and with delight felt the spray land on her skin.

A far cry from that crowded cabin 'twas indeed, and Sophie took a deep draught of the night air. They must have come out on the open sea, for she could see naught but the dark, tempestuous surface of water in every direction, and the realization that she had come this far excited Sophie. Astounding 'twas that there could be so much water in one place and she wondered how far it stretched, what lurked in its depths, whether it truly was salt of taste as one of her brothers had once told her.

The play of light across the sky exhilarated her as it abruptly illuminated the wind-torn clouds, and she felt that the true adventure of her life had begun. The sky split unexpectedly and torrents of rain dashed the ship, sluicing through her hair. She was soaked to the skin within moments of her stepping out on the deck, but Sophie did not care. A thunderstorm on the open sea was a magical and marvelous thing to behold.

The ship dipped and dived like a mere plaything cast on the waves; the wind snapped impatiently at the sails straining overhead. A jubilant Sophie clutched the rigging, completely unnoticed by the shipmen as she watched the storm break around them and they struggled to keep the vessel aright.

One of the men shouted, the others took up his hoarse cry and Sophie turned to follow their gestures. She admired the wild disarray of the coast for a moment before a flash of lightning illuminated the ragged scattering of rocks. The seamen hastened to furl the straining sails but 'twas too late, she saw even with her inexperienced eyes, for the wind and the waves had already conspired to cast the ship onto the shoals.

Chapter Five

"Rocks to starboard!"

Hugues heard the warning cry as he climbed the ladder out of the hold and he hesitated for but an instant before leaping down once more. 'Twas clear from the pitching of the ship that it had already been torn from the captain's control. Too often had Hugues been at sea not to understand their inevitable fate now that rocks loomed nearby.

He stroked Argent's nose, seeing the fear rising in the stallion's eyes but knowing there was little he could do to save the creature should the ship founder. The ramp that had let the beasts into the hold was stowed away. He would not be able to move it himself, nor would he find one to assist him with what could only be seen as a foolhardy task in the midst of this storm.

'Twas each for himself alone.

And so 'twould be for Argent. Blinking back tears of frustration, Hugues unfastened the stallion's reins from the loop where they were knotted, and removed the bridle so that the beast was completely unfettered. 'Twas the only chance he could give his faithful companion and Hugues knew it well.

The tightness that rose in his chest made his fingers fumble with Luc's palfrey's reins as he did the same, noting how the smaller beast cozied up to Argent's side. Hugues fought his tears, tangling his fingers in the stallion's mane for a long moment before he forced himself to release him.

Sophie and Luc he had to tend to, as well, Hugues reminded himself, though that thought made parting from the beast that had so long been his partner no less difficult.

"Farewell, my friend," he said shakily. No accident it seemed that Argent nuzzled his neck in that moment and he stood for a long moment beside the creature, wishing there was something, anything, he could do. Finally Hugues stepped away and strode to the ladder determinedly, refusing to recall how long they two had ridden together as he climbed to below-decks.

In his mind's eye he saw the silver foal running across the green pastures outside Pontesse's gates so many springs ago. He felt again the way his heart had leaped when his father had promised him the steed and demanded that he name him, then and there. Well indeed did he recall his father's dry comment that he had expected a more original name from a boy of eighteen, fully knighted no less, than merely Argent. Hugues smiled sadly at the recollection. But Argent it had been from that day on.

Argent. Hugues glanced over his shoulder one last time and saw the silver beast standing deceptively still, his feet braced against the floor, as the smaller palfrey stepped nervously. 'Twas exactly thus the destrier stood whenever they faced a battle, a testament to discipline despite his fear, and Hugues could bear to look upon him no more.

He had done all that he could and precious little it was.

Hugues threw himself up the last few rungs of the ladder, deliberately leaving the hatch open. Tears blinded his vision as he stumbled down the passageway to his cabin, but he told himself 'twas the pitching of the ship, the salt in the air that stung his eyes.

He threw open the cabin door just as Luc retched and coughed dryly. The boy looked up shamefacedly, but Hugues had no time for polite formalities.

"Can you walk?" he demanded tersely, noting the gray pallor of the boy's skin as Luc struggled to his feet.

"Aye, milord," he asserted bravely, but Hugues saw that he lied in the same moment that he realized Sophie was gone.

"Where is the lady?" he asked abruptly, buckling on his sword with unnecessary ferocity.

He would throttle that mad witch if she had gone above-decks, he growled under his breath. The pitching of the ship summoned the sickening thought that she might have been swept overboard. Anything but that, Hugues prayed with a fervor that surprised him, knowing that if he alone could swim of the three of them, he would give his last to see them all ashore.

"I know not, milord," Luc confessed. Hugues' heart took an unsteady lurch not unlike those of the ship. "She was gone when I awoke."

Hugues swore eloquently, scooping up the boy in one impatient gesture and making for the door. If the ship ran aground their best chance was to be on deck.

"Milord, your hauberk!" Luc cried, pointing over the knight's shoulder to the abandoned mail, but Hugues shook his head as he shouldered his way out into the passageway.

"'Twill only impede us," he answered out, hoping against hope that Sophie hadn't done anything foolish and knowing in his heart that he was being overly optimistic.

He saw her the instant he gained the slippery deck, and the breath fairly abandoned his chest in his relief, but Sophie was oblivious to all but the raging fury of the storm. Her face was tipped back to greet the slashing rain and her wet hair whipped loose around her shoulders, her braid having fallen prey to the wind's fingers long ago. Her shirt and chausses were plastered to her skin, but despite it all, Hugues was amazed to see that she was actually smiling.

"There she is!" Luc cried from his perch. Hugues almost grinned at the echo of his own relief in the boy's tone as he made his way carefully to the mast where Sophie had her grip. At least she had had the sense to stay away from the rails, he thought as he gained her side. Her delight broke through his reserves when she greeted him with a radiant smile.

"'Tis marvelous, is it not?" she demanded with shining eyes and Hugues found himself looking at the storm with a new perspective. So far he had seen it only as a threat, but now he watched the lightning shoot across the sky and acknowledged a grudging admiration for the array of forces at work around him.

"Look to the sea!" she urged and Hugues did her bidding, gathering Luc tighter to his side when the boy shivered.

What power threw the waves up in such majesty? he wondered, seeing now the myriad shades of indigo and ebony in their arching heights, marveling at the froth of white foam that graced the crest of each. Some of Sophie's excitement fired his own blood and he looked to the shore. His alarm at how close it was summarily dismissed his enjoyment of the elements.

"Luc," he shouted over the wind, and the boy's frightened gaze swiveled to his. "Should we become separated, you must hold fast to a wine cask," he commanded, watching as Luc swallowed nervously and nodded once.

"Do not abandon me, milord," he pleaded in a whisper that the wind snatched away, but Hugues shook his head adamantly as he read the words from the boy's lips.

"I vow I shall hold fast as long as I am able," he promised. He could feel Luc's fingers tighten on his shirt. Hugues turned his attention to Sophie, only to find her watching him intently.

"Dare I hope that you can swim?" he demanded, stunned when she smiled. She must have not understood his words, he reasoned.

"Indeed, it would matter little against these waves," she shouted back to him, and Hugues was forced to face the reality of that. He grimaced, but Sophie laid one hand upon his arm.

"'Twill be the will of the fates alone that determines what happens this night," she informed him, doing little to reassure the practical Hugues.

Before he could respond, the ship lurched hard to one side. The hands cried, and Hugues fancied he heard the horses scream over the wrenching sound of tearing wood. He waited with bated breath, but when the ship did not right itself Hugues glanced up just in time to see the huge wave climbing high over the crippled ship.

The deluge caught Sophie by surprise and she sputtered helplessly for a moment before she realized that she was surrounded by water. She snatched but naught came to hand, wild kicking yielding the same absence of anything solid. Sophie's chest tightened at the emptiness and she dared not intake the water that pressed against her skin from every direction. She struggled and twisted desperately and just when she thought her chest might burst she broke the surface and gulped at the air gratefully.

A shadow loomed over her anew and she barely had time to take another deep breath before the sea fell upon her once more, pushing her deep down toward whatever lay at the bottom of all this water. Too late she realized that she was alone in the sea, without ship, without planks beneath her feet, without Luc and Hugues, and she fought the icy grip of the water with renewed strength.

When Sophie gained the surface again, she thought she spied the shadowy outline of the ship, but it was astonishingly far away and no longer pitched with the waves. The familiar shape of a wine cask bobbed past and, remembering Hugues' advice, she lunged in pursuit of it, barely gaining a grip upon it before the waves washed over her once more.

This time she came up gasping with a newfound determination to survive. Her hold on the cask was precarious at best and Sophie had an idea that set her numb fingers to fumbling with the lacing on her chausses. It took another dunk in the cold sea before she had the lace in hand, but Sophie was not about to admit defeat. Despite the coldness of her fingers she quickly threaded the sturdy lace under the iron bands that held the cask together and knotted it securely.

Hoping against hope that her strategy would work, she wound her arms into the lace and held on tightly as

another wave broke over her. The cask bobbed and
dipped momentarily below the surface, but Sophie almost let out a victorious hoot when it regained the surface almost immediately with her sprawled inelegantly
atop it. She wound her hands more deliberately into the
lace, knowing she had but to hold on to ride out the fury
of the storm.

But what had happened to Hugues and Luc?

She tried to spy the ship each time she surfaced but
the night was dark, the intervals few. Once again she
thought to have glimpsed a spiked shadow in the distance that could have been the ship with its barren
masts, but 'twas much farther away than she had
thought earlier. She strained to look in the same direction again, though the waves were disorienting, but saw
naught of the ship again.

Refusing to be daunted at the thought that she might
have lost Hugues, Sophie hung on to the knotted lace,
coughing and sputtering each time she surfaced, feeling the sensation slowly drain from her chilled hands
and feet.

She could not find her knight again if she did not
survive, and that thought alone fueled her determination to ride out the storm.

Sophie awoke on a rocky beach beneath a watery sun.
She sat up and ran her hand through her hair, grimacing at the salt-encrusted tangle it had become. She was
stiff from her ordeal and stretched as she slowly got to
her feet, her hopes fading as she confronted the vast
emptiness surrounding her.

The beach was deserted as far as the eye could see.
Gulls wheeled overhead with their incessant caterwaul-
ing, and the sea stretched unbroken to the horizon like

smooth glass. Swallowing her disappointment, Sophie forced herself to look again more carefully, shielding her hand against the pale sun as she scanned the distance once more.

Naught. They were all gone. Hugues, Luc, the seamen, all of them perished at sea.

Hugues was gone. Sophie could scarce believe 'twas so, that he should pass from her life so quickly. She had been so certain that their destiny was ordained, so convinced that all was going according to plan.

Now she felt foolish to have believed in the goodwill of the capricious fates. Hugues was gone and she would never again see that fleeting twinkle of humor in his eyes, or watch the gentle way he tended his sick squire, or taste his rising passion in his kiss.

Sophie felt tears on her cheeks before she realized that she had shed them and she wiped them away in annoyance with the back of her hand. Time there would be for mourning her knight, but now she stood alone on an abandoned beach with no food or shelter and the sun was already high in the sky.

If she and Hugues were destined to be together, had she cheated the fates by surviving the storm?

That thought motivated Sophie as none other had so far. Should the fates wish to claim her, too, she would not make it easy for them. She retrieved her lace from the wine cask and laced up her sorry chausses, then briefly and thirstily considered the cask of wine before ruefully realizing that she had no way to open it. Sophie cast a glance to the sun and turned her back upon it, trudging determinedly north.

North to the standing stones. If truly they stood on the coast, she would find her way there.

* * *

The sun was sinking far on her left when Sophie spied something on the beach ahead. Her pulse quickened at the thought that it might be someone from the ship until she noted that it moved not as she advanced hurriedly upon it. Something then, some stores from the galley that she could eat or drink, mayhap a blanket to wrap herself in as the sun sank relentlessly lower. Already she could feel the chill rising from the damp sand, the pink burn the sun had raised on her flesh certain to make the night feel even colder than it actually was.

That the object was from the ship she had little doubt, for it had the look of something thoroughly wet, washed ashore like seaweed, but too large to be spawned of the sea itself. Something at one end of the drenched heap caught an orange glimmer from the setting sun and Sophie stopped in shocked recognition of that arched shape.

A horse's shoe, it could be naught else. Her heart in her mouth, Sophie advanced more slowly, rounding the great still shape and gasping aloud as she confronted Hugues' drowned stallion.

His fine bridle and caparisons were gone, his sleek silver coat dull and caked with salt, his once well-groomed mane tangled with green tendrils of seaweed, but 'twas undoubtedly Argent.

The bile rose in Sophie's throat along with a fresh torrent of tears. The stillness of the horse made Hugues' fate all the more tangible to her. Barely knowing what she did, Sophie turned and ran blindly down the beach, away from the destrier, away from the harsh demise of her dreams.

* * *

She had walked for five days when the town appeared almost magically at the crest of the cliff.

The days had blended together, the blisters on her bare feet had risen, broken, healed and risen anew, her skin had burned red, peeled and turned to yet a darker shade of brown than it had been. Sophie's hair was still tangled and salty, her nails broken and dirty, and the vision of the fallen Argent yet haunted her dreams when she dared to sleep.

Though she had found a bundle of possessions apparently from the ship on the second day, the round of salty cheese was now gone, the last drop squeezed from the wineskin that very morning. Her stomach had rumbled in dissatisfaction for so long that she barely noticed its complaints any longer. Her tongue was so dry that she could scarce recall it being any other way.

So it was that Sophie stared up at the walled town for a considerable part of the morning, uncertain whether 'twas indeed there or merely a figment of her imagination. When the sun broke through the clouds to shine on those high walls and the town remained resolutely lodged atop the cliff, Sophie resolved to climb up and seek assistance there.

What indeed had she to lose, after all?

'Twas the market that proved her undoing.

Fully did Sophie intend to ask for aid. In fact, she had made an inquiry immediately upon entering the town and had been directed to the convent, little knowing that the path there wound directly through the market square. The market was in full swing and Sophie gazed with admiration at the first few stalls of fine leather goods and lengths of silk and wool.

Then her nose caught the scent of roasted meat.

Her stomach rumbled with unheralded ferocity and her mouth watered so that Sophie feared she would drool like a dog, the hollowness of her stomach making itself known once again with a vigor. 'Twas meat and onions, Sophie was sure of it, and her guts rebelled at the delay in her acquiring any of it. She lifted her nose to the air and followed the direction of the tempting scent to a baker's stall, watching avidly as he proudly laid out fresh crescents of baked pastry.

Warm pastry filled with meat and onions.

Sophie's hunger overwhelmed her judgment and before she knew what she intended, she noted that the baker had turned away. In a flash she had pilfered the pastry closest to her and taken off at a run into the crowd.

A shout rent the air behind her but she was already on the other side of the square, jamming the savory meat pie into her mouth even as she ran. Her blood pumped with the fear that she would be caught while she shoved her way through the crowd. She heard footfalls far behind her as she ducked around carts and stalls, and sidestepped loaded donkeys and overburdened women who cursed her for throwing them off balance.

The pastry tasted divine, filled with herbs and sautéed onions, and Sophie half wished that she had the time to truly enjoy it. She ducked down a maze of tangled side streets to escape the press of the market, then gradually slowed her pace as the way wound tighter and the sounds of pursuit faded behind her.

Feeling inordinately pleased with herself, she plopped the last piece of pastry into her mouth and licked her fingertips with a cocky gesture just as a heavy hand fell on her shoulder.

Sophie jumped and would have run again, but that hand's mate landed on her other shoulder, effectively stopping her flight. She had been caught virtually red-handed and she had not the nerve to look up at her captor to see the recrimination in his eyes.

She was a thief, plain and simple. What would Hélène have said about that?

"I thought you better raised than that," Hugues muttered.

Sophie stared up in surprise. "You!" she exclaimed and he grinned outright. Had circumstances been better, Sophie might have appreciated the boyishness that gesture gave his features, but her heart was still racing.

"Aye, me," Hugues agreed readily. "Well you knew that I was coming to La Rochelle," he added, though Sophie was not as certain as he that she had known. Sophie fancied she saw relief in his regard of her for a brief moment before he became stern and she wondered, for just that instant, whether he had waited here in hope she would show up.

That stern expression dispelled any hope that he had given any more credence to what she knew about their entwined destinies, and Sophie gritted her teeth in annoyance. Hugues looked disgustingly well fed, groomed and rested and she was suddenly conscious of her own less orderly state. His paternal air was considerably less than welcome, considering their circumstances, and she drew herself up to her full height indignantly.

How many times did she have to explain this to him?

"And lucky for you that is," he said.

Decidedly uninterested in a morality lecture, Sophie shook herself free of his grip and his condemnation.

"Precious little have I had to eat since Bordeaux," she said defensively, watching Hugues' tawny brows rise in surprise. "Not that you concerned yourself with that aboard the ship."

His neck tinged red even though he did not concede the point. "Verily?" Hugues demanded curtly when Sophie thought any other mortal might have apologized for abandoning her. At her reluctant nod of acquiescence, he frowned anew and she braced herself for that lecture.

"Come along, then," he urged unexpectedly, gripping her elbow with a firmness of purpose that brooked no argument, and Sophie did as she was bid.

"Where do we go?" she demanded as she tried unsuccessfully to wriggle free, but Hugues marched her firmly down the narrow street.

"'Tis time enough you ate," he growled, as if she were no more than a persistent nuisance with whom he had to contend, and Sophie bit back a cutting response.

Was he going to feed her, then? Surely he knew she had no silver, for what other reason had she to resort to petty thievery? Her mind filled with a thousand questions that she had not the inclination to ask this stern-faced man who seemed determined to fetch her somewhere. Before long the widening of the streets and the rising noise told Sophie that they were approaching the market again.

"I cannot go back there," she protested, pulling against Hugues' hand, but he still propelled her forward.

"Aye, you must," he declared. Sophie's heart sank when they burst into the square and she saw that he was cutting a straight path to the baker's stall. A cluster of men had assembled around the stall and Sophie had no doubt her theft was the subject of discussion, for they were all frowns and sage headshakes.

Would he hand her over as a thief, then, and leave her to her fate? No time had she to plead her case, for Hugues set a swift pace and she groaned when the baker glanced up, the scowl that darkened his brow indicating that he recognized her. Mercifully, Hugues spoke before any accusations could be made.

"My ward tells me that you are owed for one pastry," he said smoothly. His *ward*? What nonsense was this?

"Your *ward*?" demanded one of the men skeptically, sweeping a glance over Hugues' neat tabard and Sophie's filthy state. She stiffened at his insult and stared him down.

"'Tis not for the likes of you to take on the debts of stealing urchins," insisted a man with a more kindly face. Before Sophie could indignantly deny that she was some common child of the street, Hugues turned his attention to the man.

"Aye, but this particular *urchin* is already my responsibility," he assured the doubtful man. The way he savored their assessment of her made Sophie itch to kick him.

Urchin was it, then? She ought to bite him, as the urchins did in Bordeaux when they were caught. That would show him of what she was made, Sophie thought dryly, and the way Hugues' grip tightened on her arm in that moment made her fear he had read her very thoughts.

"Know you how many of this one's ilk there are in La Rochelle?" asked the baker with a disparaging glance to Sophie. "Truly, you scarce will be able to make your way through the market should that greedy lot hear of your generosity."

"Meaning no disrespect, of course, milord," interjected the kinder-faced man, earning a sharp glance from his companions.

"None taken, I assure you," Hugues countered smoothly. "But, truly, my ward and I were separated when our ship foundered. Indeed, I thought him dead."

Him? Now she was not merely a ruffian but a boy, as well. Sophie's pride straightened her spine still further, for though she had survived an ordeal, still she had the shape of a woman and no mere boy. Hugues ruffled her matted hair as if she were but a child and Sophie barely restrained herself from glowering at him.

Curse him for pretending she was a boy. No matter if her garb would inspire much gossip otherwise, if not lecherous looks. Well she knew that she looked a mess, but did he have to find the matter so amusing? And what was this nonsense about her being his ward?

She was sorely tempted to set the matter straight right here and now, but the baker chose that moment to cooperate with the foreign knight.

"Indeed you know best, milord." The baker grumbled under his breath when he saw the flash of coin, but he pocketed Hugues' proffered silver hastily despite his manner. He shot Sophie a dark glance, fully communicating his awareness that she had had no intention of seeing him paid.

"And I would take three more on the weight of the recommendation," Hugues continued blithely as though there were naught amiss.

The baker recovered himself quickly, his manner becoming incrementally more friendly with this subsequent exchange, and his companions nodded amiably among themselves at the knight's resolution of the situation. Sophie felt her color rising, knowing full well that this would be the matter of discussion around more than one board this night and wishing she could flee the town this very moment.

But first she would clarify the thinking of one Chevalier Hugues de Pontesse.

Hugues could not imagine what had compelled him to claim Sophie as his ward.

If naught else, this impulsive move was sure to reaffirm her confidence in that mad idea of destiny, he worried as he completed the transaction with the disgruntled baker. He risked a sidelong glance in her direction that did naught to reassure him. Indeed, Sophie was already looking as though she were up to something and Hugues gritted his teeth in anticipation of what she would say once she gathered her thoughts.

And what defense had he?

Truly, his heart had leaped when he had spied her in the market, so certain had he been that she must have perished when she had been swept overboard. 'Twas Luc who had kept him from jumping into the waves in pursuit that night. Well he knew that he could not help them both, and the sickened boy would likely have lost his footing within a heartbeat if Hugues had left him alone.

Was it simple relief, then, that had prompted his tongue? Was it hope of her survival that had made him dally in La Rochelle two days longer than he should have? Hugues knew not and firmly resolved that he did not particularly care.

'Twas only natural that he feel some relief that she had survived, he reasoned matter-of-factly, and drew some satisfaction from the clear logic of that thought. Hugues watched Sophie make short work of another pastry as he further concluded that he would have felt the same to discover any of their shipmates alive.

Any satisfaction died abruptly with the recognition that that thought was a lie even before it completely formed. Hugues almost snorted at his foolhardiness, knowing full well that the captain's wry presence would not set his pulse to pounding as Sophie's did, even in her admittedly unkempt state.

He wanted to touch her, he realized with a shock, wanted to wash the salt and dirt from her skin himself that his own hands might reveal the smooth tan of her skin anew. 'Twas not his place to even think such a thing, let alone his task to wash her. The inappropriateness, not to mention the illogical nature, of these impulses deeply disturbed him and he gritted his teeth against them. But Hugues could not dismiss the thoughts and he clenched his fingers as he walked, painfully aware of her right alongside him, the tendrils of her fair hair brushing against his shoulder.

Unable to fight his own mind, Hugues let the thoughts come and immediately regretted the concession. He wanted to touch her and taste her and bury himself within her once more with a ferocity that startled him. He wanted to welcome her back to the land of the living that he had feared she had abandoned. The best way he could imagine to do that was to show her the pleasures he had denied her in his own haste in their single coupling.

The images prompted by that thought nearly undid him and Hugues was grateful that he was doing naught more complicated than walking across the square. He had but to put one foot solidly in front of the other until his mischievous mind regained its common sense. Uncomfortable with the intimacy of his thoughts in the public forum of the marketplace, Hugues cleared his throat and took Sophie hastily by the elbow, steering her back to his rooms.

What other option had he? Inappropriate 'twas to leave her out in full view in such garb, and he *had* claimed her as his ward. Had he not some measure of responsibility to her, in truth, if only as a fellow being whom the fates had frowned upon?

The fates, Hugues snorted silently with disgust. *That* was the kind of thinking that lay at the root of his troubles.

Hopefully Luc's bubbly presence would help him to compose himself. Hopefully the practicalities of ensuring that Sophie was properly groomed and attired would give him time to dismiss this impulsive nonsense that clouded his thoughts.

A boy. Hugues de Pontesse was not going to forget this slight any time soon.

Another pastry lined Sophie's stomach with a welcome and somewhat unfamiliar warmth, leaving her more than ready for battle. She bided her time while Hugues led her down the streets to a coppersmith's shop, even as she planned her vengeance. He hustled her through the dim interior of the shop with its dancing sun motes before she could get a good look at it and up the stairs so fast that she almost tripped. Sophie cast a scathing glance over her shoulder, but Hugues looked momentarily fierce.

"Have the good sense at least this once to hold your tongue," he muttered under his breath. Sophie considered having their imminent argument right there, but had not the chance to decide before a female voice rang out from the shop below.

"Chevalier!" came an older woman's recriminating cry. "Told you I did that there'd be none of *that* in my house."

Sophie turned to see a gray-haired woman standing at the foot of the stairs, one hand propped on her ample hip, the other waving a tiny gleaming hammer threateningly in their direction as she scowled.

"Truly I do not see your meaning," Hugues protested, but the woman shook her head dismissively.

"Think you that I have not eyes, sir?" she demanded. "A respectable house this is, and I'll not see my children corrupted with your whoring ways."

"But madame, you have erred," Hugues argued with careful innocence, gesturing expansively to Sophie. "This is but my ward, lost these days at sea. Surely I mentioned my sorrow at his loss, but blessed was I indeed to find him in the market this very day."

"A finer tale will you have to spin should you intend to take that woman upstairs in my house," the woman countered in a flat interruption of the knight's tale, folding her arms skeptically across her chest.

Ha, Sophie thought with satisfaction, an old crone sitting in the dark knew me to be a woman. *That* should give him something to think about. She turned on Hugues with no small measure of satisfaction, only to find him looking flummoxed.

"This be no woman, but merely my ward," Hugues persisted stubbornly, but the woman shook her head with determination.

"She might well have been a boy, chevalier, had she not those curves beneath her shirt," she commented dryly. Sophie watched Hugues struggle momentarily with the temptation of continuing to argue, but then he shook his head and shrugged.

"She *is* my ward," he conceded with a defeated sigh, and Sophie wondered if he would even manage to pull off this last, relatively small lie. The woman looked unconvinced and Sophie weakened toward Hugues, deciding to take up the fight herself that it might be resolved in her favor.

Clearly her knight had no talent with such delicate matters.

"Indeed, madame, he speaks the truth," she confirmed in the most demure voice she could manage and pointedly refrained from watching Hugues' reaction. Hopefully he would not give her away. Some of the doubt faded out of the woman's eyes and Sophie warmed to her theme.

"There are few with eyes as sharp as yours to see through my disguise," she said in mock admiration and the woman visibly preened at the compliment before she frowned anew.

"Well-enough mannered do you sound," the woman conceded crossly. "But pretty words will not turn aside my good sense." She squinted up at Sophie, and the younger woman steeled herself for an interrogation. "What manner of lady travels with a knight unescorted?" she asked skeptically.

Sophie thought furiously and came up with a tale that was not quite a lie.

"'Tis not my choice of travel, you must know, but 'tis the caprice of circumstance that forces this situation upon me. This knight guaranteed my protection and passage on ship, but when the ship was cast onto the shoals, we were separated. Truly I feared that I alone survived and knew not how I would continue on my way." She leaned forward to whisper theatrically to the woman. "The road is no place for a woman alone, as you doubtless know, but I simply must return to my family."

"High time it must be for you to wed," the older woman confirmed assessingly, evidently assuming that this was the reason for her return home. Sophie had but to nod and did so, unable to stifle a twinge of annoyance at a mention of her advancing age that reminded her all too well of what she had left behind in Bordeaux.

"Aye, time enough 'tis." She nudged Hugues imperceptibly when the woman paused to consider the tale, and he fumbled for his silver.

"Well enough do I understand that you will expect compensation for another breaking fast here," he said hastily and the woman's expression changed from doubt to speculation. She frowned at the silver denier gleaming in Hugues' hand in the half-light and tapped her tiny coppersmith's hammer against the palm of her hand thoughtfully.

"I have not another room," she mused, shooting a dark glance up the stairs as if she wished she did not have to turn away the coin and, sensing her advantage, Sophie looked shocked right on cue.

"*Madame!*" she whispered in mock horror. "Surely you *cannot* mean—"

"Aye, I'll not have such goings on in my home," the older woman reiterated with a firm shake of her hammer, but Sophie interrupted her tirade before it could truly begin.

"Madame, I *assure* you that my greatest gift is for the man I wed and none other before him," Sophie insisted.

The woman's gaze predictably flicked past her shoulder to Hugues. "And naught will I hear of you trying to persuade the lady otherwise?" she demanded, and Sophie willed Hugues to simply agree. Do not even attempt to lie, she commanded him in her mind, knowing all would be lost if he made such a poor effort of it as the last time.

"Nay," he contented himself with saying, and Sophie breathed a silent sigh of relief. "The lady shall have the bed," he added quickly when their prospective landlady did not smile. Still she did not smile or respond to his words, but mutely nicked the silver coin from his grip.

"A bath will you be wanting, then?" she asked with a shrewd glance to Sophie, who nodded at the very thought.

"Aye," she agreed, looking to Hugues for agreement on the next matter. "And mayhap a seamstress," she added. Hugues' curt nod of acquiescence made her smile.

"No need is there for you to travel thus any longer," he said, casting an inquiring look to the woman at the foot of the stairs.

"My neighbor plies a needle well for reasonable prices," she supplied matter-of-factly, turning away from the stairs to shout, "Émil! Chrétien! Fetch the tub for the lady upstairs and hang water to boil. Quintere! Fetch Madame de Mauléon. Work there is for her here!"

Chapter Six

"Never have I heard such lies," Hugues muttered as they climbed the last stairs. Sophie cast a questioning glance over her shoulder to him, those violet eyes wide with innocence. His stomach knotted at her expression, his conscience troubled by the tale she had spun and the ease with which she had spun it.

"Indeed?" she inquired politely. "What lies have you heard this day?"

That she would deny her own falsehoods just moments after uttering them astounded Hugues. He barely managed to push her ahead of him and into the room at the top of the stairs before he responded explosively.

"What lies!?" he demanded in amazement when the door was safely closed behind them. "'Twas not you who stood before me there?" He swept his arm toward the stairs in a broad gesture.

"Aye," Sophie retorted calmly. Too calmly, Hugues thought as she folded her arms across her chest and looked him steadily in the eye. "What precisely did you find to be a lie?"

Where to start? From his perspective it had all been a lie from start to finish.

"That you travel to your family," Hugues retorted, studiously avoiding the particular assertion that plagued him.

"My mother was said to have been from Bretagne," Sophie answered with that same quiet assurance that he found so unnerving.

"What of your husband in Bordeaux?" Hugues demanded, taken aback when Sophie looked astounded in turn. Maybe she truly *was* mad, he thought reluctantly, though still he pressed on stubbornly. "Is he not your family, though evidently he neglected to render his marital debt?"

"What husband?" she asked in what appeared to be genuine confusion.

"The man who sat beside you at the council in Bordeaux," Hugues explained patiently. "Was he not your spouse?"

"Gaillard?" Sophie asked with a wrinkled nose that eloquently answered Hugues' question.

"I know not his name," he responded tightly, not at all certain what this discussion would reveal. Was it possible the man was not Sophie's spouse? Indeed, her virginity would seem to support that argument, he acknowledged with a growing sense of dread. Was it possible she was unwed?

"He was the man who shouted to you when, when..." Words failed Hugues to describe their fateful embrace. He gestured futilely with one hand, but Sophie interrupted his objections.

"Gaillard," she asserted firmly as she propped her hands on her hips, "is my *father*." Sophie frowned for an instant, then corrected herself. "My foster father." She looked Hugues sternly in the eye.

"Surely you did not think me wed to one so much my senior?" she asked skeptically, and Hugues could not bring himself to admit that he had questioned that very same issue.

"Why, then, was he so distraught? And why would he bring his daughter to such a meeting?" he demanded in turn, not at all interested in abandoning his understanding of the situation so easily.

Sophie rolled her eyes. "A *match* he thought to make," she supplied and Hugues' heart sank at the unwitting reminder of how thoroughly he had diminished her marketability. "I knew not his plan until 'twas thoroughly upset," she added. Hugues glanced up at the smile in her voice to find unexpected mischief twinkling in her eyes.

"A good team we made," she whispered, and Hugues found himself grinning at her unexpected playfulness.

"And how much of the gray at his temples was of your making?" he teased before he knew what he was about, delighted at the way Sophie laughed outright at his jest.

"Little enough of it," she said, but Hugues had little doubt of the truth of that. She regarded him with an expression that could only mean trouble and he sobered again.

"What other lies would you claim I told our hostess?" she demanded softly. Hugues felt hot color suffuse his neck, the back of his ears becoming hot enough to fair glow in the dark.

"About your greatest gift," he managed to mutter gruffly despite his embarrassment. Sophie's widening grin made it impossible for him to continue.

"That 'twas meant for my husband alone?" she prompted. Hugues nodded mutely, dry mouthed and grateful for her meager assistance, though still he did not trust her intent.

A knock there was at the door and he opened it without thinking, grateful for the interruption but wishing all the while that he knew what Sophie was about. He watched blindly as a pair of young boys carted in the wooden tub and placed it before the hearth.

One stoked up the blaze, the other trotted back downstairs, and Hugues was painfully aware of Sophie's amused regard upon him the entire while. The second boy left as the first returned with a pail of steaming water and dumped it into the tub. The splash of the water and the reason it was being carried upstairs brought Hugues abruptly back to earth and he stirred himself.

"Time 'tis I left," he mumbled hastily, able to think only of getting out of the chamber before Sophie disrobed. "Luc I sent to find steeds and I had best tell him we have need of another," he began by way of explanation, suddenly uncertain of Sophie's plans. He flicked a confused glance across the room to find her still smiling that maddening smile.

"Unless, that is, should you intend to travel with us any farther, if you..." The words fell from Hugues' lips in an inarticulate tumble and he despised himself for not being able to retain his usual composure.

Sophie's confident nod brought his words to an abrupt halt and he swallowed nervously in anticipation of what she would say. He could only regard her mutely as the boys' departing footsteps echoed on the stairs below and she stepped deliberately toward him, every curve crying out for his touch despite her filthy garb.

Hugues clenched his hands at his sides in a desperate attempt to keep them there.

"Aye, Hugues," she whispered, and he closed his eyes against the scent of her skin. His eyes flew open in shock when she stretched up to brush her lips across his with tantalizing gentleness, her fingertips pressing lightly on his chest.

"Aye, I would travel with you," she murmured, her eyes turning smoky as she spoke, and Hugues backed up so quickly that he hit his shoulder on the door frame. He spun wildly, needing only to put distance between them, glancing back from the landing to find her still watching him silently.

"I did not lie, Hugues," she asserted. The softly uttered words launched a panic through Hugues' veins that sent him lurching down the stairs.

That he should bolt and run in response to her statement of what was obvious to them both was the last thing Sophie would have expected, and she spent the remainder of the afternoon puzzling over Hugues' behavior. That a veritable lion of a knight should run from the likes of her would have been amusing, were it not so disturbing.

Was it possible that Hugues did not find their entwined destiny that obvious?

Incredible it seemed to Sophie that he could think thus, but the longer she stitched in the quiet of the afternoon and the more she reflected upon the matter, the more evident that fact seemed to be. The pieces of the puzzle fit far too well to deny the conclusion.

Indeed, Hugues had not seemed already aware of their fate when she first broached the subject in Bordeaux. So sure Sophie had been that he had felt that same initial jolt, but now she wondered whether she had wrongly assumed his experience to be the same as her own. And since then, he had grudgingly tolerated her intrusion into his life. Hugues seemed intent on fighting their destiny, for how many times now had Sophie had to explain this most fundamental circumstance to him?

And evidently the appeal of the idea had not improved despite her explanations, judging by the way he had fled today. What had she said that was new? That she believed him to be the man for her? Surely this had already been made clear to them both, but Sophie reluctantly considered the possibility that the truth might not be evident to Hugues.

Obviously he could not be lying or otherwise trying to deceive her as to his real feelings, for time had shown the man's complete inability in that area of endeavor.

Not that honesty was such a bad trait, Sophie conceded with a smile as she stitched the seam in a new kirtle. In fact, she rather liked that Hugues could not tell a lie to save his life. Aye, an honorable man would suit her just fine.

She shook out the light green wool to check her workmanship before threading the needle anew and matching another seam. The inestimable Madame de Mauléon nodded approvingly from the other side of the room, bending back over the chemise she was piecing with enviable speed.

Renewed by the certainty she would have at least one garment by the close of the day, if not a particularly modest one, Sophie knotted the thread and began to stitch. Hélène had always said that work went more than twice as fast with two pairs of hands. And good coin she had saved Hugues by doing some of the work herself—that should render him proud.

But what to *do* about Hugues? Sophie frowned thoughtfully, knowing that evoking blind terror in the man would net her naught in the end. If indeed he was not convinced of their destiny, mayhap it would be best to leave that topic aside for now. Mayhap she should show herself worthy of his love, earn his respect as any other maid who had set her cap for a man.

Mayhap she had pushed too hard by granting her greatest gift so soon.

Hugues hesitated in front of the coppersmith's modest house, frowning at the upstairs window where a candle flame flickered patiently. It could only be a portent that Sophie was awake and waiting for him.

As a woman waited for her husband.

Something writhed within him at that thought and he struggled against the urge to walk away from the house and never look back.

Hugues could only wish, too late, that he could have had the foresight to get drunk. At least then he would have been blissfully unaware of the reception Sophie gave him and perhaps, with a measure of luck, might have forgotten the entire incident by the morning.

But past time was it for such thoughts now and Hugues reluctantly entered the quiet house, pausing for another long moment at the foot of the stairs before he sighed heavily and climbed to the top.

His heart predictably leaped in his chest when he pushed open the door to find Sophie seated beside the table where the candle reposed. She was sewing, wearing a simple chemise that was evidently new, her hair loose and cast over one shoulder, a glistening cascade of gold that she had shoved out of her way.

Hugues must have made some unwitting sound, for she glanced up suddenly from her stitchery. Their eyes met and held for a long moment and Hugues could not find it within himself to move or speak. Finally Sophie smiled and put her work carefully aside.

"Have you eaten?" she asked quietly, touching her finger to her lips as she indicated Luc sleeping soundly on the hearth. Hugues smiled affectionately at the boy's peaceful repose and when he glanced back to Sophie he was surprised to find a similar smile playing over her lips.

"I fear he must have talked you deaf," he commented with a grin and Sophie chuckled under her breath.

"Aye, he seemed glad that we met again," she agreed as she regarded Hugues thoughtfully. "'Twas quite a tale he told of the shipwreck."

"Aye," Hugues agreed, feeling very tired at the reminder of that ordeal. And well he could imagine how Luc might have embellished the tale for the telling to such a fetching audience.

"'Tis easy to be romantic about an adventure one has been carried through," he commented gruffly, curiously intent on eliminating that speculative light in Sophie's eyes. Sophie laughed as she rose to her feet. Hugues' heart picked up its pace as she approached him and he wondered what she intended to do.

Would she kiss him again?

The thought alone fairly made his knees buckle in a mixture of anticipation and dread, for he knew not how he would respond to such a test. He stood his ground despite his unruly thoughts, determined that he could and would survive any ordeal she dealt him.

Had she not urged him on before? What matter if he did lose control beneath her touch when 'twas clear he gave her what she wanted?

"Aye, but he is here and healthy because of you alone," she murmured, her voice softly seductive to his ears, admiration gleaming in her eyes.

Every fiber within Hugues leaped in anticipation when she paused a mere handbreadth before him and tipped back her chin to look him in the eye. He noted the thickness of her surprisingly dark lashes, the splash of new freckles across the bridge of her nose, the sun-kissed hue of her skin. At this proximity Hugues wished that her chemise was more sheer when his gaze followed the golden length of her throat only to find a pair of pert nipples arching the fine cloth into twin peaks.

He swallowed with difficulty and looked back to Sophie's eyes, knowing he would be unable to check his response if she touched him, even while he willed her to do so. Just when he thought she might have kissed him, she simply laid one hand upon his arm and beckoned him to the table.

"Come and eat," she urged gently as she stepped away, and his shock was followed quickly by a wave of disappointment.

She had not even attempted that kiss he had so anticipated. What had changed?

"There is stew and some excuse for wine," she added dryly, and in his surprise he could not even appreciate her unwitting bias.

"Aye, I am hungry," he agreed, taking the offered seat heavily even as his appetite unexpectedly waned.

Clearly the emptiness of his belly was clouding his thinking, he reasoned stubbornly. Obviously she was being thoughtful, for naught could have changed. Sophie wanted him, Sophie always wanted him, Sophie was convinced that they were destined for each other. This much Hugues knew without question. If she did not seem to want him right this moment, 'twas merely the fault of his own perception.

The woman's madness was consistent, if naught else.

Sophie put her work away, unwrapped a trencher of dark bread from a linen cloth and laid both before Hugues on the table. He schooled himself not to be disappointed that she did not make any effort to touch him in even the most innocent manner, telling himself that she must be biding her time. 'Twas well enough something he had wished her capable of in the past and could hardly fault her for it now.

A flagon of wine and stoneware cup joined the repast and Hugues poured himself some wine while Sophie retrieved a lidded iron pot that she had placed in the embers of the fire. The light silhouetted her when she crouched on the hearth and he admired the view as he felt the wine ease through his tired muscles.

A thoughtful woman she was to ensure his needs met before her own. Aye, that must be the way of it. He smiled to himself and sipped his wine, permitting himself to speculate for just a moment.

Mayhap 'twas not so bad to have Sophie convinced he was the man for her. Indeed, he could well get used to this scenario, Hugues conceded, returning the smile she granted him as she placed the pot on the table. The smell of stewed venison that enveloped the room when she removed the lid made his stomach growl loudly and they exchanged another of those smiles.

"You *are* hungry," she commented wryly and Hugues chuckled.

"Aye, a long day has it been." Sophie shot him a sharp look as she ladled the meat onto the bread. "And this smells good," he added appreciatively.

"The landlady offered it."

"Have you eaten?" Hugues asked when she emptied the pot onto his trencher.

"Aye, the boy could not wait and I knew not when you would be back," she confirmed mildly.

Hugues could not meet her eyes at that, for fully did he know that she must have wondered whether he was coming back at all. He knew not what to say to reassure her and the silence that stretched between them seemed so loud as to hurt his very ears. He watched her return the pot to the hearth and wished he knew how to put them back on an even footing again.

"Another meeting you had tonight, did you not?" she inquired as she returned to the table. Hugues nodded, relieved to have something mundane to talk about, even if 'twas no more than the pretense of a meeting he had arranged solely to have an excuse to linger here an extra few days. A pretense that had borne unexpected fruit, he reminded himself, for Sophie was here. That thought tightened everything within him, and he forced himself to concentrate on her question.

"Aye, and poorly it went, just as the others," he conceded with a shrug. Naught had gone aright on this venture of the Queen Regent's, but the meat was good and he savored the richness of it on his tongue, pushing the other issue out of his mind for the moment.

"And why is that?"

Hugues glanced up at Sophie's question, surprised to find her regarding him from the chair opposite with genuine curiosity. She grinned unexpectedly and he supposed his astonishment that she should be interested in such matters must have shown.

"I would like to know," she urged quite sincerely. Hugues acknowledged her assertion with a nod, taking a quaff of wine to rinse his palate before he spoke.

"'Tis the changing times," he said. He waved toward the window, and the shadows of the town spread beyond as he frowned.

"These townfolk, they think differently than the old noble lines who ally themselves with this king or that one on the basis of loyalties that have endured for generations. We do as our fathers did, as their fathers did before them." He wiped his mouth and leaned forward to emphasize his point.

"Pontesse, for example, has allied with the Capetian kings since they rose to power and 'tis inconceivable to me, or likely to my father, that that alliance could change, regardless of what the crown might do."

"My father supports the Normans because they pay their debts in a timely fashion," Sophie contributed and Hugues shot her a look. Apparently her madness was limited to a single issue, for she evidently could and did think clearly otherwise.

"Aye, and should they cease to do so, he would likely cease to support them," he suggested, watching her nod in agreement before he returned to his meal.

"He spoke exactly thus before I left," Sophie confirmed. "In fact, one of my brothers was already convinced the business of the Capetians should be courted in case shipping should be interrupted by the war."

"'Tis exactly that of which I speak." Hugues warmed to his theme, propping his elbows on the table as he spoke. "Naught does tradition and loyalty mean to them—they wish to know the advantage to them personally of taking one side over the other. Concessions they want from the crown." He tapped the blunt end of his finger on the well-worn wood as he enumerated those requests.

"Rights to hold court, freedom from taxes and levies, release from tolls, greater jurisdiction in their own councils and courts," he concluded with an expansive gesture that adequately expressed his frustration.

"But the Queen Regent did not anticipate this?" Sophie demanded.

Hugues could only shake his head. "Little authority have I to make such offers," he admitted and Sophie nodded thoughtfully.

"'Tis so important, then, to have the support of the townspeople?"

"I fear 'tis the new way," Hugues agreed with a frown. "There is silver in the towns, not to mention a gathering of folk who think like-mindedly. Truly I fear that Gascogne will be held by whoever the towns support, for the nobility are equally split over the question and feud between themselves."

"Would that you could buy up the wine," Sophie jested with a smile and Hugues laughed.

"Would that I could buy the entire vintage of the district," he agreed good-naturedly, "or summon a Norman tax collector at this most opportune moment." Sophie chuckled in turn. Hugues returned to his meal and enjoyed the golden glow that seemed to have surrounded the candlelit table.

"What will you do?" she asked a few moments later.

Hugues shrugged philosophically. "Return to Paris, make my case to my lady queen and hopefully return here with a more palatable offer."

"Will there be time enough for that?" Sophie inquired and Hugues glanced up, pleasantly surprised by her perceptiveness.

"Dame Fortune might yet ride with us," he said simply, finishing his meat and leaning back to savor the last of his wine.

His own words made him wonder whether Sophie intended to continue to ride with him, whether that was the point of her asking about his plans. Unfortunately he could think of no way to ask her without sounding rude, and the silence grew between them once more.

Sophie cleared the table quickly while Hugues sipped reflectively and watched her. She tossed the crusts of bread out into the street for the dogs, placed the dirty pot outside the door and returned to pick up her needlework before he had even finished his wine, and a new appreciation for her skills dawned within him.

"The dressmaker came?" Hugues asked as she plied her needle once more. She smiled and nodded.

"Aye." Sophie looked nervous about what she was going to say. "This chemise she made today and I the kirtle." She held up the light green cloth piled in her lap almost apologetically. "A wool surcoat she is making this night and that is the sum of it." She added in a much quieter voice, "I hope I have not spent too much of your coin."

Indeed, she had bought considerably less than Hugues had anticipated, the barest minimum of attire, in fact. "The dress is wool?" he inquired and she nodded. "And the cloak?"

"Wool, as well."

"'Tis lined?"

Sophie looked shocked. "Hugues, I would not waste your funds on fur!" she exclaimed, and he shook his head.

"'Tis cursed cold at night, Sophie, I would not have you chilled when we travel," he declared, liking the fact that he could be so openhanded with coin. "And to that end, you need wool stockings and boots, sturdy gloves, a wimple and fillet and at the very least a heavier chemise."

A little silence followed his words and Hugues enjoyed the knowledge that he had surprised her. Did the woman think he held her in such low regard that he would willingly see her freeze?

"Hugues, you have no need to spend thus on me," Sophie argued softly, and he leaned across the table to playfully tap her on the end of the nose.

"No ward of mine will dress poorly," he teased, and to his relief she smiled tentatively. "In truth, Sophie, you have naught to put upon your back," he added to reassure her, and she reluctantly nodded agreement. No need had he to tell her that purchasing a third horse had set him back far more than a few serviceable garments.

"Aye, Hugues, you speak the truth," she conceded, standing and stretching her back. "No wish have I to be a burden to you, though, and I vow to find some way to pay you back."

Hugues wondered if she had deliberately stepped out of the circle of candlelight so that he might not discern her mood. The loss of her maidenhead hung between them in Hugues' eyes and he well knew that he could scarce compensate her for the loss of that.

What were a few female indulgences, in truth? Well could he afford them and the horse could be sold when they parted ways for good. For some reason that thought annoyed Hugues and he was more stern than he intended to be when he finally spoke.

"Twice have I willingly taken you on," he chided gruffly as he likewise shoved to his feet. "Surely that should dissuade you of that notion."

Sophie's silhouette was briefly outlined as she glanced back over her shoulder to him, as if surprised by his words, but then she was climbing into the bed with a heartfelt sigh of relief.

"A pallet did she bring for you," she informed Hugues tiredly. "Mind you snuff the candle."

Hugues stood mutely beside the table, unable to believe that she had made no effort to kiss him or assault his senses in any other way. He waited before giving full rein to his disappointment, unexpectedly feeling the knave for assuming she would invite him to her bed this night. Sophie's breathing merely slowed to the same leisurely pace as Luc's, the room filled with the soft sounds of their sleeping, and Hugues realized that she had had no intention of touching him.

Had Sophie changed her mind about him?

The very thought filled Hugues with a panic that astounded him with its intensity and he almost crawled into the bed beside her to convince her otherwise before he checked himself. For what would he do once he found himself there? Force himself upon her? Never that. Beg her forgiveness? For what? For following his intellect in the right manner of any man? 'Twas unthinkable.

Regardless if Sophie apparently had changed her mind about their being destined for each other.

And the revelation that this intoxicating, undoubtedly mad woman was unerringly practical with silver, as any good wife should be, did not ease his mind in the least. And she could sew. And was thoughtful of his needs. Hugues threw back the rest of his wine, refusing to even glance to the bed where her breathing slowed to a whisper even now, refusing to even entertain the notion that Sophie would make a good spouse.

Well it seemed that he was coming too late to this conclusion.

Disgruntled beyond belief, Hugues extinguished the candle in poor temper, groaning at the hardness of the straw-filled mattress as he stretched out upon its meager length. He hauled his cloak over himself in annoyance and positively glared at the dying embers of the fire, reminding himself that he was a full knight in line for an inheritance from an ailing and aging sire.

A warrior with a reputation for effectiveness and a man not considered hard to look upon, Hugues de Pontesse knew he was eligible, whatever Sophie's ideas might be to the contrary.

Well might he know the truth, but it helped him naught to gain his rest that night, and Hugues found himself creeping out of the quiet room before the very dawn, telling himself 'twas high time to see to the horses.

"Milady, you look beautiful!" Luc enthused, and Sophie could not help but smile at the boy's praise.

"Thank you, Luc. You are most kind," she responded, letting him gallantly kiss the back of her hand like a great lord. All day she had spent alone with her needle again and 'twas good to know the results had come out so well.

Her eyes raised of their own accord to check Hugues' response, for he had said naught since the two had returned to the chamber this eve, and her heart fairly stopped at the intensity of his expression. He stepped forward with purpose and Sophie held her ground, even as her heart recovered itself and began to race.

How she wished she could dare to tell him how she had missed him this day!

Hugues silently doffed his gloves and took her hand in turn. Sophie's fingers curled around the strength of his. She was acutely aware of the differences in their skin in that moment, intrigued by the leatherlike texture of his skin, the last remnant of a callus on his thumb. She felt all atingle, alive and alert for the first time since she had awoken and found him gone. His very presence made her want to taste him once more.

"Aye, as fair as the willows of Pontesse," he murmured enigmatically just before his lips brushed the back of her hand.

Sophie shivered at his touch and Hugues glanced up to meet her eyes in that moment, almost as if he were perplexed by her response. She returned his regard, willing him to see the emotion flaring within her, and slowly his surprise was replaced by a heat to match her own. He turned her hand over and pressed a kiss very deliberately into her palm, still holding her gaze, and 'twas Sophie who closed her eyes against the pleasure that rose when the tip of his tongue flicked against her skin.

She sensed rather than saw Hugues straighten before her, knew how close he stood before he spoke or she opened her eyes. Sophie took a deep draught of his scent, reminding herself sternly to temper her response lest she frighten Hugues again.

This night she would not sleep alone should she have the sense to be careful.

"Madame de Mauléon finished your surcoat?" Hugues murmured and Sophie fancied she could feel his breath against her temple.

"Aye," she managed to respond, clenching her hands so that she did not reach for him. She waited breathlessly, certain that he would kiss her somewhere more interesting than her palm, but after a moment's pause that felt like an eternity he released her hand and she felt him step away.

Sophie's eyes flew open in surprise, only to see Hugues pacing away from her toward the door.

"Fetch it, then," were the words he tossed curtly over his shoulder. Sophie was momentarily stunned that things were progressing so differently than she had expected just an instant before.

"'Tis time we ate," he added when she did not move.

Furious tears blinded Sophie's vision and she spun on her heel in annoyance, snatching up her new cloak and tossing it over her shoulders. Leave it to a man to think of his stomach first! Undoubtedly his mind would turn to romance once his belly was filled and his senses dulled with some cheap vintage.

Sophie jabbed her chin into the air and sailed past Hugues without even a glance. So he thought her undesirable? Well, 'twould be a cold day in Hades before she offered herself to him again.

In complete confusion Hugues watched Sophie sweep down the stairs. Now what had sparked her anger? He flicked an imperious finger at Luc and the boy scampered in the lady's wake, leaving Hugues to stamp down the stairs behind the pair of them.

What did she expect him to do? Evidently something he had *not* done, but he could not for the life of him have guessed what it was. Had she not made it clear last night that she would not welcome him in her bed? All day he had spent bolstering his confidence to confront her yet again, but she was more encouraging to the gallant words of a mere boy than a salute from him.

Mayhap he had been a fool to think that touching her would prompt her desire anew; that had proved to be an untold folly. Though she had borne his touch, Hugues would not soon forget the way the pit of his stomach had dropped when he had looked up to find her eyes closed in revulsion. Truly he had gone too far.

What had happened to the woman who could not get enough of him? Was this truly the same temptress who had demanded he take her against the wall of a cramped ship's cabin? Had it truly been only yesterday that she had assured him that he was the man for her?

Much as Hugues hated to admit it, he rather missed that peculiar madness of Sophie's and he trudged sourly behind the other two, ignoring Luc's enthusiastic banter. What perversity of her cursed fates had made him amenable to her plan just as she decided to abandon it?

Gradually Luc's chatter soothed Sophie's temper and the raging urge to wring Hugues' thick neck subsided to a dull roar, only to make new room for her doubts. What did he mean, she looked like willows? Gaillard had always called them weeds with destructive roots and Sophie herself had never cared for the way they drooped to trail their branches in the water. They looked weak and melancholy and she could not imagine how Hugues could expect her to be flattered by such a comment.

Did he think her weak because she had offered herself to him so readily? That thought was more than a little disturbing and Sophie reluctantly considered the possibility that Hugues had acquiesced simply because she had made herself so available. 'Twas not likely he would have had another similar offer on that ship, and with growing uneasiness she recalled her brothers' whispered tales of their conquests.

She risked a glance over her shoulder to find Hugues staring stubbornly at the ground as he walked heavily behind her. Had he really anticipated that she would fall into his arms after such a comment? Surely 'twas not unreasonable to expect him to make some effort to court her?

'Twas a sign of disrespect, no more, no less, and Sophie would not encourage his assessment of her any further. Hugues had some work to do before she let him between her thighs again.

Weak and melancholy. Ha. Sophie squared her shoulders and stared up into the indigo sky as the first few flakes of snow fluttered down.

She would show him.

It soon became evident that Hugues had no intention of seeing much of anything that night. He had no patience with Sophie's interest in the goods at the market or Luc's delight in the snow now falling thickly, but hastened the pair of them into a smoky tavern and ordered a meal.

The potage was rich and good, the bread heavy as Sophie was accustomed to, but Hugues ate naught. She watched with trepidation as he ordered yet another pitcher of ale and consumed the bulk of it himself, much as he had its predecessor, and wondered what he was about.

By the time they left, the knight was markedly unsteady on his feet, though Sophie took little encouragement from the fact that even Luc seemed surprised at

Hugues' behavior. The very idea that he had to besot himself to forget her troublesome presence pricked her pride sorely, never mind that she could hardly refuse him if he made no effort toward her. A sorry trio they must have appeared, weaving through the quiet, snow-covered streets, Sophie and Luc trying to keep Hugues upright despite the slippery footing. But they could hardly have left him behind.

"A finer night you might have picked for such non-sense," she muttered irritably under her breath when Hugues unerringly found a small patch of ice on the cobblestones and leaned more heavily against her as he regained his balance.

"Mayhap I should sing to ease the way," he suggested amiably. She glanced up dubiously to find his eyes twinkling with unexpected merriment.

"No, milord, not again," Luc cried in mock despair and Sophie looked between them in confusion. An old joke this evidently was, but she knew not the way of it.

"Aye, singing is what is needed to make the path shorter," Hugues bellowed gleefully. Sophie could not help but laugh when he commenced to do exactly that.

She laughed not long, though, for Hugues had a commandingly deep baritone voice and carried a tune rather better than he walked at this particular moment. His singing filled the streets to bursting and although more than one pair of shutters slammed shut, Sophie found herself entranced by the ballad he sang.

Of Tristan and Iseult it told and 'twas a chanson she had not heard before, a tale of star-crossed lovers seemingly doomed to be apart. Verse after verse un-furled from his lips and Sophie marveled that Hugues knew so many of the words, even as she was amazed at the beauty of his voice. So engrossed was she in the tale unfolding that they stood before the coppersmith's house before she knew it, and when she started in surprise, Hugues ended his verse and gave her a merry wink.

"Did I not speak aright?" he breathed with mischief dancing in his eyes. Sophie coughed unwillingly at the waft of ale breath he exhaled.

"Aye," she conceded with a laugh and a wrinkle of her nose, giving him a playful shove toward the door. Hugues lolled unsteadily against the door frame as though he had intended to lean there all along, and fixed his companions with a merry eye.

"Very quiet we must be," he warned in a whisper loud enough to wake the dead, and Sophie giggled despite herself.

"Hugues, you have been singing the entire way home. Think you that no one knows you here?" she protested, but he waved aside her objections with a casual air.

"'Twas but a lullaby for all these work-weary townsfolk," he said with a grin, wagging one finger unsteadily in her direction. "One day, woman, I shall sing for you in truth." Sophie's heart leaped at his words, but she quelled her optimism sternly, for he could not mean whatever he said in this state.

"Cross yourself quickly, milady, for 'tis a curse," Luc piped up in jest. Hugues laughed as he stretched out one arm and hauled the boy close for an affectionate tussle that left Luc's hair standing comically on end.

"We had best get you upstairs while yet you can help," Sophie interjected with a smile and Hugues' brows arched high.

"Luc," he said with apparent astonishment, "the lady thinks me in a state. Have ever you heard the like of such injustice?"

"Milord, do not do it," Luc warned ominously, but Hugues was inside the door with an agility that belied his drunkenness.

"She thinks I cannot take the stairs, boy," he informed Luc airily, casting a troublemaking wink over his shoulder to Sophie. "Such an insult cannot be left to pass unchallenged."

"Milord!" Luc warned again, but Hugues lunged up the stairs at a run. Sophie gasped and ran after him, convinced he would lose his balance and fall, but he gained the landing with a victorious "Ha!" and spun triumphantly on his heel.

"God's blood," muttered Luc, and darted up the stairs in their wake.

"What say you now, Sophie?" Hugues demanded with a jubilant flourish.

His eyes glittered in the darkness above and Sophie was painfully aware of her own quick breathing after that jaunt. Before she could think of something clever for her retort, the victorious expression on Hugues' face gave way to dismay and Luc shoved her summarily out of the way.

"My pardon, milady, but 'tis always thus." The boy excused his rudeness even as Hugues groaned from the very depths of his soul.

Sophie watched in silent amazement as Luc propelled his master unhesitatingly across the room. Hugues dropped heavily to his pallet. His eyes glazed over as Luc hurriedly fetched the cinder bucket in anticipation, and the knight made ample use of it while the boy pulled off his lord's boots.

Once he had been ill, Hugues rolled to his back with one arm over his eyes, his snores filling the room but moments later. Luc looked up to Sophie with an apologetic grin and shrugged.

"Seldom enough does he drink that I mind it not," he said, and Sophie smiled at the boy.

"Well indeed do you tend him," she commented, and even in the shadows she could see Luc's color rise at her praise.

"'Tis only when something is amiss," he explained, casting a look to his unconscious hero and dropping his voice. "I fear this message of the Queen Regent's has not been well received."

"Aye, it must be that," Sophie agreed with a heavy heart. She closed the door and strolled back to the center of the room. Luc's words had dismissed any faint hope that Hugues was disturbed about her.

"I fear to strike a flint with such a smell of ale," Luc said with a frown. Sophie laughed aloud before she realized that he was completely serious.

"Aye," she agreed more soberly. "Enough light there is from the snow to serve us."

"Aye. Sleep well, milady."

Chapter Seven

The dream came back that night when Sophie finally did fall asleep, and she struggled against it when she saw that familiar coastline rise in her mind's eye. Not tonight, she pleaded, even as her footsteps led to that ominous clearing and she shivered at the chill of the stones as she drew abreast of them.

She closed her eyes stubbornly against the sight that would greet her within the circle. Whatever force governed her dreams would have none of her avoidance and eventually she was compelled to look. Her gaze lit first on the fire burned down to embers, as it always did, and she felt the hairs prick on the back of her neck when she dared to look to the cloaked figure.

Would it be Hugues or the woman who greeted her this night? Sophie almost could not bear to see and she cringed as her gaze lifted unerringly to the spot, only to find it vacant. She gasped aloud and spun around, searching the clearing to no avail.

Sophie stood alone before the dying fire.

She darted outside the circle of stones, but the wild coastline was abandoned and there was no one within sight, just the surf pounding relentlessly on the rocks below. The moon shone through fitful clouds overhead, the fog hugged the shoreline and the great stones cast their chill over all.

Alone.

A terror a thousand times more terrifying than confronting the mysterious stranger washed over her and Sophie barely stifled a scream as she sat bolt upright in bed.

The snow still fell gently outside the window, its light illuminating the wool-clad curl on the hearth that was Luc. The knight still snored quietly on the floor beside her. The scene exuded a peaceful intimacy and Sophie choked back her tears unsteadily. She pulled the covers up to her chin, forcing herself to lie back and stare at the beamed ceiling as she struggled to steady her breathing and make some sense of her dream.

If Sophie had seemed offhand the previous day, by the time Hugues reluctantly pried his eyes open the next morning she was positively skittish in his presence. In fact, 'twas so out of character to see her nervous that it took his fogged mind a moment to accurately assess her mood. When she silently broke bread at the table and passed him a portion without even glancing up, her hand immediately retreating to her lap, the evidence was inescapable and Hugues could only imagine that he was somehow at fault.

After all, his memory of the previous evening was shaky at best.

One way he knew to cheer his sisters was the spending of coin and he conceded that 'twould be worth a bit of silver to see Sophie smile again. His suggestion that they go to the market was greeted with a quick, mute nod, quite unlike the feminine enthusiasm he had anticipated, and Hugues looked to Luc in confusion. The boy shrugged and Hugues leaned across to speak to him while Sophie fetched her cloak.

"I pray I did not give offense last night," he murmured, and to his immense relief the boy immediately shook his head.

"Nay, milord," he confirmed pertly. "But you did sing."

Aye, that would have been typical. Hugues cast a glance after Sophie, found her still occupied with her cloak, and frowned anew. Often had he been told that his voice was fine and he could not imagine that that should have offended her. A thought occurred to him and he turned back to Luc.

"What did I sing?" he asked, worried suddenly that it had been that lewd tavern verse he had recently learned that had sprung from his lips.

"Tristan and Iseult," Luc whispered as Sophie turned expectantly toward them.

Hugues shook his head in growing puzzlement. Perhaps the tale of two lovers left dead by a tragic combination of errors had not been the most romantic choice, but there were worse ones, to be sure. He rose slowly to his feet, painfully aware of both the aching in his temples and Sophie's refusal to look him in the eye. 'Twas time enough he learned what troubled her.

"Well it seems to me that you have need of some gloves," he commented gruffly, using the words as an excuse to take her hand. To his surprise her fingers trembled within his and Hugues looked to her face to discern the source of her distress.

"As you wish," was all she said with remarkable demureness. Then she tried to pull her fingers away. Hugues tightened his grip slightly on her hand and she turned to him, pinning him with an imploring glance of those pale eyes.

"What is it?" he whispered, but Sophie only shook her head mutely. He watched helplessly as her tears rose and he noted now the purple shadows beneath her eyes, though he could not fathom a reason for either sadness or sleeplessness on her part.

"I would not speak of it," she murmured brokenly and pulled her fingers abruptly from his. She would have turned away, but Hugues gripped her arm and would not let her slip away so easily.

"Surely it cannot be so bad as that," he soothed, not knowing what else to say. A single tear caught the light as it spilled over her cheek and Hugues turned her toward him, gently grasping her other arm as her tears began to fall in quick succession. Still she refused to look up at him and he urged her closer for lack of a better option, closing his own eyes when she huddled against his chest and cried like a child.

What was he to do? How could he heal her hurt if she would not confide its cause?

It seemed to Sophie that she would never smile again and she was more than certain that Hugues also was becoming convinced of that fact. Repeatedly he tried to entice her with some trinket or other, but she refused all. No need had he to be spending good coin on her that she would not likely be able to repay.

Especially if they were not destined to be together after all.

Naught else could her dream have meant, and difficult as the truth was to face, Sophie was struggling to come to terms with it. How could she tell him now that she had erred? Surely he would think her a madwoman if she changed her mind after having surrendered her virginity.

And the worst of it was that her growing feelings were not so easily dismissed as her dream might have liked to dictate. Sadly, she was growing to like Hugues and the more set he became on bolstering her sagging spirits, the more she appreciated his charm. And she could not deny the way her blood rose each time his eyes met hers or he touched her hand. She still wanted Hugues, more even than she had originally, were such a feat possible.

The wintry sun barely warmed her face and she shivered in the marketplace, rubbing her hands together absently while she fretted over her tangled emotions. Hugues was immediately before her, but she could not summon the strength to deny him a small smile of greeting.

"No case can you make for being without gloves," he argued, his eyes twinkling irresistibly as he cupped her shoulders and smiled down at her. Sophie opened her mouth to protest but found he spoke aright.

"You name it truly," she conceded, and he grinned victoriously, fairly sweeping her off her feet as he guided her directly to a stall he must have already discovered. The most marvelous gloves were displayed therein, but when Sophie would have backed away from their certain expense she found Hugues blocking her retreat.

"Too expensive are they," she hissed, but his answering chuckle told her that he would not be easily swayed.

"Should you insist on letting me purchase only one gift, it shall be a worthwhile one," he countered firmly.

The broad warmth of his palm at the small of her back was Sophie's undoing, for she felt the shape of his hand as surely as if 'twere against her bare skin. She closed her eyes against the sweet pressure as her imagination supplied any lacking details.

Had Hugues any idea how she had missed his touch? When Sophie opened her eyes an instant later the gloves were right before her and the proprietor was regarding her avidly.

"A green pair have I in fine Cordovan leather to match the lady's cloak," he suggested, holding up the gloves trimmed in fur. Sophie shook her head quickly at the sight of the beautiful gloves, certain they cost more than one of Gaillard's shipments to the Norman court.

"Something simpler I would like," she demurred and the proprietor obligingly turned to the more reasonably priced selection of his goods.

"What of this pair?" Hugues indicated gloves the very shade of freshly churned butter. The proprietor's brows raised speculatively and Sophie's heart sank.

"Hugues, too expensive are they," she protested, losing herself when he pulled her closer as if they were lovers true. When he bent to whisper in her ear, she knew without doubt that he would have his way, for she could not think clearly enough to argue with him.

"But try them," he murmured against her hair and Sophie glanced up to find the proprietor smiling indulgently at them. Hugues' thumb made some persuasive move against her spine and she reached blindly for the gloves.

"Lined with squirrel," the man opposite intoned in a voice designed to close the sale as Sophie slid the luxurious softness over her fingers. She turned her left hand to show Hugues the fit and the proprietor nodded with pride. "My wife does the cutwork," he confided. "Well you can see that she has a fine eye for such things."

"Aye, she does indeed," Hugues agreed easily. Another move of that thumb sent Sophie's right hand into the yellow glove's mate.

"Fit as though they were made for the lady," added the proprietor when Sophie said naught.

"Aye," Hugues confirmed. The way he bent over her made Sophie's pulse ring so loud that she could think of naught but kissing him. "Do you like them?" he murmured, his face so close that their noses almost touched. Sophie looked to his lips before she could stop herself and dropped her gaze.

"They are beautiful," she confirmed breathlessly, caring naught about the gloves, but Hugues grinned happily and haggled briefly over the price.

The men concluded their negotiation, exchanging pleasantries in the wake of the deal, and Sophie turned away, trying to tell herself that 'twas the warmth of the fur lining that caused that cold trickle of sweat on her palms.

Hugues caught up to her, offering his elbow with a jubilant smile now that he had accomplished his objective. Sophie shook her head as she slipped her fingers into the crook of his arm, realizing that she felt better just to see him so pleased.

How was she ever going to turn away from this man?

The dream stalked Sophie again in the dark of that night and though she had been expecting it, she tried desperately to escape its grip. When her footsteps drew her unwillingly near the great stones, she struggled futilely against the confining cocoon of sleep. She shivered helplessly at the cold emanating from the stones, hearing herself moan when the embers of the fire were revealed. But a moment longer and she would be forced to confront either the cloaked figure or the vacancy where it should be and she fought anew.

"Sophie!" The urgent whisper drew her back to earth and her eyes flew open.

The dark beams of the ceiling became clear despite the shadows and she gasped in relief, reaching for the silhouette that was Hugues before she even thought. Her tears broke and the flood of relief that rushed through her made her oblivious to the way he gathered her close or the words he murmured into her hair.

She had escaped the dream. 'Twas all she knew, and she was safe from the terror of its vision. Hugues rocked her gently against his chest and she gradually felt her racing heart slow, the steady pulse of another heart beneath her ear awakening something entirely different within her.

"Better?" Hugues inquired softly, pulling away far too soon for Sophie's taste but she nodded. She felt his regard upon her but did not look up, even when his fingertip traced the curve of her cheek and brushed her hair out of the way.

"Often do you have nightmares?" he asked quietly. Sophie nodded again and wiped ineffectively at the remnants of her tears.

"Aye," she agreed flatly, and Hugues' thumb made short work of the tears on her cheeks.

"Would you speak of it yet?" His words revealed that he understood she had had one the night before, as well. Sophie risked an upward glance, and something melted within her at the compassion in his eyes.

"I cannot," she admitted and he nodded once, his gaze dropping to her lips seemingly by accident.

Hugues' thumb followed his gaze, his nostrils flaring as the pad of his thumb slid across Sophie's bottom lip. She parted her lips at his touch and his gaze flicked back to hers once more, though this time the passion flared there again. Sophie leaned toward Hugues and he stumbled quickly to his feet.

"My pallet," he said hastily with a gesture to the offending object and Sophie fancied he swallowed with difficulty before continuing.

"Should you be fine, I would leave you sleep," he added gallantly. Sophie sighed shakily as she regarded the vast expanse of empty mattress beside her.

She had done it again. And the last thing she wanted at this moment was to be alone. She turned back to find Hugues watching her avidly and decided to risk the asking.

"Could you but hold me for a while?" she demanded softly and their gazes locked for a long moment across the shadows of the room. When she sensed he might refuse, she could not keep herself from begging even as she cursed her own weakness.

"Please, Hugues," she added quietly and he took a ragged breath before nodding and returning hesitantly to her side.

Hugues was uncharacteristically clumsy about climbing into the bed, though Sophie was simply so relieved that she minded neither that nor his fidgeting with the coverlet. She settled into the curve of his shoulder. The way he stiffened told her that he had not expected the move, but Sophie ignored him and within a few heartbeats his arms closed securely around her. She sighed with satisfaction, inhaling deeply of his scent in the process, and felt truly safe once more as she drifted off to sleep.

Hugues for his part counted the four beams on the ceiling over and over again, first from one side, then the other, desperately trying to come to terms with holding Sophie so close for naught but sleep.

Had he ever ached with such longing for another woman? Hugues could not recall and supposed that was a blessing, for if he had, 'twas an ordeal best forgotten. When he had seen that look in her eyes again, he had wanted with every fiber of his being to kiss her. But well enough did Hugues know that his desire was at such pitch that he would not be able to stop there. And what manner of man would take advantage of a woman so distraught from a nightmare?

In truth, to be held was all she had wanted and likely another would have served that purpose as well as he. Hugues frowned and glanced down at the golden beauty nestled contentedly against his side, resisting the urge to shake her until she remembered that she wanted *him*, that they were destined for each other. He sighed in frustration and Sophie murmured a sleepy protest at his movement, even while Hugues forced himself to think of more prosaic matters.

A nightmare. What could haunt a soft woman with steel in her spine? Naught had she backed away from since he had met her, save perhaps himself, Hugues reflected wryly. Indeed, her departure from Bordeaux and survival on the coast spoke of an audacity rare in the fair sex, though a quick downward glance confirmed that she carried her share of that fairness, as well. Hugues gathered Sophie tighter to his side.

If he could fight only her nightmares for now, he would willingly do so, and one day, destiny or no, he would win more than that.

* * *

When the sun lit the thick windowpanes Sophie awoke and stretched contentedly, freezing for an instant when her toe encountered a decidedly hairy and muscled calf. The night's events flooded into her mind again and she turned to find Hugues regarding her indulgently.

"Sleep better?" he demanded in a low growl that awakened everything within her at once, and Sophie nodded quickly.

"Aye," she conceded nervously. "Thank you."

"'Twas naught." Hugues stretched luxuriously, himself, the resultant slipping of the linens revealing that his broad chest was bare. Sophie felt her cheeks redden and she tried not to look at the tangle of tawny hairs, more than cognizant of the fact that her fingers had been entwined there at some point during the night.

"A fine morning it looks to be," Hugues said heartily as he swung his legs over the side of the bed. Sophie followed the gesture without thinking, the sight of their muscled length making it suddenly difficult to breathe.

Had Hugues slept with her nude? In truth, she had no idea, and the very thought was more than disturbing. He spared her a wink as though he enjoyed her discomfort and Sophie could have swatted him for showing none himself.

"'Tis by far the best night's sleep I have had since we came here," Hugues commented further when Sophie remained stubbornly silent, absently running one hand over the stubble on his chin. He shot her a piercing glance that fairly stopped her heart with its intensity before he continued. "We will share the bed from this point on," he affirmed flatly and Sophie gasped aloud.

"But Hugues, 'tis improper," she began, not knowing how she would keep from touching him if he were so close at hand.

Should they not be intended for each other, she had no business being intimate with him and there was no way she would have temptation so readily available. Hugues leaned over her, bracing his hands on either side of her hips to make his argument.

"Did your nightmare return?" he asked softly and Sophie could only shake her head. Curse him for being so close and making it impossible for her to even think. And well he knew that she had not had the nightmare again.

"Nay," she conceded, and he shrugged his shoulders good-naturedly.

"Then only logical it seems that we both enjoy a solid sleep," he concluded matter-of-factly, rolling out of bed before Sophie could protest.

"But—" She began to argue once he had put some distance between them, but Hugues merely shook his finger in her direction.

"The matter is settled," he said firmly as he prodded Luc's shoulder.

And perhaps 'twas not so bad an idea, Sophie consoled herself, knowing there was precious little chance of changing Hugues' mind. And she would welcome a few nights' sleep without the threat of the dream reappearing. She rolled out of bed in turn and pulled up the linens with an unexpected lightness of heart, blissfully unaware of the way Hugues watched her legs when she had her back to him.

'Twas that morning that the Normans occupied La Rochelle.

The increase in knights on the streets was the first indication and Hugues noticed it immediately as the market opened. An idea he had had to fetch some bread so that he would not be tormented further by the shadowy silhouette of Sophie's legs beneath her chemise, but both his task and his torment were forgotten by the change in atmosphere.

Hugues hurried back to their rooms without appearing to do so as soon as he spied the Norman nose guard on more than one knight's helmet. The insignia that he noted en route confirmed his suspicions. Hugues had to get out of sight before he was identified, and he took the stairs three at a time back to the room, then dropped to sit before the window to watch events unfurl.

"Have you the bread?" Sophie inquired in confusion and he shook his head impatiently.

"Nay," he said curtly. "Best send the boy."

The Normans had quietly infiltrated the town and Hugues did not take that as a good sign. As far as he could determine, business was continuing as normal in the streets below, the arrival of the foreign knights accepted as though 'twere usual.

It could only be that the townsfolk supported the Norman crown. Hugues could determine no other reason they would be so amenable to such an infiltration. Strictly speaking, La Rochelle was held by the French crown, but his lukewarm reception at those meetings and this occupation seemed to indicate that 'twas another crown that held the hearts and minds of the townspeople.

Which left Hugues, sole emissary of the French crown, as an unwelcome visitor in a rather awkward position at the very least. It seemed Hugues had erred

in lingering yet longer in La Rochelle while he sought
some way to ensure that Sophia accompanied him.

Now what to do? A sense of vulnerability washed
over him as he watched the foreign knights stroll down
the street below, and he wished pointlessly for his hauberk, undoubtedly rusted somewhere in the depths of
the sea. Granted he still had his blade, his wits and a
reasonably adequate steed, but he was alone and well he
knew it.

Not quite alone. Hugues cast a sidelong glance to Luc
and Sophie as she bade the boy not be fooled into buy-
ing yesterday's leavings. What was he thinking? The
boy might be asked the identity of his lord.

"Tell no one of your identity," Hugues counseled
Luc, and the boy hesitated on the threshold. He felt
Sophie's regard on him and sensed her confusion but
did not look to her, not having fully formed his plan in
his mind and knowing she would expect an explanation. But a moment more he needed to think this
through.

"What is amiss, milord?" Luc asked in a voice that
revealed his youth all too well.

"The Normans have landed," Hugues confirmed
tersely, disliking the way Sophie's brows drew together.
"If you must fetch bread, make haste." Luc ducked his
head in a curt nod and disappeared down the stairs.

Had Sophie any idea what difficulties they were in?
Could she not see that the longer they stayed here, the
more likely he was to be challenged by the Normans?
Well he should have headed for Paris two days past,
when Sophie's sewing was completed. He cursed his all-
too-ready trust. Indeed, their landlady might have betrayed his presence already, and Hugues looked over his

shoulder as if expecting to find her on the threshold with a bevy of Norman knights.

His presence. That was the key. Hugues nearly kicked himself for being so dim-witted. Sophie had naught to fear, for she was Gasconne and her accent would readily tell the tale. Luc was too young to be much of a threat to anyone and Hugues came to the painful realization that 'twas his presence alone that endangered the others. He watched Luc step quickly along the street below and confronted a troubling thought.

Should he leave them?

The idea was more disturbing than it should have been and Hugues carefully sought the reason. The boy he had pledged to protect, and well it could be that the very thought of breaking this vow unsettled him. Sophie he had willingly claimed twice; however, he knew as well as she did that these had been matters of expediency, no more, no less. She drew alongside him to look out the small window and he dared to glance in her direction.

The way her new kirtle hugged her slenderness disconcerted him as it had over and over again since he had first seen her wear the garment, its color and fit combining with Sophie's strength to remind him of the Pontesse willows. 'Twas almost as if she had read his mind and chosen the garment to heighten his image of her, but Hugues knew that that could not be.

He should leave her and he knew it, but the very idea bothered him more than was logical. Indeed, her security was threatened by his presence, if he were to acknowledge the truth of it. Hugues frowned at the floor and tapped his toe impatiently. He sat back on his stool discontentedly, wishing the sun would hurry and complete its course, that 'twould be evident whether the knights were staying or passing through.

He would leave her here, Hugues resolved, ignoring the lurch in his chest. Indeed, he had bought her clothes and she could have the horse he had already acquired for her. He would leave her silver, pay the landlady and he and Luc would leave this very day.

Telling himself he was satisfied with his decision, Hugues shoved to his feet and commenced to pace the room.

Sophie knew there was something in the wind, but Hugues frowned so forbiddingly throughout the day that she had not the nerve to ask. He paced the length of the room and back so many times that she thought she would scream in an echo of his own evident frustration. What on earth was the matter?

Could it be that he was missing her touch as much as she missed his? Sophie watched him covertly through her lashes, her gaze drawn to his right hand clenching and unclenching as he walked. She imagined those fingers closing around the back of her neck, around her breast, or around her buttocks, and her blood rose. Indeed, she had thought him close to touching her so many times these past days, but he had turned away time and again, and she could scarce believe that that was what drove his pacing now.

She started when he finally spoke to her as the shadows began to lengthen.

"Sophie, mayhap you could go to the market," he suggested gruffly and Sophie had a fleeting sense that he was concerned with larger matters than a morsel to eat. He flicked an apologetic glance to her and Sophie relaxed her suspicions. 'Twas a reasonable enough request, as the bread was long gone, though she could not understand why he had insisted on sending her rather than Luc.

"Aye, Hugues, I am hungry, as well," she agreed, pulling her cloak over her shoulders. No need was there to make a fuss about such a small thing, for 'twould be accomplished before the matter could be settled by argument. And well enough would she welcome a draught of fresh air. "Have you a preference?"

"Nay." Hugues shook his head quickly, so quickly that Sophie again had a feeling that he was not telling her something important. She regarded him for a long moment but he simply held her gaze with an innocence that might have aroused her suspicions more had she not seen how poorly he lied before.

"Have you any silver?" he asked softly. Sophie flushed, realizing he must think her very bold for staring him down thus instead of simply asking for some coins.

"I have not," she admitted in a quiet voice. Hugues poured a dozen pieces into his palm and silently handed them to her while she watched in shock.

"Hugues!" she protested. "'Tis too much!" Would he have her buy everything she saw for sale?

"You should not be without a few coins in your purse," he said with a noncommittal shrug. "Well have I intended to give you some and now is as good a time as any."

Something *was* amiss.

"What need have I of coin when you are always at hand?" Sophie demanded skeptically. The color that flooded Hugues' neck confirmed all of her suspicions.

"Sophie, make this not harder than it is," he urged softly as he closed the space between them. He tipped her chin up with one fingertip and Sophie closed her eyes beneath his touch, his gentle appeal dissolving her concerns.

"I would have you with a few coins of your own," he murmured. When she felt his breath on her cheek, Sophie wished fervently that he would kiss her.

When no kiss came she opened her eyes. The tenderness in his expression made her wonder what had dissuaded him. Had his desire for her truly expired?

"But, Hugues, 'tis so much," she protested one last time, but he pressed her fingers closed over the coins and Sophie savored the weight of his hand upon hers.

"I want you to have it," he said with quiet resolve and Sophie could only nod when he bent his will upon her thus. If he felt the need to be so free with his coin, she could scarce refuse. 'Twould be easy enough to repay, for she had no intention of spending it.

"If 'tis what you want, Hugues," she agreed and for some reason he seemed to find that amusing. Sophie glanced up at the sound he made beneath his breath and caught him smothering a smile. His eyes glowed with more than humor, though she had not the chance to name that warmth.

"Aye, 'tis what I want," he whispered, his hand sliding beneath her chin as his lips closed over hers.

Sophie closed her eyes in mingled pleasure and disbelief when Hugues' tongue slid between her teeth, and she gripped his shoulders as the room spun around her. Her hands found their way into his hair, the abandoned coins scattering around her feet, and his grip closed around her waist, urging her to her toes.

How had she survived these days without his touch? How could she have questioned his desire? Sophie felt that they were back in balance once again and delighted in the roughness of Hugues' whiskers as he nuzzled her neck.

She smiled at him when he pulled away with evident reluctance and he smiled down at her as though they shared some private joke. His expression changed suddenly, as if he had just recalled something, and Sophie frowned at the abrupt transition before his words made his thoughts clear.

"Go," he urged. "The boy should eat soon."

Luc. Sophie flicked an alarmed glance to the boy seated before the window, studiously pretending not to have noticed anything going on in the room, and flushed scarlet. What had they been thinking of?

Naught but each other.

"Perhaps you should enjoy more than the bed this night," she whispered mischievously and the heat flared in Hugues' eyes anew. Sophie watched the conflicting emotions play across his face for a moment before he turned aside.

"Go," he muttered and Sophie smiled as she did his bidding. She crouched and gathered up the scattered coins, hastily shoving them into her pocket.

True enough, Hugues would be breaking his vow to their landlady by joining her in bed, but she would not tell of it and she would ensure that they did not waken the boy. By the time she returned from the market she was certain Hugues would have conquered that obstacle in his mind. She waved jauntily to him from the doorway, momentarily surprised to find him curiously withdrawn.

"Au revoir," she said pertly and she fancied that Hugues' lips thinned before he answered.

"Aye," he said so quietly that she barely caught the words. "Au revoir, Sophie."

There was a sadness in his tone that seemed unwarranted, but before Sophie could question it he turned to Luc, asking the boy to point out the differences in armor between Normans and Franks. Sophie frowned to herself, uncertain whether she was missing something. Then she shook her head dismissively and hastened down the stairs to the market.

"Bloody Thouars and his Franks," muttered a knight behind Sophie in the market in his coarse foreign accent. "Run the lot of them through, we will."

Sophie suppressed a grimace of distaste as she carefully pocketed her change and gathered up the meat pies she had bought.

The Norman knights she had encountered thus far were an uncouth group, as far as she could discern, their loud boasting and jostling of the few women in the market convincing her that Hugues was on the right side of things. No need had they of such men in Gascogne, she reasoned. 'Twas bad enough to have them as near as here in Bretagne.

Another knight in a ridiculous Norman helmet commented about taking on the ineffective French knights and Sophie raised her chin a proud notch, knowing that *her* French knight was far from ineffective. Well could she imagine that Hugues would make minced meat of one of these men and she nearly turned to tell the sorry creature that, before the fullness of the truth hit her between the eyes.

Hugues was a *French* knight.

La Rochelle was now occupied by Normans.

Sophie spun on her heel and ran from the market, even as she cursed Hugues' sorry hide under her breath. She would kill him if he had dared to believe he could leave without her. She gathered up the fullness of her troublesome skirts irritably as she darted down the narrow streets.

No consolation was it that everything made perfect sense now, that her sense that something of greater import was transpiring had not been wide of the mark. If he had made it out of town without her, she would hunt him down, if only to give him a piece of her mind. How dare he abandon her here? 'Twas *she* who was deciding whether or not they were truly destined for each other and she would not have him forcing her hand.

If in truth she had to give up Hugues, Sophie would do so when she was good and ready to do so, not a moment before. It occurred to her that this might be the fates' own way of dealing with the change of plans and she hastened her footsteps, determined to intervene in something that would so affect her life.

The fates could *not* change their mind at this late date, she concluded fiercely, a growing determination to fight their interference dawning in her chest.

Would she defy the fates for Hugues? The very thought fairly took her breath away, but Sophie inhaled deeply and plunged onward. Mayhap she would and she vowed that the fates themselves would rue the day, not she.

She rounded a corner and the coppersmith's house came into view. Sophie told herself that it meant naught that no candle burned in the dark second-floor window, but her heart pounded in trepidation as she took the stairs two at a time. The room was empty, as she had known it would be, and Sophie slammed the door back against the wall in frustration while angry tears blurred her vision.

Curse Hugues de Pontesse *and* the bloody fates.

"Paid the rent, he did," came the landlady's voice from the bottom of the stairs, and Sophie took a deep breath before she turned.

"He would," she muttered in perverse annoyance, propping her hands on her hips. Curse him and his ethics. Hugues probably thought he was doing her a favor or something equally ridiculous. She glanced down the stairs at the landlady who stood watching her speculatively.

"Not his ward, were you?" the older woman demanded shrewdly. Knowing 'twas moot to deceive the woman further, Sophie sighed in frustration.

"Evidently *he* thought that to be the extent of it," she replied, watching that tiny hammer catch the light as the woman tapped it thoughtfully against her palm.

"I was to tell you on the morrow that he had left you a steed," she mused, casting another sharp glance to Sophie. "But perhaps 'tis best to tell you now."

If Hughes had left her a steed, then he had bought one, as well, Sophie thought excitedly, certain that the two beasts would be stabled together.

"Where is it stabled?" she demanded breathlessly, and the older woman smiled at her excitement.

"At Hubert Ridell's." She turned and gestured out the door and to the left. "Two houses down, around the back." Sophie leaped back down the stairs, hoping against hope that she was not too late.

"You've not missed him by much," the woman commented when Sophie reached the bottom of the stairs, and Sophie impulsively kissed the woman's leathery cheek.

"Go," she urged quietly. "And may Lady Luck ride alongside you."

Chapter Eight

Luc was stalling and Hugues knew it.

The boy had dragged his feet leaving the chambers, forgetting his saddle blanket deliberately, Hugues was certain, so that they would have to return to fetch it. Now he dawdled with the saddles and Hugues had no doubt what he was about. Luc was fond of Sophie and did not want to leave her behind, though he would not dare to voice his objection.

Hugues frowned and finished saddling his own steed with ready expertise, shooting the boy a dark look as he made quick work of even the palfrey's harnessing. Luc glared balefully back at Hugues, but the knight had no time for such theatrics. They were off later than he had hoped and could well have far to ride this night to outrun the reach of the Normans.

"Should you ride at the pace you work, you will likely find yourself alone on the road," he warned his mutinous squire. Defiance flashed in Luc's eyes but he nodded obediently. Hugues sighed, softening slightly toward the boy. No fault was it of his that he was young and that Sophie had caught his heart.

"Oftentimes the hardest road is the best one," he added more quietly. Luc regarded him for a long moment before the disbelief faded from his eyes.

"Aye, milord," he agreed halfheartedly. At his concession, Hugues swung up into his saddle. He knew there was no way to convince the boy that he had done aright.

Indeed, he was hardly convinced of that himself.

Hugues had a heavy heart and set his lips determinedly as he urged his steed forward. Sophie would be fine, she was a survivor, she was Gasconne. Indeed, she would be better off without him, and in time his conscience would leave him be over the matter of abandoning her here.

"Chevalier Hugues de Pontesse!" rang out an imperious feminine voice from the back of the stables. Hugues twisted in his saddle, surprised to find the lady herself descending upon him in a storm of fury.

His heart leaped when she snatched his stallion's reins without fear, but he immediately quelled its wayward response, reminding himself that Sophie would be endangered only if she was with him. The horse sidestepped nervously, but Sophie held her ground stubbornly and Hugues roundly cursed the beast's inexperience under his breath.

"Already I bade you farewell," he managed to say with a calmness that belied the emotion churning in his gut. Sophie glared up at him and Hugues knew in that moment that he would not get out of the stables without a fight.

"Think you that 'tis as easy as that?" she demanded, positively spitting sparks as she confronted him.

"'Tis you alone who would complicate matters," Hugues lied. He was certain she would see right through him, and half wished that she would, but Sophie turned abruptly aside as though she could no longer bear to look upon him. There, he consoled himself at the pang of guilt that shot through him. 'Twas true enough that she had no regard for him.

"Is your vow so worthless as that, then?" she asked softly and Hugues inhaled sharply at the confirmation of her sole interest. She wanted his protection, no more, and well he knew that she was safer without it. The accusation that his word was of no value stung, though, and Hugues found his tone much more caustic than he had intended.

"'Twas a mere matter of convenience and well we both knew it," he answered. Had the light been better, he might have thought that Sophie blanched at his words.

"More I thought there was betwixt us than mere convenience," she snapped, and the truth in what she said made Hugues feel the knave.

Aye, he acknowledged to himself, much more than that there was, and 'twas for that alone that he would give her more of a chance. In truth, he owed her an explanation and 'twas not his plan, but merely his execution of it without counseling her, that was at issue.

"Well enough should you know that I would not endanger you," he began to explain in a low tone, but Sophie would have none of it. Her eyes flashed in the dim light of the stables and Hugues realized that she was too furious with him to listen to reason.

"Spare me your sweet words," she hissed. "You ply them at will to win your way with me." Her words sparked Hugues' anger anew, for he had had naught of his way with her, as far as he could see.

"Me?" he demanded sharply. "'Tis not I who have had my way, milady, of that I assure you, for when you cannot control the scene, you want naught of it."

"What nonsense is this you speak?"

"Think you that I have not seen how you turn away in revulsion from my touch?" Hugues whispered, leaning down from his saddle to close the space between them. Vaguely he noted that Sophie looked perplexed, but his frustration had already seized the reins and he could not check it now.

"But I—" Sophie attempted, but Hugues summarily interrupted her.

"Spare me *your* sweet words," he growled. "And spare me also your mad tales of destiny, your sultry looks and the tempting sway of your buttocks. Well you know that I would have had you a hundred times these past days had you not turned me aside with your maidenly distaste. Different I thought you, Sophie, woman enough to admit what you wanted, but in truth you are as like any other *lady* I have known, promising what you cannot or *will not* deliver."

He drew himself up and took a deep breath, briefly amazed that Sophie seemed struck dumb, before he continued harshly. "'Tis but a measure of my perversely enduring regard for you that I leave you now. Though ration is clearly not one of your strong suits, should you trouble yourself to reflect upon it, you would see that your survival is better assured *without* my protection in this Norman-infested town."

With that, Hugues hauled his helmet over his face and touched his spur to his mount's side. The stallion's resultant movement pulled the leather bridle effortlessly from Sophie's fingertips. Still consumed with his anger, he gestured imperiously to Luc, who meekly trotted his own horse out into the fading light, apparently unwilling to tempt his master's wrath yet further.

And well-advised he was to do so, Hugues thought sourly, pausing in the portal to glance back to an uncharacteristically silent Sophie one last bittersweet time before riding away.

"Again I bid you adieu, milady," he growled, despising the way his vision blurred. Unaccountably annoyed with himself, he spurred his steed hard and made for the gates.

Sophie collapsed weak-kneed against one of the stalls, struggling to come to terms with what Hugues had just revealed.

A measure of his regard for her. She bit her lip and clutched those words to her heart, barely able to accept that he had *any* regard for her, let alone enough that he would want to ensure her survival. To think that he had thought *she* was not interested and did not wish to force himself upon her, 'twould almost have been funny had it not been so tragic.

In fact, he *still* thought as much, and she roused herself to look around the stables. Only one other palfrey was stabled there and she stared at the beast for a long moment, knowing that 'twas undoubtedly the steed Hugues had bought for her.

She could follow him.

Sophie folded her arms across her chest indecisively and frowned at the hay-strewn floor. And tell him what? That he was wrong? That she had only wished to refrain from frightening him anew that she might win his heart?

That she feared they were no longer destined for each other?

Sophie gasped aloud as the truth became painfully clear. Hugues was in danger. He had already admitted as much to her. Could it be that they were no longer destined for each other because he was doomed to perish in his attempt to evade the Normans?

It made perfect sense now that she thought it through, for they would have been gone from La Rochelle long before this invasion had the sea voyage gone as planned. The shipwreck could well explain the change in their path and the resulting changes in their destinies. It was all painfully clear now that she had found the key. Sophie was in the wide stall harnessing the palfrey before she knew what she intended to do.

She could not let Hugues ride unknowingly to his death. Precious little there was that she could do, but she *could* warn him.

And perhaps, she hoped desperately, *that* would change the course of their destinies yet again.

"His horse he keeps here," came a gruff Breton voice as she hastily harnessed the palfrey, and Sophie glanced behind her in alarm.

Three men stood silhouetted against the winter sunlight in the street beyond. Seeing that two wore mail, she stepped behind the chestnut mare, hoping against hope that she would not be seen.

"No destrier is there here," argued one of the other men and Sophie's heart sank in recognition of his Norman accent. Looking for Hugues they were and she knew for certain that 'twas not for any good end.

"'Twas here when I swept the stables," the first replied. Their footsteps echoed on the stone floor as they advanced into the stable. Sophie held her breath, certain they would be able to hear the pounding of her heart should they come any closer. "He cannot be long gone, but only one of his palfreys has he taken."

"This other beast is his?" the Norman demanded. Sophie crouched still farther behind her horse, praying 'twas dark enough that they would not see her feet. One of the men drummed his fingers impatiently on the side of the stall, the proximity of the sound fairly making her jump.

"Aye, a destrier and two palfreys he had," the local man confirmed with a wry laugh. "Perhaps this one he left as a gift to me."

"He had paid his debt?"

"Aye, in silver and in advance," the local man confirmed, evidently proud of his keen business sense.

"Then the horse is tribute to our lord king," the Norman concluded. Sophie's heart stopped completely even as the local man gasped aloud. Were they going to try to take her horse? Then what would she do? She could hardly walk in pursuit of Hugues. Sophie tightened her grip on the mare's bridle, determined to keep the beast.

"Fool Frenchman even left the beast harnessed," came another deeper Norman voice and the two knights chuckled together condescendingly.

"Have you need of a saddle, Gaston?"

"Mayhap my squire," agreed the second good-naturedly, and Sophie heard his footfall as he stepped into the stall.

'Twas now or never, Sophie resolved in that instant. This would be her last chance to have the element of surprise on her side. Grateful that she had managed to harness the horse before they had arrived, she hauled herself up into the saddle with a shout.

"What the—?" the Norman cried in shock as the mare bolted at Sophie's unexpected cry.

Barely had she time to note the shock on his face before he flattened himself against the wall of the stall and the chestnut palfrey brushed past him in her flight. The other Norman looked just as stunned when the horse burst out of the stall. Once free of confinement, the horse needed no urging to make for the street beyond.

"'Tis his whore!" cried the local man. In shock that he could mean her, Sophie looked back in time to see him shake a fist at her.

The Norman knight's face contracted in rage as he lunged in pursuit and Sophie kicked the horse's flanks in panic. The palfrey responded instantly, hurtling recklessly down the cobbled streets, dodging carts and peasants with wild agility, and 'twas all Sophie could do to hang on for the wild ride.

Mayhap she should not have kicked the horse, she realized, ducking as a dangling sign loomed before her and narrowly missing a blow that would surely have dismounted her. The mare showed no signs of slowing her pace, the confusion around her feeding her frenzy to escape, but any thoughts Sophie had of stopping her died in the next instant.

"Stop that thief!" the Norman knight shouted behind her, and Sophie gasped at the audacity of his lie. A man daringly reached for her bridle but the mare would have none of that and danced sideways into the market square. It seemed to Sophie that every eye was turned upon her but she leaned down over the horse's neck, talking softly to the beast and urging her to make haste.

"Close the gates!" cried another, launching panic through Sophie's veins. She gritted her teeth and eyed the distance to the portcullis, determined to outrun them even as the cry was taken up.

The mare seemed equally resolved and her pace increased as the call to close the gates swept through the market, passing ahead of them like wildfire. Sophie watched the sentry dart back inside the gatehouse and cursed him heartily. The ominous creak of the wheel that held the iron gate told her that his fingers had not fallen useless, her fervent wishes to the contrary.

The mare's nostrils flared as she surged forth and cleared the clutter of stalls. Naught but a stretch of cobblestones stood between them and the gate. The portcullis inched downward and Sophie whispered encouragement to the beast. The shadow of the wall fell over them, then that of the gatehouse itself, the loud cranking making Sophie hunker lower and squeeze her eyes shut as they passed beneath the falling iron gate as swiftly as the wind itself.

The last rays of sunlight warmed her shoulder and she sat up in amazement, then fell down into a crouch in the saddle when the gate hit the ground in the horse's wake with a force that set the very earth to quaking.

Sophie laughed even as the palfrey gained the road, a clatter of hooves and the echo of solid Norman cursing adding to her jubilation. The gatekeeper's voice rose in anger far behind her as he argued about raising the gate just after he had been commanded to lower it but the wind carried his words away. Sophie's heart leaped when she spied two figures on the road far ahead of her, just before the forest shadows closed over the path, and she watched the distance close between them in rising anticipation.

*   *   *

Hugues was somewhat less enchanted to see Sophie, particularly with a party of Norman knights on her heels.

"What in God's name are you about?" he roared when she drew within earshot. To his satisfaction, she looked utterly astonished by his greeting.

"I thought only to warn you that you were endangered," she responded with some measure of meekness. Hugues cocked a thumb to the knights approaching, guessing that she had no idea she had been followed, though that did little to temper his fury.

"Why did you not simply serve my head on a platter, should you so wish my demise?" he countered hotly. Sophie's confusion changed abruptly to horror when she saw the men in pursuit.

"N-no idea had I," she stammered, her mare stepping nervously as though it sensed her agitation, but Hugues swept aside her apologies.

"No time have we for talk," he interrupted. "Haste must we make into the forest if we hope to outride them."

"But, milord, 'tis the enchanted forest Brocéliande," Luc objected, earning himself a sharp glare from his master.

"No enchanted forests are there in this world, boy."

To Hugues' dismay Luc shot a suspicious glance over his shoulder and still delayed. "'Tis said they have hunting packs of werewolves at the court of Brocéliande," he cautioned. Hugues could not help but roll his eyes that this nonsense was keeping the boy from doing his bidding, especially since Sophie seemed to be weighing Luc's words.

"Well served you would be to learn the difference between myth and truth," he snapped irritably, slapping the rump of Sophie's mare when she hesitated alongside. "Hasten yourselves or we shall all be worm food by sunset."

"But—" Luc tried to object once more and Hugues spurred his horse impatiently.

"Naught is there in this woods that is not in any other forest," he said sharply, annoyed at the way the boy looked between the advancing knights and the forest as though assessing the comparative risk. Sophie's mount disappeared under the shadow cast by the trees and Hugues raised an imperious eyebrow as he regarded his squire.

"Now," he commanded flatly and Luc's lips thinned in displeasure but he kicked his palfrey's flanks obediently.

He would likely wring the necks of both of them himself before the sun set, Hugues thought with gritted teeth and cast a glance over his shoulder, not at all happy with how close the Norman knights were. His stallion closed the distance to the forest in quick strides, the coolness of the shadows falling over him making Hugues shiver with what could have been dread when he unaccountably recalled Luc's words.

'Twas the absence of the sun, he told himself firmly. No more than that.

Luc cast a suspicious eye into the forest on either side as they rode and to Hugues' dismay the hairs on the back of his own neck prickled. Naught was there to fear in this woods over any other, he reminded himself, old wives' tales to the contrary. And Brocéliande itself was but a tale told to gullible children around the hearth and not any place of this earth.

Sophie dropped back to ride closer to his side and he was unaccountably glad that they were riding in a fairly tight pack, even as he tried to dismiss the eerie sense that they were being watched. Thousands of creatures were there in the forest, Hugues reasoned, and 'twas only natural that such woodland creatures eyed invaders.

Aye, that was it.

A shout carried into the muted atmosphere of the forest and Hugues looked back to find shadows clustered in the sunlit opening to the road. The pursuing knights seemed to be arguing and he guessed there were those among them of like mind as Luc.

Lily-livered Normans, he concluded with disgust. His fingers moved of their own accord to touch the hilt of his sword as though 'twere a talisman.

"'Tis so quiet," Sophie whispered. It seemed to Hugues that her words carried farther than they ought to have, as though the trees passed them from one to the other, and he struggled to curb his overactive imagination.

"Perhaps 'tis best not to talk," he responded quietly before he could check the words, hating the smug look of satisfaction that Luc shot in his direction. He shivered with the sense that his own words were being carried along that same network to disappear deep into the shadows of endless trees.

Hopefully they would be able to clear the woods without having to stop and sleep, he thought. Then he recalled just how extensive the woods of Brocéliande were said to be. And the old tales did place the enchanted forest in this area, that much of the fable Hugues did recall.

Three days' ride if the witches chose to let you pass, as long as a lifetime if they did not. Hugues swallowed carefully and gripped his reins, reminding himself sternly that there *were* no witches in this world anymore, if in fact there ever had been any.

And this was no Brocéliande, merely the hunting reserve of some local lord. 'Twas as simple as that.

'Twas impossible to tell how much time had passed beneath the canopy of trees, for the shadows fell so thick that the passage of the sun could not be discerned. It had been cool when they had first ridden out of the late-afternoon sun and it stayed thus, making Sophie glad of her warm gloves and surcoat.

She was well aware of Hugues' nervousness beneath his stoic expression and it puzzled her, as did Luc's superstition. The forest felt welcoming to her, not forbidding, and 'twas all she could do to check her urge to wander off into the woods and explore its hidden mysteries. It seemed to Sophie that she had never seen so many shades of green or such variety of leaves and she longed to look fully upon the minuscule white flowers that she glimpsed clustered on the ground in the distance.

She hoped it took some days for them to reach the other side of the woods.

At length they were forced to stop to eat and give their horses some respite. The three beasts huddled together in the midst of the well-trodden path with much the same expression as Hugues and Luc. Sophie laughed at the lot of them, liking the way her laughter carried into the trees, but Luc cringed at the sound.

"Milady, you must not awaken the witches," he whispered and Sophie laughed anew at his fears.

"Luc, 'tis but a forest and a surprisingly peaceful one," she chided, watching Hugues nod vigorously.

"Aye," Hugues agreed firmly and she sensed he was trying to convince himself as much as the boy. "No witches are there, here or anywhere," he added, taking a solid bite of bread as if to enforce his point. Luc looked as if he might argue the issue but Hugues shot him one of those quelling looks and the boy sighed, nibbling at his own bread without interest as he scanned the forest around them.

"I fancy I hear water running," Sophie mused a moment later, tilting her head to listen carefully. "Aye, 'tis just off this side of the road." She grasped her palfrey's reins, fully intending to lead the beast to the stream.

"Milady, do not leave the path!" Luc cried, and Sophie froze midstep to regard him in astonishment.

"Surely you jest," she retorted but the boy shook his head wildly, his bread completely forgotten in his agitation.

"'Tis said that those who leave the path in Brocéliande never find their way again," he warned, darting covert glances into the woods on either side as though he might spot one of those lost souls wandering aimlessly an arm's length away.

"Never have I heard such nonsense in my life." Sophie laughed, her gaze rising to meet Hugues' dubious one.

"'Tis easy enough to lose one's way in the woods," he remarked noncommittally, and she wondered whether he put any stock in Luc's tale at all. "And sounds can carry deceptively clearly."

"Aye," Sophie conceded reluctantly. "Well could it be farther than it sounds, for I cannot see a glimmer of water." Hugues came to stand beside her, cocking his head for an instant to listen, then gazing off into the distance as well.

"Aye, I hear it, too," he admitted, frowning into the woods. "Should there truly be a stream, it will likely cross the path sooner or later." He cast an apologetic glance to Sophie. "I would not waste time searching the woods for its bed." Sophie nodded at the logic of Hugues' argument, and looked up to find his regard still upon her.

"Angry are you, then, that I followed to warn you of your danger?" she inquired softly, and Hugues seemed to find her question amusing. He tried unsuccessfully to smother his smile, then grinned outright.

"Lucky you are that the Normans had heard tell of Brocéliande or you would have been responsible for bringing that danger directly to me," he teased, and Sophie flushed.

"I meant no harm, but they were going to steal the horse," she explained, but Hugues brushed her words aside.

"Of no matter is it," he conceded gruffly.

Sophie forced herself to ask the question that haunted her. "Mean you, then, what you said?" she murmured and Hugues' gaze caught hers once more for a long moment.

"Aye, I would see you safe," he growled as though embarrassed by the admission, and looked off into the shadows once more.

"Nay, not that. The other," Sophie urged. Hugues turned slowly back to face her, the color rising to redden his neck.

"Aye," he admitted in a low voice after a long moment, and she saw the truth of it in his eyes. His voice dropped as he continued, his gaze locked with hers with an expression that made her heart leap. "Aye, that I meant, as well."

"Good," Sophie whispered, barely giving Hugues time to digest the word and its implications before she stretched up to kiss him.

If he was surprised to learn that she cared for him as well, he recovered quickly enough, Sophie acknowledged with pride. She loved the way his arms closed uncompromisingly around her. His tongue slipped into her mouth as she cupped his strong jaw in her hands and the passion flared between them anew. Sophie arched against his strength and Hugues gathered her closer, the stubble of his beard grazing a path along her jaw as he nibbled his way to her ear.

"Ride with me," he whispered urgently and Sophie could only nod, so weak had her legs become with his kiss. He kissed her again lingeringly so that the forest spun around her, then lifted her up into his saddle with a wink for her and a whistle for Luc.

"Mayhap we can reach an inn this night," Hugues growled into her hair when he had swung up behind her, and a trill of anticipation rolled through Sophie's veins. She closed her eyes as Hugues' fingers found their way beneath her cloak and latched unerringly on her breast, caressing her nipple to a point through the wool of her kirtle. To imagine his touch on her bare skin again made her fairly swoon and she turned in the saddle to lean against him and press a kiss against his chest.

"It matters not," she murmured, closing her eyes with satisfaction when Hugues' arms tightened around her.

Well it seemed to Hugues that they should have fair reached Paris by the time the stream did cross their path. Its trickling had become gradually louder before it finally came into sight, sparkling with some light of its own within the darkness that blocked out the sun.

If indeed the sun was still aloft and of that Hugues had his doubts.

The horses quickened their pace at the promise of a drink and he gave his steed its rein, leaning down to give Sophie a leisurely, thorough kiss. She sighed and arched against him, her hands sliding over his shoulders to lock around his neck, and something within Hugues surged with pride.

This was more like it, he reasoned, more than pleased to find Sophie back to her previous passion. The promise of the magic they would make this night dismissed all other thought from his mind. No quick loving would there be this time, he resolved with a smile, drawing back to watch Sophie slowly open her eyes.

"Why do you laugh?" she asked lazily, and he grinned even wider.

"'Twas but the thought of you trying to walk on the morrow that amused me," he murmured, and was satisfied by the answering flare of heat in her eyes.

"You shall simply have to carry me," she answered easily and, liking the sound of that, Hugues bent to kiss her again.

"Milord!" Luc cried and Hugues conceded that the boy did have a tendency to be annoying. "You cannot let the horses drink of this stream!" he protested.

Hugues shot him a look of outright confusion that was not entirely the fault of Sophie's kisses even as he instinctively snatched up his horse's reins. The beast snorted impatiently at being denied his drink when 'twas right before his nose, but Hugues stayed him while he attended Luc.

"Whyever not?" he demanded tersely.

"'Tis enchanted," Luc insisted and Hugues barely restrained himself from rolling his eyes as he released the stallion's reins.

"No enchantment is there in this water," he explained patiently, dismounting to lead Sophie's palfrey to the stream, as well. The mare bent immediately to drink and Hugues propped his hands on his hips when Luc continued to hold back his own steed.

"'Twill put them under the witches' spell and they will carry us off into the woods," he insisted in a hoarse whisper. Hugues shook his head and reached for Luc's palfrey's reins.

"They shall expire shortly without it," he countered evenly.

Luc pulled his horse abruptly out of Hugues' reach, and the knight stifled a twinge of irritation. "I cannot let him drink." Luc maintained wildly. Hugues ran one hand through his hair with exasperation.

"Think upon the matter carefully, boy," he said in his firmest tones. He noted with satisfaction that the boy was in fact listening to him. "The beasts have been running hard all day and have had naught to drink since dawn. 'Tis cruel to deny them a drink of any kind now, be it enchanted or no."

"'Tis simply a chance we must take?" Luc demanded quietly after a long pause, and Hugues nodded unequivocally.

"Aye, lest the poor creatures be unable to carry us clear to the other side of Brocéliande."

That thought seemed particularly compelling to Luc, and Hugues wished he had thought of it sooner when the boy's eyes flashed with outright fear. Without another protest he dismounted and led his palfrey to the stream, his brow drawn tight with worry, and watched the beast drink thirstily.

Sophie slipped from the saddle and cupped her hands to drink before Luc's horrified eyes, swallowing the water apparently without ill effects of any kind. 'Twas a good idea and Hugues realized at her blissful expression just how thirsty he was. So hastily had they left that he had not had the opportunity to fill his own wineskin.

Hugues glanced at Luc's horrified expression and concluded 'twas time to set the boy's fears to rights. Without a word he knelt by the water himself and cupped his own hands to drink.

"Milord," Luc warned in shaky tones, "the witches will put you under their spell." Hugues met Sophie's gaze over their cupped hands, seeing that she, too, had anticipated the boy's objection.

"Nay, 'tis but a tale you have been told," he answered carefully, watching a stray drop of water trickle from the corner of Sophie's lips and barely quelling the urge to retrieve it when it slipped down the neck of her kirtle. All logical arguments evaporated from his mind with the disappearance of that droplet and he forced himself to make some attempt to think coherently.

"Already has one witch claimed me," he murmured for her ears alone and Sophie chuckled outright at his jest.

Luc drew alongside them as Hugues drank of the stream. The boy licked his lips and watched his lord carefully, as though any detrimental effects would be immediately visible. With great leisure and apparent enjoyment, Hugues drank another draught of the icy water and washed his face with abandon.

Seized by a curious lightheartedness and certain the boy was taking these superstitions learned at his granny's knee far too seriously, Hugues abruptly frowned as though puzzled by something. Sophie immediately reached for his arm.

"Hugues, what ails you?" she demanded quickly. He said naught but clutched at his stomach, seeing out of the corner of his eye that Luc was watching avidly.

"I know not," Hugues admitted slowly, endeavoring his best to sound perplexed while secretly amazed that neither had seen through his ruse. "'Tis most odd." He let his voice waver and fade, and lifted his eyes to focus on some distant point in the woods.

"'Tis the witches!" Luc hissed in alarm.

"Hugues?" The pressure of Sophie's hand increased slightly.

Hugues stood slowly like a man in a daze, then clutched his chest and stumbled to one knee as if stricken by some invisible lance. Certain he could not keep from laughing much longer, he toppled backward to great effect without harming himself, a trick he had learned wrestling with his master when he had squired, and rolled to his back with a heartfelt groan.

"Struck him dead they did!" Luc exclaimed in horror. Hugues felt Sophie's hand drop to his brow.

"Hugues?" was all she asked and though there was concern in her voice he knew she schooled herself to avoid frightening the boy.

"He has been claimed by the witches, milady," Luc gushed, his fright evidently getting the better of him despite Sophie's efforts to the contrary. Hugues gauged the boy's position by his voice and struggled to keep from revealing himself too soon. "We must get him out of the forest. He should never have drunk of the water.''

"Do not be ridiculous," Sophie countered with firm practicality. "I also drank of the water and still I stand before you."

"Oh, nay, nay," Luc moaned with newfound fear. "'Tis only a matter of time before they claim you as well, milady, and then I shall be all alone in the forests of Brocéliande. What shall become of me? Whatever shall I do?"

Reasoning that he would get no better cue, Hugues sat up abruptly and grasped Luc by the upper arms, savoring the shock that transformed the boy's face.

"Drink of the water," he commanded with a grin. When Sophie conquered her surprise and began to laugh, the boy shortly followed suit, the three of them laughing uproariously together.

"Deliberately did you trick me," Luc accused as his color rose, and Hugues affectionately tousled the boy's hair.

"Aye, that I did, for you had need of it," he responded genially. His tone grew more serious as he looked the boy in the eye. "Naught is wrong with the stream, Luc, so take a good draught. Long might it be afore we see another."

"Aye, milord," he agreed reluctantly and bent to drink, though not without some lingering vestige of hesitation.

Hugues chose to ignore that, straightening and running one hand through his hair as he turned to face Sophie. She was struggling not to laugh outright again and he grinned unabashedly at her.

"You fair had me fooled, as well," she charged.

Hugues hooted. "*Fair* had you fooled?" he repeated skeptically and she laughed that he had seen through her tale. "What ails you?" He mimicked her concerned voice, watching her flush as she swatted him playfully across the shoulder.

"What expect you of us when you feign death?" she accused with a chuckle. Her expression changed subtly as Hugues gathered her up against his chest.

"Naught else, I suppose," he conceded happily, bending to kiss her anew and reveling in her ardent response. He lifted his lips from hers a long moment later, and enjoyed the way her features had softened in passion.

"Make no mistake, Sophie," he whispered as he pulled her against him so that she could not fail to note his own response to their kiss. "Fully alive am I."

"Aye, and I shall expect you to do more than talk about it this night," she retorted mischievously, her eyes sparkling as she danced out of his embrace.

"Think you that I cannot make good on my promise?" Hugues called after her in a bantering tone. Sophie laughed and reached for her mare's bridle.

"'Tis more a question of willingness than ability," she teased unrepentantly.

So she would question his intention to have her fully this night. That disillusion could easily be put to rest. Hugues grinned in anticipation as he descended upon her and she giggled when he scooped her up and dropped her purposefully into his saddle.

"Willingness aplenty will you witness this very night," he threatened under his breath. Sophie flashed him a wicked smile, confirming her approval of this turn of events with that single gesture.

"'Tis all talk from you," she countered with a dismissive wave of her hand.

Hugues chuckled at her accusation and reveled in the levity of his heart. He filled his wineskin from the stream, then swung up behind Sophie and pulled her close. When she snuggled against him, he wondered how soon he could command a stop without appearing overly anxious.

But perhaps there was naught wrong with being anxious, he thought when Sophie turned to press a kiss beneath his jaw that fairly heated his blood to boiling.

Chapter Nine

❦

They forded the shallow stream and the hardwood trees gave way to cedars, the air filling with their refreshing scent. The ground was softer, and the thick carpet of fallen boughs combined with the scent to give a spring to the horses' steps, despite the amount of time they had been traveling. These trees seemed of less stature and Hugues fancied that he could see the sky through their uppermost boughs, noting with satisfaction that it seemed to be decidedly dark.

His steed hesitated and Hugues glanced to the path ahead. The way was less easily discerned here under the cedars. No undergrowth was there to mark the forest floor other than the path, a smooth brown layer of discarded boughs stretching evenly in all directions beneath the trees. The space between the tree trunks seemed most broad directly ahead and Hugues urged his mount in that direction, fairly sure that 'twas the path they followed.

Was it but his fancy that the trees closed ranks behind them or that the way seemed narrower as soon as they stepped upon it? The three of them fell silent, as none dared to voice the fear that they were becoming lost in the woods, and they rode thus for what seemed a long time.

Hugues's certainty in his choice faded with the waning light and 'twas not much longer before he halted his horse to gaze about him into the trees. No sign was there that they followed the true path, nor indeed any path at all, and he frowned at the cedar trees that innocently confronted them on every side.

In fact, 'twas difficult to tell exactly which way they had come.

"Water do I hear again," Sophie contributed softly. Hugues cocked his head to listen. The stream it must be again, he reasoned, but his ears told him differently, for the sound of rushing water was louder than the gently flowing stream could have made.

"'Tis as good an objective as any," he muttered in frustration and Sophie looked at him with understanding.

"You spoke aright when you said 'twas easy to become lost in a woods," she reminded him. Hugues forced a smile with difficulty, not wanting to worry her unnecessarily.

He appreciated her reminder that forests could be confusing in their own right. Luc said naught, but Hugues had not to look at him to know the direction of the boy's thoughts. And naught could he say that might ease his mind, especially now that they were unequivocally lost.

"Undoubtedly the path will be clearer in the morning," Hugues concluded with what he hoped sounded like conviction. Sophie smiled confidently, but Luc merely looked troubled as they headed in the direction of the rushing water.

Now they were well and truly off the path, for the trees pressed in on either side as if they would prevent the riders from passing, their branches entangling their clothes. Hugues' stallion folded his ears back and ducked his head stubbornly while he forced his way through the trees, the very image of a decent beast forced to endure the direction of an idiot.

Branches snapped on either side as they pressed onward, and it seemed to Hugues that their passage made an inordinate amount of noise. No trick was it that the trees seemed somehow disapproving of the entire circumstance, but he cajoled the horse on as the sound of the water grew distinctly louder.

Without preamble they burst out of the woods as if the very trees had spit them out in disgust, the stallion balking when he found himself unexpectedly knee-deep in water. Sophie gasped in delight and the two palfreys plunged into the water immediately behind them as Hugues gazed about himself with of amazement.

'Twas such a peaceful spot they had stumbled upon that he could not quite reconcile its proximity to the forest that he had imagined so hostile toward them. This stream was wider and deeper than the last had been, if indeed it had been the same course of water, and it ran at an energetic and sparkling pace. The gnarled trunks of old cedars bent over the water on either side as though they would drink of the clear depths, but the span of the river was open to the night sky and Hugues tipped his head back to look briefly at the stars.

To his left the land rose abruptly, the crest towering above them evidently still within the bounds of the forest, for its line was a leafy silhouette of still more trees against the indigo sky. A godsend that high land was, for Hugues could scale the bluff to get some bearings before they started out in the morn. The line of the road should be evident enough from that height, he reasoned, and 'twould be only a matter of time before they were back on their way.

The rushing sound came from the left, as well, and Hugues guessed what they would find, even while he urged his horse upstream. Sophie murmured in wonder when they rounded a crook in the stream and came upon a glistening waterfall, the water etched silver in the starlight as it fell from that height to linger in eddies and pools before rolling out to swirl around the horses' hooves and then hasten on its way.

"We shall rest here this night," Hugues said, pleased when Sophie turned to him with shining eyes.

"'Tis a most beautiful spot," she enthused, and he felt himself smile in anticipation despite his worries. After all, their way would be clear on the morrow and this was a magical place.

"'Tis a trickery," Luc contributed sourly as his palfrey splashed to the bank and clambered onto the shore. "Should we dare to sleep, we shall not awaken for a hundred years."

"Then mayhap we have need of such a long slumber," Hugues countered amiably as he followed suit and dismounted, not intending to let the boy's nonsense affect his mood.

This night he and Sophie would explore each other, he thought with rising excitement. The way she smiled when he lifted her down from the saddle told him that her thoughts had followed a similar path.

"Milord, do you truly not understand?" Luc insisted. "'Tis but a prank of the witches to enslave us forever within Brocéliande."

Enough was enough.

"Luc." Hugues turned on the boy with a tone that brooked no argument. "No such place is there as Brocéliande. 'Tis but a myth, a tale told to children that they will stay in their beds at night." He gestured to the woods surrounding them, refusing to acknowledge a sense that the trees themselves were listening to his words.

"This is but a forest like any other. And like any other forest, 'twas easy to lose our way within it. On the morrow you and I will climb this bluff to find the direction of the road. 'Tis most logical and most simple. There is no magic or trickery involved and I would have you curb your tongue about such matters."

"But milord—" Luc protested one last time, his conviction fading.

"But *naught,*" Hugues interrupted. "Need have we all of sleep. Mind you fasten your steed securely and get yourself some." With that he turned away to tend his own beast with practiced ease, that Luc might settle into sleep sooner.

"'Tis Brocéliande and well I know it," Luc muttered stubbornly under his breath but Hugues chose to ignore the assertion. Let the boy think what he would as long as he did as he was bidden with a minimum of argument.

Now that the moment of their liaison was upon them, Hugues felt considerably more awkward and he hesitated to join Sophie. The fire on the lip of the bank beside the swirling pool had burned down to embers. Luc was snoring softly downstream. Sophie had stretched out on Hugues' blanket near the fire and a slim crescent of silvery moon rose above the trees. Well it seemed that naught could be more perfectly contrived, but

Hugues checked that the horses' reins were securely fastened for the hundredth time and shifted his weight from one foot to the other uncertainly as he covertly watched Sophie.

An elusive creation of the moonlight she seemed to be with her thick golden braid draped over her shoulders and her long hand trailing leisurely in the water. No sign was there of the robust gold of her skin in this light or of the strength that so fired his longing for her. Tonight she appeared as pale and insubstantial as a moonbeam, and Hugues wondered fleetingly whether his Sophie had been replaced by some water nymph who eerily bore her very likeness.

Would she truly welcome him into her embrace? Boldly indeed had he planned to pleasure her again, but this image of a more delicate creature fostered doubts in Hugues' mind whether his loving would be adequate. He gripped the stallion's reins and lingered in the shadows of the trees, uncertain what to do.

"Hugues?" Sophie demanded softly, her voice no more than a whisper on the wind, and his heart leaped at her call.

"Aye," he responded awkwardly, knowing with that uncanny sense the very instant that her gaze landed upon him.

While Hugues watched, Sophie smiled sunnily and rose to her feet, the sound of her light tread on the riverbank reassuring him somewhat as she approached. She paused before him and Hugues marveled at the beauty of the smile she granted him.

"'Twas but a jest that you had not the will," she teased gently. He chuckled nervously before he could stop himself, but the way their gazes clung brought his laughter to an abrupt halt.

"I would not compel you." He fumbled with the words, but Sophie closed the minute space between them with a quick step. Her hands rested lightly on his chest and Hugues could not help but look down into her face.

"Do you want me, Hugues?" she murmured. He could only nod. "And I want you," she confided softly, her fingers entangling with his as his pulse leaped.

"Let us show each other how much," she urged, and gave his hand a firm squeeze.

If her confession had encouraged him, the grip of her fingers convinced Hugues that she was no moonbeam. Still tentative, he framed her face with his hands, savoring the softness of her skin beneath his own rough fingers, and bent to gently kiss her. Sophie leaned against him and opened her mouth to his embrace with a soft sound of surrender, her hands clasping around his waist, and he slipped one hand into her hair to caress her nape.

She moaned and a flurry of little signals confirmed her very earthly state: the insistence of her fingers now beneath his tabard and fanned against his bare back, the nipples that bore twin marks into his chest, the demanding tongue that darted unabashedly into his mouth. Sophie ground her hips against his erection impatiently and the last vestiges of Hugues' doubts were swept away.

"Nay," he whispered into the curve of her ear as he gripped her hips and put some minute distance between them. "This time I vowed 'twould be slow." She shivered at the fan of his breath against her ear and Hugues kissed her earlobe before pulling back to look into her eyes, wide with incomprehension.

"Know you not what I mean?" he demanded softly, hearing the affection in his own voice.

Sophie shook her head quickly, as if embarrassed, before smiling shyly.

"Show me," she urged, her quiet words almost making it impossible for Hugues to remain true to his objectives. He schooled himself to keep the pace slow, though, and maintaining that handspan of distance between them, he reached for her braid.

Sophie watched him untie the band that held it fast and Hugues was glad the dexterity of his fingers did not abandon him. He handed her the band when 'twas free, their fingers brushing for an instant and drawing their eyes to each other in a shock of mutual awareness. Hugues felt the air between them heat and he held her wide-eyed gaze with a smile as he carefully unbraided the plait.

When his fingertips brushed her neck, Sophie closed her eyes with a sigh, and once her hair was loose he could not resist the urge to bury his fingers in the thickness of it at her nape. Sophie made some incoherent sound at his touch and leaned back within his caress, the way her lips parted inviting Hugues' kiss. He brushed his lips gently across hers, and lifted the mass of her hair to spread it over her shoulders in glorious disarray.

He unlaced the neckline of her kirtle next with the same methodical movements, the impertinent juts of her nipples echoing his own state. He traced the outline of one through the wool with his fingertip and when Sophie gasped at his touch, he bent to caress the point with his lips. She was melting in the heat between them and he reveled in the knowledge that 'twas his touch that did this to her, even as her kirtle fell away and he caught his own breath at the vision of her.

The moonlight played with the shadows of her chemise, making Hugues imagine again that 'twas some water nymph who bewitched him with loose hair and a hauntingly sheer garment. Determined to convince himself that Sophie was real, he knelt before her, running his fingertips up her legs from her bare ankles to the hem of her chemise.

He glanced up to find her watching him and smiled as he curved his hands around her knees. Slowly he slid his hands up the smoothness of her thighs, the chemise lifting on his forearms, and her slender beauty was revealed to him. Hugues felt something tighten within him when the tawny curls at the juncture of her thighs were bared to his gaze. His grip tightened around her hips, his thumbs tracing the smooth curve of her pelvis before his hands locked around her waist.

Sophie gasped when his tongue first touched her, but Hugues barely noticed her surprise, lost as he was in the intoxicating scent of her arousal. He pulled her closer and felt her hands land on his shoulders even as his tongue burrowed into those curls in search of her tender spot.

She lost her balance and leaned against him, her grip tightening on his neck, and Hugues knew he had found what he sought. His hands slipped to cup her buttocks that she would not stumble even as he caressed her with leisurely expertise. Her skin heated and Hugues heard the involuntary sounds she made, but still he continued undaunted at the same leisurely pace until Sophie gasped and trembled convulsively from head to toe.

"Hugues," she whispered shakily, and he noted with satisfaction the reddened hue of her flesh. He smiled to himself and traced an upward path to her breast, suckling the nipple with that same leisurely thoroughness.

"Hugues, please," Sophie urged in a trembling voice. He paused to meet her gaze as he cast her chemise aside, noting the flush on her cheeks, the glitter in her eyes.

"Thrice will you find your pleasure before I find mine," he murmured. Sophie fairly swooned at the promise in his words. Seeing that she intended to argue the point, he kissed her, his fingers finding that tender spot and caressing it until she arched against him helplessly, her cry swallowed in his kiss.

"Twice that is," she whispered weakly against his throat and Hugues grinned.

"The third will you have to work for," he vowed, savoring Sophie's shiver of anticipation as he scooped her up into his arms and carried her purposefully to the blanket laid out on the bank.

When the dream came to Sophie much later that night, she greeted its arrival with a sense of anticipation for the first time in her life. Never before had she been impatient with its leisurely pacing, never before had she tried to rush inside the circle of stones. She could not help but turn immediately to the place the cloaked figure usually occupied, and relief surged through her at finding the stranger standing silently opposite.

So certain was Sophie that 'twould be Hugues' visage she would see now that the threat to his existence had been thwarted, she looked without hesitation to the cloaked figure's face, trying to discern the features despite the shadows of its cowl. It advanced at a pace she now found annoyingly slow and she fidgeted impatiently as she waited for Hugues to reveal himself.

The figure lifted one hand to its hood and Sophie felt a twinge of dread that the fingers seemed much smaller

than those of Hugues. Her panic rose when she noted
the narrow span of the shoulders beneath the cloak,
caught the glimmer of a green gem at the neck, and she
tried desperately to stop the unfurling of the dream now
that she feared the way of it.

The motion of that hand continued unerringly,
though, and Sophie watched helplessly as the hood was
gripped and lifted. She saw naught but an eerily pale
pair of eyes boring knowingly into hers before she
jerked herself upright.

Sophie struggled to steady her breathing as she huddled beside the river, the dancing water rushing alongside, Hugues' blanket discarded around her ankles. He
mumbled something in his sleep beside her and turned
toward her. The way his hand snaked around her waist
and pulled her closer prompted Sophie's tears to rise.

Impossible that this was not meant to be, she thought
fiercely, tears blurring her vision while she watched the
knight sleep beside her. Impossible that she should both
win his regard and save him from danger, yet the fates
would deny him to her. Sophie had half a mind to defy
the fates outright when a splash brought her to her
senses.

Startled, she twisted to find the source of the sound,
taking a long moment to pick out the woman's figure
beside the base of the waterfall.

Evidently the other woman thought herself alone, for
she discarded her cloak to unselfconsciously bare her
flesh to Sophie's gaze. Sophie fairly gasped aloud at the
woman's form in the moonlight. The dark curtain of
hair falling over her shoulders and down to her knees
echoed the cascade of water behind her. She stepped
now into the water and her hair spread over the surface

of the pool like a dark veil, stretching farther and farther as the woman waded yet deeper into the pool.

Though she knew she was spying, Sophie could not tear her eyes away from the woman's beauty, could not close her ears when the other began to softly sing. The words eluded Sophie but the tune was hauntingly beautiful, foreign and familiar at once, conjuring images of stories she had heard as a child, of fearless knights and beauteous maidens, of dragons ferocious and towers tall to be conquered.

The shards of her own disturbing dream were all but forgotten as Sophie was transfixed by the woman's graceful movements. She wondered at finding another here in these seemingly empty woods, but then the song swept even those concerns away. Sophie leaned on her elbow to unabashedly watch the woman bathe, feeling an inexplicable link between them.

"Sophie," Hugues murmured sleepily some time later, stirring restlessly when Sophie ignored his appeal. She felt him roll over behind her, felt the weight of his hand on her hip, but could not turn away from the woman in the pool.

"Sophie?" he asked a little more emphatically, but Sophie shook her head.

"Hush, Hugues," she chided in a whisper. "Can you not hear the song?"

Sophie sensed Hugues' confusion but ignored it, their words evidently having drawn the attention of the bathing woman. The woman's head snapped up and she looked directly to Sophie, the force emanating from her stunning Sophie with its intensity.

An invisible cord between them suddenly drew taut and Sophie felt the woman's gaze bore into her with a ferocity she had experienced not long past. Sophie shivered in recollection of her dream and knew without a doubt that the woman's eyes would be pale beyond pale.

So this was the way 'twould be. Her path lay with this woman now, no longer with Hugues, for whatever capricious reason of the fates. Would the dream always guide her choices thus? On some level, Sophie rebelled against the knowledge of what she must do, even as she recognized that she was powerless to turn from the path chosen for her.

Mayhap she had already pushed the patience of the fates too far by following Hugues from La Rochelle. Well it seemed that they were intent on her parting ways with him, one way or the other.

Sophie closed her eyes and felt the relentless draw of the woman's personality, the awareness that she had much to learn from her growing more resolute with every passing moment.

And what of Hugues? Indeed, it seemed he would have been poorly served by having the likes of her at his side, should these visions haunt her for the rest of her days. The thought saddened Sophie beyond compare and she felt a tear stumble over her cheek at the bitter realization that she loved this knight enough to want a better mate for him.

"Sophie, what is this?" Hugues demanded behind her, but she could not look away from the woman to reassure him.

Indeed, what could she say? Her path lay with this woman now, Sophie knew no more than that, and 'twas clear that the woman knew that, as well. She raised one hand to Sophie in a beckoning gesture and Sophie rose mutely to her feet.

"Sophie, where do you go?" Hugues asked urgently and she spared him a small smile at the concern in his words. He looked completely perplexed and Sophie sadly touched his cheek in a gesture of farewell, taking one last opportunity to commit his features to memory. Her heart swelled with love for this man and fairly broke with the awareness that she must part ways with him, especially now, but the fates would not be denied.

"I go with this woman," she explained softly, her words evidently doing little to enlighten Hugues. He glanced uncomprehendingly to the woman waiting patiently and frowned.

"Do you know her?" he demanded. His frown deepened when Sophie shook her head.

"Not yet," she conceded, and his expression grew positively thunderous.

"Naught do you know of her, yet you would go with her?" he asked incredulously. Sophie could but smile.

"Aye, Hugues. 'Tis my fate to follow her," she explained simply, stunned at the pain that flickered through his eyes before he composed himself again.

"Long have you insisted that 'twas your fate to be with me," he countered hotly. Sophie felt his dismay as keenly as her own, but knew not how to make the change clear without hurting him.

"No longer, I fear," she admitted gently. "Something has changed, I know not what, but that path is no longer clear to me." She turned and would have walked away but Hugues gripped her shoulders, forcing her to face him anew.

"What nonsense is this?" he demanded vehemently. His eyes blazed angrily and Sophie thought he might bodily shake her. "After this night we have shared, you would say this to me?" His grip tightened on her shoulders in his anger but Sophie held his gaze determinedly, wishing she knew some way to make him understand.

"Your virginity have you granted me," Hugues reminded her fiercely. "A gift you vowed belonged to the man you would wed alone." His voice softened, his grip loosening as his hands slid to frame her face. He looked bewildered and she fancied a tear glinted in his eye. "Was that all a lie, Sophie?" he whispered and there was no mistaking his pain.

"Nay, Hugues, never that," she vowed, touching his cheek, his jaw, the leaping pulse at his throat as she sought to reassure him.

"What, then? What has changed, Sophie?" he asked impatiently. His brows drew together in a tight frown.

"Everything has changed, Hugues. In a dream it came to me," she explained, reaching up to touch his face once more as if in apology.

"A dream?" he repeated in disbelief. "You would abandon me for some whimsy in the night?"

"No whimsy 'twas, Hugues, but a vision of what should be," she insisted softly. "Like the vision I had of you the night before we met."

"And what of that vision? Is its value naught now? Well I thought that we each had regard for the other, well I thought that we might make our path together."

Sophie's heart leaped but she refused to read any implication into his words. He was angry with her for leaving him, no more, no less. Perhaps 'twould be best if she made the matter most clear to him.

"No more do I dream of you, Hugues, and I cannot deny the sign," she confirmed quietly, watching disappointment cloud his eyes before he turned abruptly away and feeling terrible for so hurting him. Hugues' back straightened stubbornly, but naught could Sophie say to ease his hurt and well she knew it. She had pricked his pride and that would not be easily repaired.

"You would leave us, then?" Hugues asked hoarsely once more as if unable to believe her intention. Sophie simply nodded, despite the fact that he could not see her gesture. No words were there to ease his pain and she would not try lest he see her own.

"But last night..." Hugues began before his voice broke and he gestured mutely with one hand. The agony in his eyes when he turned to confront her fairly dismissed Sophie's resolve. She closed her eyes against her tears, cursing the fates for forcing this choice upon her, and fingered Hugues' tabard as she fought for the words.

"'Twas the most magical night of my life," she whispered unevenly. Hugues shook his head uncomprehendingly.

"Then stay," he urged, but Sophie shook her head in turn.

"You must know that I would if I could," she insisted, tears blurring her vision. She stretched up to press one last kiss to the uncompromising line of his jaw.

"Adieu, Hugues," she whispered unsteadily, biting her lip as she turned away.

Sophie slipped into her garments blindly, achingly aware of Hugues' silence behind her even as her own tears threatened to rise and choke her.

"Any difference would it make to know that I meant to ask for your hand this morn?" he asked softly when she was dressed, and Sophie spun on her heel to find the truth shining in Hugues' eyes. Her own tears rose in a torrent at the sight of what she wanted most offered to her so simply, but 'twas no longer hers to take.

"Hugues, I cannot," she whispered and he turned away, the shock she had dealt him evident in his expression.

Sophie turned and glanced up through her misery to the woman still standing mutely hip-deep in the pool. That awareness snapped like a whip between them, compelling her to follow her instinct's bidding. Unable to risk a backward glance she squared her shoulders and walked down the riverbank, away from Hugues, away from the love she had been so sure she would call her own, away from the love he was offering, away from the love she was no longer free to claim.

"Sophie!" Hugues called urgently one last time, but she could not turn now and risk losing her conviction. 'Twas this that she had to do, this alone, though Sophie cursed the fates for cheating her. Her heart ached, the ground blurred before her as she walked and she stumbled more than once on the path to her destiny.

"Should you follow the base of the cliffs on the morrow, you will find yourself clear of the woods by sunset," the woman in the pool said now to Hugues, her voice as silvery as the moonlight. "A road is there that will lead directly to Pontesse. Well are you needed there in these days of crisis, Chevalier Hugues, and I bid you make haste lest you arrive too late."

Her words hung in the night air and Sophie knew as she picked her way along the bank that Hugues would be gone far from her side in but a day. The very thought made the bile rise in her throat. Had she truly done aright? She raised her gaze to the woman patiently awaiting her, now garbed on the bank ahead, and it seemed to Sophie that she nodded once in reassurance.

"Long have I been waiting for you," she said, but 'twas the pale luminosity of her eyes that truly convinced Sophie, not her words.

They were indeed the eyes she had glimpsed in her dream and any hope that she might have been mistaken died then and there.

Sophie had not the nerve to look back to Hugues until they were sheltered by the woods where he could not see her gesture, and even then she glanced quickly over one shoulder, knowing somehow that her companion would disapprove.

Hugues stood alone on the bank, silhouetted against the trees, his hands on his hips, his brows drawn in a thunderous scowl. Sophie almost smiled to herself at the realization that that expression usually seemed to be connected with something she had done, and she sighed shakily, filled with a sense that she would not see him again. As Sophie watched, he kicked a rock into the river with a vehemence that surprised her, before he turned away and shouted at Luc that they must hasten home.

He should have seen it coming, Hugues concluded sourly as he rode along the surprisingly clear path at the foot of the cliffs. After all, had he not thought her mad from the very first? And was it not the act of a madwoman to simply disappear into the forest with a complete stranger?

Truly he had been mad as well to let Sophie simply walk away, to not force her to see the foolishness of what she planned to do, to not persuade her with logic. One could not simply trust another on the basis of some misguided direction of the heart, or instinct, or fate, or whatever one chose to call it. The world was a danger-

ous place, and all the more treacherous for fools who
followed such whims. Too late had that reminder come
to Hugues' mind to be of any use at all and he grimaced under the shadowed canopy of the trees.

To what fate would she come now? And why had he
let her follow this path? Annoyance with himself, with
his failure to think rationally despite his pain, flooded
through Hugues while he rode. He should have stopped
her, should have persuaded her from this foolhardiness, but nay, too concerned had he been with his own
anguish at her rejection of his offer to think clearly.

And by the time he had composed himself, the two
women had disappeared without a trace.

Why had he not been born with a facile tongue, with
the ability to woo women with sweet words? Why had
he been unable to tell Sophie that he was concerned for
her safety? Would that have stayed her? He knew not,
but wished he had tried.

Would she have stayed if she had known that he loved
her?

True, he had made clear his intention to offer for her
hand, but well he knew that women did not assume that
the two ideas traveled hand in hand. And well he knew
how they treasured such words of love. A fool he had
been to not confess the fullness of his feelings when he
had had the chance.

For that chance might never present itself again,
judging by the way she had disappeared. Would he
never see Sophie again? Never hear her laughter sparkle at some simple jest, never again cringe when she set
out to argue with him? 'Twas not even the dawn and
already he missed her presence, her certainty in completely illogical concepts, her perceptiveness and ability to find the precise way to reassure his fears.

Would a confession of love have made a difference?

Hugues squared his shoulders to face down the disappointment welling within him at the realization that he knew not. A simple answer that question should have provoked, a resounding aye to his way of thinking, but Hugues knew not whether 'twould have made a whit of difference to Sophie. Already did she know that he held her in high regard. He had made that clear enough in the stables in La Rochelle, and little enough difference had that made.

Her choice had she made, whatever his thoughts about it, and little enough was there he could do now since he knew not where she had gone. Somehow, Hugues suspected that the other woman would ensure that he never found them.

And there was that ominous warning about Pontesse, a warning that managed to pull at Hugues' heart despite all the other troubles assailing him. Indeed, he had been away longer than he had intended. Of what did the woman speak? Was his father fallen yet more ill? Hugues sat straighter in the saddle and took a deep breath, recalling himself to his responsibilities.

Indeed, Sophie had claimed she no longer dreamed of him and from a woman who put so much stock in her dreams, there could be no greater rejection.

Hugues closed his eyes against the bite in her declaration, knowing that Sophie and the web she had spun around his heart would not be so easily dismissed from his own dreams, regardless of what awaited him at Château Pontesse.

The woman led a surprisingly quick pace through the forest and Sophie struggled to keep up with her, bursting with a thousand questions but too breathless to ask a one of them. Brambles tore at her hands as the woman traced a path indiscernible to Sophie's eyes, the trees pressing more tightly around them, the shadows falling deeper, the very air growing denser. Finally, just when Sophie thought they could force their way no farther, they burst unexpectedly into a small clearing.

'Twas not more than twenty paces across, but the winter sun peeked over the trees, illuminating the sheltered patch of ground to little avail. The air was crisper here, cleaner, and the early sunlight made Sophie feel as if she was inhaling pure light after the ominous shadows of the forest. She heard a trickling while she looked around, and concluded that the stream must run nearby. A hut leaned into the shadows of the trees on the far side. Blackened stones in the very center marked a fire pit, the remainder of the open space crowded with a tangle of growth.

With the lateness of the season, most of the plants appeared deadened, their branches leafless, those leaves that remained dried and brown. Sophie took a step into the tangle of growth and was immediately assaulted by the scent of mint. Closer examination revealed a small green leafed plant stubbornly growing under the shelter of the other dormant plants. Sophie had stepped on it and now she reached down to rub its leaves, releasing that fresh scent once again.

Suddenly it seemed that her nose was awake for the first time in her life and she discerned a spicier smell along with the mint. Her fingers found the deadened branch that exuded the scent but she knew not its name, nor the name of the one beside it that made her think of the stuffed fowl that Hélène used to roast. The tangled undergrowth took on a clarity in Sophie's eyes when she cast another glance over it, the myriad different plants and their scents becoming distinct to her as she looked.

"How many of them do you know?" the woman inquired softly. Sophie glanced up and saw that pale regard fixed upon her, the woman's arms folded across her chest.

"I know few of their names," Sophie admitted, wondering if she imagined the way the woman's lips quickly thinned.

"And their uses?" she demanded sharply.

"I know not what you mean," Sophie responded carefully and this time there was no mistaking the woman's displeasure. The sunlight shone full on her face as she turned to finger a plant, frowning in thought, and Sophie saw that the woman was much older than she had originally believed.

"'Twill be more difficult than I anticipated," was all the woman murmured now, turning abruptly and stalking to the hut. So many questions had Sophie that she could not simply let the woman walk away, and she plunged through the knee-deep tangle of growth in pursuit.

"Wait!" she called. The woman paused on the threshold of the cabin. "I do not understand. What will be more difficult? Why does my path lie with you? Who are you?"

The woman turned slowly and regarded Sophie with what could only be amazement. "Do you truly know naught of this?" she asked quietly, her expression hardening when she noted Sophie's confusion. She closed the space between them with quick strides and Sophie struggled not to squirm beneath the knowing expression in those pale eyes.

"Do you not then know who I am?" the woman whispered, and Sophie could only shake her head.

"Nay," she managed to say. To her amazement the woman seemed to find that amusing.

"Melusine am I called," she declared, looking directly into Sophie's eyes. Sophie knew from the intensity of her expression that the name should have meant something to her and felt a failure because it added naught to her understanding.

"Know you not the tale of the Melusine?" the woman asked in disbelief. Sophie shook her head quickly again.

"My...my mother would not permit the telling of the tale," she confessed heavily, startled when the woman facing her laughed outright.

"Did she not, then?" she mused, an enigmatic smile playing over her lips as she seemed to note every sign of Sophie's discomfort. "Perhaps 'twas a wise choice she made, for the tale is not a pretty one," she added in a low voice that Sophie had to strain to hear, then turned away once more.

"But why am I here?" Sophie demanded in desperation, seeing her chance to have her questions answered rapidly fading. Melusine glanced over her shoulder and smiled knowingly before she shook her head.

"You should know the import of your choice before 'tis made," was all she said, ducking into the hut before Sophie could ask anything else.

Chapter Ten

Gervais, the chatelain's son, met Hugues at the gates to Pontesse and Hugues immediately knew that matters had gone awry in his absence. At least there were some things in this world that a man could rely upon, he thought sourly, refusing to look to the dormant willows trailing their yellow fingers in the icy river.

"How goes it, Gervais?" he asked when they had exchanged greetings, slowing his steed's pace that the man might walk comfortably alongside. Gervais sighed and frowned.

"Well indeed did I think the Michaelmas tithes settled afore you left, but there are several disputes in the village outstanding over the harvest."

"My father did not hold court to arbitrate this?" Hugues demanded in surprise, the court being the one function he could usually rely upon his father to maintain. Gervais looked uncomfortable for a moment, then glanced quickly to Hugues before he spoke.

"The lord is less than well," he confided, and Hugues' heart lurched.

"He is ill again?" he asked with a dry mouth, feeling positively skittish when Gervais nodded.

"He has taken to his bed these last weeks and indeed it seems to me that he has grown quite feeble," Gervais confirmed, and Hugues refrained from shuddering with an effort. His skin prickled at the thought that he would have to go into the sickroom to greet his father, his imagination conjuring up the smell of illness that so terrified him.

And his father, his *warrior* father, was undoubtedly even more frail than the last time he had seen him. Hugues swallowed with difficulty and forced himself to concentrate on practical matters.

"Has news come from Fontaine yet?" he asked, referring to Louise's pending delivery. He disliked the way Gervais grimaced. He dismounted, sparing a nod for the ostler and shooting a glance to Luc to confirm that the boy would tend the beasts. Hugues matched pace with Gervais as they strode toward the portal to the hall, and disliked that the man had held his silence so long.

"Out with it," he urged impatiently.

"Actually, sir, Louise herself has come here from Fontaine," Gervais admitted reluctantly.

"What nonsense is this?" Hugues was shocked, unable to fathom why his sister would do such a thing, and Gervais gave him an apologetic smile.

"It seems she thought the birth might cheer your father," he offered, and Hugues bit back a retort with difficulty. 'Twas the thought of two invalids underfoot that distressed him. Louise's intentions had been good, that much he would concede, but he hoped desperately that he could avoid seeing either of them before they were hale again.

"What trouble has Justine conjured up in my absence?" he asked, hoping that at least one member of his family was healthy, but he was disconcerted once more when Gervais frowned thoughtfully.

"Naught that I know of," he confessed heavily, shooting Hugues a look that spoke volumes. "But too quiet is she, to my thinking."

Hugues rolled his eyes and grinned, clapping the other man on the back as they ducked through the portal. "Good instincts have you, Gervais, and I suspect you speak aright. 'Tis fair enough to suspect that Justine is always making mischief, no less when she acts the innocent."

Gervais laughed. "Aye, sir."

"And your own father? He is well, I hope?" Hugues asked politely. Gervais' enthusiastic nod sent relief surging through him. There, someone was healthy.

"Aye, he insists on terrorizing us all," Gervais confirmed with a grin that Hugues returned, glancing up to find that same gentleman descending upon them.

Gervais' sire bustled with the efficiency of an experienced chatelain, his manner no-nonsense, his bearing as official as a royal seneschal, his energy belying his age. Eduard's hair had been gray as long as Hugues could recall, though now it had lightened to a thick mane of snowy white that made him appear even more dignified.

"Welcome home, sir," he greeted Hugues formally, nodding in curt dismissal to his son, who tactfully slipped away. 'Twas not Gervais' place to hear Eduard's news for the lord's son and heir, and although Hugues appreciated the older man's awareness of social propriety, he hoped the chatelain he chose would tell him the news from below the stairs, as Gervais did.

"I thank you, Eduard," Hugues returned with equal formality. "I trust my father is well?"

"I fear he is not, sir," Eduard returned calmly. "He has requested your presence." Hugues' heart sank that news of his arrival had already reached his sire. Now 'twould be impossible to delay his visit to the solar at all.

"I understand there are several matters in the village to be settled," Hugues commented, earning a censorious glance from the older man.

"Court must be convened by your father's dictate," he countered frostily. Should his father be unwell, 'twas unfitting for the villeins to be left unattended and Hugues saw it as his familial responsibility to tend to Pontesse's estates, be it against formal convention or no.

"Certain am I that were he aware of the oversight he would convene one," Hugues retorted evenly. "Notify the villeins that their complaints will be heard the day after the morrow, if you please."

He turned to the stairs, unwilling to argue the niceties of protocol with the older gentleman lest he lose his temper. Too much was there fraying at the edges of Hugues' composure, Sophie's abandonment doing little to bolster his confidence at having to face his fading sire.

"But your father—" Eduard began, but Hugues spun on his heel to make the matter clear.

"Will arbitrate, of course," Hugues confirmed flatly, hoping that his father could in fact manage to do that. "'Tis simply a matter of arranging the court for his convenience, out of respect for his current condition. Surely we cannot expect the villeins to put their own matters aside because of my father's illness. Please see to the matter this very day, Eduard."

Without giving the man any further time to protest, Hugues strode toward the stairs to the solar. After all, he had best put this obligatory visit behind him.

"Hugues!"

Hugues looked up to see Louise descending upon him and grinned as he picked her up, feigning difficulty in lifting her petite form. She pecked him affectionately on each cheek in turn.

"Fairly bursting with child are you," he teased and her blue eyes danced as she laughed in protest.

"No gallant are you to so boldly state that," she accused happily. Hugues widened his eyes in mock amazement at the size of her belly. In truth, he was pleased to see her as healthy with this pregnancy as she had been with the last, though her swollen womb seemed inordinately large in contrast with her own size.

"'Tis impossible not to comment when you are so round," he jested, sparing a pat to his sister's stomach. "Well it seems to me that this one is reluctant to show his face. Ten months is it now that you have kept him hidden away?"

Louise looked as though she would make some clever retort, but suddenly her face crumpled and Hugues bent over her with alarm.

"What is it?" he demanded. Louise did not answer immediately, but simply breathed quickly several times, then straightened carefully and smiled weakly up at him.

"'Tis naught as yet," she concluded bravely, but Hugues saw the brief flicker of fear in her eyes.

"Jean is here?" he asked, and was dismayed when Louise shook her head.

"Matters he had to attend at Fontaine." She laid one hand on Hugues's chest when he frowned. "Look not so stern, Hugues," she chided. "Almost a month have I been here and the world cannot stop for a child."

"Michel is here?"

"Aye, he plays with Papa in the solar," Louise confirmed with a nod. Her eyes glazed and she gripped Hugues' arm once more.

"Eduard!" he shouted over his shoulder. "Send a runner to Fontaine to fetch Jean. The babe is coming!"

"Not yet, Hugues. Jean will come in a panic," Louise scolded. "And the babe will surely take its time."

"You will need him afore the babe arrives," Hugues retorted firmly, drawing a small smile of concession from his sister.

"Aye, better 'tis not to count on the likes of you in a sickroom," she teased and Hugues chuckled despite himself. "'Tis but small consolation that you think less of yourself for being ill than anyone else does."

"Enough of your badgering or you will have the babe here in the hall." His gruff words were rewarded by the tinkle of Louise's laughter.

"Oh, Hugues, 'twill be days afore the child arrives and poor tempered will I be if I must pass all of it alone in the solar," she protested, but her argument provoked little change in her brother's resolve.

"Jean will be here soon enough and my head will he have if you are not abed and resting."

Louise pursed her lips in dissatisfaction, but Hugues ushered her back toward the stairs. When she inhaled sharply on the third step, he took but one look to her face before sweeping her up easily and carrying her up the remaining stairs.

"Well it seems that I am not so heavy after all," she quipped and Hugues shook his head with amusement.

"In your old chambers are you?" he asked, continuing down the hall at Louise's nod.

"Such a romantic you have become," she teased now. At her jest, Hugues was dismayed to feel his neck heating. "Has our Hugues lost finally his heart?" she whispered mischievously when they reached the doorway to the chamber, but Hugues refused to give her any encouragement.

"Nay," he responded flatly, setting her on her feet and closing his eyes against the smell that carried to his nostrils from his father's chamber at the other end of the hall.

'Twas the poultice that Eduard had brought Hugues' sire for years beyond recall whenever he had been feeling less than himself. The distinctive combination of herbs triggered Hugues' instinctive response to illness now as surely as the sight of an invalid.

He had to go in there, he thought, gritting his teeth as he glared at the closed door.

"Poor Hugues," Louise whispered sympathetically beside him and he barely noted the gentle brush of her fingertips across his brow. "What worse foe could you face than a solar full of invalids?"

Fearing suddenly that he had offended her, Hugues turned to his sister sheepishly. "Glad I am that you are here," he protested, certain that their father had taken pleasure in her presence, for who could not delight in Louise's lightheartedness? She smiled again, and laid a hand upon his arm.

"I understand, Hugues. Always has it been difficult for you to see those you love fall ill," she murmured, her fingers pressing against his arm. "But go now to Papa while you can yet speak with him," she advised, and Hugues saw the truth he had been avoiding reflected in her clear eyes.

"'Tis bad?" he asked hoarsely and Louise sighed.

"'Twill be passed soon enough, I fear," she confirmed softly.

Hugues squeezed her fingers in turn, then squared his shoulders and strode toward the closed door. He hesitated but an instant on the threshold, his heart pounding in his ears, an encouraging smile from Louise setting his knuckles to tap on the wood before he knew what he was about. An answering call came from within and there was naught to do but step inside to bid his father farewell.

The Lord de Pontesse was on his hands and knees, playing with his grandson.

The sight so stunned Hugues that he froze in the doorway, momentarily wondering whether he had returned to the wrong château. Michel leaped onto the old man's back with undisguised delight and Hugues' eyes widened in alarm.

The two-year-old granted Hugues a sunny smile and dug his heels into his grandfather's ribs with all the might he could muster. Hugues grunted in sympathy when his father's eyes widened momentarily, then the older man lifted his chin and fairly glared at his only son.

"Have you forgotten to close the door or has that faithless beast of yours finally kicked you in the head?" he demanded by way of greeting. Hugues felt his color rise as he quickly closed the door. "Know you not how easily a child can catch a chill in these draughty halls?"

"My apologies, Father," he muttered, struggling to understand what Louise had been talking about as he stood awkwardly by the door. If anything, his father seemed healthier, and decidedly more surly, than before his departure. Indeed, Hugues could not recall when he had last seen the man out of bed, let alone cavorting on the floor.

"Dismount, chevalier," the older man instructed the boy, but Michel pouted.

"But—" he protested, and the lord's eyes flashed with anger.

"Dismount, I bade you," he snapped. "Well enough a knight should know to obey his lord," he added frostily.

Michel did as he was told with less than his usual good nature, that bottom lip trembling as he gained his footing and eyed his grandfather warily. The glare the older man granted the boy as he struggled to his knees explained all to Hugues. The color that tinged his sire's ears when he did not, or could not, rise farther was more than eloquent.

His father had not wanted to be abed when Hugues arrived.

"Luc was hoping for your help with the horses," Hugues contributed in an effort to cheer his confused nephew, watching Michel's face light up with the promise of going to the stables.

"Argent likes me," he confided to Hugues as he trotted happily toward him. Hugues scooped the boy up and swung him around with a hoot of greeting, coaxing that smile back to the boy's face.

"Argent is not here," he felt obligated to explain, feeling his father's eyes upon him. Michel met his gaze with a frown.

"Why not?" he demanded. The perfectly natural question left Hugues momentarily uncertain of what to say. How to explain to a child that the horse was dead? What had Jean told him of such matters? Or what did Jean intend to tell him?

"I ride him no longer," Hugues said simply, relieved when the explanation seemed to satisfy the boy, then braced Michel's weight on his hip as his tone became confidential.

"But another steed have I now, and he has sore need of a name. Mayhap you and Luc could think of a good one together," he suggested and Michel squirmed in anticipation. Hugues put him down and the child scampered out into the hall as fast as his little feet could carry him.

"Eduard! Gervais!" Hugues called out after the boy, following him to the top of the stairs. "Ensure that Luc and the ostler know Michel is underfoot!" To his relief Gervais appeared at the bottom of the stairs to take the boy's hand with a wink and Hugues turned back to confront his father, still on his knees on the floor.

"Can you not see that I require your assistance?" the old man demanded testily.

Hugues declined to comment on the wisdom of his father's frivolity and crossed the room quickly to extend a hand. His father's grip was still strong, but the older man's fingers felt as though they grasped at him and Hugues struggled not to recoil. 'Twas his father clutching at his shoulder, not some stranger, though 'twas only with difficulty that he could reconcile this weakened figure with the bear of a warrior his sire had been.

"Have we no help left in this place?" the lord grumbled impatiently while Hugues virtually carried him back to the bed. "Cursed cold 'tis in this room and not a flicker of a blaze to be found. And where is Eduard? Another poultice do I need, so chilled am I."

Hugues assisted his complaining father into bed and pulled the bed linens up, struggling not to notice the older man's bony knees or the pallor of his skin. "'Tis good to see you well, Father," he commented, and the old man shot him a sharp look.

"Ha!" he snorted. "Not dead yet am I, is what you mean. Is that not the only reason you return on occasion? To confirm the status of your inheritance?"

"Well enough do you know that that is not the reason," Hugues retorted, forcing himself to remain calm in the face of these familiar accusations.

"I shall leave the estate to another," the older man claimed wildly, shaking a thin finger in his son's face. "To the girls shall I leave it and naught will you be able to say about it."

"Should you not continue to manage Pontesse, 'twill scarcely be of worth to anyone," Hugues responded to the customary charge.

"Oho. So you, a mere pup of thirty summers, now know better than I how to run an estate," he challenged, but Hugues refused to rise to the bait.

"A good teacher had I once," he countered, holding his father's stubborn gaze, "who counseled me not to let a week slip past without a court for the villeins."

His father's nostrils flared but he could hardly take offense at the impertinence, for well enough he knew that he alone had taught Hugues of business matters.

"Fully did I intend to call one this week," he answered hotly, "should the villeins bring their cases here to be heard."

"'Twas exactly thus I told Eduard," Hugues confirmed. His words brought the old man bolt upright in bed.

"Not dead yet am I!" he shouted with remarkable tenacity. Hugues lost his temper at the promise of those tired accusations coming to the fore once more.

"Nay, you are not," he countered sharply, jabbing one finger through the air at his sire. "But neither are you alive. How many years have you lain up here, afraid to choose your path?"

"Afraid?" The Lord de Pontesse imperiously drew himself up still taller. "You dare to call me a coward?"

"Aye, a coward you have become," Hugues argued, knowing even as the words left his lips that he would regret them later, but he was powerless to check their flow. "The man who knighted me would have chosen his way—life or death and naught in between. How can you lie here, day after day, the smell of this swill of Eduard's filling your nose while you lie abed and snarl at all who surround you?"

"Not dead yet am I," his father insisted and Hugues looked him right in the eye.

"I do not contest your claim," he stated. "I merely ask whether you are yet living."

The lord's mouth opened and Hugues thought for a brief instant that he might confess something, but then he snapped it shut, his eyes flashing as he pointed emphatically to the door.

"Get out!" he cried. "You will not have the satisfaction of seeing me take an easy death."

"Fine!" Hugues shouted back. "Fight for your life! I would applaud your efforts. 'Tis your peaceful vigil in anticipation of death that I cannot countenance, for surely Death has kept you waiting long enough to lose your patience!''

With that Hugues left his father's chamber, as he had so many times before, slamming the door in his wake. Louise watched him sadly from the end of the hall, but he had no interest in her recriminations, nor those of the other members of the household who watched his departure in wary silence.

Certain to find solace among simpler creatures, he stomped in the direction of the stables, wishing that he had not had the misfortune to lose both his heart and Argent on one trip.

It snowed the first day that Sophie flew.

Well it seemed that she had been grinding roots to powder forever, struggling to distinguish each plant from the other by scent alone, visualizing the usefulness of each. Always did Melusine ask the questions, never did she supply Sophie with a straight answer, simply allusions to ruling planets and signs and gods long departed from this domain.

Sophie was bone tired from the long hours of labor, the exhaustion of constantly straining for the correct response and the struggle to remember what Melusine did tell her. Knowing that Hugues could not be more than a fortnight gone did little to bolster her resolve, for it seemed the time had passed with agonizing slowness.

If indeed the rest of her life passed at this pace, she would have time aplenty to regret being without him.

The snow lightened Sophie's heart when she discovered it falling thickly outside the cabin that morning, the very way it fluttered to the earth making her want to laugh aloud and dance. She flung her arms wide when she carried the bucket to the stream and spun around like a carefree child, leaning back to catch a snowflake on her tongue. At the sudden feeling that she was being watched, she cast a guilty glance over her shoulder and scampered to the stream, hastening back with the full bucket in anticipation of another day of work.

To her surprise Melusine had kindled a fire in the middle of the hut on the earthen floor, the smoke meandering up to find the hole in the roof that served as a chimney. The bulk of the smoke stayed within the hut, but Sophie blinked against it, appreciating the warmth it cast at the very least.

"'Tis said that even the Christians' god rested after but six days," Melusine commented with apparent idleness, her strangely pale gaze locking with Sophie's across the room. "Perhaps this is as good a day as any to take our leisure."

"What shall we do?" Sophie asked quietly. The idea of spending an entire day enduring Melusine's assessing regard was enough to make her want to work instead, despite the ache in her shoulders.

"We shall talk." A coy smile played over Melusine's lips. She arched one brow and Sophie swallowed carefully. "Surely you have questions?"

"Aye," Sophie confirmed, her heart beating faster with the promise of learning something new. "Many indeed have I."

Melusine nodded slowly. "I will answer but one," she said flatly, setting Sophie's mind racing as she tried to decide which one to ask.

Why was she here? Why was Melusine teaching her? What was her choice? And curiously, more questions about the future and distant events popped into her mind, as though she expected Melusine to read doings beyond her sphere. Where was Hugues? How was he? Would she be with him again?

To Sophie's surprise the question that fell from her lips was none of these and one on which she regretted wasting her opportunity as soon as she heard her own words.

"What is the tale of the Melusine?" she asked. Something flashed in Melusine's eyes before she smoothly gestured for Sophie to take a seat.

"Perhaps there is more to you than meets the eye," she mused, but Sophie barely noted the words before the older woman drew herself up. Mayhap 'twas but a trick of the dim light and smoke, but she seemed to change subtly, the years dropping from her visage, an intensity emanating from her that held Sophie in thrall.

"Once upon a time," she began as a mischievous smile made a fleeting dance across her lips, "a nobleman was hunting in the woods and became lost. His name is not of import, but he was young, fair of face and tall, a veritable prince among his peers.

"'Twas May Eve and the hunt was a celebration of a sort traditional on his family's lands, a markedly practical one that would not only assert the bounty of the land but also provide for the board on the May Day feast. Only natural then 'twas for the nobleman to give chase to a particularly large hind that darted across his path, though the beast led a merry chase deeper and deeper into the woods. When the hind finally lay dead at his feet, he realized that he stood absolutely alone in the woods. Not a whisper carried to his ears to hint at the location of his companions."

Melusine took a sip of water and threw a handful of dry plants onto the fire. The smoke immediately smelled slightly sweeter and a pleasant sense of well-being flowed through Sophie as she leaned back against the wall.

"As I said, he was young and strong and not to be distressed by such an occurrence. Confident of his own ability to find his way home alone, he collected his kill and rode back in the direction he believed he had come. He rode and rode and rode, and still there was no sign of his companions, not a sound in the woods to betray the presence of another soul. He sensed the darkness falling about him and felt a flicker of dread, for the trees seemed to grow denser, not thinner, and this forest had a reputation for being bewitched.

"Not a man to entertain such childish fancies, he resolved to spend the night in the woods, for surely his path would be more clear on the morrow. He heard a stream and followed the sound, realizing as he knelt on the bank to drink that there was another sound behind the trickle of the water. Singing 'twas, he realized in wonder, and filled with the promise of finding another in these woods, he rushed toward the sound, astonished when he burst into a glade and discovered a woman at her bath.

"He was so surprised at his find that he could but gape in wonder, for no reason could he see for this woman to be bathing so deep in the woods. As he stood stunned on the bank, he noted her beauty, realizing at the same time that she was unaware of his presence. Never had he been one to spy, but well it seemed he could not help himself and he crept back beneath the shadows of the trees to covertly watch her.

"Who knows what went through his mind or his heart that night as he watched the young woman bathe? It seemed that he could not look away. Indeed, it seemed that her song crept through his ears to weave a snare around his heart and he could think of naught but touching her. When the woman turned in his direction as though she had heard his very thoughts, he had not even the reason left to be surprised that she knew he was there. He had not the will to deny his urges when she waded out of the water directly toward him.''

Another handful of herbs was cast on the fire and Sophie had a sense that things around her were not as they seemed. Motion there was in the most mundane items. The legs of the table curled into lion's feet before her eyes, the three-legged stool sidled up closer to the fire, the walls themselves curved in to surround them like a great womb.

She cast a glance to Melusine to find her eyes unnaturally bright and glittering, the dark hair flowing loose over her shoulders writhing with a life of its own. Curious 'twas but none of this repulsed Sophie, or perhaps she had not the will to stir herself to such response. She simply sat and watched the dance around her with fascination.

''They loved that night on the forest floor,'' Melusine continued softly, ''and the dawn came too soon for both. The nobleman fell asleep and when he awoke he could feel the heat of the midday sun on the canopy of the trees but of his lover there was no sign. He sought her all of that day, but found her not, finding himself instead on the edge of the woods not far from his family château when the sun touched the horizon. With regret he turned his back on the woods and went home, where he was greeted with delight, the hind he had killed roasted for the meal that very night.''

Melusine fell silent and Sophie frowned into the shadows. ''Tis all?'' she demanded in surprise and the older woman shot her a sharp look.

"Oh, nay," she confided. "The tale has but just begun." She took another draught of water and licked her lips slowly before she continued. "Two new moons had come and gone when a stranger presented herself at the portal of the nobleman's family estate. The young nobleman's father had passed in the interim and now the nobleman stood as lord of all his family's domains, the weight of his responsibilities hanging heavy on his brow.

"'Twas the woman from the woods who stood before him, and for a long moment it seemed this fine young man might deny her tale, but she curved her hand about the roundness of her stomach when he hesitated. He understood the import of her move, according to those who were in attendance, for he accepted her immediately afterward, announcing to all that she would be his bride, that the babe she bore would be his heir.

"Her name she gave as Melusine and naught else would she say of her heritage. The people in the nobleman's home assumed that she was of common blood and ashamed to admit her roots before the nobleman. By her own admission she had lived in the forest for years.

"No denying was there that he was besotted with her, though, and those surrounding him took reassurance in the strength of the love that seemed between the two. After two different soothsayers had pronounced the child to be his, people were inclined to be indulgent over his choice. After all, he was a handsome young man who charmed all who met him and lord of his own manor. Why should he not have his will?

"The night after their nuptials he came to his new wife, summoning a bath for her in their chambers in recollection of that previous night, but to his astonishment and dismay she forbade him to stay. Never again could he watch her bathe, she decreed. This alone was her demand from the match.

"The nobleman was not pleased by this condition, for he had fond memories of their first night together and savored the recollection of Melusine's sleek nudity, but she was adamant. When he persisted, she declared flatly that she would leave if ever he dared to watch. Convinced that she would disappear with his child and heir just when he had made her his own, the nobleman reluctantly agreed.

"Well it seemed to the nobleman that his Melusine's beauty increased tenfold every day that she bore his child, and tales of his good fortune spread far and wide. Always was his hall filled with guests, and the nobleman suspected that many created business to discuss with him that they might gaze upon the perfection of his bride. In his own eyes she was unsurpassed in elegance and grace, and as time slipped by he came to long for that one sight she denied him."

Once again the older woman paused to cast herbs on the blaze that had died down to glowing coals and Sophie watched transfixed as the fire gobbled up the dry stalks. The smoke that curled from them seem blue to her and filled with fanciful shapes—faces and feathers and curious beasts.

"Melusine was ripe with child when the nobleman finally broke his word. He hid himself behind the draperies surrounding their bed early one evening, convinced that his wife had not detected his presence when she had the tub filled. When the servants had left, she carefully barred the door and peeled off her clothing leisurely. The nobleman ached with desire when she dipped one toe gracefully into the water to test its temperature.

"She supported the weight of her womb with one hand, the candlelight playing lovingly over her soft curves, and he wondered how he would control himself to wait, for well he knew that he could not risk betraying his presence. His wife stepped fully into the water and raised the spare bucket high, laughing to herself in delight when the water splashed over her nudity.

"'Twas then that he saw the sight that would haunt him for the rest of his days."

The older woman paused, and despite the unusual languor stealing through her, Sophie found herself leaning forward in anticipation.

"What did he see?" she asked, seeing the gleam of Melusine's eyes in the shadows.

"He saw a tail," she said softly and with great relish. "A great, thick, serpentine tail that coiled in the water and filled the tub where his wife's legs should have been, a tail with scales of green and yellow."

Sophie shuddered in horror and the other woman leaned closer to her. "Aye, well you can picture his response. He revealed himself in that moment, I am afraid, screaming accusations at his wife of witchcraft while she called him all manner of names suited for those who break their word.

"Their arguing brought a barrage of servants, but none could enter because of the locked door. When the lord and his lady finally opened the door to confront the assembly, naught seemed amiss to any other eyes. Except, of course, that the lord declared he was casting out his wife.

"All were scandalized by this turn of events, for they could not imagine what fault the lord might have found with his lovely, pregnant wife and he refused to speak of it. Naught else did Melusine say before she took her departure and naught did she take with her but that which she had brought herself. Great sympathy was there for her when she walked out of that château with her chin held high, and though many offered to help her, she disappeared into the woods and never was heard from again."

A silence filled the hut much as the curling tendrils of smoke did and Sophie frowned.

"What about the child?" she demanded. Melusine only shrugged her shoulders.

"Many different tales are there of that one's fate," she said with a frown of her own. "Some say that the babe born was a serpent in truth, others that the lord was forced to kill his own spawn. Some insist that the Melusine lives still in the woods with her child and together they torment the lives of men. Others insist that she made her way to the sea with the babe and back to her rightful home beneath the waves. Still others maintain that her spawn walk among us, but one flaw within them revealing the taint of their heritage." The fire crackled silently for a moment until Melusine softly sighed.

"'Twas long ago and far away and no one can truly know the way it went."

This last it seemed to Sophie was added with a measure of regret, but she had not the opportunity to question the older woman before she abruptly stood. Sophie watched numbly as Melusine retrieved some herbs from the bundles tied in the low rafters, a crock of fat, a mortar and pestle. The older woman set the lot on the floor before Sophie, holding out a bunch of dried plant as was her wont.

"Name it," she commanded with typical curtness. Sophie recoiled from the foul smell of the dry bundle stuffed beneath her nose.

"I know it not."

"But you should," Melusine snapped. "Thorn apple 'tis, its flowers large and fluted when they open at night, its fruit spiked. Venus rules it, though its beautiful bloom is one of deceitful charm, for 'tis a killing plant."

Melusine broke a chunk off the dry root, dropped it into the mortar and handed the stone bowl to Sophie. "Grind it fine," she dictated, taking an experimental sniff of the root left in her hand. "Strong this one is, for 'twas harvested in the seventh moon."

Sophie nodded, trying to commit this information to memory despite the muddled state of her mind. Melusine pulled the finer roots from another thick root, more twisted in shape than the last, and held it out to Sophie in the palm of her hand.

"Name it," she demanded. The younger woman tentatively sniffed the tuber, rubbing her fingers against it.

"I cannot," Sophie admitted reluctantly, but Melusine leaned closer.

"Then feel it," she ordered. "And tell me something of it."

Sophie closed her eyes and sniffed the root again. The image that rose to her mind's eye was startlingly clear and she did not think upon it before she spoke. "White peaks I see," she said, "with dark caverns beneath them." She opened her eyes, saw Melusine's satisfied smile and shook her head in confusion.

"Good Sight have you," the older woman commented and Sophie felt a surge of pride at the first compliment she had been granted. "Monkshood 'tis called, or wolfsbane by some, and you see aright, for it comes from the high hills where 'tis said that never the snow does melt. By Saturn 'tis ruled and what does that tell you?"

"That it summons the darkness if used with a heavy hand," Sophie responded promptly. She was gratified when Melusine nodded.

"Aye, a root of power, of mysteries, of deadliness and remorse. Handle it with respect," she instructed, breaking off a segment of the root and adding it to Sophie's mortar. "And this?" She offered a trio of wizened berries, each the width of her finger.

"Another child of Saturn?" Sophie guessed and Melusine nodded curtly.

"Aye, and one always to be used in threes, for 'tis the mark of Atropos, who used it thus to cut the thread of life. Harvest it at first light when its strength is highest."

Sophie frowned at the reference, but Melusine had already tossed the berries into the bowl and picked up a handful of dried leaves. She crushed them beneath Sophie's nose, watching expectantly all the while, and Sophie immediately recognized the scent.

"'Tis what you have been throwing on the flames," she said. Melusine nodded again.

"Yet another of Saturn's spawn," she confirmed, taking a sniff of the leaves herself. "Henbane, Jupiter's Bean, conjures the dead, it does, and their presence strengthens the Sight."

Sophie ground the leaves into the pungent powder mixed beneath her pestle, repeating Melusine's words in her mind that she might recall them later. The older woman jabbed a finger into the compound and rubbed the result experimentally through her fingers to check that it was ground finely. She nodded, adding a handful of animal fat into the bowl, and mixed it together with her hands.

"Shed your clothes," she bade Sophie in a tone that brooked no argument, a curious light in her eyes when she glanced up. "And I shall teach you to fly."

Sophie hesitated, but when Melusine stood and shed her own, she followed suit, the sweet smoke that filled her nostrils seeming to dispel her reservations. Melusine unbraided Sophie's hair, spreading it over her shoulders with something that could have been affection, then lifted the bowl as if in offering.

"Spread it on your skin," she whispered, those eyes shining with eerie brightness. "And may Dame Fortune guide your path."

Sophie paused for a moment, then dipped her fingers into the warmth of the unguent and spread it over her stomach and breasts as Melusine indicated, then over her arms and down her thighs. As soon as the concoction touched her skin she felt her flesh heat in response and it reddened angrily beneath her very gaze. The tingle penetrated her through and through, her ears ringing when she leaned to smooth the grease down her legs.

"The soles of your feet," Melusine directed, and it seemed her voice came from leagues away. Sophie lifted one foot unsteadily and bent to smooth the salve there, but suddenly the floor dropped away and she seemed to tumble helplessly forward, the darkness of the earth swallowing her whole before abruptly parting to reveal the star-spangled night sky.

Chapter Eleven

Sophie felt the tingle of the winter wind on her skin and smiled at the sensation, spreading her arms wide and arching high, delighting in the clarity of vision that had been granted her. Like a dream it was, this flying of Melusine's, but yet more vivid, and Sophie wondered at the marvel of how thoroughly her mind deceived her. Far below she saw the tops of the trees, the tiny speck of the hut surrounded by the snowy blanket of the clearing and she laughed aloud in delight as she spun effortlessly in midair.

Sophie looked down again and a fine thread caught the light, running like a quicksilver river between her navel and seemingly right through the roof of the hut far below. She flew farther and the silver ribbon did not restrict her or grow taut, magically stretching to cover the extra distance. She did not dare to touch it, could not even feel it coming from her belly, but its very presence was curiously reassuring and Sophie turned her face back to the stars with a lightened heart.

Sophie thought suddenly of Hugues and the wind rushed past her ears with frightening intensity that made her curl up defensively. She crossed her arms protectively across her bare chest, shivering in the chill of the wind, before she found herself abruptly within a crowded room.

The transition was alarming in its suddenness and Sophie blinked, wondering at such a convoluted dream. Truly the dead were aiding her Sight, for this seemed as clear as real life. Women gathered around a draped bed, the concern etched on their features making them oblivious to her presence, and Sophie crept closer, curious as to what was going on.

A man on the far side of the room looked up suddenly and Sophie's heart stopped when she recognized Hugues looking directly at her. A thoughtful frown briefly darkened his brow before he shook his head and turned his attention back to the bed. Why had she been brought to him again? Because she had but willed it? Or because there was yet something unfinished between them?

Before Sophie could reflect upon this or the reason for his frown, a woman screamed in agony and the assembly pressed closer to the bed, the women murmuring soothing sounds.

"Push not so hard, for the child will come in its own time," a stocky older woman advised as she purposefully rolled up her sleeves. Sophie easily identified her as a midwife and liked not the scowl that darkened her brow.

Clearly 'twas a birthing, but why were there men in the chamber?

The woman in labor screamed again and the fear hit Sophie as surely as if she had walked into a wall. The woman was afraid, to be sure, but 'twas another who felt with such intensity and drew Sophie ever closer.

A girl, she thought, feeling a oneness with the unborn babe that astonished her. An exhausted girl, but one who wanted fiercely to see the light, one who was frustrated by the failure of her own infant form to meet the demands of what was surely a trying birth.

Compassion overwhelmed Sophie and she rose above the group of women without taking the time to think about how to accomplish it. A tawny-haired woman writhed on the linens below and Sophie noted the fear and helplessness etched on the faces of those who surrounded her. She grimaced when her womb contracted and Sophie felt the babe's panic grow.

Turned 'twas and its time to right itself was quickly passing. Sophie saw the child struggle to turn as clearly as if she were in the midst of the ordeal with it. She closed her eyes and felt the relentless crush of the woman's womb push it onward as though it surrounded her own body. 'Twould die thus, Sophie realized, tasting the babe's fear at that realization, and before she knew what was happening she was directly above the straining woman.

The child was too tired to manage the turn herself. She had been fighting long and was in dire need of assistance. Sophie looked expectantly to the midwife, alarmed to find indecision etched on those heavy features.

"Turn the babe!" she cried in her mind, but the woman paid no heed to her words.

An invisible barrier there was between Sophie and this scene and she cursed her newfound knowledge that 'twas no more than a vision. How could she help this child if she was powerless to intervene? Surely there could be no reason to be granted a vision of an unnecessary death. She was already a healer and understood well the usefulness of her knowledge.

Would that this midwife could know what to do.

The woman in the bed gasped and a flood of crimson stained the linens. The smell of the blood assaulted Sophie's nostrils and she marveled anew at the detail of the dream.

But the babe was tiring, filling Sophie with an urgent desire to assist that could not be denied. She eased closer to the midwife, uncertain how to compel the woman to save the child. The woman moved aside, making a slight space for Sophie, evidently without realizing what she had done, and the unconscious gesture gave Sophie new hope.

"Turn the child," she whispered urgently into the woman's ear, bending her will upon her. The midwife lifted one worn hand tentatively in the direction of the laboring woman, as though she knew not what she did, and Sophie's excitement rose.

The heavy hand dropped in indecision even as Sophie knew the child rolled one shoulder desperately within the confining womb. Time was sliding away and soon 'twould be too late to help this one who fought so valiantly. Sophie knew she could not let the matter be and she put her lips directly to the midwife's ear.

"Turn the child," she commanded but the midwife made no immediate response. Desperate to help, Sophie let her voice rise to a shout that she might be perceived. "Slide your hand into the darkness and turn the child. Grasp anything you can! Do it now or the babe will die!"

The midwife blinked once, her face blank as she unthinkingly plunged her hand into the woman's wet heat. The waiting women watched her gesture with alarm, and the laboring woman gasped anew at the intrusion. Sophie was aware of naught but the child's jubilation when those worn fingers closed resolutely around her shoulder.

She knew the instant the babe was turned and instinctively pressed closer to the bed that she might have an early glimpse of this one she had aided. Was this child particularly important? Had Sophie been specifically summoned to attend her in her time of need? The woman pushed with Herculean effort and the babe unexpectedly burst forth into the world, her tiny fingers locked around the midwife's thumb.

The surrounding women jostled each other in their desire to see, but Sophie heard neither their cries of delight nor the mother's grateful sobs, all her attention focused on the infant before her. The midwife wiped the mucus quickly from the infant's nostrils and Sophie smiled when the baby girl gave a bellow fit to wake the dead.

A will of such a magnitude could only be destined to survive, Sophie thought admiringly, grateful she had had the opportunity to assist this one's arrival, if only in some ethereal world of visions. What purpose had this one in the world that her arrival must be so ensured?

Or was this but a premonition of something that would come to pass?

Mayhap 'twas merely a vision of the good she could do once she had mastered Melusine's healing arts, Sophie reasoned, and not a specific incident, present or future, at all. Sophie knew not and she glanced over the assembly, seeking some indication of how to interpret the scene, not knowing what to think when her gaze fell again on a familiar figure.

Why was Hugues here?

Was this the woman who was or would be his wife?

That thought was sobering and Sophie turned away from its implications, looking to the babe as she was washed. Who was this child? Was her arrival of particular import to Sophie? Were their paths destined to cross again?

"Such debts are not easily repaid," Melusine remarked dryly in Sophie's inner ear, almost as if Sophie's thoughts had summoned her presence.

"Praise be to God," Hugues said with wholehearted relief and Sophie's chin snapped up at the sound of his voice.

Again his gaze traveled right through her and she glanced about her, marveling at the unfolding events, even though she realized that none detected her presence here. Sophie drifted toward the ceiling as she took this in, watching almost absently while Hugues shook hands heartily with a dark-haired man who looked exhausted enough to have delivered the child himself.

Look to me, Hugues, Sophie demanded in her mind. Make this clear to me.

He glanced quickly in her direction and her heart leaped that he had heard her, before he checked the gesture to turn back to the other man as though naught had occurred. Sophie's heart sank and she fought against the inevitable thought that followed.

Had she concluded aright that they were no longer meant for each other? She thought of Melusine's tale of her namesake and wondered if she, too, was destined to live out her days alone. That disturbed her deeply, but still Sophie could not dispel the notion that 'twas critical for Hugues to acknowledge her this night.

But he had not. Whether he could not or simply would not she did not care to know. Blinking back her tears, Sophie deliberately turned her back on the out-breaking celebrations and stretched for the stars once more.

Sophie awoke naked on the hard floor of the hut with her surcoat tossed over her, her muscles cramped, her skin still greasy and irritated from the salve. She rolled over with an effort, to find the fire long since burned out, the morning sun filling the crack between the door and its frame.

How much time had passed?

Her tongue was thick and dry, her vision blurred and a pounding took up residence between her ears when she forced herself to sit up. Sophie drew the softness of the squirrel pelt lining tighter about her and noticed Melusine watching her silently from the far side of the cabin, her eyes glittering in the shadows like pale gemstones.

"You alone must choose," was all she said, her voice deeper than usual. Before Sophie could request an explanation, the older woman rose and slipped outside with a light step, leaving Sophie to sort the tangle of her thoughts in solitude.

"Rather glum you are looking for a new godfather," Jean commented as he drew alongside Hugues. The unexpectedness of the other man's presence made Hugues start as he abandoned his thoughts.

"'Tis but the weather," he said by way of excuse. Hugues distrusted Jean's smug grunt in response as he braced his hands on the parapet. The sharp sidelong glance Hugues caught did little to ease his discomfort that Jean had seen through him, but the other man turned back to his perusal of the ripening countryside.

The hills of Pontesse were turning verdant again as the soft spring rain ceaselessly fell. Hugues realized as he stood alongside his brother-in-law that his head and shoulders were soaked, but the air was so warm with springlike promise that he had scarce noticed it.

Five months it had been since he had left her there in the woods. Five months and every moment of it an eternity. To Gascogne and back Hugues had been once more on the Queen Regent's mission and then to Paris again but all for naught, as the townspeople had cast their lot with the Normans. The tax collector Hugues had hoped for had not shown his face until after the allegiance was pledged, which showed the run of his luck as well as anything else, he concluded wryly. And to cap the matter, Jean would have no more cheap Gascon wine to fill his cellars.

"At least the old man survived the winter," Jean remarked idly as if he had followed Hugues' own thoughts, and Hugues nodded in turn.

"Aye," he agreed. "'Tis Justine alone who can cheer him."

Jean chuckled under his breath. "True enough, and one can only wonder at how much time she has spent in his company."

"She wants something, likely as not," Hugues commented, knowing his sister as well as any.

"Likely she is to get it, the way she has been charming him," Jean contributed dryly.

"Aye. Never could he deny her anything." The two men's eyes met in mutual understanding. Something flashed in Jean's eyes and Hugues dreaded his next words before they even fell.

"What of your Sophie, Hugues?" he demanded quietly. Hugues felt the color rise on his neck.

"I know naught of her," he responded grimly, wishing Jean would look to the countryside once more instead of watching him so carefully.

"Well I thought that you were destined for each other," Jean remarked. At that, Hugues could not stop his own snort of derision.

"As did I," he retorted, flinging one hand wide with frustration, and he turned to face the other knight. "Yet she stood before me in the woods and told me that her destiny no longer lay with me."

"I did not think destiny so readily swayed," Jean commented. The sentiment was so close to his own thoughts that Hugues could but snort again.

"Nor did I," he muttered, folding his arms atop the parapet and leaning on them with dissatisfaction. "Nor did I."

The silence between them was no more easy than the previous one had been and Hugues wished Jean would disappear so he could give full vent to his frustration. Talking of Sophie simply gave new life to his annoyance with her and showed more strongly how illogical her choice had been.

How could she give herself to him with such abandon then part ways with him the next morning? He had pleasured her, he had made sure of that, and her behavior was completely inexplicable in light of that.

"Perhaps she thought she had something to do before your destiny to be together could be fulfilled," Jean mused, and Hugues shot him a wry glance.

"The woman does not think," he growled. "She but *feels*."

Jean grinned and Hugues looked away in annoyance. "Perhaps, then, she *felt* there was a hurdle to be leaped first."

"Perhaps she is truly mad," Hugues retorted sharply. He was not in the least pleased when Jean laughed outright.

"Nay, Hugues," he said when he sobered. "No madwoman could capture a clear-thinking man's heart so surely."

Hugues' head shot up and he looked his brother-in-law right in the eye. "What madness is this?" he demanded. "No heart of mine has been captured."

"Nay?" Jean inquired archly, and Hugues' ire rose still further at his presumption. "Why then do you stand in the rain like a lovesick squire? Five moons have passed since your return and not yet have I seen you smile."

"My responsibilities wear heavy," Hugues answered defensively, hearing the ineptness of his excuse even as he voiced it. Jean merely arched one dark brow at the lack of conviction in his tone and Hugues sighed reluctantly in concession.

"I could not believe she would cast me aside," he admitted, shaking his head as he gazed unseeingly out over the lands that would one day be his to govern. "So surprised was I that I simply rode away as she bade me and now oftentimes I wonder..."

"Wonder what?" Jean prompted, his eyes bright with curiosity.

"I wonder if she was but testing me," Hugues concluded quietly, glancing up to find his brother-in-law's thoughtful regard upon him. He shrugged and pushed away from the parapet in annoyance, shoving one hand through his damp curls. "But then, who can even speculate at the path a woman's thoughts might follow?"

"Well it seems to me that it might be worth finding the answer to that," Jean mused thoughtfully. It took but a moment for Hugues to nod in agreement.

"Aye," he agreed and even as he spoke the idea gained appeal in his mind. "Aye, 'twould be good at least to know."

"Now that Easter has passed, we will return home. Ride with us to Fontaine, Hugues," Jean urged and Hugues found himself drawn to the idea.

"Let us ride out this week," he concurred. His resolution was growing with each passing moment. Jean's grin flashed for an instant before he smothered it.

"Come out of the rain," he invited. Hugues grinned in turn, feeling unexpectedly optimistic about this decision.

Mayhap Jean was right and Sophie needed to resolve something with the woman in the woods before they could be together. Mayhap she had been simply testing him and he should never have left her. Mayhap she was mad. Hugues was intrigued to realize that it mattered not. Simply the thought of seeing her again lightened his heart more than it had been since his return home.

Dusk was falling when Sophie finished tying the tender spring herbs she had harvested that morning into bundles and hanging them from the ceiling of the hut to dry. She stretched, recited the litany of their names and ruling planets once more as she scanned her handiwork and absently acknowledged the exhaustion that had become such an integral part of her days here. She draped her cloak over her shoulders and headed toward the stream to wash.

Her thoughts flowed easily to Hugues, as they often had of late, and to her troubling vision. Had that scene happened anywhere other than within her mind? No doubt had Sophie that Melusine's salve had prompted the illusion and she wondered for the hundredth time whether she had truly left the hut or simply become lost in complicated dreams. And what did such a vision mean?

A chance look at her filthy kirtle reminded her once again of Hugues, for 'twas none other than the one he had had made for her in La Rochelle. Sophie's eyes clouded with tears as she noted how worn it had become these past months, and she determinedly continued toward the river. She had turned him away, had she not? This now was her path, this learning from Melusine.

Was it not evidence enough that her recurring dream had abandoned her here?

A familiar song carried to her ears and Sophie hesitated in the undergrowth, reluctant to interrupt Melusine's bathing. She drew closer to the edge of the shadows and peeked out through the branches to find the older woman hip-deep in the pool where Sophie had first seen her, her long hair spread out around her like a dark fan. Melusine seemed unaware of Sophie's presence, for her song continued unabated, and there was something enchanting in the way she reveled in the water that compelled one to simply watch.

One long note finally ended her song and Melusine dived into the water unexpectedly. The sight of something decidedly not a foot made Sophie gasp aloud before the other woman disappeared completely into the shadows beneath the surface.

She took a step backward into the woods, trying to determine exactly what she had seen even as the details of Melusine's tale crowded into her mind. Melusine herself surfaced directly in front of Sophie before she could sort her thoughts. Sophie gasped again in surprise, the way the other woman's bright gaze locked with hers telling her that her presence had been detected long before.

"Upset you look," Melusine purred in a low voice and Sophie shook her head mutely in response.

The older woman smiled mysteriously as she approached and Sophie could not help but watch transfixed as she drew nearer the bank and her hips rose out of the water.

"Indeed, one might say that you look as though you had seen an old tale come to life," Melusine mused in that same knowing voice.

Sophie could neither answer nor move nor look away from the pale thighs that were drawing clear of the water.

"Well you should know that centuries have passed since the Melusine of that old tale reputedly graced this earth," she added. Unable to tear her gaze away, Sophie swallowed with difficulty as the woman stepped into the shallows.

Perfectly normal knees became visible next, then calves that could have belonged to any woman. Sophie's breath came more quickly as she nervously awaited the sight of Melusine's feet, but the woman stepped to the bank with a grace that belied the presence of any tail or fin. The second slim foot rose out of the water to join the first, putting any such suspicions to rest. Sophie glanced up to meet Melusine's eyes, unsure of what to think until she met the smug confidence in those pale eyes.

"What did you see, Sophie?" Melusine asked in a hushed voice. Sophie knew in that moment that Melusine knew exactly what she had seen, that her eyes had not deceived her and that Melusine was but playing a game.

"Who are you?" Sophie demanded, and the woman's brow rose eloquently.

"Already have I told you that I am Melusine," she countered calmly, reaching for the kirtle she had left on the bank. "Naught else do you need to know."

"But where did you come from? Why do you live here? What of your family?" Sophie asked. The impertinent questions fell quickly from her lips once she had begun.

"I cannot remember," Melusine responded flatly, impaling Sophie with a glance that effectively silenced her questions. "Should you make demands of me, ask what you truly want to know," she dictated coldly.

Sophie dared more than she would have imagined possible just moments sooner, her revulsion making her bold.

"What is my choice?"

The question hung between them for a long moment. Melusine hesitated for an instant before she continued methodically drying her skin. Sophie feared she had pushed too far when the silence continued so long that the shadows seemed to grow deeper, but Melusine turned to face her once she was dressed.

"The Melusine made her choice," she said softly. Her gaze held Sophie's own.

"She chose to be alone," Sophie concluded, earning a curt nod from her tutor.

"Aye, she did, but why? You cannot know the end without the reason."

"Because her husband betrayed her," Sophie guessed. The way the older woman's brows rose told her that she was wrong.

"Surely she could have guessed that anyone would try to gain something expressly forbidden to him," Melusine mused. Suddenly Sophie saw another side to the tale that she had not perceived before.

"She said that apurpose," she breathed in surprise, frowning as she thought out the implications. "She knew 'twould only be a matter of time before he broke his word should she force him to make such a vow."

"Mayhap," Melusine commented noncommittally, but Sophie had seen the flash in her eyes before she looked away.

"But why?" she pondered aloud and the older woman looked up again.

"Perhaps her curse weighed heavily upon her," she said in a speculative tone. Once again, Sophie had the sense that Melusine was not guessing, but she dismissed the thought as quickly as it formed.

"Then why would she have married him?"

Melusine sighed and looked off into the shadows of the trees with a frown. "Mayhap she would choose to be of this world instead of the world of shadows. Mayhap she thought that love alone could strike the balance," she whispered shakily.

Before she knew what she was about, Sophie reached out and touched the older woman's shoulder of her own volition for the first time, aware of naught but the other woman's pain, which she felt as keenly as if 'twere her own. Melusine's hand crept over Sophie's though she did not look up.

"But when she tested his love, he cast her out," Sophie concluded in a murmur that was not contested. The woods grew silent around them as darkness fell and creatures settled for the night, the steady trickling of the stream into the pool behind them the only sound.

"You are one of us, Sophie," Melusine said finally, though the younger woman had to strain to catch the words. "We two are of the spawn of the Melusine, one foot in this world and one in the other. 'Tis that alone that grants the Sight, that and the purchase price we pay. Times are changing and intolerance of we who are different, we who were once revered, grows by the day. 'Tis not an easy choice you must make in these troubled times, but those there have been before you."

"What choice?"

"The choice of the world in which you will dwell." Melusine turned and regarded Sophie for a long moment in a way that sent a chill through the younger woman's bones. "The world changes, Sophie, and makes our choices difficult no matter which side we select. But we who have already paid the price cannot take it back."

"What is this purchase price of which you speak?" Sophie whispered, unable to quell a certainty that she was not going to like the response. Melusine sighed and frowned at the ground in thought.

"The Sight does not come without its own price," she conceded finally. "You must be aware of that before you make your choice. Be aware, too, of the toll the world will extract from you for acknowledging the Sight." Melusine smiled sadly and shook her head. "Yet should you not confess to having this gift, 'twill wither and die."

She glanced up and the sharpness of her gaze held Sophie's captive. "This then is the double bind of your legacy. Should you use the Sight, others will persecute you. Should you deny its presence, it will truly leave you, but never will its purchase price be repaid.''

"What purchase price?" Sophie demanded hoarsely again. Melusine's fingers tightened briefly over hers and she struggled to dismiss her growing sense of dread.

"Each of us bears a mark of the Sight." The older woman chuckled wryly under her breath. "Some admittedly more openly than others."

"I bear no such mark," Sophie denied quickly, but Melusine glanced up at her with that knowing smile.

"Do you not?" she murmured in a low voice and Sophie was suddenly afraid. "Times change, child, and mayhap just as we hide, so do our marks."

She slipped to kneel on the ground and drew a circle in the soft dirt of the bank with her fingertip while Sophie watched with trepidation. The signs for the planets were quickly etched in, the houses and ascendant. Melusine paused to look up at Sophie expectantly when she finished.

"'Tis my chart," she confirmed, recognizing the first horoscope she had learned to draw, and Melusine's nod was acknowledgment enough. Melusine's fingertip dropped deliberately to the chart and she granted Sophie another look. Reluctantly Sophie stepped forward and eyed the location of her imperious finger.

"'Tis the fifth house," she said, not knowing what to make of this.

"And what is there?" Melusine demanded. Sophie shrugged.

"Naught," she concluded, the house being conspicuously devoid of planets.

"Aye. The fifth house 'tis that governs your first child," Melusine whispered, and Sophie recoiled in horror.

"You cannot know this," she argued, but the older woman said naught and Sophie panicked anew.

Could her mark be a barren womb? 'Twas impossible. She was young and healthy in every other way. Doubt grew in Sophie's mind, even as she considered casting the Sight aside for the hope of a child.

"The purchase price has already been paid," Melusine murmured as though she had guessed her very thoughts. Sophie turned away from the incriminating chart.

"Nay," she said, her voice growing firmer as she argued. "Nay, it cannot be thus. No desire have I to hide from the world and live out my days in the woods," she insisted angrily. Melusine's lack of response only fueled her anger.

"Well could I have Hugues instead of this," she snapped and gestured broadly to encompass the woods. The older woman nodded slowly as Sophie backed away.

"Aye, you could," she agreed easily, the confirmation making Sophie's heart leap. She *would* have Hugues, she *would* have that life outside the woods, with or without the Sight and its cursed purchase price.

"I will go to him," she informed Melusine, turning on her heel to do exactly thus.

"Is this, then, how you would make your choice?" Melusine called after her, but Sophie stalked resolutely back to the hut. "Think upon your path, child, before you cast all aside. Would you deny, then, everything you have learned?" Melusine's words slowed Sophie's pace. "Would you deny this gift you have, this ability you have honed all these months?" Sophie turned and looked over her shoulder to the woman kneeling on the riverbank.

"I love Hugues," she said simply.

"And love will conquer all?" Melusine demanded archly, her sarcasm reminding Sophie of that haunting tale once more. "It has not worked for us in the past," she added softly, but Sophie shook her head adamantly.

Naught would she have of this nonsense.

"I am *not* of your kind," she retorted hotly, barely noting the pain that flashed briefly in the older woman's eyes. "I *refuse* to be of your kind. No mark do I bear of the Sight and I will have my Hugues!" Sophie spun angrily and stalked into the woods, her tears rising when Melusine's final words carried to her ears.

"But will your Hugues want *you* should your womb prove barren?"

At least Luc approved wholeheartedly of their path, even if Hugues had some residual doubts about the wisdom of seeking out Sophie. She could have gone back home to Bordeaux for all he knew, and he fought against a curious inner sense that she was still within the woods. Illogical 'twas and he would not put any stock in it.

Even if she was there, he knew not whether she would come with him, despite Jean's assurances. What would he do if she turned him away once again? Hugues lifted his chin stubbornly and confronted the shadow of the forest growing on the horizon.

He had to speak with her once more, to know for certain that she wished no part of him.

"Hasten, milord, that we might gain the woods by nightfall," Luc urged enthusiastically. Hugues granted the boy an indulgent smile.

"Never thought I to see you so anxious to pass within Brocéliande yet again," he commented, enjoying the way the boy's ears turned scarlet.

"Our duty 'tis to save our lady Sophie," he responded earnestly.

"Mayhap she will not see the matter thus," Hugues pointed out carefully, but Luc shook his head.

"'Twill only be because the witches have her under their spell," he insisted. Hugues wished 'twere really that simple.

"May Eve, 'tis," he reminded the boy. "So certain are you that you should pass within the trees on this night?"

Luc swallowed visibly and eyed the approaching line of trees. "This I would do only for you and lady Sophie," he murmured. Hugues felt his surprise show upon his face, but the boy was oblivious to his response as he peered into the distance.

"See you lights, milord?" he asked and it seemed to Hugues that the boy's voice wavered just a little. He glanced up and did indeed see lights, spots of fire along the line that marked the beginning of the forest.

"No witching lights are they, Luc," he reassured the lad, "but fires set by very human hands for May Eve. See the shadows surrounding them?" And indeed the silhouettes of people were discernible around the flames. Hugues frowned at the realization of how many were gathered at the edge of the woods.

They drew nearer and he would have asked, but one of the men brandished a burning torch high above his head and shouted to the others.

"Know this night that the witches can be conquered!" he cried, and something went cold within Hugues at the agreement rippling through the crowd.

"'Tis the night of their weakest point, the night that we can banish them to the other side once and for all!" He waved his torch and Hugues watched in horror as myriad flaming torches were held aloft.

"Burn the woods!"

"Kill the witches!"

The crowd roared and surged under the eaves of the forest, the bobbing torches swarming like an invading army of fireflies as they dipped deeper into the woods.

"Nay!" Luc cried when torches were dropped and larger flames took hold within the woods. Hugues grasped the reins of the boy's palfrey, restraining him with an effort while he quickly considered what to do.

Was Sophie within the woods?

Fires were already raging within the trees to his left and he watched torches becoming mere pinpricks as they were carried still farther. The trees beside the road leaped into flames as torches were dropped into them and the crowd roared their approval, even as Hugues spurred his destrier.

He could not take the chance that Sophie might perish thus. And precious time to waste did they have to ride to the waterfall and back before the fire engulfed them.

Luc shouted close on his heels and he did not waste his breath telling the boy to wait, for he knew the order would be ignored. His horse balked as the shadows of the trees fell over them. The acrid smoke rose to Hugues' nostrils as well, but he urged the stallion ever onward. This was the road he had taken out of the woods, Hugues was certain of it. The very thought that Sophie was within a day's ride made him wish the horse could run faster yet.

If she was still there.

Hugues refused to let himself think upon that, concentrating instead on outrunning the flames that spread with eerie glee. The trees were cast in strange orange and yellow shadows and he heard them falling far behind him as they submitted to the roaring will of the hungry fire. The sounds of the peasants' cries grew more distant and his steed settled into a pattern as the immediate threat of the flames dropped away from the road itself.

They had to get out by the dawn, Hugues realized, hoping against hope that he could navigate his way back to that clearing. All the tales of witches in the woods he had ever heard returned to haunt him, the charge that they could not be found unless they were willing, the idea that one found them only when one was enchanted and drawn into their web as unsuspecting as a fly.

Hugues closed his eyes against the sting of the smoke and hoped he had not committed them to a path of no return.

Hugues found the footpath that veered away from the main way, and cast a glance over his shoulder. The fire was far behind them now, but its golden glow was still within vision and Hugues nervously spurred his horse on. Their pace was slower as the path was less worn and he admitted that they would be hard-pressed to even gain the waterfall before the flames were upon them, never mind make it back out of the forest.

"Too late will we be," Hugues called to Luc, seeing the boy's lips set in a grim line when he looked back again. He leaned over his saddle and urged his destrier yet faster, setting a reckless pace through the pressing undergrowth and hearing the footfalls of Luc's palfrey accelerate as he followed suit.

The horse snorted unexpectedly and Hugues' head shot up, his eyes widening in disbelief at the sight of a woman standing stock-still in the middle of the path ahead. He had but a glimpse of her green cloak before his steed swept around her, but Hugues' heart leaped in recognition and he scooped her into the saddle on his way past. She gasped and pummeled his arm as she struggled for release, the sight of those flashing violet eyes making Hugues want to laugh for joy.

"Sophie!" he breathed, and her fighting halted abruptly as she stared up at him. Belatedly Hugues realized that he wore his helmet and that she could not see his face. An instant later the matter was resolved, the undisguised delight on Sophie's face setting Hugues' reservations aside.

"Hugues!" she exclaimed in delight, framing his face in her hands as if she could not believe he was here before her. 'Twas much like the greeting she had given him before, and Hugues' heart swelled with possessive pride. Clearly she had changed her mind yet again and he was glad Jean had managed to persuade him to return to the forest.

"Luc!" he called over his shoulder. "Turn about— we may yet outrun the flames!"

"Milady!" Luc shouted when he spied Sophie before Hugues, his worried frown breaking into a grin. "Afraid we were for your welfare."

"What is wrong?" Sophie demanded quietly. Her expression sobered when she caught a whiff of the fire. She frowned and met his eyes in puzzlement.

"The peasants have set fire to the woods," he informed her softly. Sophie lifted her nose to the wind and concern filled her eyes when she looked back to him.

"'Tis close," she whispered and Hugues could but nod.

"And fast approaching," he concurred, spurring his mount back in the direction they had come.

"Wait!" Sophie cried out, gripping his shoulders with a strength that surprised Hugues.

"We cannot wait," he growled, but she shook her head quickly.

"Melusine," she said, and he assumed she spoke of the woman she had followed instead of staying with him. "I cannot leave Melusine to such a fate." Despite Sophie's entreaty, Hugues was not particularly inclined to risk his life for the woman who had prompted Sophie to cast him aside.

"Sophie, there is no time. We may not make our way through the woods even now," Hugues argued, resenting the time they were already wasting over this matter.

"I cannot simply leave without warning her," Sophie regarded him with something akin to horror. Reluctantly Hugues conceded the sense in her words.

"She is not with you?" he demanded sharply. Sophie quickly shook her head, an intriguing flush rising over her features as she looked shyly up at him. This blushing Sophie Hugues had not seen before and he watched in fascination as she licked her lips nervously.

"An argument we had," she admitted uneasily. "And I thought to leave her."

"But where would you go?" Hugues asked, not daring to trust the hope budding within him. "Bordeaux lies the other way."

Sophie's flush deepened yet again and she risked a quick glance up to Hugues. "She told you that Pontesse lay this way," she confessed in a voice so small he had to strain to hear her words. Shock stopped his heart for a long moment, then it seemed he would not be able to restrain his glee, though he permitted himself no more than a chuckle of delight.

"So it does," he agreed happily. Sophie looked up just before Hugues bent and kissed her breathless. "A debt do I owe to this Melusine for making you see the way of things," he growled when he paused to take a breath, enjoying how flustered Sophie looked in the wake of his embrace. "We shall indeed seek her out first."

Chapter Twelve

They gained the clearing around the hut in record time and Sophie slipped from the saddle while Hugues looked back to check the progress of the fire. 'Twas close behind them, he noted with a sinking heart, the orange glow closing fast on either side of the clearing, the roar of its voice filling his ears. Soon the clearing would be encircled and he tasted his fear, uncertain what they would do.

"Melusine!"

Hugues cast a glance up to the sky while Sophie's cries for her mentor rang in his ears, noting the heavy clouds scurrying across the moon. A fitful wind tossed the tops of the trees, undoubtedly helping to spread the flames more quickly, and he shivered, thinking that 'twas indeed a witching night.

Sophie was scrabbling in the dirt on the threshold of the hut, and he wondered that she was not calling out any longer. He saw her frown as something in her hand caught the light. She shook her head dismissively, then she turned to him with a stricken countenance.

"She is not here!" Sophie cried in dismay. Hugues' destrier needed little urging to hasten forward.

"Sophie, the fire is fast upon us," he reminded her tersely.

"The pool," she exclaimed as he drew alongside her. "She was at the pool when I left."

"How do we get there from here?" He thought the water might serve them well whether Melusine was there or not.

Sophie directed him and the horses moved quickly, nervous as they sensed the proximity of the fire. When the reflection from the surface of the pool glimmered through the trees, both beasts instinctively rushed forward and plunged into the icy water.

"She is not here," Sophie whispered brokenly against Hugues' chest.

His lips thinned in frustration as he guided his steed into the middle of the pond, and he could only hope the pool was deep enough to protect them until the fire passed. The trees on the side of the river they had just abandoned leaped into orange and scarlet flames, crackling so loudly that the horses jumped nervously. Sparks jumped into the sky and Hugues slipped from his destrier's back, pulling Sophie down into the water before him and holding her close.

"She is not here," Sophie murmured again. Hugues stroked the back of her neck reassuringly, checking that Luc had followed his lead into the water.

"Mayhap she smelled the blaze," he whispered, hating that he could do naught to ease her tears.

She did not respond but merely burrowed her face in his chest, and Hugues held her close, warily watching the way the flames jumped from one treetop to another. They easily crossed the river that way, the carpet of flickering orange spreading across the opposite bank and racing off into the distance.

Hugues looked back the way they had come and could see only raging flames. A sweet scent on the breeze drifted to fill his nostrils despite the strong smell of the burning. He felt Sophie fiddling with something and looked down to find her turning a bright object over in her hand.

"What have you there?" he asked quietly, and she shot him a watery glance.

"'Twas on the threshold," she answered, holding the token up to his view.

A silver figure 'twas, finely wrought, a setting made in the shape of a woman holding a large oval green stone, which glowed with a pale luminosity. The woman's hair was long and intricately detailed, twining over her shoulders and around the stone, twisting over the serpent's tail that coiled thickly where her feet should have been.

"A melusine, 'tis," Hugues commented, recognizing the figure from old tales he had been told as a child. He took the piece from Sophie and admired the workmanship of the pin, noting that it had a hook on one side on the back. "Was this hers?"

"I know not," Sophie confessed. "Never have I seen it before."

"And 'twas on the threshold?" he asked. Sophie nodded quickly before him.

"Pressed into the dirt 'twas, right in the middle."

"Mayhap she meant for you to find it," Hugues guessed. "Said you not that her name was Melusine?" Sophie nodded again.

"A sign it surely is from her to you that she knew of the fire and made her way from here safely," he reasoned, liking the way Sophie's tentative smile lit her eyes.

"Truly you think so?"

"'Tis only logical," he concluded. He was surprised when Sophie chuckled and leaned her cheek against his chest.

"I have missed you, Hugues," she whispered, sending that surge of pride lurching through his veins again. He had not the chance to savor it, though, before she tipped her head back and regarded him with a thoughtful frown.

"What brings you into the forest this day?" she demanded as though it had just occurred to her that 'twas odd for him to be there, and Hugues fidgeted in discomfort. He struggled to look away, but Sophie refused to relinquish his gaze and he knew he would have to answer her, sooner or later.

"Well you should know that I missed you, as well," he muttered with no small measure of embarrassment, losing his footing on the riverbed when Sophie leaped for his neck with a whoop of delight. They fell backward into the pool, but Hugues cared naught, for his Sophie's enthusiastic kisses blotted all else from his mind.

The sky managed to grow lighter despite the heavy clouds and Hugues guessed that 'twas just before the dawn that the rain started. Spring rain it was, light but persistent and enough to chill one to the bone. Though the front of the fire had long passed the glade, the surrounding trees still burned and the embers hissed in the first drops of rain.

Soon the air was filled with steam and the acrid smell of devastation. Sophie huddled close to Hugues and he felt her shivering, but he was loath to leave the water just yet. His own feet were numb from the icy pond, his new hauberk a chilly burden that he longed to shed.

Luc was paler than Hugues would have liked, and even the horses trembled in the early-morning light. But there was naught to be gained by risking their way before the fire was truly extinguished and Hugues waited, albeit impatiently.

The light rain gave way to a more purposeful drizzle as they stood huddled together, and the hissing embers gradually fell silent. Eventually the steam ceased to rise from the blackened woods and Hugues waited but a bit longer before making his way to the bank. He clambered ashore, feeling the soil before allowing his horse to follow suit, scanning the horizon for some sign of persistent flames.

Naught but destruction greeted him from every side. Indeed, even the birds had been silenced and Hugues shivered, unable to believe that a lush green forest had thrived on this very spot but a day past.

Good time would they make this day and Hugues conceded the luck of that as he turned back to his bedraggled companions. He helped Sophie climb to the bank, the fullness of her sodden kirtle and surcoat conspiring against her in the task. He lifted Luc into his own saddle, a glance to Sophie confirming that his concern for the boy was mirrored in her eyes.

"How soon can we reach shelter?" she asked.

Hugues pursed his lips thoughtfully before he spoke. "Fontaine by nightfall, mayhap." Her lips thinned briefly. She brushed her fingertips across Luc's brow and met Hugues' eyes again.

"I fear we shall have to do better than that," she murmured. Hugues' gaze flew back to the boy, now dozing, and he carefully swallowed the lump that had risen in his throat.

"What know you of this?" he asked hoarsely and Sophie almost smiled.

"Five moons have I spent learning the craft of healing," she supplied in a low voice, drawing Hugues' amazed gaze to hers. "He must be warmed, and soon." Hugues immediately reached for the clasp of his mantle, but Sophie laid her hand on his to stop him.

"Nay, Hugues. Need you have of its warmth yourself," she argued practically and he wondered how he had ever thought her mad. "But hold him close against you as we ride that he might share your warmth," she advised while Hugues found himself nodding agreement.

He helped Sophie to mount Luc's palfrey, then mounted his own steed, looking down at the boy for a long moment. Ill he looked, and Hugues swallowed carefully, schooling his fervent desire to flee.

"He needs you, Hugues," Sophie said as though she understood his dilemma. The very thought gave him surprising strength and he lifted the boy carefully against him, wrapping his mantle around them both.

"Aye," he agreed slowly, frowning at the chill in Luc's skin. "Aye, that he does."

As Hugues gazed down at the pale boy, something changed subtly in his perception. The very act of keeping the boy warm could help him, and the realization that there was something he could do in the face of illness diminished his sense of powerlessness before it.

"What will you do?" he asked Sophie. She thought for a moment before she responded.

"Warmth he needs to counter chill. So, heat and dry garments will he have at the soonest chance and hot broth in his belly. Should he begin to cough, there are common herbs to clear his throat and nose. 'Tis likely any garden will have one or two of them." Her words did more to diminish Hugues' fear than he might have expected.

"You can help him, then?" he asked with no small measure of surprise. Sophie nodded and smiled.

"Aye," she returned confidently, indicating the way Hugues held Luc. "As can you."

As could he. Hugues cast another glance down to the sleeping boy and concluded that he liked the sound of that. No mysterious force that could not be engaged was illness, but a dark rider whose ways of war could well be known. A formidable foe 'twas undoubtedly, but one that could be conquered nonetheless.

Hugues nodded with satisfaction, gathering the boy closer to the heat he felt returning to his limbs, and nodded to Sophie. "Let us make haste to Fontaine," he urged and at her smile of agreement, gave his destrier his spurs.

The sun was still glowing dusky red high above the western horizon when they reached a château with four tall towers at the corners of the curtain wall. The structure rose from a slight hill, a slow-moving but broad river curling around its back and leaving but one approach. The road angling up to the gates could be watched with ease and there was little doubt that it was being surveyed now, for the hairs on the back of Sophie's neck were prickling.

Sophie stared up at the imposing facade in amazement, certain they could not be allowed into such a sumptuous estate, but Hugues called a greeting to the gatekeeper without reservation. Well-known here he seemed to be, for the gatekeeper hailed Hugues cheerfully by name, even stepping out of his post to bow to the arriving knight.

"What need you?" Hugues demanded of her. Sophie forced her mind to return to more immediate matters.

"A warm room, hot broth, dry garments for the lot of us," she said, sparing Hugues a glance and disliking the way his usually hearty golden coloring had seemed to pale.

"Wearing your mail, are you?" she asked curtly. The way he colored guiltily was all the answer she needed. Anger flowed through her at his casual disregard for his own health, followed quickly by a fear of losing him so soon after their paths had twined together once more.

"Hugues de Pontesse, have you not a whit of sense about you?" Sophie demanded curtly as she dismounted. She tossed her horse's reins aside impatiently and rounded the beast to confront Hugues angrily. "What possible good do you think to do holding that boy against the cold press of steel?"

"Abroad we rode," he insisted stubbornly, dismounting carefully himself. Luc he still cradled against his chest, even as he leaned over her with flashing eyes to make his point. "Only sensible 'tis to travel armed in these days."

"Aye, especially with the perilous path we traveled this day," Sophie countered in a voice heavy with sarcasm as she placed her hands on her hips.

"No man can know what he will meet on the road," Hugues responded.

"And well indeed your mail has served you on this trip," she snapped. "Had you been caught in that blaze, your mail would have ensured you burned to a very crisp.'' The very thought made the bottom of her stomach drop out, but she plunged on.

"As 'tis, it may bring you a wet cough in your chest.'' She emphasized her point with a jab of her finger to his chest, the chill of the steel making her shiver with just that touch.

"Hugues,'' she began anew, unsure whether she intended to curse him or tell him of her fear, but words failed her, and tears welled up to blur her vision. Hugues looked as though he would interject, but the unexpected sound of another voice fairly made them both jump instead.

"Might I assume that this is the Sophie of whom I have heard so much?'' a hearty male voice demanded.

Sophie's color rose when she turned to meet the twinkling eyes of a tall, dark-haired knight. She looked to Hugues, wondering what on earth he had said about her, only to find him looking decidedly uncomfortable.

What *had* he said about her? Annoyance filled her again, her emotions running ragged after the ordeal of this past day, and Sophie stubbornly blinked back her tears to force a smile for the man before her.

"Sophie, I would have you meet my brother-in-law, Lord Jean de Fontaine,'' Hugues muttered as though he, too, had been caught off guard by the interruption. The other man bent low over Sophie's hand and brushed his lips against the back of her hand.

"Enchanted,'' he murmured against her skin, sparing her a covert wink when Hugues positively bristled at the intimacy.

Serves him right, Sophie thought with satisfaction and she stifled an answering grin. The very cheek of Hugues to discuss her with another while she had been certain he was gone from her life forever had earned him no less.

"The pleasure is indeed mine," she responded coquettishly, enjoying Hugues' thorough dissatisfaction with this turn of events. "Is this then your château?" She deliberately let her awe filter into her voice.

"Aye, all mine and my father's before me," Jean confirmed proudly. "Mayhap I could have the pleasure of showing you its charms?" he asked with an impish grin that Sophie could not help but return. Jean was a mischief maker, there was little doubt of that, but he was an engaging mischief maker nonetheless.

"Need have we of warmth and dry garments, not a guided tour," Hugues retorted sharply and Jean laughed outright.

"Indeed, I forget myself before such a lovely lady," he apologized gallantly.

Sophie thought that perhaps he overplayed his game with that comment, but Hugues looked sour enough to curdle fresh milk. Jean stood back and indicated the portal to the hall with a sweeping gesture of invitation while Sophie struggled not to gape at the wealth surrounding her.

The gates they had passed were located in the middle of the curtain wall between two towers. The two towers opposite them framed a three-story structure that housed the lord's residence. The curtain wall over the gates had been particularly thick and Sophie guessed that the guards' quarters were directly over their post.

"A beautiful château have you," Sophie murmured, but Hugues snorted behind her with what could have been disdain.

"New construction," he scoffed disapprovingly. Jean grinned indulgently for Sophie.

"Château Fontaine has stood but fifty summers," he informed her, "unlike some ancient châteaux hereabouts."

"Were you of Fontaine not such a headstrong lot, your homes might survive longer," Hugues growled, prompting Jean to laugh.

"Aye, a family tendency have we to become involved in particularly nasty squabbles," he agreed easily, but Sophie had not the chance to sort out that enigmatic remark, for they had ducked into the portal. She blinked as her eyes adjusted to the relative darkness, the hall higher and wider than she might have guessed from the outside.

"'Tis beautiful," she mused.

"Aye, for *new* construction, 'tis not all bad," Jean conceded with pride, urging them forward as he called to his chatelain and ignored Hugues' poorly concealed "harrumph."

A woman rose from the cluster of people gathered around the hearth and Sophie started as she recognized the woman from her vision of the birth. Her warmly welcoming smile made Sophie wonder for a moment if the woman had in fact seen her on that night.

Had she truly witnessed something that had occurred?

Indeed, she had not given that possibility much consideration. Sophie scanned the hall disconcertedly, but found naught familiar about it.

Had this woman recently borne a child? Another glance to Jean convinced her that he might have been the man with Hugues in her dream and she bit her lip nervously, wondering about the babe.

Had the child survived?

"Welcome to Fontaine," the woman greeted them with a friendly tone. She was directly before them, no flicker of recognition in her bright blue eyes.

"My sister Louise," Hugues supplied from behind Sophie. "The *Lady* Fontaine."

Louise looked taken aback by her brother's particular emphasis on her title, but Jean only laughed again. Sophie looked over her shoulder to find Hugues gritting his teeth. The sight of Luc cradled against his chest brought her back to her senses.

"Sophie, this is," Jean informed his wife. The way Louise's eyes widened in surprise indicated to Sophie again that Hugues had been free with his tongue, and she stifled the urge to set him straight on the spot.

"So pleased am I to meet you," Louise enthused.

"And I you," Sophie returned politely, gesturing to the boy. "I fear Luc may be falling ill from the chill we have had—" she began, but got no further. Louise's hands flew to her cheeks in dismay at the boy's lack of coloring.

"Of what were you *thinking*, Jean?" she chided, beckoning to the politely hovering chatelain with brisk efficiency. "Our guests are chilled and wet. Arnaud, have a fire kindled in the children's room—they can sleep with us this night. Dry garments will our guests require, hot baths and have Gaston bring venison stew and warm wine. A tunic of Jean's will fit Hugues well enough, I imagine...."

Sophie checked Luc's skin once again after she climbed out of the luxurious warmth of her bath, and was reassured that his color seemed to be returning. Now he appeared to be but asleep and she smiled as she tucked the blanket still higher around his chin, then wrapped another about herself and basked in the glow of the fire raging on the hearth. Her belly was filled with a hot and spicy stew, and a robust red wine that must have been a good Gascon vintage surged through her veins.

Indeed, one could easily become accustomed to life at Fontaine.

Hugues she had not seen since he had carried Luc here, and she could only hope he had had the good sense to remove his mail shortly after he had left. When she had reminded him to do so, he had given her a firm kiss as his sole reply in the clear sight of everyone, leaving her blushing beneath Jean and Louise's eyes when he ducked out of the room.

Sophie would have to get even with him for that impertinence and the very thought made her smile in anticipation.

A tap at the door returned her to her senses and she called a welcome. Louise smiled as she ducked through the wooden portal.

"How is Luc?" she asked.

"He but sleeps now."

"Good." She smiled as she crossed the room, offering a bundle of pale violet cloth to Sophie. "A kirtle and chemise I have brought you," she said, and Sophie was astounded at the softness of the wool when she took it.

"I cannot take something so fine," she protested, but Louise waved off her objection.

"Then 'twill rot, for it fits me no longer," she pointed out, patting her slightly rounded stomach. "Two children have quite destroyed my figure."

Sophie gave the slender woman a speculative glance before she slipped into the chemise, resolving that this was as good an opportunity as any to ask her questions.

"How old are they?" she asked with what she hoped was nonchalance and Louise laughed.

"Do not start me talking of them," she advised good-naturedly. "Well does Jean complain that once I start upon the matter, I cannot leave it rest." She dropped to a seat by the fire, sparing a maternal glance for Luc, gathered up her knees and watched Sophie dress. "Angels they are to me both, though Michel—" she wagged one finger "—has lately shown his father's own tendency to make trouble."

"The eldest is he, then?"

"Aye, but two summers old and as sure of himself as a lad of twenty." Louise stood and helped Sophie with the laces on the side of the violet kirtle, cocking her head to one side as she assessed the fit of the garment. "Suits you well, it does," she mused, grimacing when she regarded Sophie's waist. "To think that once I was so slim." She sighed and shrugged her shoulders.

"Still slender you are," Sophie pointed out, but Louise rolled her eyes as she glanced down to the fullness of her breasts.

"Jean says he likes my new curves well, but I would rather they were less again," she pouted, cupping one's weight experimentally. Louise pursed her lips in dissatisfaction as a wet stain immediately spread from the point, and she shrugged her shoulders ruefully.

"Well it seems that you will soon meet my newest angel," she commented in reference to her leaking milk.

"One you bore recently, then?" Sophie asked. Her heartbeat accelerated when Louise nodded matter-of-factly.

"But five months past 'twas," she agreed, surveying her kirtle with a frown. "Come braid your hair in my chambers, for 'tis time she was fed. Shall I call another to watch Luc?"

Sophie turned back to the sleeping boy and shook her head. "He will be fine," she concluded, following Louise nervously to the lord's solar.

"Stand not on ceremony here, Sophie," she chided when her guest hesitated on the threshold of a lavish bedchamber. "Already do I feel that I have known you long."

Sophie closed the door behind herself, watching as Louise lifted a bundle from the cradle near the hearth. A serving girl slipped back into the shadows and her lady smiled gratefully, even as she cooed to the fidgeting babe. Sophie crept forward, barely daring to look but unable not to, jumping when Louise gasped as the baby latched onto her nipple.

"Thirsty she is, my little Alexandria," Louise commented with a breathless laugh. "And such a will, I know not where she gets it."

Sophie stopped beside Louise and watched the child nurse, not knowing what she had expected to feel, but surprised that naught assaulted her. 'Twas a babe, much as any other, and Sophie fought against her disappointment.

"Lovely she is," she forced herself to comment, earning a sunny smile from Louise.

"Aye, and eyes of blue just like mine," Louise supplied with maternal pride. "I do so hope that they do not change as she grows, for she has Jean's dark hair and 'tis a lovely combination."

The baby suckled contentedly, her pace slowing gradually, and she took Louise's shift to the other breast in stride. As Sophie watched, those tiny lips pursed less and less frequently, the babe's breathing slowing, as well. Louise draped the child over one shoulder and the tiny belch that resulted made both women giggle.

"Would you like to hold her?" Louise asked and Sophie nodded agreement.

The child stirred as she settled into Sophie's arms and Sophie touched the softness of her cheek with one fingertip. 'Twas the same child, she knew it well as she cradled the babe against her chest, just as she knew without a doubt that this one had not the Sight.

No legacy did this little one carry, no purchase price had she paid. She was but a child much like any other and Sophie realized that anything of that night had faded from the child's mind.

She realized as she rocked the sleeping babe that she had hoped for that bond to still be as strong between herself and this child. A kinship she felt, to be sure, for they had joined together in adversity, but 'twas not that recognition she had known with Melusine. Suddenly Sophie felt very alone.

Melusine had been right, she realized now, and the truth was somehow easier to see here in the comfort of Fontaine than it had been in the woods. Sophie was different than other mortals; she was of Melusine's kind, as much as she might wish to be otherwise. Tears rose to blur her sight once again, but Louise's hand on her arm recalled the other woman's presence to her.

"Children you will have of your own one day, Sophie," Louise murmured with a reassuring smile, the words making Sophie ache inside. Nay, not that for her, not if Melusine spoke the truth fully. She shook her head mutely, not knowing how to explain how she felt, but Louise gathered her into an impulsive hug.

"No godmother has Alexandria," she said impulsively, granting Sophie a smile. "Already has she been christened and Hugues declared as her godfather, but I would ask you to share in watching over her." Sophie parted her lips to protest, but Louise shook her head adamantly in anticipation of her words.

"Things you know, Sophie, well can I see it in your eyes. 'Tis not my imagination that this one is special. Teach her for me."

"But I know not where I will be when she is older," Sophie countered helplessly. Louise's firm headshake effectively silenced her protest.

"My brother is a man of good sense and stubborn once he knows what he wants. Think you that none saw you flush when he kissed you?" she demanded with a teasing smile. "Well do I think that you will be close for a long while."

Sophie's heart leaped at the idea, but she could not pretend the matter was settled, nor even that she was sure all could come aright. This curious sense of isolation unnerved her, as did her new conviction that Melusine had spoken the truth, and she knew that she would have to reflect hard upon her choice before she accepted Hugues.

If indeed he wanted her.

"I know not what will happen," she began, but Louise's finger on her lips silenced her.

"None knows what will happen," Louise said flatly. "Promise me only that you will teach my child should the opportunity arise." The two women looked into each other's eyes for a long moment and Sophie saw Louise's concern for her "littlest angel."

"Well you know that I would do my best," she vowed, and Louise's eyes glazed with tears just before she gathered Sophie close.

The babe protested at the crush that disturbed her slumber and they parted with a laugh. Sophie watched Louise proudly kiss her daughter's cheek as she carried her back to the cradle. Sophie's hand slipped into the pocket of her kirtle seemingly of its own accord and she fingered the pin she had transferred there, biting her lip as she considered the legacy she had gained.

Hugues was roughhousing with Michel in the hall when he spotted Sophie hesitating at the foot of the stairs. He set the young ruffian immediately on his feet and stood himself, running one hand through his hair and smiling when her gaze lit upon him. She returned the smile but something in her demeanor made her look sad, despite the way Louise's kirtle flattered her coloring. He noted with pleasure that she had not coiled up or covered her long blond braid and he was tempted to unplait its length and spread that shining gold over her shoulders.

"Luc is not well?" he ventured to guess when he drew near, but she shook her head in quick denial.

"Nay, he is fine," she confirmed in an uncharacteristically subdued voice. Hugues frowned, unable to fathom what else might trouble her.

"What is it, then?" he asked gently, noticing only now the tears welling in her eyes. She looked away, but he put one finger under her chin and forced her to face him. "Tell me," he urged, wanting only to make everything right in her world.

"'Tis the children," she said unsteadily and he saw that she struggled with the words. Their eyes met briefly and Hugues hoped his expression was encouraging when she glanced down at her hands.

"I fear that I will not bear any," Sophie confessed in a low voice.

Hugues was completely taken aback at her words. Well could he assist with that, he thought, but he restrained the impulse to tease her when she was so distressed. The idea that had tormented him leaped to the fore of his mind and he impulsively resolved to make his case now, when the opportunity for success seemed unusually good.

"Should you not take a man to husband, 'tis unlikely you will," he concurred readily, taking her slim hand within his and daring to look to her eyes. Sophie seemed to be holding her breath and Hugues could only hope that was a good sign.

"Well you know that I cannot take a bride until my inheritance is gained, but I would ask you to consider my offer," he said all in a rush, and was disconcerted when Sophie's tears spilled onto their entwined hands.

"What troubles you?" he demanded in alarm. "Surely the thought is not so terrifying?"

"Nay, nay." Sophie shook her head quickly, looking up at him once more. "Indeed, I would want naught else," she confessed. The words set Hugues' heart to pounding. He grinned, but she placed her hand on his chest, the concern in her eyes stopping his rejoicing before it had quite begun.

"What if I could not bear you a child?" she asked.

Hugues shrugged in confusion. "Sophie, 'tis a possibility all who wed must confront," he responded, distrusting the conviction in her eyes. "Are you saying that you know beyond doubt that our match would be barren?"

"Aye," she confessed.

What a thought. Hugues knew not what to say for a long moment and he fingered her slim hands within his own.

No children. He cast a glance behind him to Michel cavorting under Jean's watchful eye and almost smiled at the boy's antics before Sophie's assertion rang again in his ears. He turned back to find her regard serious upon him.

"How know you this?" he asked quietly, cupping her chin in his hand that she might not look away. "Have you been injured?"

"Nay, Hugues, but I know it all the same," she responded with conviction, tapping on her breast. "My heart tells me 'twill be so."

"Your heart tells you?" Hugues could not help but scoff in his relief. "Sophie, spare me this frivolous nonsense. Should you not have a reason to anticipate no children, we shall take the gamble just as any other couple."

"A reason have I," she murmured, and he bent low to catch the words. "Melusine 'twas who told me 'twould be thus."

"And the reason?" he prompted.

"That I am different."

Hugues waited, but it was clear Sophie had no more to say. He raised his brows in an eloquent expression of disbelief, struggling not to mock something his intended apparently took very seriously.

"So, on the word of a madwoman in the woods, I am to cast you aside?" he demanded.

"Call her not that," Sophie whispered, but Hugues shrugged in frustration.

"Call her what you will, her word will not sway my intent." He paused when Sophie gripped his hands tightly within hers.

"But what if she spoke aright?" she asked, her own difficulty with the idea reflected in her eyes.

"She could not know such a thing," Hugues insisted, as much to reassure Sophie as himself.

"Hugues, what if she did?"

Hugues framed Sophie's face in his hands, sliding his thumbs across her cheeks to wipe away the last vestiges of her tears, wishing he could find the words to assuage her fears.

"I would wed you, not your womb," he whispered. "Should a barren match be our destiny, we will face it when the time comes."

Sophie closed her eyes and Hugues pressed a kiss to her brow, touching his nose to hers when she looked up at him once more. She reached up and pushed the weight of his hair from his forehead. The sad smile that played over her features made Hugues dread her words before she spoke.

"I wonder if you will think thus a decade from now," she mused sadly. With that charge, Hugues lost his temper with the entire debate.

"Sophie!" he exclaimed angrily. "Can you not see the madness of what you say? Would you truly turn me aside solely on the basis of this possibility?"

She shook her head mutely and he stalked a distance across the floor, unable to believe she could conceive of an excuse so completely insane, then jammed a hand through his hair as he closed the distance between them once more.

"This issue alone stands between us?" he demanded curtly, encouraged beyond measure when she nodded silently.

"Is it not enough?" she asked innocently, and Hugues fairly spat in frustration.

"Half a mind have I to haul you to bed and prove you wrong," he growled irritably and, to his surprise, Sophie chuckled through her tears.

"I would not have you disappointed," she whispered shakily.

"Sophie, such a fate I cannot imagine at your side," he confessed readily, liking the glow that came to her eyes.

"But promise me that you will think upon it," she urged and Hugues shook his head adamantly.

"Nay," he insisted. "My offer stands as made and 'tis you who must reflect upon that."

Her expression softened at his assertion and, unable to resist temptation, Hugues kissed her deeply, savoring the way she trembled against him and ignoring Jean's appreciative whistle.

Sophie's dream came to her that night in the solar of Fontaine and she knew not whether to welcome its arrival or not. Well it seemed that she hesitated as long as she could outside the circle of stones, dreading that she would feel that sense of isolation again and that she would stand alone by the glowing embers.

Finally, relentlessly, her footsteps carried her within the circle despite her objections and she shivered yet again as the shadow of the great stones fell over her. She stared into the orange coals for an eternity before she risked a quick glance to the spot the figure usually occupied.

It was there and she knew not whether to be relieved or afraid.

Once she had looked up, the figure began to approach and Sophie could not look away. The shoulders seemed broader, but she could not be sure if 'twas what she saw or what she wanted to see. A glimmer at the throat of the cloak made her gasp in recognition.

'Twas the pin Melusine had left her and Sophie feared she knew the identity of the cloaked figure. She fought against its approach, willing Melusine to disappear, willing her to leave Sophie to her choice that she might truly be with Hugues. The figure's pace did not slacken and suddenly the shadowed cowl filled all of Sophie's vision. Those hands rose and she recoiled in terror, refusing to look into the face of her tormentor.

"Sophie!"

She dared to look again as the hood was drawn back, the figure's visage melting into the concerned features of Hugues.

Hugues. His grip on her upper arms tightened when she did not respond and he shook her and repeated her name urgently once more.

"Hugues." She whispered his name brokenly, feeling her tears start to gather as he smiled gently at her.

"Aye. I am here," he murmured when he saw that she was awake. "'Tis all right now."

Sophie started to cry and Hugues gathered her close, the scent of his skin reassuring her as much as his soothing caress on her back. She sobbed against his strength helplessly, uncertain whether 'twas truly all right despite his assurances.

For she knew not whether she had seen him in her dream or not until she awoke.

Chapter Thirteen

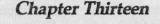

The first clue that not all was well when they arrived at Pontesse several days later was Justine stomping across the cobbled courtyard toward them, and Hugues stifled a groan at the determination in every line of his sister's figure. Too quiet had she been for too long and he saw now that he had been foolish to grow accustomed to her new demeanor. She stopped directly before him before he had even dismounted and rested her hands on her hips, her hazel eyes snapping in fury as she spared not a glance to Sophie or Luc.

"Time enough 'tis that you troubled yourself to return," she snapped by way of greeting. "Papa is being absolutely impossible and well do I expect you to talk some sense into him."

"Is he well?" Hugues asked, and that familiar trepidation burgeoned when Justine shook her head.

"A cold he has and 'tis making him sour and surly," she retorted tartly. Fruitlessly Hugues tried not to imagine his father being yet more difficult than he had been this winter past.

"Tell me not that he has denied you something," Hugues asked dryly as he swung out of his saddle, incurring a baleful glare from Justine.

"No jest is this, Hugues," she retorted. "Reasonable enough is it for me to wed, yet he will not give his word."

"What nonsense is this?" Hugues demanded as he turned to face her, knowing full well that his father had been trying to find a suitor to meet Justine's taste and his own lofty ambitions for his favorite child for some years.

"I have found a man," Justine supplied with an impudent toss of her tawny locks. Something in her manner immediately fueled Hugues' distrust of his sister's intentions.

"And who might he be?" he asked tolerantly, folding his arms across his chest.

"Look not like that, Hugues, he is a wealthy merchant from Venice." Justine's eyes shone as she spoke and Hugues struggled to avoid showing his disappointment. He reached to help Sophie dismount so that Justine might not see his answering frown, realizing that Sophie had not missed his gesture.

"Fit enough are you to tend the horses?" he asked of Luc to fill the awkward silence, then smiled when the boy nodded enthusiastically.

"Aye, milord," he assured his master. Hugues could not resist the urge to tousle the boy's hair affectionately, still relieved that he had so quickly recovered from their ordeal. This one would do him credit once he earned his spurs, of that Hugues had little doubt.

"How romantic for you to be wooed by a mysterious foreigner," Sophie commented lightly.

"I do not believe we have met," Justine retorted haughtily, and Hugues gave his sister a censorious glance.

"Sophie is my intended and you would do well to mind your scanty manners in her presence," he chided, prompting an unrepentant grin from his youngest sister.

"So formal are you, Hugues," she returned. "'Tis only that I must grow used to being the lady of the manor." She pranced across the courtyard with an affected step and Hugues heard Sophie stifle a laugh behind him.

"Two weddings will there be, then," Justine concluded as she spun on her heel to face them anew, her eyes fairly dancing with delight. "Hugues, you must talk to Papa and make him see the way of things, you simply must."

"Justine, he is surely only concerned for your happiness," Hugues said in defense of their sire, but Justine was not impressed by the argument.

"Suspicions he has of every man, Hugues," she pleaded, pouting prettily for his benefit. "And I *love* Guilio. Surely that is evidence enough that I will be happy."

Hugues sighed heavily, wishing 'twere indeed a guarantee of happiness. He stifled the urge to ask whether this Guilio loved Justine or what guarantee she had of his financial situation, knowing that Justine would not appreciate the turn of his thoughts.

"I will talk to Papa," he conceded reluctantly, mentally bracing himself for yet another argument, and Justine threw her arms happily around his neck.

"Hugues, the very best brother you are," she enthused, and he chuckled despite himself.

"Your only brother am I," he felt obliged to remind her, but Justine's mood could not be so easily dispelled.

"And still you are the best," she reiterated, pressing an affectionate kiss to his cheek. "Sure I am that Papa will see it our way."

How easily Justine assumed that he would take her side! Hugues thought to point out that his father and he seldom saw eye to eye on anything anymore, but decided not to risk shattering his sister's delight with such a cynical comment.

"When shall we meet this man who has stolen your heart?" he asked instead, watching Justine dance before them to the portal.

"Tonight he comes to the board," she whispered conspiratorially and Hugues was momentarily scandalized.

"Justine! Surely you did not invite him to the table when our sire was so opposed to his offer?"

Justine's lips set mutinously in an expression that Hugues found all too familiar, her eyes turning hard as she tipped her chin stubbornly and met his gaze.

"Well do I know what I want and no one, not even Papa, will stop me from having it," she informed him angrily, spinning on her heel to stomp into the hall.

Her behavior embarrassed Hugues and he could not think of what to say to Sophie in excuse. The silence that followed Justine's departure confirmed his suspicion that Sophie did not approve.

"Well it seems that one would never doubt what others are thinking at Pontesse," Sophie murmured finally from just behind him.

Hugues grimaced as he turned to her. "Justine has been indulged overmuch by my sire, I fear," he muttered, watching Sophie's fair brows rise in a gesture that said it all.

"Never would I have guessed," she teased as she smothered a smile and Hugues chuckled aloud.

"The storm will pass," he promised. "My father has never had the will to stand against Justine when she digs in her heels."

"Well can I imagine," Sophie satisfied herself with saying.

Hugues squeezed her hand affectionately as they entered the hall, feeling his nervousness rise as he tried to anticipate her response to his home. Would she find it lacking in comparison to Fontaine? Sophie ran one hand over the fitted stone wall as her footsteps faltered and Hugues watched her gaze about the hall in amazement.

Would she approve of his home? Of the hall that would become their home? He turned and scanned the expanse quickly himself, trying to look at the hall as though he had never seen it before, noting the green-and-white banner of Pontesse's unicorn hung over the hearth, the carving high on the stone walls. He glanced back, saw a smile playing over Sophie's lips and his heart began to pound.

"Hugues, 'tis beautiful," she whispered in evident awe and he released his breath with pleasure.

"Finer than Fontaine?" he demanded. Her eyes twinkled merrily as she wrapped her hands around his elbow and leaned close.

"No flimsy new construction this," she teased.

Hugues felt his neck heat at her jest. "I like that it is older," he answered defensively, the tightening of Sophie's grip on his arm drawing his gaze back to her.

"Aye, Hugues, 'tis better thus," she agreed wholeheartedly. "Strong roots has Château Pontesse and little is there not to admire about that." That she would so closely echo his own thoughts confirmed for Hugues the wisdom of the match he was making and suddenly he was anxious to hasten toward it.

"I would have you meet my father," he urged, but Sophie shook her head quickly.

"Nay, I would let you speak with him first," she demurred. Hugues noted her uncharacteristic hesitation with amusement.

"He is not so frightening as that," he teased, and was pleased when Sophie smiled.

"Family matters have you to resolve first," she reminded him quietly and he nodded in reluctant acknowledgment of her assessment. There was this business of Justine's to be settled and his sire was almost certain to not be in a social mood over after that.

"And I would have you be certain," Sophie added, her words reminding him of her mad conviction that she would be barren.

"Certain I am," he assured her firmly, determined not to be swayed by such whimsical nonsense, but understanding that she could not be rushed. "But should you yet have doubts, we will wait."

She did not respond to that, so Hugues kissed her quickly, then summoned Eduard with a wave that her needs might be tended in his absence.

Hugues heard his father coughing before he finished climbing the stairs, and he grimaced at the sound of the older man trying to break the phlegm in his throat. His footsteps slowed and he looked up to the closed door of the solar, unable to imagine how he would manage to face the spectacle of illness in full flower.

He glanced back to Sophie, though he knew not why, relieved that she immediately noted his hesitation and hastened to the foot of the stairs.

"What is it?" she asked and Hugues gestured helplessly with one hand.

"My father—" he began, but a renewed tirade of coughing from above drowned out whatever else he might have said. Understanding dawned on Sophie's face as Hugues watched, and she held up one hand.

"Wait but a moment and I will give you something to take him," she insisted and Hugues was more than happy to agree to the delay.

"Have you any elecampane?" she demanded of Eduard, who nodded agreement.

"Aye, candied 'tis."

Sophie waved that technicality aside easily. "'Twill do well enough. Hot water will I need, some honey, a knife and dare I hope you have aniseed?"

"But of course, milady," Eduard responded briskly, evidently responding to Sophie's own efficient manner, and Hugues bemusedly watched the pair of them bustle away.

"Well-equipped kitchens have we here at Pontesse, make no mistake, for the lord has a fussy palate," Eduard enthused. "Before she passed, the lady insisted on naught but the best and ever have I endeavored to follow her dictate."

Several moments later Hugues found himself holding a steaming mug of some brew that prompted him to clear his own throat. Something about it rose to tease his nostrils, some recollection it prompted dancing just beyond his reach. He frowned and tried to place the scent but could not.

"He should drink it while it is yet hot," Sophie urged when that cough carried to Hugues' ears and made him hesitate anew.

"You would not take it to him?" he asked hopefully, but Sophie just smiled and gave him a light push of encouragement.

"'Twill not be so bad, you will see," she promised.

Reluctantly Hugues conceded that she might be right. Difficult 'twould be indeed for his father to be as much of an ogre as he anticipated. He took a deep breath and one last look at Sophie's smile before carrying his offering up the stairs.

Though little enough did Sophie know of his father's ways, he realized, too late to turn back.

Hugues tapped on the door and entered as bidden, just in time to watch his father launch a globule of phlegm toward his chamber pot. He cringed in revulsion at the sight but his father chortled with satisfaction when the missile made its mark with a small splash.

"What is that you bring?" the older man demanded when he glanced up, and Hugues carried the crockery mug to the bedridden man.

"'Tis a hot drink to ease your ills," he replied, deeply uneasy to be so close to someone so thoroughly sick. His father sniffed experimentally and grimaced.

"Like no brew of Eduard's does it smell," he commented sourly, shooting Hugues a sharp glance. "Taken it upon yourself to finish me off, have you?"

"Nay," Hugues responded angrily to the all-too-familiar accusation. His father was consistent, if naught else. "A healer is there here."

"A healer from whence?" his father demanded suspiciously.

"Of what import is that?" Hugues retorted, but the older man folded his arms across his chest stubbornly.

"Some are healers and some are killers," he insisted. "I would know which you have hired."

"And you would tell this from whence they came?" Hugues asked skeptically, earning himself a testy shrug.

"'Tis as good a mark as any."

"From Brocéliande she hails," Hugues grumbled in annoyance for lack of any easier answer, but his father snorted in derision.

"There be an answer that tells all," he muttered, sniffing once more at the proffered mug as though tempted by its scents.

"Like your mother's sweets does it smell," he mused thoughtfully, and Hugues knew 'twas so as soon as the words left his sire's mouth. That was the vaguely familiar scent that haunted him and he sniffed at the brew himself with new appreciation.

"Aniseed it has in it," he told his father, and the older man nodded thoughtfully.

"Aye. Always did she make aniseed pastries at Yule," he recollected, giving his son another sharp glance. "No accounting is there for Saxon taste," he commented sourly, though he eyed the cup anew, and Hugues stifled the pang that shot through him at the casual dismissal of his mother.

"'Twas said you should drink it while 'twas warm," he prompted and the older man's eyes narrowed in suspicion once more.

"Drink of it yourself," he retorted.

Would these suspicions never end? Hugues shook his head in frustration but did as he was bidden, taking a long draught of the hot liquid under his father's assessing gaze.

The rush it prompted within him took him aback, a tingling spreading to his very fingertips as his chest expanded until he thought it might burst. His eyes watered and he coughed when the tingle filled his nostrils, then he shook his head and took a deep breath, astounded to find his breathing clearer.

Hugues met his father's regard in astonishment and the older man reached for the mug.

"Give that to me," he growled. "A fine son you are to bring me a cure and drink all of it yourself."

The man grasped the mug in both hands and drank greedily of its contents, the cup only falling aside when 'twas empty, and he began to cough uncontrollably. Tears ran freely from his eyes and his face grew so red that Hugues was alarmed.

Mayhap the brew would kill him, Hugues thought, for he had been himself surprised at its strength.

"Sophie!" he shouted, helplessness flooding through him anew.

"*Sophie!*" he cried again when there was no response, watching his father fight the coughing spasms.

Hugues' sire grimaced as he coughed and he wagged one finger weakly in the direction of the chamber pot. Hugues fetched the vessel, placing it by the bed just in time for his father to launch an enormous wad of phlegm into it, followed quickly by a second and a third. His frail figure convulsed with the coughing and he curled into a ball on the bed, the linens twisting about him. Hugues feared that Sophie had mixed too strong a brew, that the cure alone would kill his sire.

Where was she? And what should he do?

Abruptly the coughing stopped and his father propped himself up on one elbow to wipe his brow and drop one last missile into the pot with satisfaction. He blew his nose thunderously and wiped the tears from his eyes, breathing deeply and blinking once before meeting Hugues' dubious gaze.

"A fine elixir, that," he commented with hearty approval. "Already do I feel better. Well-advised you would have been to bring it to me days ago before I had suffered thus." Hugues was spared from responding to that accusation by a light tap at the door.

"Hugues?" Sophie peeked around the door.

"And who might you be?" the older man demanded abruptly before his son could respond. Hugues felt his color rise at his father's impertinence.

"Sophie is the healer of whom I spoke," he informed his sire quietly and the man positively glared at Sophie.

"Make me another mug of this brew," he demanded, but to Hugues' astonishment Sophie shook her head in refusal.

"You cannot have another before nightfall," she said quietly. The older man's color rose indignantly at this information.

"Who are you to deny me this?" he asked imperiously. "Lord I am of my own manor and no impertinence will I tolerate from a mere healer."

"You cannot have any more for 'twill be too strong," Sophie explained mildly. "Another brew will I make you that will soothe your throat until nightfall."

"But only half of the last did I have, for Hugues here drank of it first," he complained bitterly. Hugues bit his tongue rather than defend himself, knowing this to be a battle that could not be won, and Sophie looked quickly to him.

"Half is but enough for now," she concluded readily, and he wondered how much she had guessed of what had transpired. "Well enough did all hear that the coughing from that half fair ripped *you* in half."

Hugues watched his sire draw himself up regally in the bed and fix Sophie with that look that brooked no argument, the look he had learned to fear when he was but a child.

"I want another cup of brew." The older man bit out each word with determined precision, but Sophie appeared unmoved by his demand.

"And you shall have it at nightfall," she repeated pertly, smiling cheerfully to the two astounded men. "If you will excuse me, I shall make that other brew."

The door closed quickly behind her and an uneasy silence filled the solar as Hugues and his father struggled to come to terms with what had just happened. How could she have so readily defied his father? Hugues felt his own annoyance rise and he had half a mind to pursue Sophie to ensure that his father's demand was met. The Lord of Pontesse he was and none here had the right to defy him.

"Cheeky lot, healers are," his father finally growled, to Hugues' surprise. "See that she does not take it into her head to leave before I am well."

"Aye, Father," Hugues agreed, struggling to hide his smile.

"And what is so amusing about my desire to become well?" his father demanded sharply and Hugues immediately sobered.

"Naught, Father."

"And naught should there be wrong with it," his father muttered, then coughed up and spat once again as though to emphasize his point. "Well I see that you do not leave, so other business must you have with me," he observed slowly. "Out with it, then."

Hugues pulled up a stool and sat deliberately, deciding how best to broach the matter of Justine's intentions. He looked to his father and their gazes locked for a long moment before Hugues cleared his throat.

"Justine tells me you two have a disagreement," he began, watching his father's brows shoot up.

"A disagreement? Aye, one could well call it that," his father confirmed irritably. "Though how she expects me to sit by and let her cast aside her opportunities for some foreigner of no repute, I know not."

"She says she loves him," Hugues felt obligated to explain, not in the least surprised by his father's snort of disapproval.

"And love will keep her warm and fed for the rest of her days?" he demanded. "A commoner and a foreigner both is no match for a woman of noble birth like Justine. Expectations has she, though little does she know it, and I would not have her find herself trapped years hence."

"Have you met the man?" Hugues asked quietly, and his father grimaced.

"I would not sully myself with his presence," he retorted, sneering anew. "But a common merchant is he."

Hugues folded his hands together before him and stared down at them for a moment before he responded. Well did he want to avoid arguing with his father, but if the issue was Guilio's common birth, 'twas best to resolve it now. Only a matter of time was it until Sophie's heritage became a similar issue and Hugues found that the charge of being of merchant stock struck particularly close to home.

"Jean says that many merchants are better established than the nobility," he countered calmly.

"Ha! Well does that figure, for Jean is a fool. Never should I have allowed Louise to take his hand despite his inheritance. That man will see an early grave, mark my words." Hugues' sire wagged a finger in his direction. "A fool is Jean de Fontaine with all his fine opinions and a cretin to explain them readily to all and sundry. Little stock indeed would I put in any defense put forward by the likes of him."

"But you have not met the man who Justine wishes to wed?"

"No need have I to meet him," the older man snapped, his color rising as his anger grew. "Well enough have I explained to Justine that I would not see her wed a mere merchant. He is beneath her status and a woman of Justine's charms should always, *always* marry higher."

"How long must Justine wait for the king himself to demand her hand before she weds another?" Hugues demanded quickly, his own temper beginning to slip. Always had his father had a distorted idea of Justine's appeal. Although she was admittedly a pretty girl, she had a viper's own venom when aroused and he for one was fed up with these high expectations of a spouse. He shoved to his feet and glared at his father.

"No younger is she getting, yet you would have her continue to wait for this magical match. Perhaps your expectations are too high."

"The Count of Burgundy requested for his son and *heir* to meet her a fortnight past," his father growled irritably. "But Justine would hear naught of it."

"Well, now Justine will hear naught of abandoning this Guilio," Hugues responded, his patience rapidly expiring.

"Speak not his name in my chambers!" the old man shouted as he sat up and pointed at his son accusingly.

"Make no mistake, Father, this matter will not disappear in the night!" Hugues shouted back.

"Were you not gallivanting around the countryside all the time, well you might have stopped this before it had begun!"

"I?" Hugues demanded angrily. "I stop this? You 'tis who are lord of the manor and well you know that much is said if ever I dare to interfere in any matter here!"

"'Tis not your place to usurp me!" The old man rose to his knees, his face red as he cast accusations at his son.

"Usurp you?" Hugues repeated incredulously, closing the distance between them with deliberate steps. "Always have I sought only to assist you, but nay, you would plunge the entire estate into chaos rather than accept the aid of any other than Eduard."

His father's chin shot up and his eyes flashed as he defiantly met Hugues' regard. "A stubborn lot you are, just like your mother," he accused. The unfairness of that charge sent Hugues spinning on his heel before he could do something he might regret.

"Obstinacy being a trait foreign to you?" he could not help but mutter.

"Well did I hear that impertinence!" his father cried out behind him.

"No impertinence is it to note the truth," Hugues dared to counter, and the old man clambered unsteadily from the bed in his anger to shake a finger at his son.

"Lord I am of this manor still and you will do my bidding," he raged. "Your sister must be relieved of this

ridiculous notion, and should you not persuade her
from it, no heir of mine will you be.''

A terse silence hung between the two men and
Hugues stared his father in the eye in disbelief. To wipe
away his entire legacy on a whim of his stubborn sister's was beyond unfair and Hugues gritted his teeth,
determined not to give his sire the satisfaction of a show
of temper.

''You cannot do this,'' he seethed, but his father
merely shook his head calmly.

''I can and I will,'' he insisted quietly, a cold light
settling in his eyes as each assessed the other's resolve.

Hugues saw the determination in his father's eyes and
knew there was no argument that would change his
mind. His own anger dissipated, leaving him feeling
weak in the knees. He tore his gaze away, frowning for
a long moment at the floor as he struggled with the
emotions that rose in his chest and threatened to choke
him.

His father would commit Pontesse to ruins rather
than grant him his rightful legacy. Two decades he had
worked in preparation, to not only be worthy of his he-
reditary title but to be capable of maintaining the estates. Now 'twas all for naught. Ways aplenty there were
to avoid inheritance and Hugues knew that if his father
was truly so determined, he would bequeath Pontesse to
the Church rather than leave it to his hand.

'Twas almost too much to bear and Hugues found he
had naught to say.

''I shall check on your elixir,'' he murmured quietly,
turning to make his way to the door, missing the consideration that flickered through his father's eyes at his
response.

* * *

Sophie spoke to herself as she wandered through the extensive herb garden beyond Pontesse's kitchens, reciting the names of the herbs under her breath along with qualities she had learned about them. Something she needed to restore the balance of fire in the lord's body, for 'twas more than clear that he was a fiery type.

'Twas the abundance of water in his system that troubled him, for it unbalanced his natural order. Cleansing fire she needed, to clear his breathing, and Sophie knew not precisely the plant, so she wandered along the paths, reciting her ceaseless litany while she sought the elusive ingredient.

"What are you doing?"

Sophie's head shot up at the unexpected question and she found Hugues' younger sister, Justine, watching her, her arms folded across her chest.

"I seek the herbs to make your father an elixir for his cold," she informed her, then frowned down at a clump of calendula and spoke to herself once more as she considered it.

"Fire 'tis true, ruled by the sun," she recalled in a murmur. "'Tis strongest plucked when the sun is in Leo, but a love charm 'tis, and sign of unfaithfulness." Sophie shook her head and moved on. "Nay, 'twill not do."

"A witch you are," Justine charged, and Sophie looked up, surprised at the unexpected assertion.

"Nay, I am but a healer," she clarified, but the younger woman pointed at her as she advanced.

"Nay, nay," she insisted. "A spell 'tis that you chant. I heard it well."

"'Twas no curse," Sophie countered indignantly. "I am but trying to recall the qualities of the plants that I might make the best choice."

"Nay!" Justine argued, her voice rising. "You mean to poison my father! You mean to cast a spell upon him!"

Eduard poked his head out the kitchen door as Justine's voice apparently carried to the room beyond, his expression inquisitive. Justine ran toward him, gesturing back to Sophie, who stood alone amidst the plants in quiet amazement.

"A witch is she!" Justine proclaimed. Sophie watched the chatelain grow more thoughtful. He apparently gave credence to the girl's accusations. "She will cast a spell upon Papa!"

"Justine," Eduard pointed out in a deferential tone, "already has this healer made a brew that has aided your sire immensely."

"But that is just their way," Justine insisted, glancing to Sophie with evident trepidation. "'Tis thusly she means to gain your trust."

"I know not how to cast a spell," Sophie defended herself quietly, but that new light in Eduard's eye did not completely fade.

"Perhaps 'twould be best if you prepared the lord's brew before me," he suggested tactfully. With that single comment Sophie understood that Justine's fears had been given consideration beyond their merit.

"As you wish." She nodded acquiescence reluctantly, not liking this turn of events but knowing that she had naught to fear from such false charges.

"What goes on here?" Hugues inquired when he entered the kitchens to find Eduard watching Sophie while she worked. Justine and the cook watched the pair carefully in turn.

"She is a witch," Justine hissed.

Hugues could only shake his head dismissively at his sister's nonsense, wondering what was truly in the wind. Sophie did not look up from her task, though she colored slightly at the charge, making Hugues consider whether 'twas the first time it had been made. No one else looked surprised at Justine's words and Hugues regarded them all with amazement.

"Sophie is a healer," he insisted in a flat voice, running one hand through his hair wearily. "Eduard?" he asked, and the older man shrugged quickly as though he sensed Hugues' displeasure with this turn of events.

"A reasonable idea it seemed to watch her prepare the brew for your father, as he is the Lord of Pontesse," he said defensively.

"So I have been made to understand," Hugues muttered, shaking his head when Eduard looked at him inquiringly.

He moved behind Sophie, wondering if she was as annoyed as he would be in her place, and watched her scrape the sugar glaze from what he assumed to be the candied elecampane. An uprooted plant with a woody stalk reposed on the table beside Sophie's work, emitting a sweet scent.

"What is this?" he asked her in an effort to discover her mood, bending to sniff of the leaves appreciatively. "Like honey it smells."

"Aye," Sophie granted him an appreciative smile. "Angelica 'tis."

"To soothe the throat?" Hugues prompted, well aware that their discussion was being listened to avidly. Evidently well aware of the same fact, Sophie grinned mischievously while she rinsed and diced the angelica root.

"Aye, and to invoke the protection of the archangel Michel," she supplied, a twinkle evident in her eye before she bent over her work once more.

Hugues smothered a smile himself at the aptness of her choice, and leaned against the table beside her. Justine snorted with disbelief, but they both ignored her. Eduard cleared his throat delicately.

"I thought to have someone drink of the potion before sending it to your sire," he suggested carefully. The very suggestion annoyed Hugues, but he refused to let his anger gain the upper hand again so readily. Sophie poured hot water over the mixture and stirred the lot carefully as he watched.

"A fine idea, Eduard," Hugues concurred, instead of giving vent to his real opinion. "As I drank half of the last at my father's insistence, I will drink half of this one, as well." The chatelain's eyes widened and he shook his head in quick disagreement.

"But—but you cannot," he stammered, even as Hugues held up one hand to silence his fussing.

"Only reasonable it seems that my father and I should continue to ingest the same substances," he argued, pleased with the logic of this and particularly enjoying Eduard's discomfort with the idea.

"But I cannot allow you to do so," Eduard objected. "Son and heir of the lord are you and 'twould be unfitting—"

"Jump not to such ready conclusions, Eduard," Hugues advised dryly, meeting Sophie's eyes with a wry grin as he lifted her brew to his lips.

* * *

Hugues' conundrum of how to sort matters between his sister and his sire was further complicated by the fact that he did not like Guilio Masenti.

Or perhaps 'twas made simpler, he reasoned as he picked at a stew served that eve, for now he could protest the match on the basis of something other than Guilio's social class.

Hugues slanted a glance down the table, covertly watching the man flirt with Justine in an effort to pinpoint exactly what disturbed him. Were the man's garb a reliable indication of his wealth, Hugues would have had to concede that his pockets were indeed heavy, for the damask of his tabard had the richness of weave seen only in cloth genuinely from the East.

The hilt of Guilio's blade was elaborately jeweled, his manners perfection, his grooming immaculate, his coloring exotically dramatic. Glossy dark hair and flashing dark eyes combined with a sparkling smile and a laugh that came easily and often to produce a man that Justine was undoubtedly not the first to find charming.

But still Hugues was not satisfied. The sharp look the man shot his way, which Hugues undoubtedly was not intended to intercept, did little to reduce the knight's uneasiness. 'Twas not enough to dissuade Justine from the match, to be sure, but still, Hugues' fleeting first impression unnerved him.

Hugues rose at the end of the meal, fully intending to take the time to talk to Guilio in the hope that he had misread him, but the sight of Eduard brought him to a halt. The chatelain stood numbly at the base of the stairs, his countenance ashen, and Hugues wondered immediately what was amiss.

"Eduard, are you all right? You look to have seen a ghost," Hugues jested when he reached his side. Eduard granted him a curious look that gave Hugues chills even before he responded.

"I thought to take dinner to my lord," he explained slowly as though unable to believe even his own words, glancing down at the tray still in his hands. He looked up to Hugues once more and shook his head.

"Dead he is, sir," he whispered.

Hugues felt his mouth drop in shock even as the hall behind him fell silent. Whispers broke out, then nervous chatter, but Hugues was running up the stairs, his heart in his mouth, to see for himself.

The solar was deafeningly quiet in comparison to the room downstairs and Hugues hesitated on the threshold. His father looked to be asleep when he nudged open the door. Half expecting the old man to jump and start shouting that he had disturbed his slumber, Hugues stealthily crossed the room until he stood looking down at his sire.

There was no mistaking the lack of animation in his visage, the curiously complete stillness of his father's form. His chest no longer rose and fell, his eyelids no longer twitched. Peaceful he looked but 'twas evident to the most casual observer that this house of the soul stood empty.

He was gone.

Even knowing that his sire was finally at rest did little to quell the sadness welling up in Hugues' chest. He stubbornly blinked back the tears that rose at the thought that never again would they shout at each other as they had these past few years. Free his father was of the illness that had long plagued him and even though

Hugues already missed his cantankerous presence, he hoped the old man was at peace.

Maybe his wife had had aniseed pastries waiting for him.

The frivolous thought made Hugues smile through his sadness and he looked down at his father for a long moment, committing the man's features to memory while he yet had the chance. This would be their final parting, then, and without questioning the impulse, Hugues reached out to take his father's gnarled hand. He refused to be dissuaded from the chill that permeated the flesh even now, and shook hands with the corpse lying before him.

"Godspeed to you, milord," he whispered shakily, his mind guiltily filling with all of the unfair charges he had thrown at his sire these past years. "Wrong I was in saying that you refused to live, for even to Death did you give a good fight."

He sensed another behind him and composed himself quickly before he realized 'twas Sophie who crossed the room with light steps. She paused beside him and touched his father's brow, his pulse point, his chest, before finally glancing up to Hugues.

"Slipped away in his sleep, he did," she murmured, summoning a tiny smile as she watched Hugues' reaction carefully. "'Twas easy for him, Hugues," she added, to dispel Hugues' last fear.

"Aye," he agreed hoarsely, letting her take his elbow and urge him back to the door. Eduard stood there, his expression still disbelieving, and Hugues gripped his shoulder.

"We shall make our way of it, Eduard," he assured the chatelain, who nodded quickly in agreement.

"Aye, milord," he agreed, but when he might have said more, Justine burst into the room, shoving the chatelain aside.

"Is it true?" she demanded, wild-eyed. "Is Papa dead?"

"Aye, Justine. He passed in his sleep," Hugues confirmed heavily.

"Passed in his sleep?" his sister scoffed, shooting a hostile glance to Sophie that Hugues instinctively distrusted. "Be not so credulous, Hugues. The witch killed him."

Chapter Fourteen

"Justine! Guard your tongue!" Hugues was clearly shocked at his sister's assertion, but naught could match the cold that settled around Sophie's heart at the unwarranted accusation.

To be called a witch and a murderer in one blow was a devastating insult. The malice that gleamed in Justine's eyes told Sophie that she would not be easily swayed. How could she think such a thing? Had they not watched her prepare the elixir? Had they not seen that there was naught to fear? Evidently not, for even Eduard was looking uncomfortable, and though Sophie looked to him openly, he refused to meet her eyes.

Melusine's warning rang in Sophie's ears and she wondered now if she had erred in returning to the world of normal mortals. Would this ignorance and suspicion follow her all her days? She glanced to Hugues to find the red rising on his neck as he controlled his anger and suddenly wished she had not brought this rift, however unwittingly, into his household.

"Sophie is a guest in our home and my intended, as well you know," Hugues scolded sternly, but Sophie barely heard his words, her attention captured by the hostility in Justine's eyes. Was such hatred truly di-

rected at her alone? And for what? She had done
naught but try to help the old lord, but well enough
could she see the fear with which she was regarded.

"Surely you cannot intend to wed a witch?" Justine
gasped. "Wickedness aplenty has she brought to Pontesse and only a fool could fail to note her influence."
This charge cut Sophie to the quick, reminding her all
too well of Gaillard's charge that she could not help but
bring ill luck to those around her. Was she truly a curse,
then?

"What nonsense do you speak?" Hugues demanded
impatiently, folding his arms in a posture that suggested he was unlikely to change his mind.

Something curled up within Sophie at the realization
that his defense of her would not stop with this incident should she take his hand. A wife that brought
scandal and did not bear sons. Indeed, in this moment
it seemed that she was asking too much of the man she
loved.

"Papa is dead!" Justine fairly shouted, her color
rising like Hugues'. "Can you not call this wickedness?
No sooner had she set foot on the threshold than he
sickened and died. Surely there could be no clearer
sign?"

"'Twas you who met us in the courtyard to tell us of
Father's illness, as I recall it," Hugues pointed out
dryly, but Justine merely tossed her hair defiantly.

"Did he not grow worse that very day? All in the hall
heard him cough after her elixir, did they not? Did he
not then turn against me and my wishes? How can you
not see the truth arrayed before you?"

"Indeed, I would ask you much the same," Hugues
retorted coldly. "Before we even arrived, you two had
quarreled, for this you told me in the courtyard, as

well." Sophie watched the younger woman carefully, her heart sinking at the realization that Justine was not to be swayed by Hugues' logic.

"'Twas but the portent of her coming that influenced events, then," she argued, incurring one of Hugues' indignant snorts.

"You cannot insist upon such nonsense." He dismissed her charges with a shake of his head and frowned as he deliberately took Sophie's hand within his. She wondered if he would feel her trembling or sense her dismay, but the warmth of his hand simply folded around hers as he pulled her closer. "Too much is there to be done to concern ourselves with this," Hugues said.

"Nonsense?" Justine repeated, her voice rising to an hysterical pitch as Hugues brushed past her to leave the solar. Sophie stepped quickly past her, painfully aware of all eyes in the hall below avidly watching the argument. Hugues gave her fingers an encouraging squeeze but she had not the heart to respond, so certain was she that she saw the same condemnation reflected in the eyes of all who watched.

"Nonsense you call it that this woman has killed our sire?" Justine demanded wildly. "Magical elixirs she gave him, Hugues —" she dropped her voice to a whisper "—and naught do we know of what was in them. This you cannot deny."

Hugues hesitated on the stairs and looked back up at his sister. "Of both draughts did I drink, as well," he reminded her carefully, but his level tone did not deceive Sophie. His temper was wearing thin and well she regretted that this burden had been added to his shoulders on her account.

"Young and strong you are, Hugues," Justine sneered. "And already was Papa on death's threshold."

"Enough!" Hugues exploded, jabbing a finger through the air in his sister's direction, his eyes flashing, and Sophie stepped quickly backward, stunned at this uncharacteristic show of temper. "Too far do you push my tolerance on this day of days! Bite your tongue in this regard and content yourself with paying your respects to your sire."

"*I* push your tolerance?" his sister repeated sarcastically, pointing a finger directly at Sophie. "'Tis you who would shelter the murderess of our sire within these very walls!" An expectant silence fell in the hall below as Hugues leaped back up the stairs, his brows drawn together in a thunderous scowl.

"Always must you stir the brew, Justine, and on this day I will hear no more of it!" he shouted, fit to rattle the gates themselves. "Your sire lies dead beyond and before you have even paid your respects, you are set on disrupting the lives of all. Lucky indeed will you be if my fiancée chooses to overlook this insult out of deference to the strain of the day."

The two siblings glared at each other for a long moment, then Justine's eyes narrowed. Hugues turned away and stamped back down the stairs to Sophie's side. Before all, he took her hand once more and deliberately interlaced their fingers.

"You cannot ignore this, Hugues," Justine warned in a low voice when he began to descend the remaining stairs. Sophie watched Hugues' nostrils flare as he struggled to control his temper yet again, but he did not hesitate in his path.

"Your charges are inappropriate and ill timed," he growled as he cast a deprecating glance over his shoulder. "I had thought you better reared than this."

Justine blanched at the accusation, and with that parting shot Hugues turned and descended the stairs, resolutely tugging Sophie in his wake. Mercifully Justine held her tongue and Sophie kept her head bowed, feeling the air fairly crackle with hostility in the hall. They reached the floor and Hugues paused to look around at the curiously silent assembly.

"Have you naught with which to occupy yourselves?" he demanded irritably, and the tension was eased somewhat. When Sophie looked up, the household was returning to its business, but not without a fair measure of covert glances in their direction. Hugues sighed and she squeezed his fingers as she watched the tension ease out of his shoulders.

"Sorry I am about your sire," she whispered. Hugues shook his head, turning to face her with a sad smile, and slid his finger under her chin.

"Never did I actually expect him to die," he mused, dismissing his frown with obvious effort. He tipped up Sophie's face and stared into her eyes for a moment. Sophie fancied he saw just how deeply Justine's words had cut, for his lips thinned abruptly.

"Sorry I am about Justine," he murmured, his fingertips caressing her cheek gently as he stared down at her. "She is upset, I wager, and knows not what she says." The excuse sounded like what it was, even Hugues' deep tones giving it little credibility. Sophie shook her head, and Hugues' brows rose questioningly.

"She knows precisely what she says, Hugues, and indeed she speaks the truth," Sophie argued softly.

"This charge will not go away and it will not be the last leveled in my direction."

"What is this you say?" he demanded unsteadily, his grip tightening on her fingers, but Sophie could only shake her head.

"She is not alone in her suspicions," was all she could say. She looked away so that she would not be forced to see the acknowledgment of the truth in Hugues' eyes, and missed the flash of fear that lit them instead.

"Sophie," he murmured under his breath with surprising urgency, but when she might have turned back to him another voice brought their conversation up short.

"I would extend to you my most sincere sympathies," Guilio interjected smoothly, and Sophie fairly jumped at his surprising proximity. So focused had she been on Hugues that she had not heard him approach. Hugues looked similarly taken aback, blinking once or twice to collect himself before glancing to the other man with evident reluctance.

"Thank you," Hugues accepted quietly, but he did not release Sophie. Still he held her hand trapped within his, his other hand cupped beneath her chin.

"Guilio Masenti," the other man offered, and Hugues nodded curtly.

"Aye," Hugues agreed. Apparently unaware that the man had also offered his hand, Hugues resolutely held Sophie as he met the other man's eyes steadily. She could feel Hugues' disapproval and wondered at it, for it seemed most unlike the knight to be deliberately unencouraging. Truly the man had interrupted at a most inopportune moment, but still Hugues' unfriendliness seemed unwarranted.

"Well do I recall our introduction. And my sister has mentioned you," he added. Despite the charm of the other man's flashing smile, Sophie had an uneasy sense that he was up to no good. Hugues held the man's gaze for a moment, then turned deliberately back to her, clearly signaling that he intended to return to the business at hand, but Guilio had no intention of being so easily dismissed.

"Unfortunate it is indeed that we must make each other's acquaintance under such sorry circumstances," he continued glibly and Sophie watched Hugues' lips tighten in annoyance. "As you undoubtedly know, Justine and I were but awaiting your father's approval to wed."

Hugues barely suppressed a snort, his gaze holding Sophie's long enough for her to note the ironic light in his eyes. "Aye, and long you would have awaited it, 'tis true," he limited himself to commenting when he did turn. Guilio glanced up in surprise, his eyes narrowing slightly.

"Indeed?" he inquired archly.

"Indeed," Hugues confirmed. "My sire was set against the match, as I am certain you both had discerned."

"I had thought he might change his mind," Guilio proposed. His gaze never wavered from Hugues' own. Hugues shook his head, reluctantly stepping away from Sophie as it became clear that this conversation would not go away, but still he kept a grip on one of her hands.

"Unfortunately, Justine inherited her resolute nature from our sire," he said flatly. Sophie watched Guilio's nostrils flare in irritation, his lips tightening as he glanced quickly away, then back to Hugues, that charming smile once again in place.

"I can only assume that the lordship passes to you now, as the only son?" he asked and Hugues drew himself up taller.

"Mayhap you and Justine are well matched, for indeed you both show the same inability to consider the appropriate timing for your comments," he snapped with uncharacteristic testiness. "I would remind you, sir, that my sire is not yet cold and the discussion of the passing of his estate at this time could only be considered most inopportune." To his credit, the other man looked momentarily embarrassed.

"I beg your pardon," Guilio apologized quickly, "but business interests have I to attend to in Venice and I would know the status of my offer before I am compelled to leave."

Sophie was stunned at the callousness of this claim, marveling that the man did not make his bid on the basis of any tender feelings he held for Justine. Apparently Hugues was similarly surprised, for his features tightened and he shot the other man a cold glance.

"Surely you cannot expect that I would so readily disregard my father's wishes on this matter?" he demanded sharply, and Guilio looked momentarily taken aback.

"Well I had understood that you two did not see eye to eye," he said tentatively, but Hugues swept away his objection with a wave of his hand.

"True enough it is that we did not agree on every matter, but on this one—" he paused to look Guilio squarely in the eye as Sophie watched in amazement "—on this matter we are in perfect accord."

With that Hugues turned and gathered Sophie's hand into his once more, then began to leave the hall. "I would speak to you yet this day," he muttered to her determinedly before Guilio clutched at his sleeve.

"Think you that I am not good enough for Justine?" he demanded acidly. The way his face contorted in anger made Sophie more certain of her earlier assessment. "Think you that mere merchant blood is inadequate to mix with your line?" Sophie gasped at his audacity, but Hugues' face had set into a mask that did not hide his rising fury.

"I think naught of the kind," he snapped, though Sophie wondered at the truth of it.

Had he not seemingly made up his mind about Guilio before they had even met? And what of herself? Indeed, she did not even know if she was of merchant stock. And how would Hugues respond to learning that she was a child of the Maying, to boot?

Suddenly Sophie did not want to hear whatever Hugues intended to say to her.

"God's blood, you nobles are all the same!" Guilio charged, drawing the interested gazes of all still lingering in the hall. "Be at least man enough to confess that 'tis my class that troubles you."

"Naught has this to do with your class," Hugues insisted hotly and Sophie could bear to hear no more. She surreptitiously pulled her hand from Hugues' grip, relieved and disappointed to see that he was engrossed enough in the erupting argument to not notice. She stepped behind him while he argued heatedly with Guilio, then, when he glanced away, turned and fled the hall.

She could not stay here, Sophie thought wildly as she ran, feeling her tears start to rise. She could not make Hugues compromise so much of what he wanted simply to be with him. Indeed, she loved him too much to compel him to make the choice he seemed bent on making. Too much was at stake, for always would the suspicion of her craft follow her and that could only taint the reputation of his house.

This was but a taste of what would inevitably be repeated over and over again through the years. The very promise of that made her stumble over the threshold to the courtyard, but she picked herself up, her vision blinded with thick tears that would not fall.

And what of her own lineage? Naught did Hugues even know of that, though indeed he seemed so fixed on his path that she did not doubt he would take it all in stride. A barren witch born of the Maying. He would never live down the shame of taking such a woman to wife and she could not permit him to follow such a foolhardy path.

Yet well enough had Sophie seen that Hugues carried a fair measure of his sire's stubborn nature himself and she knew that her words would not convince him to forswear his intention to wed her. Tears flowed down her cheeks unchecked as she gained the stables and took a deep breath of the sweet scent of straw, knowing now what she must do.

Melusine had been right and Sophie had chosen wrongly.

A bitter revelation 'twas, but there was little she could do to mitigate its sting. Once already had she disregarded Melusine's advice and naught but pain to herself and those she loved had been her reward. She had made her choice out of love, but the cost to be borne for living in the world was too high to bear, too high for her to ask Hugues to bear.

She had to leave Pontesse, for 'twas only time without her would enable Hugues to see the truth. Taking a shaky breath, Sophie summoned the ostler and asked him to saddle her palfrey.

"Aye, a fine evening 'tis to take a jaunt in the meadows," he agreed heartily as he saddled the beast with experienced hands. "Will you be wanting someone to ride with you?"

"Nay," Sophie demurred quickly, hoping she had not refused so quickly as to arouse the man's curiosity. "A busy day it must be for all in the château," she added, but the ostler frowned.

"But late 'tis for a lady to be about. Certain you are that you do not intend to go far?"

"Nay," Sophie lied, again afraid her haste would reveal her deception. "I thought to ride just to the river." She was relieved when the ostler grinned.

"Aye, a mighty river 'tis. All the way to Nantes and the sea winds the Loire," he asserted as proudly as if he had wrought its path himself, and Sophie's heart leaped. Nantes! Had not Gérard said that the stones were reputedly west of Nantes?

"Verily?" she asked politely and he nodded.

"Aye. Mind you watch your step, for the waters are yet high, even this late in the spring."

Sophie nodded and accepted his assistance to mount, certain he would hear the excited pounding of her heart. For no short jaunt in the meadows did Sophie intend to take. Though she knew not what she would do when she reached there, she knew that she had to find the standing stones of her dream. Should this river truly run to Nantes, 'twas clearly destined that she follow its path directly there.

Hugues noticed Sophie's absence but moments later, though every time he thought to seek her out, it seemed another presented himself at his side with something to be resolved. The villeins had been anticipating a court the following day and the oldest villein had cornered Eduard into promising a new court day as soon as possible. Friends and relatives had to be notified, preparations had to be made for at least Jean and Louise's imminent arrival. The cook wanted the menu confirmed for the following three days of mourning; the priest demanded that the household fast for two days. There was, of course, a shortage of good wine in the cellars and a hunting party needed to be organized that the board would be adequately stocked for all the guests.

And there were the accounts. No reassurance was it to Hugues to discover that Jean had spoken aright. The costs were shockingly high, the revenues shockingly low, but at least his sire had kept thorough records. No old loans had Hugues to repay as Jean had complained, and for his father's keen business sense he was once again glad. Hugues stared at the records scrawled in the older man's hand and let the sense of loss fill him for the first time as he sat alone in the hall that night. In the silence he was unable to dismiss the thought that if he but climbed the stairs his father's cantankerous tones would rise anew from the bed.

But the solar was still, as was the rest of the keep.

Hugues looked around the dark hall with a speculative eye and considered the responsibility that had fallen on his shoulders that very day. So long had he trained, and now that the moment was upon him he was suddenly afraid that he would not be adequate for the task.

He swallowed his trepidation and rose awkwardly to his feet, feeling the ache in his shoulders as he stretched, and let his lips pull into a smile. He would have Sophie by his side. Sophie, who gave him such strength. Sophie, who always knew how best to assuage his worries. Hugues grinned outright at the realization that he could now offer fully for her hand, and some of the weight of his burden slipped away as he strolled to the threshold and looked out into his home cast in moonlight.

He should find her this very night, he thought impulsively, for the air was warm with the promise of summer and the moon was bright overhead. He should take her out to see the willows in the moonlight, those willows so reminiscent of her graceful strength, and make his proposal there on the banks of the river.

But nay. Hugues spared a glance to the moon and acknowledged the lateness of the hour, knowing full well that he had no right to disturb Sophie's slumber for such an illogical bit of whimsy. He grinned anew at the thought that she alone might appreciate it and shook his head in amusement.

Truly the woman would skew his thinking should he listen to her for the rest of his days, he conceded, not at all surprised at how little that promise troubled him.

"Milord, they are gone!"

Hugues opened one eye groggily to find Eduard shaking his shoulder with an urgency that contrasted sharply with his usual reserve. The brightness of the sunlight made him close that eye again, though he roused himself with an effort and propped himself up on his elbows. He must have fallen asleep sitting at the table in the hall, he realized as he acknowledged the protests from his cramped body, and he shivered in the chill of the morning air.

"Who is gone?" he asked without real interest.

"Justine and Guilio," Eduard wailed and Hugues came abruptly awake.

"What is this?" he demanded, watching the chatelain wring his hands.

"They are both gone, their beds have not been slept in and no one has seen them since your argument with Guilio."

"But where would they have gone?" Hugues asked, his mind still shaking off his heavy slumber. "And to what purpose?"

"Milord." Eduard's tone dropped and Hugues looked to him questioningly. "I fear they have eloped."

"Before the funeral?" Hugues demanded skeptically, unable to believe that even Justine would be so cavalier. Eduard nodded but once and Hugues' heart sank.

"It seems Justine confided in one of her ladies," he revealed in an undertone and Hugues fell back in his seat in amazement.

Eloped. Run off like common peasants to make their match. Who would have believed that Justine would do this thing?

And what should he do? Send others in pursuit? But unlikely 'twould be indeed for Justine to meekly accompany several of his men-at-arms back to Pontesse. He should go himself, if any were to go, and Hugues briefly considered the merit of that before shaking his head slowly. Nay, she had not listened to him yesterday and she would not today.

"Shall I have horses saddled and men made ready?" Eduard prompted, drawing Hugues back to the present with a jolt. Hugues watched astonishment dawn on the older man's visage as he slowly shook his head.

"Nay, Eduard," he said in a low voice. "She has made her choice and I would respect that right."

"But milord—"

"But naught, Eduard. If indeed Justine desires this match so much as to flee without her family's permission, then I would not stand in her way," he declared flatly, noting how the barest hint of disapproval tightened the chatelain's lips before he composed himself once more. No matter if he did not trust Guilio himself, Hugues added silently, for 'twas Justine who would mark out her days with him. 'Twas only reasonable in this matter that her choice be respected.

Mayhap indeed Justine and Guilio were meant for each other if they were so determined to make their match that they would boldly forfeit her dowry. No small sum had the old lord set aside for his youngest child's match and Hugues frowned that Justine would be so foolhardy. Successful merchant or no, Guilio had been so impulsive that Hugues wondered if he knew what he had cast to the winds.

Justine's dowry was forfeit and with it Hugues' own inheritance.

The realization hit him like a brick and his head bowed for a long moment before he reluctantly pushed himself to his feet. Had he not failed in this, his father's last demand? Had his sire not made it clear that Pontesse would not be his if Justine made this match? Naught else could Hugues do but cede to his sire's demands, even at this late date. Hugues caught his breath awkwardly, well aware of Eduard's scrutiny, but did not know what to say or how to tell him of this realization.

In that instant he knew that only one could ease his mind and help him see his way through this conundrum.

"Have you seen Sophie this morn?" he asked, somehow forcing the words out despite the tightness in his chest. To his dismay, Eduard shook his head.

"Nay, I have not seen her since your father's passing," he answered, and Hugues realized that he had not seen her since then, either. So busy he had been and so late the hour that he had assumed she had quietly retired, only realizing now how atypical of Sophie that would have been. He forced himself to control the irrational rise of fear in his throat.

"Please find the lady, Eduard, as I would speak to her as soon as possible."

Eduard must have caught the controlled urgency in his tone, for he scurried off, leaving Hugues waiting impatiently by the fireplace. What seemed like an eternity passed while Hugues tapped his toe and fancied that the sun had already risen to zenith before a breathless Eduard returned.

"She is gone as well, milord." He confirmed Hugues' worst fears in a single phrase, and Hugues was dismayed to feel his chest tightening anew.

"What is this?" he demanded impatiently. Why would she leave? Where would she go?

How could she have left without speaking to him?

"None have seen her since last eve when Justine..." Eduard's voice faltered and Hugues' mind effortlessly summoned the recollection of his sister's ugly charges. He closed his eyes against the understanding of Sophie's pain, straightened suddenly and strode for the stables.

He would find her, regardless of where she had gone, find her and somehow convince her that Justine's accusations meant naught. Did she not know yet that he meant to have her as his bride? Did she truly believe that Justine's nonsense could sway his heart?

"Milord, where do you go?" Eduard implored, his footsteps pattering in Hugues' wake. Hugues cast an impatient glance over his shoulder. "I mean to find the lady," he declared, blinking as he strode into the sunlight in the courtyard but not easing his pace.

"But milord," Eduard protested.

Hugues ignored him and beckoned to the ostler. A quick survey of the stables revealed the absence of the chestnut palfrey he had acquired in La Rochelle and his heart plummeted.

"When did the lady Sophie depart?" he demanded abruptly of the ostler and the man looked momentarily stunned. He glanced over his shoulder to the empty stall and Hugues watched the heavyset man visibly swallow.

"Last eve 'twas, milord," he admitted reluctantly and Hugues exploded once more.

"Last eve! Over the night has a lady been missing from the estate and naught was said?"

The ostler looked decidedly uncomfortable now, glancing quickly from side to side as though hoping something or someone would appear to save him. "She said to take but a short ride, milord, and in truth, so busy was I with horses coming and going, what with all the messengers, that her departure fair slipped my mind." He swallowed again and dared to flick a glance to Hugues, who simply shoved one hand through his hair in annoyance.

"Arnulf," Eduard chided when Hugues said naught, "never have I seen such a shocking breach of conduct. Indeed, never have I known you to be so slipshod—" Hugues held up a hand to stop his tirade and looked the ostler in the eye, only interested in one thing at this late point.

"Where did she go?" he asked softly, his throat tightening when the ostler shrugged helplessly.

"In truth, milord, I know not, for she said little—" Suddenly he frowned, his eyes lighting as he evidently recalled something, and he almost grinned as he met Hugues' regard once more. "Nantes," he asserted. "I told her in passing that the Loire traced a path all the way to Nantes and the sea and it seemed that she was most interested."

Nantes. Hugues frowned in thought. The name of the Norman port did little to enlighten him, until suddenly he recalled Sophie's determination to reach Bretagne. Had she not said that her natural mother was said to have been from Bretagne, as well? Suddenly it all made sense to Hugues and he gestured to his own steed.

"Saddle the beast as quickly as you are able," he commanded. "I ride out this morn." The ostler responded with a curt nod, summoning two squires with a shout as he turned to do his lord's bidding. Hugues pivoted, intending to fetch his mail from the hall, only to meet a concerned Eduard.

"But milord, this you cannot do," he protested with a frown. "Responsibilities have you here...." Hugues permitted himself a dry snort of what could have been laughter at the very thought.

"Quite the contrary, Eduard," he replied, urging the perplexed man back out into the sunlight. "Justine has ensured that naught of Pontesse is mine, least of all its responsibilities."

"What is this?"

"My sire's last demand was that I stop Justine from making this match, for if she did, he vowed to disinherit me," Hugues explained, watching the older man's eyes widen.

"But this he cannot do," he protested.

"Well you know that he would have bequeathed the lot to the Church had he been so set on seeing me penniless," Hugues responded in a low voice. The other man's expression revealed that the shot had found its mark.

"Surely you cannot mean to take this threat seriously? Surely the old lord spoke only in anger?"

"I know not, Eduard, and so must take him at his word alone."

Eduard digested this assertion for a long moment before fixing Hugues with a skeptical eye.

"But you ride in pursuit of your sister?"

"Nay," Hugues said, grinning outright at the look of shock that crossed Eduard's features. "I ride in pursuit of my bride." He savored the weight of each word upon his tongue, but Eduard positively bristled at this piece of news.

"What nonsense is this? The very estate of Pontesse hangs in the balance and rather than persuade your sister to abandon her folly, you ride in pursuit of a witch you mean to wed?"

"Aye." Hugues nodded with satisfaction to hear his intent so plainly voiced. "Aye, that I do. Justine has made her choice and now I would make mine."

"But Pontesse—"

"Will endure with or without me," Hugues interjected, meeting Eduard's gaze steadily as his voice dropped. "Know that I cannot so cavalierly disregard my sire's wishes," he added, waiting for understanding to flash in the older man's eyes before he turned away.

* * *

"You do know that the old devil was only trying to frighten you?"

Hugues glanced up from adjusting his cursed stirrup to find Jean leaning casually over the side of the stall, his eyes bright in the darkness. Fine time his trap chose to break. He would have Luc's head for not tending matters better.

"Nay, I know no such thing," he said. He turned back to his task, silently cursing how long it was taking him to get on the road.

"Well, I do," Jean asserted, patting the stallion's glossy rump.

"How could you know such a thing?" Hugues demanded impatiently.

To his surprise Jean laughed aloud. "How soon you forget that 'twas I who was forced to endure all his tales of his only son."

"No time is this for such jests," Hugues countered irritably, dropping the uncooperative stirrup and swinging up into the saddle with a vengeance. Jean snatched at the stallion's reins and pulled the beast up short, forcing Hugues to meet his regard once more.

"No jest is this," he said. "Your sire was proud of you, Hugues, and on no account would he want you to cast the estate aside."

"Then he should not have said as much."

"Perhaps not, but there is little enough he can do to repair the damage now," Jean reminded him. Hugues sighed and frowned, deciding in that moment to confide in his brother-in-law.

"In truth, Jean, I cannot think to do it without her," he confessed. "Already so much has happened that I am fair bewildered and overburdened with the task."

He paused as he sought the words, unable to look up and meet the mockery he was sure to find in Jean's eyes.

"I need her strength," Hugues added, hearing his words echo in the silence of the stables.

"And when you find her?" Jean asked after a pause and Hugues looked up in surprise to find the other knight's expression thoughtful, not mocking. Jean grinned, evidently noting Hugues' surprise. "Truly you do Louise a disservice to think that I know not what you mean," he charged and Hugues felt his color rise.

"I meant no offense," he began, but Jean waved off his apology.

"And none is taken. I need only know whether my neighbors at Pontesse will be honorable folk or clergy."

Hugues laughed and shook his head. "I know not," he confessed, "for I know not what Sophie wants. Indeed, I cannot even be sure to find her."

"You will," Jean asserted with a confidence Hugues was far from feeling. "Do you intend to ride alone, then?"

"Aye, but I thank you for the offer."

Jean paced beside Hugues as he rode out into the sunny courtyard and halted his steed. The two knights regarded each other in silence for a moment, then grins broke out simultaneously on their faces and Jean offered his hand.

"Godspeed and good fortune to you," he said heartily and Hugues shook his hand gratefully. They nodded to each other and Hugues spurred his destrier on, feeling more positive about the future than he had in a while as he rode out the gates.

Chapter Fifteen

Dusk was falling when Hugues caught a glimpse of a rider far ahead of him on the winding road. His pulse quickened but he schooled himself to keep an even temper lest he be disappointed by simply another traveler. He had made good time this day, the destrier thundering down the road that wound alongside the river at a steady pace, and it almost seemed too good that he could have found Sophie so soon.

The road ahead curved into the dying sunlight, a glimpse of a palfrey's chestnut rump and a rider with a dark green cloak setting Hugues' spurs into his mount's side in encouragement. He considered the wisdom of shouting out to her, but knew not what to do, so overwhelmed was he with mingled excitement and relief.

'Twas then that he noted the lateness of the hour, and that Sophie rode alone, and rage that she had taken such a chance with her life won the day.

"Sophie!" he shouted, gratified by the way she pulled her horse up quickly and spun to face him. He savored the complete shock in her expression as his destrier rapidly closed the distance between them and gave full vent to his annoyance without another thought.

"Have you not a whit of sense, woman?" he demanded impatiently when he drew alongside. "Of what were you thinking to ride off alone? Know you not what manner of brigands haunt these roads, searching for unwary victims?"

"You followed me," Sophie whispered in evident amazement, her soft tone temporarily taking the bluster out of Hugues' sails.

"Of course I followed you!" he shouted when he had recovered himself. "Think you that I care naught for your welfare? Time and again have I taken you under my protection, yet still that very fact surprises you. Again I ask, have you not a whit of sense about you?"

Sophie drew herself up taller, seemingly having recovered from her surprise, and steadily met Hugues' regard. "Responsibilities have you now and certainly 'tis not unreasonable to think you have no time for a murdering, lowborn witch."

Hugues looked at Sophie in openmouthed astonishment. "Never have I called you this," he protested weakly, but Sophie only shook her head.

"No need had you, for there were plenty of others to make the charge," she stated flatly and he saw now how Justine's suspicions had stung.

"She is gone, Sophie," he informed her. She shook her head once again and Hugues thought he glimpsed tears in her eyes.

"It matters not, for she would not be the last," she declared. Hugues impulsively laid a hand over hers, only to find it trembling.

"I care naught for this," he whispered urgently, not missing the hopeful light that dawned in her eyes before she determinedly quelled it.

"But others do," she countered with annoyance. "Hugues, you cannot so jeopardize the reputation of your house, and well enough do I know it."

"This, then, is why you left?" He needed to know the truth.

"Aye, and well you know it," she agreed impatiently. "I would not bring this burden upon you."

Hugues tightened his grip over her fingers, wondering how he dared to ask what he really wanted to know. "But do you love me, Sophie?"

The question hung unanswered for a long moment in the air between them and Hugues began to fear that she did not. His chest tightened at the very threat, when Sophie looked up and impaled him with her pale gaze.

"Aye, Hugues, I love you truly and have from the very first," she confessed heavily. "Indeed, I love you well enough to want better for you than I can bring."

Hugues squeezed her hand within his and grinned, unable to believe the magnitude of his luck. "Well you know that I think there is none better."

Surprisingly his words did not seem to please Sophie, for she pulled her hand abruptly away and frowned. "Hugues, my effect upon your holdings cannot be so readily dismissed."

"Not unless I have no estates."

Sophie shot him a sharp glance. "What nonsense is this? Your sire is dead, Pontesse is yours to administer. Think you that I am so feeble of intellect that I would not see this simple fact?"

"I have walked away from Pontesse," Hugues confessed, watching carefully as Sophie's shock melted to outrage.

"Walked away? Mean you that you have declined your inheritance?"

"Aye."

"Are you quite mad?" she demanded angrily, and for some reason the accusation struck Hugues as incredibly funny. So long had he thought her touched in the head that her charge seemed unspeakably hilarious and he could not stop his laughter once it started.

"Mayhap 'tis my *destiny*," he gasped when he could manage to speak, the very words launching another volley of unwilling laughter. Sophie's lips twitched as she regarded him, but she stubbornly did not join his enjoyment.

"You *are* quite mad," she commented when Hugues wiped the tears from his eyes some moments later, and he made some effort to compose himself.

"Aye, well enough is it said that one can only recognize one of like mind," he charged with a chuckle and this time Sophie leaned over to swat him across the shoulder.

"I am *not* mad," she contested hotly, cursing when her fingers contacted the mail concealed beneath his tabard with a resounding smack. Hugues raised his eyebrows eloquently at the futility of her strike, not to mention the damage she had inflicted on herself, and she laughed aloud this time.

"Incorrigible you are," she charged, but her sparkling eyes belied her tone.

As their eyes met and held, Hugues felt everything quicken within him at the familiar sense that they two were alone in the world. Her laughter died and the sound of the running river filled his ears, reminding him of that evening they had spent in another forest, seemingly so long ago. His gaze dropped to Sophie's lips and he recalled the wild taste of her, his loins filling with longing for the feel of her beneath him once more. Her lips parted, her breathing quickened and Hugues knew that their thoughts were as one.

"Sophie," he began, easing his mount closer to hers, but she backed quickly away.

"Why did you leave Pontesse?" she demanded breathlessly. Hugues met her gaze, saw her fear and wondered at its cause.

"Justine and Guilio eloped last eve," he said carefully and Sophie gasped in surprise before she frowned.

"But what has that to do with Pontesse?"

Hugues looked away for a moment, then met her gaze once more. "My sire vowed that he would disinherit me if I could not persuade Justine to forswear Guilio, as he did not approve of the match."

Sophie laid a hand on his arm and Hugues closed his fingers over its slender strength. "He cannot have meant it, Hugues," she insisted. "'Twas but a cry of his own feelings of helplessness." Hugues sighed, entangling their fingers carefully.

"It matters naught," he whispered, not daring to watch Sophie's response to what he had to confess. "For I could not bear the burden of it without you at my side." What seemed to Hugues to be an awkward silence enfolded them and he took a deep breath, determined to plunge to the finish now that he had begun.

"I love you, Sophie. I love your strength and your softness, and I would not be without you, regardless of what others would say."

"But, Hugues." She leaned closer and he saw her eyes were glazed with tears. "I am not even of legitimate birth." He frowned, but Sophie pressed one fingertip to his lips before he could protest. "My adoptive mother claimed that I was a child of the Maying and that my mother gave me up in shame."

Hugues lifted her hand from his lips and kissed her palm. "It matters naught without Pontesse, and perhaps less than you think even then." Her tears fell then, like scattering jewels, and Hugues plucked her from her saddle to hold her close before him.

"Where do you ride?" he whispered into her hair. "Back to Melusine?"

Sophie shook her head against his chest and sniffled unsteadily. "Nay, to Vannes."

Hugues frowned anew. "I know it not."

"West of Nantes, 'tis, in Bretagne, and 'tis said there are great standing stones there," she explained, but her words did no more to enlighten Hugues.

"But why?" he asked softly. The way Sophie shrugged told him that it was going to be another one of *those* answers. He smiled to himself and hugged her close as she spoke.

"In my dream there are always such stones," she confessed shakily and his hand slipped to massage the nape of her neck as he recalled the terror those dreams left her in. Pride surged within him at her intention and he marveled anew at her strength. Indeed, what other woman would be so brave as to try to face those nightmares single-handedly?

"And as my mother was said to have been from Bretagne, I thought..." Her voice faltered but Hugues could readily discern the hopeful direction her thoughts were taking.

"Well it seems that this once your heart has guided you on a most logical path," he said gruffly, deliberately ignoring the surprise on her face as he tied her palfrey's reins to the back of his saddle. He looked

down at Sophie and grinned, inexplicably glad that
there was something he could do to please her.

"I will take you to Vannes to see the stones," he
vowed firmly. Her resulting smile was not in the least
disappointing in its brilliance.

It was early June when they reached the coast and
climbed the rise to face the stones.

Naught else had been said about their respective
concerns while they traveled, but Sophie often awoke to
find Hugues staring at the sky, his lips pursed, his hands
folded behind his head as he evidently reflected upon
some matter. Little effort did it take to guess what he
was thinking; she suspected that time was making him
miss the responsibility of the estates he had inherited.

Could he truly be happy with just her, away from the
responsibility he had spent most of his life training for?

Despite that concern of Sophie's, and Hugues'
thoughtful nights, a comfortable companionship had
grown between them and well enough Sophie knew that
she flourished beneath both Hugues' kisses and his
teasing. He had been adamant that any further rela-
tions between them wait until they were wed, his insistence upon that course having changed naught, and she
found herself wishing more than once that it could always be just the two of them as 'twas now.

And again, that thought brought her back to the
question of whether he could truly live fully without
Pontesse.

The sun was setting in orange splendor over the ocean
as they approached the standing stones. Sophie's pulse
quickened when she saw that they stood tall and cold
exactly as her dream had portrayed them. They gained
the summit of a small rise as the last wedge of the sun

disappeared over the horizon and it fairly took Sophie's breath away to see the mist rolling in from the sea.

So clear her vision had been of this place she had never seen that she could scarce believe it truly existed. Indeed, she had never even seen the sea before the dream had begun to haunt her.

She slid from her palfrey's back and closed her eyes, filling her ears with the sound of the waves breaking on the rocky coast, struggling against her familiar trepidation. Hugues remained silent beside her but she drew strength from his very presence, giving him a grateful smile when she opened her eyes.

Not knowing what would greet her there but knowing she had no choice but to look, she took a deep breath and strode toward the circle of stones that she knew so well.

A thousand footsteps did it seem to take to close the distance, the chill of night permeating the wind as Sophie silently walked forward. Her mind played tricks on her, contorting the shadows into familiar shapes much as it had that night in Melusine's cabin, but she ignored its games even as she tried to slow her heart's frantic pace.

Sophie hesitated at the perimeter of the circle and glanced back to Hugues. He stood with the two horses, watching intently, the wind lifting his cloak around his shoulders and tousling his hair. The very sight of him redoubled her resolve and Sophie smiled, though she knew he could not see the gesture, before she stepped within the circle of stones.

The wind scuttled through the enclosed space, sending a few errant leaves dancing across the smooth grass of the empty clearing. No figure awaited Sophie there, no embers of a dying fire glowed to her left. She exhaled slowly with disappointment, unable to name precisely what she had expected, and looked about with new eyes.

A clearing 'twas simply. A clearing surrounded by stones, of massive size to be stood on end thus, but otherwise not remarkable. And naught was there here to fear.

Inexplicably relieved once she had absorbed the shock, Sophie spun on her heel, letting the wind tug her cloak and kirtle into broad circles. No more would this dream haunt her nights, she knew without a doubt, and she laughed aloud, spinning faster and faster as she called jubilantly to Hugues.

"Hugues! Come quickly, Hugues!" she shouted, hearing his heavy footfalls advancing and the jingle of the horses' trap.

"What is it?" he demanded, his worry evident in his tone, and Sophie stopped spinning to greet him with a sunny smile.

"Naught!" she declared happily and he dropped the reins, closing the distance between them with quick strides. Sophie laughed again at the dawning conviction in his eyes that she *was* mad and spoke before he could voice his fear.

"There is naught here," she said more emphatically. "'Tis here that my dream summons me, but there is naught here, naught to fear." Relief replaced the concern in Hugues' expression and he gathered her close with a grin. "Never again shall I have the dream, I am sure of it," she confided triumphantly.

"That indeed is reason to celebrate," he concurred, and Sophie's heart soared as his lips closed demandingly over hers. She stretched to her tiptoes and tasted him fully, convinced that any hurdle could be conquered now that the threat of this dream was behind her. Hugues 'twas for her, of this she was certain, and no more would the dream dictate her life.

They were both breathless when Hugues finally raised his head, and Sophie grinned at him unrepentantly, her passion so long denied now well and truly roused. "Well it seems that you do not intend to wait for the nuptials," he charged, deflating Sophie's optimism with a single stroke.

"Hugues," she began, fully intending to discover whether his thoughts on Pontesse had truly changed as she suspected, but he interrupted her.

"What is that? I thought you said there was naught here?"

Sophie turned and, sure enough, where the embers had glowed in her dream, something glimmered softly. Sure she was that naught had been there before, but she trailed behind Hugues, gasping in unison with him when they bent to find something silver catching the light.

"Like a pin 'tis," Hugues muttered, scrabbling at the surrounding dirt with his knife to release the object, Sophie peering over his shoulder all the while. He lifted it, flicked the dirt away and offered it to her gaze.

A figure wrought in silver 'twas, its style reminiscent of another such she had seen, though this was of a knight, every detail of his mail intricately cast. Even the insignia on his tabard was discernible and Sophie squinted in the growing darkness as she picked out the figure of a rampant unicorn embossed on his chest. She turned the pin over to find that it was evidently half of a clasp, for only a sturdy silver loop did it bear.

A thought occurred to Sophie and when she met Hugues' regard she saw that he had come to the same conclusion.

"Have you Melusine's pin?" he demanded, but Sophie was already digging in her pocket for it. She produced it and glanced to Hugues again as she noted the similarity of the pieces. Her fingers trembled as she matched hook to loop under his watchful eye, and the two fitted perfectly together with a decisive click.

The knight took the left side of the stone, his every curve matching the lines of the melusine's hair and tail so identically that there could be no doubt the two belonged together. Sophie touched the pale stone reverently and swallowed carefully before she looked up to Hugues.

"She was here," she asserted. Hugues nodded but once.

"Aye," he agreed. "And evidently she knew that you would come." Sophie had not the chance to point out the intuitiveness of Hugues' conclusion, though it indeed made her smile, for he was back on his knees again, digging in the dirt.

"Something else there is, buried yet deeper as though the pin was just to mark the spot," he said and Sophie dropped to her own knees, brushing dirt out of the way as he loosened it. A smooth and dark surface was revealed and her anticipation rose. A cry of recognition burst from her lips when Hugues pried a leather-bound book from the earth.

"'Tis her ephemeris!" she declared with delight, but Hugues looked no more enlightened at this news. Before he could ask for an explanation Sophie lifted the book from his limp fingers, flipping through the pages with their familiar symbols. "The book of the planets. 'Tis necessary to chart a horoscope for a patient."

"You can read this?" Hugues gasped incredulously, but Sophie could only return his regard in surprise.

"You cannot?" she asked and Hugues chuckled aloud.

"Nay. Know you not that this is written in Arabic, the language of the Moors?"

Sophie knew her surprise must show on her face, for she had known no such thing. "Well I thought the script looked curlier than that in Gaillard's books," she mused, fanning the pages absently. A loose sheet of parchment fluttered to the ground and she cursed herself for being careless with something so valuable even as Hugues retrieved the leaf.

"Now this I can read," he asserted with some measure of pride, and Sophie looked uncomprehendingly at the sheet when he passed it to her.

"I cannot," she confessed, unable to make any sense of these quite different squibbles, and Hugues grinned.

"'Tis a genealogy," he informed her, tracing the generations with his fingertips and reading the names from the parchment. "Many generations are there, as you can see, but just look here. For example, one Desdemona of Castile wed a certain Eustache, said to be Count of Saint-Lazare, in 1182 and they spawned a daughter, name of Melusine, five years later. This Melusine was then wed to Amaubin, Lord of Lorient, in 1200. He died not long after, in 1207, but his widow was evidently pregnant, for she bore a daughter in 1208 and the line ends here. Mayhap she has not yet been wed or borne a child."

Hugues squinted in the fading light at the parchment. "Her name looks to have been Sophie and, oddly enough, the surname Mauclerc has been written in brackets after her name.'' Sophie's eyes popped at that, but Hugues did not seem to note her surprise as he puzzled over the sheet. ''Never have I seen this convention, for if she had wed a man named Mauclerc, his full name would simply have been listed below hers.'' He shook his head in confusion. ''I know not what is meant here.''

''Hugues!'' Sophie managed to gasp and he looked finally to her as she gestured wildly from the book to herself. ''Mauclerc was the name of my adopted family.''

''The vintners? Indeed?'' Hugues pursed his lips. ''Perhaps, then, these are of your kin.''

''Hugues!'' Sophie fairly shook him, his logic was so tardy behind her fleet-footed intuition. ''Hugues, this Sophie is *me*.''

He regarded her in astonishment, his skepticism slowly giving way to speculation. ''How old are you?'' he demanded abruptly.

''My nineteenth summer will this be,'' Sophie asserted and Hugues bent over the parchment again. This time when he looked up, the doubt was banished from his eyes.

''Then Melusine was your mother?'' he asked uncertainly.

''Aye, aye,'' Sophie agreed quickly, surprised at how easily she assimilated this information. Had there not been an intuitive bond between them right from the beginning? Had not Melusine known her very thoughts before she had herself? ''Do you not see what perfect sense it all makes? Why else would she claim we were of the same kind? Why else would she leave this genealogy for me here?''

Hugues reflected upon this silently. "She wanted you to know that you were not a bastard born of the Maying," he concluded finally and Sophie nodded in delight. "Truly 'tis a gift from mother to daughter."

"And what a marvelous gift she has given me in this," she enthused, not noting the consideration still lingering in Hugues' eyes.

"Sophie, know you fully what she has granted you in this?" he inquired softly. She looked to him in surprise.

"Knowledge of my heritage," she offered tentatively. Hugues smiled and nodded.

"Knowledge of a noble lineage, no less," he asserted, tapping the parchment anew. "Born of nobility are you, my Sophie," he added in a low voice when she did not respond, and Sophie felt her mouth fall open. A lineage such as this granted her the right to take Hugues' hand and her pulse raced at the very promise implied by his words.

"But," she protested, almost by rote, but Hugues shook his head slowly.

"Your objections are naught now," he whispered forcefully. "For well enough you know that I care little for the petty suspicions of others."

"You mean to take Pontesse?" she asked, her heart in her throat, and Hugues nodded slowly.

"The more I reflect upon it, the more I suspect 'tis my destiny," he confirmed with a smile. "As, I suspect, are you. Come home with me, Sophie, for I need you by my side."

The catch in his voice revealed that he was less certain of her response than he would have liked to have been. That very fact tore at Sophie's heart so that she immediately reached to frame his face in her hands.

"Very well," she conceded with mock reluctance. "I shall have to take you both if that is your best offer."

"The best offer you are likely to receive today," he growled with a possessiveness that made her heart sing as he scooped her up and nuzzled her neck.

Any response Sophie might have made was instantly drowned in her awareness of Hugues' touch. A lifetime of this was almost too much to hope for and well she knew that she could withstand any ignorant accusation with the power of Hugues' love and faith supporting her. Her grip tightened on the book as Hugues kissed her with satisfying thoroughness, and Sophie realized that in leaving this gift, Melusine was granting her approval of both Sophie's match and her choice.

"Well it seems to me that a song might be in order," Hugues commented when he gazed down at Sophie some moments later, and her surprise at his suggestion was so complete that she laughed aloud.

"No ale have I spotted hereabouts," she teased.

Hugues grinned. "No need have I of ale to sing my lady a ballad," he affirmed, the warmth in his eyes sending a flush over Sophie's cheeks. He touched her jaw and smiled down at her. "Still you have doubts that I mean to have you as my bride?"

"Nay, a stubborn lot are you from Pontesse," she countered and Hugues chuckled.

"Aye, we are that," he agreed. "Come, Sophie, 'tis said for this sacrament one has no need of a priest. Mayhap 'tis better thus between us."

Sophie watched mutely as Hugues laced his fingers into hers and drew her outside the circle of stones. The wind careened in from the sea, lifting their cloaks and their hair, bringing the tang of salt and the vestiges of mist in from the water, even as the moon climbed into the indigo sky.

Hugues carefully placed her book within his tabard without breaking her regard and entwined their fingers so that they stood facing each other with interlocked hands. Sophie tipped her chin to gaze into his eyes when he began to speak firmly, even as she felt the tears begin to stream over her cheeks.

"I, Hugues de Pontesse, take thee, Sophie, named Mauclerc but born of Melusine of Saint-Lazare and Amaubin of Lorient, to be my wife, to honor and to cherish. . . ."

'Twas hours later before Sophie was granted her song and she smiled sleepily as Hugues lifted her carefully from the tangle of discarded garments. He leaned back against one of the stones, placing her between his legs, her back against his chest as they faced out to sea. He drew their cloaks over them both and wrapped his arms around her, pulling her close and pressing a kiss into her hair before he lifted his voice in song.

A ballad he sang this time and Sophie smiled to herself at the romantic words, savoring the rumble of his voice against her back, the weight of his arms around her, the satisfying ache between her thighs.

Something near the water caught her eye and she flicked a disinterested glance that way. Her eyes widened as she picked out the figure of a woman walking toward the sea. The woman dropped her cloak and her pale skin glimmered in the moonlight, her dark hair falling loose to her very knees as still she walked away. Hugues' voice did not falter and Sophie knew he did not see the woman despite her proximity, which made her wonder if her mind was playing games once again.

As if she had heard Sophie's very thoughts and meant
to dissuade her of that notion, the woman turned in that
instant, her familiar pale gaze locking with Sophie's
knowingly as she smiled.

Sophie's lips parted in amazement, but Melusine
turned and walked on, testing the temperature of the sea
with one graceful toe before stepping into the salty water. She strode away from the shore without hesitation,
the water rising higher and higher, spreading her hair
out like a dark cloak across the surface, yet still she
walked.

Sophie's hand rose to her lips when the water crested
Melusine's shoulders. The only thing that stilled her cry
was the realization that she alone could see the woman's rapidly disappearing form. And Melusine faltered
not in her pace. Even as the water closed over her head,
Sophie fancied she could still see her walking relentlessly on, her hair finally pulling away from the surface
and disappearing beneath the surface of the sea.

She was gone.

Sophie fingered the silver pin Hugues had fastened on
her cloak to seal their vows as she came to terms with
the sign. Melusine was gone from this earth, that much
was clear. Now she wondered whether her mother had
even survived the fire in the woods, unable to explain
how the ephemeris had come to be here in Vannes otherwise.

What, then, had happened to Melusine? Was this yet
another tale of which none really knew the end?

And what of the legacy she had granted Sophie? Well
did Sophie know that her learning had only just begun,
that Melusine had started her on a quest for understanding that would endure through all of her days. She
marveled anew at the generosity of her mother's gift,

her heart stilling at the possibility that there would be none for her to similarly instruct if her womb indeed proved barren.

But a moment passed before Sophie recalled Louise and Jean's child, Alexandria. Suddenly her witnessing of that birth made sense, and she saw it as a sign that their fates would be entwined. Had Louise not insisted that Sophie promise to take the child under her care should the need arise? In that instant, Sophie understood with a curious certainty that this child would become as her own, though she knew not how, why or when.

And the legacy would endure for another generation. No matter that the child bore no mark of Melusine's spawn, for she would still learn. Mayhap the time of such marks was passed, as was the time of Melusine's forest, whether it had truly been Brocéliande or not. Times changed, but the wisdom endured, passing from one to another in an endless chain that stretched unbroken across the centuries.

Perhaps eventually, Alexandria would teach another the way. Sophie smiled at the very thought, but no sooner had the possibility warmed her heart than a familiar voice echoed in her ears.

"Blessed be," whispered Melusine from some inexplicable source, and Sophie could but smile at the sense of well-being that filled her at her mother's unexpected blessing. Sophie's thumb slid over the cool green stone and her earlier contentment returned to flood through her with a vengeance.

She had Hugues, she recalled, curling closer to his warmth and lending an ear to his song once more. She had made her choice for love and surely there could be naught better than that. Melusine had made her own

choice, in truth, and though Sophie knew not what it
had been, well she knew that the other woman was
contented with her path. Hugues' voice rose as he
reached the climax of the tale and Sophie smiled secre-
tively to herself.

Aye, blessed indeed she was.

*   *   *   *   *

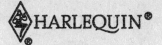

THE VENGEFUL GROOM
Sara Wood

Legend has it that those married in Eternity's chapel are destined for a lifetime of happiness. But happiness isn't what Giovanni wants from marriage—it's revenge!

Ten years ago, Tina's testimony sent Gio to prison—for a crime he didn't commit. *Now* he's back in Eternity and looking for a bride. *Now* Tina is about to learn just how ruthless and disturbingly sensual Gio's brand of vengeance can be.

THE VENGEFUL GROOM, available in October from Harlequin Presents, is the fifth book in Harlequin's new cross-line series, **WEDDINGS, INC.** Be sure to look for the sixth book, **EDGE OF ETERNITY,** by Jasmine Cresswell (Harlequin Intrigue #298), coming in November.

WEDS